Rules of the Campfire

Book One from Stories in Glass

Paul Moore

Cover design copyright © 2019 by Niki Lenhart
nikilen-designs.com

Published by Water Dragon Publishing
waterdragonpublishing.com

ISBN 978-1-946907-74-5 (Trade Paperback)

FIRST EDITION

10 9 8 7 6 5 4 3 2

1

"MYSTERIES OF THE MIND are hiders in the dark, waiting to be exposed by guided light." Dr. Abrams clutched his lapels firmly and pursed his lips before continuing. "We, who guide the light, are burdened by oath to tend the field of shadows which spring into silent silhouettes and scatter through the shards of shattered shade. Be vigilant we must, applying luminous logic from our lighthouses of learning. This endeavor demands earnest devotion."

The doctor swung his head toward the aide waiting in his doorway and widened his eyes in anticipation. When psychiatric aide, Jarvis Douglas returned his gaze with a dispassionate expression, the doctor asked impatiently. "Riveting, don't you think, Mr. Douglas?"

Jarvis knew the opening lines from past years. "New graduating class, sir?"

"That's right. Lilliputians."

"It's fine as usual, Doctor."

"Perhaps overly eloquent? I can nuance on the plane."

"Oh, hey, I got Dr. Milton waiting." Jarvis reminded the doctor why he was in his office. "He needs your notes on the John Doe."

The doctor pointed to a blue notebook on the end table. "Be sure to thank him for seeing the patient." Abrams gave Jarvis a wink. "Keep your eyes on Milton today. He's got a fun surprise coming. Mum's the word."

"Sure. You have a good flight. See you in two weeks."

"And, Jarvis, remind him he has my budget meeting this Friday."

Returning both hands to his lapels, Dr. Abrams inhaled. "Mysteries of the ... ahem ... Mysteries of the mind ..."

2

HARBINGER INSTITUTE
April 1, 2025
John Doe's Room

O N THE WAY to patient Doe's room, Jarvis gave Dr. Henry Milton his briefing. "He ate breakfast. Otherwise, he's same as the report."

"Did he have a good appetite?" Dr. Milton thumbed through the report as he asked questions. "Is he still non-communicative?"

"Ate everything. Even licked the jelly right out the little box. Still ain't talkin'. Just clutches his blue marble and smiles. Not a dumb, lost-my-frontal-lobe kinda grin. It ain't like a doubled-up-his-med kinda smile. He looks happy. Most likely goin' to jail, but don't seem to care."

Dr. Milton changed gears from walking-while-reading speed down to a molasses shuffle. Outside the door to John Doe's room, he stopped. "I don't see anything about marbles or jail here," he said. "Why is he going to jail?"

"Trespassing, sir. Abrams didn't tell you how they found him?"

"I see his vitals, admissions, and a Post-it note:

John Doe. Possible amnesiac with hypothermia. No appetite. Non-communicative but alert. Process and identify.

That's all I have."

"Dr. Abrams didn't mention we found him naked and shivering in the doctor's parking garage?"

"No."

"Looks like Doc Abrams passed extra paperwork your way."

"The private garage? On site? How did he get in?"

Jarvis Douglas shrugged and sighed. "Abrams is holding him for ID and evaluation. Then, if he ain't somebody, he's going into the system."

Dr. Milton craned his neck to peek into the room.

John Doe sat in bed, leaning back on his pillows, sipping coffee. Tucked into his elbow was a six-inch, clear, azure-hued globe. His focus was on the window ledge, where a strutting pigeon held his attention.

Milton observed from the hallway until the pigeon flew away. Then he entered the room and pulled a chair to the foot of the bed. "Good morning," he said. "I'm Doctor Henry Milton."

Doe turned his face toward him slowly, smiling but speechless.

"Are you ready to speak today?" Dr. Milton asked. "Want to tell me why you're here?"

John Doe let his smile slip a little at the questions. His eyes moved up and to the right, as if searching for an answer. After clearing his throat, he spoke softly. "Why am I here? That's been a big question in my circle for some time. Otis Beckley is the name. I have stories for you. I have stories, stories within stories, stories about stories, and ..." Otis pulled his big blue marble from the crook of his elbow and held it in front of his face. "I have stories imbedded in glass."

"Well, Mr. Beckley, I like stories." Dr. Milton sat in the chair at the foot of the bed and slumped, melting downward into the seat like an old pillow nestled into a familiar resting place. "What sort of story do you have for me?" he asked, while reaching in his pocket for a pen and pad.

"True stories. Somewhere in the telling is something you need to hear."

"First, Mr. Beckley, do you have family we can contact?"

"Call me Otis, Doc. My family isn't part of the story. Move on, I have a lot to tell you."

"It's fortunate I'm a good listener with a lot of time. We'll discuss family later."

"Perfect, Doc, we're a match made in Heaven."

"Okay, where do you want to begin?"

"We should start on the moon."

"The moon?"

"Our moon, Doc. The silvery moon." Otis pointed his finger to the ceiling and dropped his smile. "We could have used you. We were imprisoned in a box by an angel having a nervous breakdown."

"An angel on the ..." Dr. Milton caught himself, reached into his pocket, traded his pen and pad for a digital recorder, and stood up. "I'll be recording," he said, while placing the recorder on the pill cart by the bed.

After sinking back into his chair, the doctor waggled a finger toward his patient. "Okay, I'm listening. You were on the moon with an anxious angel."

"Kae'Lairy. Kae'Lairy's the name of the angel. The mighty Kae'Lairy."

"Tell me what you think I should know. I'll listen."

"I'm beginning with a campfire of angels on the moon." Otis tugged his lip. "The moon is where I first visualized a tangled mess of knots as links in a chain. I mean that figuratively, of course. As Dorothy likes to say, 'I try to be clear.' Doc?"

"Yes, Mr. Beckley?"

"I'm sorry. You haven't been introduced to Dorothy. I'll slow down."

"That will be fine. Relax and trust me to listen."

Otis squeezed his eyes and squirmed under the covers. Finally, after a long exhale, he spoke at length.

"The dance ..." Otis paused. "I'm searching for words." He turned his eyes away from the doctor and looked out the window before continuing. "l,ike the pollen dance of the honey bee, the angel dance is unevolved, forever trustworthy, and sealed into their species as a birthright. To be allowed to witness and understand the secrets of the dance was a privilege. The way they finesse their communication is fascinating."

Otis nodded, as if affirming to himself he was approaching his story properly. "The angel, Kae'Lairy began the dance by walking into the circle of campfire light. He paused, undetected, at the edge of the fire. Being undetected by the angels at the fire was the first step in the dance. To walk, unseen, among his brethren was a demonstration of higher rank.

"The two unaware watchers at the campfire, Jederic and Barabajyl, sat facing the fire. Jederic was singing and strumming a guitar. Barabajyl, silent, stared into the flame."

Otis turned his gaze back to the doctor and spoke without the hesitations of a man not sure he was taking the right path. "Adding sharp discomfort to his demonstration of superior rank, Kae'Lairy let the customary greeting, *Peace*, go unspoken. 'I am the mighty Kae'Lairy,' he announced to the surprised angels. 'Messenger of the Lord, hero of the big war, bondsman without peer, and the one to whom you will give all your attention.'

"The two watchers were made more uncomfortable as Kae'Lairy took a seat next to the fire without first having offer of hospitality. Under the rules of the campfire, he was signaling no peace was guaranteed.

"Jederic and Barabajyl looked at each other with nothing more than a tilt of the head to ask what the other had done to deserve veiled threats. After eye contact, they nodded, then moved into poses revealing their attitude over the sudden disruption.

"Jederic remained seated, placed his *guitar* on the ground, and turned his body until he was facing Kae'Lairy. His pose signaled a willingness to listen.

"Barabajyl stood and turned his back to the fire, vulnerable to attack, but protesting his treatment.

"Smoothly, without a word spoken, Jederic and Barabajyl set limits on accepting Kae'Lairy's authority. Despite the wonder I felt for having witnessed the dance, the spoken words that followed frightened me.

"Kae'Lairy began with an effort to share his confusion." 'I have in mind the differences between angels and humans,' he announced. 'Fire,' he said, while holding his hand toward the flame, 'highlights a difference between our two species. When a human stares into a campfire, he ignites a center in his brain that resides in a realm somewhere between serendipity and imagination. An angel simply appreciates the artful design of a near-static image composed of swirling shades of light in full dervish frenzy.'

"Kae'Lairy placed his hand inside the flame and stared into the fire, speaking as if forced to say the words. 'Another difference of perspective, while contemplating a fire on the moon, would be in the understanding of creation itself. A human would smugly insist you can't have a fire on the moon. *No atmosphere, no oxygen, no fire.* For good measure, he might throw in a denial of the guitar. *No atmosphere, no vibration, no sound.*'

"Barabajyl walked to Jederic's side and sat. Their mutual willingness to listen displayed in matching poses.

"After removing his hand from the flame, Kae'Lairy turned his eyes toward the two watchers. 'An angel of the Lord,' he said in heartier voice, 'would humbly avoid responding to the denial, but would judge the human response internally as, *No context, no humility, no clue.* The differences make for an uncomfortable servitude for our kind and a future full of surprises for the human.'

"Finally, after addressing issues of easy agreement with his brothers, Kae'Lairy tilted his head to allow his eyes to be searched, telegraphing he was going to challenge them with issues less easily understood. 'I feel the divide between angel and human,' he said. 'I understand the divide between loyal and fallen. What I want to resolve is a rift among loyal angels, yet to happen. There is a flaw in the rules of the Lord.'

"Without waiting to acknowledge the changing poses of the watchers reacting to his pronouncement, Kae'Lairy held out both his hands. In one hand, a blue sphere, recognized as a library of archives. Kae'Lairy placed it on the ground and announced his intention to play a recording of a twenty-year-old radio broadcast from earth.

"In his other hand, he displayed our prison. Both watchers recognized it as the box of the bondsman. No angel wanted to be placed into that box. Now, with their complete attention diluted with the distraction of fear, Kae'Lairy activated his marble and commanded, 'Listen.'

"This," Otis said, as he placed his orb next to Dr. Milton's recorder, "is the very marble Kae'Lairy used to play the radio broadcast."

Otis touched his marble and fell back into his pillows. Along with Dr. Milton, he listened.

3

"GOOD EVENING, FRIENDS. We meet again. Let's get started. I've harnessed 50,000 watts of power to push my humble show into your hungry ears. Are you ready?

"Get your finger off the speed dial. Remember, no calls tonight. Be patient. Gather your facts. Withhold your doubts. Prepare to slip into some thoughts, uncomfortable.

"But first ... before we step off into an unfamiliar zone, let's do something normal. My sponsors have wares to sell. When we return, I'm going to introduce you to a group of gentlemen with an incredible story. If you have a brain in your head, you'll scoff at them. I have them booked for three nights. What will you believe on Wednesday?

"GreenBob40, the answer is 'yes'. Everyone, continue to email my website. I'll consider your questions, but be patient. Monday to Wednesday is not going to be a straight path.

"Okay? Let's make some sponsors happy. We will be right back. This is Bill Elliott on station WNGS."

*   *   *

"Okay. We are back. Let's begin. What does Doctor Who say? *'First things first, but not in that order.'* The obvious thing to do is start at the beginning, but this story began eons ago. We'll begin just four decades ago, in 1965, with an old friend from college, David Blank. Hello, Dave."

"Good evening, Bill."

"Get your sleep today, Dave?"

"Eight straight and one old man nap."

"Good. You'll be fresh. I know you want to turn the phone over to your two colleagues, but I need to set a little background."

"Let's get to it, Bill."

"Tell us all what you were doing in 1965, as a young man in the service of your country."

"In 1965, I was part of an elite military map making team."

"How elite, Dave?"

"Just four of us."

"Four of you in the unit, or four of you in the entire military?"

"We were the only unit of its kind."

"In the summer of 1965, you took part in a mission. How did your mission begin?"

"Captain Hollis walked into the barracks and said, 'Let's go. It's tropical.' We grabbed our bags for a tropical mission and, six hours later, we were on a bald knob of an extinct volcano in the Amazon forest."

"That is a very impressive level of readiness, Dave."

"We were always ready, pre-packed to travel anywhere at any moment."

"Anywhere?"

"Yes sir, we had duffel bags for Siberia, Sahara, Amazon, and Paris, France. We trained in all of those locations."

"I can imagine the extreme climate gear, but what did you need for Paris, France?"

"Wet gear. Waders, water resistant jumpsuits, headlamp, goggles. We mapped the sewers. I added personal items to each bag. Cologne, Levis, a snappy Riviera-style shirt, greasy kid stuff, Beatle boots and condoms."

"Ah, the optimism of youth, but you didn't get sewage, sex and glamour did you."

"No. Harsh climates were the norm."

"So you wound up in the Amazon for, how long?"

"Our orders were to map in concentric circles, from the landing zone outward, until the chopper returned in three months."

"Three months?"

"Correct, Bill. We expected extreme training. It was the unexpected events ... very, very bizarre."

"Okay, folks, there's the setup. It's time to identify and do business. When we come back, we'll see how the curious can morph into the strange and become bizarre. Welcome to my roller coaster. This is Bill Elliott. We'll be back."

4

THE BILL ELLIOTT SHOW
ON AIR MONDAY – 2005

"WE'RE BACK. I have just one announcement before returning to the Amazon. I've managed to book a hot author for Thursday's show. In his new book, *Power and Perversion,* author Albie Gentile explores theories of how the sexual peccadilloes of very strong world leaders have changed global events. Kaiser Wilhelm a prudish bisexual? Thomas Jefferson a barn yard predator? We will sort out the truth and the fiction of these claims, and more, when we speak with author Albie Gentile this Thursday night. Tune in.

"OK ... Still with us, Dave?"

"Right here, Bill."

"You used the word 'bizarre' to describe your experience."

"Yes. Very, very bizarre."

"Okay, let's start with the mildly odd and work our way up to the 'very, very'. When did you begin to think something about this mission was a little odd?"

"The night we landed. Our helicopter pilot was the first person I had ever seen use night vision goggles. He also used a device that directed us to our landing coordinates. In 1965, I thought global position software was science fiction. The screen on the pilot's control panel interested me a great deal."

"In 1965 the goggles and GPS screen would be very interesting."

"Yes, Bill, but not bizarre. I would say the first hint of the bizarre was the smell."

"The smell?"

"Yes, I was the flora and fauna specialist in the group, but it was the security specialist we called Lockjaw who brought it to our attention."

"Okay. Would you tell us what he noticed? How did he bring this bizarre thing to your attention?"

"I think he said, 'Hey guys, we aren't where we're supposed to be.' We were watching the helicopter rise up and cross the moon. It was the smell that caused him to check the tree line. Those pointy little splays at the tops of the trees confirmed his nose. We were in a stand of spruce."

"That does seem unlikely, Dave."

"It wasn't something Captain Hollis thought was important. He snapped us back to reality, and the chain of command, by declaring, 'If you start in Arizona and fly due south for six hours you wind up in the Amazon rain forest. If you jump out of a helicopter in the middle of the night and find Christmas trees, then you've found Christmas trees in the Amazon. If you want to discuss the predictable range of tree varieties, before we set our tents, you are a candidate for a three-month tour of latrine duty.' The captain gave us our focus back, I guess you would say."

"Did that end the discussion?"

"Only for the night. Even the captain wanted to discuss it in the morning."

"Tell us about your first morning. What did you find when you woke up?"

"Corporal Schellert woke me at about 0200 hours for guard duty. I spent the morning staring across the camp at our fire and listening to the forest. The bird calls and jungle chatter convinced me we were in a tropical environment. When I stood up for a comfort break, I realized I'd been sitting next to a sassafras tree."

"Sassafras? The root beer tree?"

"Root beer and tea, yes. I was certain the sassafras was out of its environment."

"You discovered at dawn's light that you were in an environment alien to the Amazon rain forest. Am I right?"

"Well, yes and no, Bill. The forest environment was consistent with the flora of the Ozark mountain range, but the animals were certainly Amazonian. As the sun rose, the howl of a jaguar woke everyone still sleeping. Monkeys and exotic birds gathered around us, watching. We found ourselves staring at something unusual as well. There were surprise gifts next to the campfire."

"Surprise gifts? Tell us about those gifts."

"Somebody on guard duty missed something. When first light penetrated the morning mist, a heap of bright yellow, orange, red, and electric blue suddenly became impossible to ignore."

"Dave, I can't imagine your captain was pleased with the performance of the guards that night."

"He was angry and loud. I could almost smell the latrine duty.

"Lock responded to the situation by grabbing his rifle and bulling his way up a tall spruce. The only response I could come up with was to poke at the pile with a stick and ask, 'What is this?'

"Captain Hollis responded with sarcasm. 'Well, Blank,' he bellowed, 'I'm just the captain. I wouldn't want to infringe on your expertise, but it looks to me like a pile of dead parrots and a stack of apples, blackberries, pears, and what the hell is this?' He poked at a round, light green ball. 'It's as hard as a rock,' he said. 'It's a bumpy damn softball.' He kicked it in my direction and waited for an answer.

"I felt a little better knowing I had the answer. 'It's an Osage orange, sir. Very inedible. Sometimes used as an insect repellent. There are also a couple toucans and a macaw ... sir.'

"Mapping with the rest of the unit suddenly felt less like training and more like an adventure. I most definitely wanted to explore this region."

"Dave, I don't want to downplay the weirdness of these events, but would you confirm to our listeners that we haven't yet reached a level of weirdness that fulfills your description of this experience being very, very bizarre?"

"Without a doubt, Bill. We aren't there yet."

"At this moment, you and Corporal Schellert are on shaky ground with the captain."

"That's a fact, Bill."

"Lockjaw is up a tree in a very different sense than you are. Am I right?"

"Ha. Yes, Lock is literally up a tree, searching the ground for signs of human life. He had the high spot in the area."

"Did he find something of interest?"

"Not immediately. Schellert ran binoculars up the tree. Before he climbed back down, Lock announced he had vision for up to three miles."

"Did he see signs of human habitation?"

"No sir, but he reported one interesting and unusual observation."

"What was that, Dave?"

"He saw the tips of palm, capirona, and kapok. These are all traditional Amazonian trees, common to the rain forest. Their fronds and branches were peeking above a wall of thick green vines. We were camping in the bull's-eye of a five- to six-mile-wide circle of temperate zone woodland, ringed-in by vine covered cliffs. The separation appeared to be a clear and sudden distinction."

"A clear and sudden distinction between two types of forest? Is that what you're saying?"

"Yes sir, separated by a circle of cliffs covered with a thick wall of vines."

"That's ... What's the word, Dave? That's weird. How did Captain Hollis react?"

"He ordered me to dig a latrine, told Schellert to organize the supply tent, and sent Lockjaw to scout the immediate surroundings. He added, 'We'll map our way to the vine wall.

Concentric circles, gentlemen. We'll get there when we get there.' Hollis was his usual unflappable self."

"How long did it take to map your way to the vines?"

It never happened, Bill."

"Why?"

"That night we did guard duty in double shifts. When the sun rose in the morning, once again, we had the same sampling of fruits and birds lying next to the fire. Someone in this forest was extremely gifted at stealth, and the captain changed our orders. He authorized Lockjaw to disperse deadly response weaponry to each of us, then told us to chow down and get ready to travel."

"That sounds ominous."

"Just precautions, Bill. Three of us did a perimeter search. Hollis gave Schellert orders to ..."

"Yes? Orders to do what, Dave?"

"Orders to investigate the vine wall. Schellert had a white smoke canister to announce he reached the wall, and a red canister to signal human contact. When we saw the white smoke... Joe Schellert didn't return to camp. Early that afternoon, we went looking for him. We found his body an hour later."

"What happened to him?"

"He collected leaves, then he died horribly."

"Explain."

"We found the spent smoke canister in a small clearing. In the weeds, at the tree line, we found something ... something unrecognizable. It was Joe. We had to stare at his grotesque remains way too long before we were sure it was him. His face was misshapen. His hands were so swollen they looked like flippers. Blisters, big as lemons, covered his skin. He was partially disrobed. There was a stick in his throat. I think he died while trying to clear a breathing hole."

"What did this to Joe Schellert?"

"Poison ivy, Bill, just poison ivy."

"A really potent strain?"

"Potent and fast acting. We were so far, far outside our training. The next sixty seconds were a blur. When it was over, everything was fundamentally changed."

"OK, Dave. I know this isn't easy. You were a team. Tell us what happened in those sixty seconds."

"I don't want to give the cold facts, Bill. I don't want to leave images of horror. I want to memorialize these men with some sort of balance."

"Go ahead, Dave, let's not let the horror stand cold. Tell us what we should know about your friends."

"Joe Schellert was a kid, really. We tagged him with the nickname, Kid. He liked to remind us he was the 'youngstest amongst us'.

"Like most kids stepping into manhood, he was afflicted with the usual rookie habits. He liked the girls, and he liked to tell stories about them. His most often repeated story was about his girlfriend back home. On his last day before induction, he took her to a lake outside of town. He said it was a spot with a romantic view.

"One week into basic, he got a letter from her. She was suffering from a severe case of poison ivy. She went on to say the barmaid at *Froggy's* was suffering from the same affliction, caught at the same location, and both of them hoped he had a double dose of the misery.

"He laughed it away and added, 'I'm not allergic'. He was just a typical smart, stupid, kid."

"I'm sorry he didn't have more time, Dave."

"Yes, Captain Hollis, the oldest, had more time to mature. The army was his family., and among his family, he was legendary. As a sergeant in Korea, he sewed his own finger back on while he and his very green squad were pinned by mortars. He used his sewing kit and hummed *Mills Brothers* tunes until he finished. The effect on his squad was just what he intended. They thought he was nuts, but they lost the look of run-away fear. His squad took on the look of men girding to do what they needed to do. They survived the war a highly decorated unit.

"I believe the only time Captain Hollis ever went absent from being in charge during a bad situation was when he reacted to the sight of Joe Schellert's remains."

"How did he react?"

"He walked two steps into the tree line and began to throw up."

"This wasn't his first taste of death, Dave. The sight must have been horrific."

"Nauseating."

"Did everyone react the same way?"

"No, Lockjaw broke away from Schellert just before the captain became ill. He kept to his training, walking the tree line of the clearing, looking for movement.

"I took two steps back, and froze. That's where I stood, my mind trying to chase my thoughts until it was all over.

"Captain Hollis, between bouts of retching, spotted Schellert's collection of leaves, picked the bag up and placed it in his pocket. I wish I was thinking faster, but too late, I said, 'That's not a good idea, Captain.'

""Nobody knows what's really going on when they're puking. Hollis tapped his pocket and grinned. 'It's poison ivy,' he said, while wiping his face with his sleeve. 'Just poison ivy. I'm like Schelleret, I'm not allergic.' He said it with the same conviction of experience Schellert used when telling the story of how he lost his first love, but an awkward look crept onto his face as he realized what he'd just said. After a round of dry heaves, he removed the bag from his pocket and tossed it on the ground.

"Feet stuck in place, I looked over my shoulder because Lock was introducing something new to think about. 'Human contact,' he said. 'We have movement, three-sixty.' He was on top of things. His mind was keeping up with events, while I just stood and watched.

"We did have movement and human contact. Rocks began to unfurl into human shape. Bushes began walking.

"Captain Hollis regained his composure quickly. He saw the posture of the approaching humans and read the intent in their posture, hands up, heads down. The universal body language of submission and nonaggression. He drew his sidearm but barked, 'Hold fire. Hold fire.'"

"Dave, it might have turned into a massacre. Lesser men would have killed a lot of people that day."

"The captain did fire a warning shot into the air, but the little gray men came all the quicker. These little guys were three to four feet tall. They were fast.

"Several of them brushed past me, but Captain Hollis was given a wide berth. Like iron dust to a magnet, they rushed to Lockjaw's side, formed a circle, turned their back to him, and faced the two of us. Their posture changed from submissive to defensive.

"In 1965, Lockjaw was a six-foot-two chiseled fighting machine. He towered over the circle of tiny defenders, looking out of place and confused."

"How did you ever figure out what was going on, Dave?"

"An old guy, named Smerdis, walked out of the circle and over to Schellert's remains. In another display of universal body language, he put both hands over his forehead, then slapped them both against his legs while he turned in a single circle.

"Captain Hollis tried a universal move of his own. Holstering his sidearm, he tried to offer his hand.

"Smerdis responded by scurrying away from the offer. He pointed to Schellert, then he pointed back to the captain.

"Recognizing we all understood, Smerdis added the shrug, the two palms up, the arms spread wide, and the head shake. I took it to mean nothing could be done. Sometimes, confusion is better than understanding.

"The captain was already scratching his arms against his shirt. He stared at blisters growing on his fingers; and began trying to discreetly rub his crotch. His posture drooped, but he quickly reverted to being in command. He asked me and Lock if we itched. We both assured him we were good.

"Lock tried to make a joke. ' So what now, captain? Cut off the itchy parts and sew them back on later?' Not to be outdone, the captain replied. 'Easy for you to say, you didn't put the damn bag in your pants pocket. They both smiled the same funny smile, then Captain Hollis changed his expression to resignation and exhaled a phrase. 'So long, men.'

"Then he did it. As quick as a blink, he redrew his sidearm, nodded to Smerdis, then placed his firearm to his head and performed an act of self-mercy."

"Awful, Dave. Very decisive, but awful. How did you and Lock react?"

"We stood there, heads swiveling, stomach churning, and minds spinning. Two friends were gone in horrifying fashion. We were far from home in a wooded clearing, inside a lost world, and surrounded by impenetrable poison ivy. Our only hope for clarity came from the presence of strange little men we believed couldn't understand our questions. The only certainty was, we weren't trained for this."

"Thank you, Dave. Allow me to interject something here. You are about to start a three-month relationship with a culture you don't understand. If I were you, considering they ignored you in a time of danger and ran to protect Lockjaw, I might feel like Lockjaw was safe, but you were not very important to these people. Did you ever bridge that gap?"

"I think you should ask Lock about that. He was a witness to that very, very bizarre part of the story."

"This is only the very bizarre part, then? Maybe it's time we turned it over to Mr. Lockjaw. I may need you later, Dave. Will you be available?"

"Just a phone call away, Bill."

"Good, thank you. Get your sleep. You know what we need to do at high noon tomorrow."

"I'll be ready."

"Excellent. OK, Lock, I have some housekeeping questions."

"Fire away."

"You come from a culture with a strong imperative to honor the dead with ceremonial burial. I understand the little people ... Let's stop calling them that. What did they call themselves?"

"Savant. They called themselves Savant."

"The Savant. They discouraged you from going near the dead. Did they have any ceremony?"

"They tossed a couple inches of dirt and leaves over the bodies and sat down. I didn't recognize any signs of mourning. They shared pouches of berries, chatted, and laughed together over the next few hours. Dave and I sat with them, observing and decompressing. We invaded their world and showed them we could kill ourselves. I was expecting some hostility or mistrust. There wasn't any sign they were even capable of hostility until the eagle incident."

"OK, let's hang on that. It's time for a break. This is Bill Elliott, and here are the sound bites that pass for news."

5

THE BILL ELLIOTT SHOW
ON AIR MONDAY – 2005

"HI FOLKS, WE'RE BACK. I want to jump right in with my guests again, but my veteran listeners know what's coming. It's time for my standard post news-break rant.

"I watched the cable channels again today. What I saw was models and performers, repeatedly reading the opinions of the network owners, titillating peeks into the unnatural lives of celebrities, corporate promotion in disguise, political correctness training, and vitriolic childishness from both of our two most powerful private clubs: the demolicans and republicrats. Do we really want those dysfunctional, self-serving mobs to engineer our thinking for us? Shouldn't we all be thirsting for something better than a thin veneer of tortured spin designed to steer us away from building our opinions from the facts up? Don't be a voting bloc. Be an American.

"This is day 742 of repeating the same complaint, and I've been on air ... let me check my calendar here ... oh yes, 742 days.

If this deplorable situation changes, I promise to come up with a new rant.

"Okay, let's get back to our guests and learn a little more about their human contact.

"Lock, I've been reading my emails on the break. I have some human contact with our listeners I would like to tell you about. The mail seems to be running about eighty percent that you are liars and nineteen percent that you are loons. Military veterans are especially skeptical. Many of them suggest you reveal your unit designation. They would like to check the records. Are you willing to do this?"

"No, we are not, Bill."

"Could you explain why, Lock?"

"I've used the freedom of information act to verify our existence and came up cold.

Apparently, Dave was in Ft Leonard Wood for engineering training during the entire 1965 portion of his service. I don't even seem to exist. Schellert was reported AWOL and never found. Captain Blank retired without leaving an address or banking information for pension purposes. Those official records are lies. If you try to verify any of us with surviving family, you will find we are all childless orphans. That much is true.

"Are you guys here to correct those records, Lock?"

"No, Bill. I believe your listeners will forget our old adventure when you introduce Asitr. Asitr's story is still alive. Dave and I are here, on your advice, merely to introduce him to your audience."

"Yes, Lock. You've been very cooperative. Asitr, dear listeners, is the name of the third guest we'll be speaking to this evening. He's going to be the focus of tomorrow and Wednesday's show as well. Lock, are you appearing on my show for any financial benefit?"

"Good heavens, no. We have no money problems. I think you can verify that yourself, Bill."

"Just teasin' the folks on the other end. It's part of my job. Oh, and by the way, Lock, the one percent that doesn't believe you are liars or loons has a question he wants me to ask you guys."

"Yes?"

"This fellow says he used to pack your chutes when you were in training. He wants to know if you remember Carmelita."

"Oh, boy. Wet brown eyes as big as saucers, lashes three inches long, and a funny way of acting stubborn. Sure, I remember her. You must have spoken to Ol' Frenchy. He's a parachute packer of the first order. We last saw him at Ft. Huachuca, during desert training. Could you get his phone number off the air?"

"Can do. Eyes as big as saucers? Three-inch lashes? Carmelita sounds peculiar, but let's get back to your story before I get us further off track. An incident with an eagle is where we left the audience. No, no wait. This question is just to appease my curiosity."

"Yes?'

"How did you get the name Lockjaw?"

"I earned it In Viet Nam after being put into a situation where I strongly disagreed with my mission instructions and found it difficult to either accept the situation or rebel against it. I had a recent tragedy on my mind. One day, a chatty newbie in my unit asked our handler what the hell my problem was. The handler told him I had a bad case of Lockjaw. I began to answer to it and later introduced myself with the name. John Smith, my orphanage name, never had any appeal for me. The name I earned just stuck."

"I was curious. I never got around to asking you earlier. We'll hear more about that disagreeable mission tomorrow, but help me get back to your story. I believe you were going to tell us about an incident with an eagle."

"Yes, the only time I witnessed a violent act by a Savant in all the time I lived with them. It happened after we left the clearing."

"Did you all leave together?"

"Yes, we ate dinner at our camp. I invited them to follow us and we offered them C rations. They nibbled to be polite. Two Savant slipped off and came back with some delicious tea, fruits, and a vegetable soup. Dave and I devoured it.

"Although they ignored Dave at the clearing, they were very sociable to him at the camp. He did make one interesting friend. A monkey joined the party by strolling up next to Dave and picking through his bowl of fruits. He selected a big blackberry and offered it to him. Dave and I were the only ones there who seemed to think that it was an unusual thing to see. Dave declined the berry. Later, he told me he couldn't help but think about the places monkeys like to put their hands."

"I'm with Dave on that, Lock. Did the monkey become aggressive?"

"No, but he wasn't finished with being fascinated by Dave. He sat down in front of him and began poking around his clothes. 'It's army standard issue, fellah,' Dave said. He was wearing one of those Fidel Castro caps with the stiff brim and the flat dome. The monkey removed the hat and put it on his own head, crossed his arms, and smiled. All of us laughed and the monkey joined in. I laughed even harder because, to me, Dave's laugh sounded more like a chattering monkey than the monkey himself."

"Sounds like the mood is getting better."

"We were breaking some deep tensions, but it wasn't going to come that easy. All of us had a startle reaction when the eagle crashed the party. He dropped down smack in the middle of us with a thud, clutching a macaw in giant talons. The macaw took all the force of the landing. Just like that, the monkey was gone, running into the trees while holding Dave's cap firmly on his head.

"The macaw kicked frantically. One wing flapped awkwardly. The eagle hopped into the air and came down again with all his weight on top of the bird. It stopped fluttering.

Satisfied it was dead, the eagle started pulling feathers from the carcass, ignoring us as if we weren't significant in his world. Smerdis, not much taller than the bird, made us significant when he kicked it in the chest

"The eagle flew off, circled us a couple times, then dropped the macaw. The carcass landed in the center of our group. Smerdis looked at me and gave me a familiar set of signs. Arms out wide, palms up, shrugged shoulders, and the shaking head. He was telling us, for the second time that day, nothing could be done."

"Hold on Lock. A bird of prey doesn't act like that. He would have to be starving before he would attempt to eat his kill so close to people. If he was that hungry, why drop his dinner?"

"And a monkey doesn't act like that either, Bill. We were in a different world. The monkey was acting normally for that world, but the eagle ... All the dead birds at our campfire had been killed by the eagle. It was something new for the Savant, but it was expected. It had been prophesied. It's how the Savant knew I was coming. Dave and I didn't understand at the time, but I would hear about it soon. I would tell Dave about it a few days later."

"I don't understand that, Lock. Why?"

"Dave and I were separated that night. He stayed at our camp and I traveled to the Savant encampment."

"A dangerous decision. How did they convince you to separate?"

"Universal language again. They took my hand and started walking. They motioned for Dave to stay."

"For me, that's difficult to understand. I would be thinking that maybe you were some sort of prized sacrifice or Dave was going to get eaten. Why did you trust them so much?"

"We just did. It seemed appropriate at the time."

"Where did they lead you?"

"It was getting late and difficult to see under the forest canopy. The cliffs threw shade onto the lower region. We walked downhill from the campsite to some piled up leaves near a water source."

"Were you inside their encampment?"

"I was in an area where many of them slept. I could hear them murmur to each other off and on. The water was the last thing I remember hearing before I fell asleep."

"I want to stop you there, Lock. We're creeping closer to the really, really bizarre events, and I want to involve my wildly off-base audience in a little research. Conspiracy theories are fun, but on my show, we try to gather information before we settle on an opinion.

"I'm talking to you, dear listener. I've never seen this many Emails so irrationally certain. So, there is no need to hear any more information before conclusions are made? Herbert Spencer has a quote that eloquently shames what you guys at home are doing.

"I'm calling for audience participation time. Help me out. Send me that quote. I'm going to need it very shortly, but I'm telling you now, there is no CIA botanical warfare plot, and the Masons haven't even been mentioned. Where do you come up with this stuff?"

"Believe me when I say we are not telling tall tales. What I'm asking you to do is settle down. Don't be dismissive. Nobody is on the right trail. So, Lock, set us straight. Where were we?"

"First morning in the Savant encampment?"

"Tell us about your first morning."

"I woke up to very pleasant sounds. Birds with perfect pitch, contented purring from a large cat, the gurgle of water, and the giggle of a child. When I opened my eyes, I saw I had fallen asleep under a massive, sprawling, black walnut tree. Just ten feet above ground level, and directly over my head, a jaguar draped across a thick branch. Sitting next to him, a naked child smiled down at me."

"Lock, you're being a little nonchalant. I would have jumped out of my skin. What did you do?"

"I smiled back. The boy waved and scrambled down the branch, disappearing behind the tree. The big cat followed him."

"What a way to start the day. What came next?"

"Breakfast."

"Breakfast?"

"Yes. A bowl of blackberries."

"Mr. Lockjaw. I'm trying to lead you into telling us about your ceremonious meeting with the rest of the tribe."

Bill, I believe telling your listeners about the beauty around the encampment is important. I want them to know what the Savant enjoyed for so long and how much they lost."

"Okay. Please, do."

"In the small depression where I was eating breakfast, the source of the water's sound wasn't visible, but it was constant and melodious. I had to stand before I actually caught sight of flashes of reflected light on the trees. Nobody had to take my hand and lead me. I began walking in the direction of the water.

"As I approached, and the view became less obstructed, I was overtaken by the clarity of the spring, shining like a faceted sapphire. It glowed and flickered soft colors onto a limestone cliff.

"My view of the forest changed as I walked. The closer I got to the spring, the bigger the changes. There were flowers; moss as thick as sheep's wool but soft and lustrous. The trees, large and small, could have been designed by a bonsai master. They were all majestic, interestingly shaped, or bearing fruit. Exotic birds sat in the branches. Jaguars and monkeys found places in the trees where they could sun themselves near the gurgling water. I was in the grips of sensory overload.

"Suddenly, I was there, standing at the edge of the spring, looking straight down into a round, limestone-walled hole filled with water so clear I felt I could see forever. My knees got wobbly from vertigo. The water barely darkened as it got deeper. Some sort of flowering greenery was clinging to the smooth walls. The plants swayed back and forth in rhythm to the upward surge from the depths where this jewel was born. It was the crown of a glade filled with irrational beauty. The Savant told me it was their throne of long life. I will remember it forever.

"On the other side of the spring, people enjoyed their morning. An old woman launched herself out over the water, clinging to a grapevine wrapped around a branch of an oak tree. As she let go the vine, she whooped like a child. Her joy was comforting.

"When she came to the surface, a jaguar and a small child swam over to her. She chattered at the boy and pointed in my direction. When the child turned his head to look, I recognized his smile. He was the boy in the tree. Once again, I reflexively smiled back and waved to him. Slipping under the water, he swam like a dolphin until he reached a small rock outcropping near the rope swing. A set of stone stairs ensured that this would be a favorite exit from the spring."

"You mentioned one other thing about the spring, Lock. Tell us about that."

"You mean the water flow? The hole in the cliff?"

"Yes. You said the overflow disappeared into a wall of rock."

"That's true. The water spilled over smooth stone and ambled along until it split into smaller waterfalls downstream. These little falls gathered again into one final fall, straight down, and into a hole in the cliff. The hole swallowed up all the water flowing out of the spring. The flow, similar to the life story of Asitr, comes from one source, splits into separate channels, then rejoins for a mysterious, undetermined ending. Soon, we'll see what's at the end of the flow."

"Lock? More on that later. We will return to life in this little Garden of Eden after another break."

6

THE BILL ELLIOTT SHOW
ON AIR MONDAY – 2005

"EVERYBODY BACK? I think we are on time to finish this up today and move on to some surprises tomorrow. Don't miss tomorrows show. We're going to have corroboration to go along with our story. don't miss it. Okay... Lock."

"Yes, sir."

"You are standing at the edge of the spring. I imagine you wanted to dive in?"

"You bet, Bill."

"You didn't get the chance right then, did you?"

"No, sir."

"Tell us why."

"Smerdis appeared with a group of men and started organizing. He pulled me by the arm and led me to a log as the Savant began to gather together in a group. There were nearly a hundred of them. As they all began to settle in, I couldn't help but notice, every one of them was looking at me.

"I felt like they were waiting for me to say something, announce something. I felt foolish just standing there nodding and smiling.

"Smerdis let me know I was expected to sit on the log. The young boy with the jaguar stepped forward and sat next to me. The jaguar strolled up and curled at his feet. The only man present, who looked older than Smerdis, emerged from the group and stood in front of me, posturing with his arms folded over his chest, savoring some sort of big moment in front of his tribe."

"Sounds like he was going to be the master of ceremonies."

"Something like that, Bill. It turns out he was the first of many speakers. Reciters, I should say. I didn't know it at that time, but he was the first in a long line of Savant men and women who were going to stand in front of me and orate. Did you ever watch a foreign film with subtitles in yet another foreign language, Bill?"

"Can't say I ever have. Don't think I would ever want to."

"That's how I felt at first. It made me feel a little impolite and self conscious. I sat and smiled like a beauty pageant contestant, worrying I would fall asleep like that. Eventually, I began enjoying the sing-songy nature of the language. I started getting into the rhythm. I wasn't surprised later when Asitr described the language as very binary. Also, I took to getting involved in watching the audience reactions."

"People watching?"

"No. Watching the audience for plot clues. I had the uncomfortable feeling I was going to be a part of this production. I was sure the boy with the jaguar was a central character."

"How so?"

"Numerous times during the day all eyes were on the young boy. I began to notice that when the audience was celebrating an event in a story the boy would look either pleased or embarrassed. There were times the audience would exaggerate a stern look, and he would look ashamed. When they cried, he cried. When they laughed he would sometimes turn red in embarrassment and sometimes beam like a comedian who just brought down the house. There were numerous parts of those monologues that the audience clearly anticipated. They would join in unison to make sound effects.

"Sound effects?"

"Yeah, Bill. When the first speaker was telling his story, he went through the motions of throwing a spear. When he let go, the entire audience joined together with a sound like f-f-f-f-f-foop. The old actor strutted around as if he had just hit a hole in one. The audience showed their displeasure at his achievement by shaking their heads, hissing, and waving their arms, as if they were shooing him away. The second time that happened they cheered.

"This continued all day. I was surprised when it was suddenly over. Three men came forward and led me back to my camp. They slipped off into the forest, leaving behind hot tea and a delicious walnut and grain cake held together by an aromatic honey.

"That night, Dave had a hundred questions, and I had a thousand. We talked well into the night about mysteries we couldn't solve. We had facts and clues aplenty but not the right life experiences to prepare us to begin understanding."

"Hold on, Lock. Say that again. You had clues and facts but not enough experience? What does that mean?"

"We were in the same boat as your audience, Bill. We wanted to know what the military had to do with this. What did they know? Why were we dumped like sacrificial lambs onto this spot on earth? How did these people seem to know we were coming?

"The questions we asked each other were round holes with square answers. We explored avenues of understanding based on false assumptions. The answers were to come to me in just two more days. Five more days for Dave."

"Lock?"

"Yes, Sir?"

"I want to get to the moment you first started figuring out some of the right questions to ask. I'm skipping ahead to the afternoon of the third day of these orations. The second to last speaker is on the stage. You know where I'm going?"

"I believe you would like me to tell you about the thing that almost made me mess my pants."

"You got it, Lock. Before you tell us, let me just inform my audience of one thing."

"It's your show, Bill."

"People ... The kid with the jaguar has a name. His name is Asitr. Yes, he will be our main guest. Asitr will tell us some of the stories that Lockjaw heard. Hopefully, he'll tell us in English. Right now, however, those stories will remain every bit as much a mystery to us as they were to Lock when he watched them being told at spring-side. You are about to hear at which point Lockjaw started asking questions that were more to the point than the ones he and Dave asked each other around the campfire. Take it from there, Lock."

"Third night, about an hour before dusk, a young man with a tortured face is telling something very painful to the audience. Everyone is crying. When I feel a tug on my sleeve, I see no one is crying harder than the little boy, Asitr. I know he wants to say something to me, but is struggling to speak. His facial expressions cycle through emotions. Sorrow, great joy, and emotional pain often come with tears, and Asitr had all these emotions dancing across his face at the same time.

"I was confused. I wanted to embrace him, comfort him. Then, he gathered himself and said the most unexpected thing: 'When I last saw you, we were friends. My name was Gaipon. My foolishness broke your heart. When I was your grandfather, I was Sylvester Long. The world knew me as Buffalo Child Longlance. As your grandfather, I left only one thing from my life to your father. Your father left it to you.'

"How did he know about Gaipon? The gift from my father? I knew he was referring to a 78 RPM record. How did this little boy know about that, and how did he speak in English?

"Asitr pointed to the speaker and continued, 'Chin Feathers MacDonald is telling the story now. You will see, I now know how to sing it right. If you are any grandson of mine you will sing along.'

"The speaker, who had taken a name so familiar to me, began to sing, in English. '*What am I gonna see when I go and see the movies. What am I gonna do when I dream about 'em that night*'.

34

"I grabbed Asitr by the shoulder. ' What did you say? What?' That was the most response I could manage. There were so many reasons this shouldn't be happening.

"Asitr stood up and joined the rest of his people. When he stood, they all began to sing along. They were singing the same song I carried with me on a 78 RPM record. The recording was the only thing I inherited from any member of my family. It came along with a note from my father. The note read,

I *never knew your grandpa, but he left me this. It must have been all he had.*

It is all I have. Do better with this start than I did.

Love, Daddy

"The singing continued. ' *Listen to the music. It's so loud I want to join in. Listen to 'em play. They're very good. I wanna play too.'* My lip started to tremble. I stood up to sing, but felt faint, and sat back down...'*Shufflin' down the road. Just lookin' in the windows. Easy as it goes. Nothin' matters to me'.*

"Asitr stopped singing, grasped my elbow, and locked eyes. ' I have lived lives of lies,' he said, 'but I tell you truly. You are my grandson, and the last family I will ever have.'

"I stood stunned, encircled by the singers, staring into Asitr's face, wobbling in a waking faint."

"Mr. Lockjaw, we have a lot to prove. It's time for some local commercials."

*   *   *

"Hello again, and welcome back. Before I get this last segment of tonight's show pulled together, I want to thank my audience. You've come through again. Earlier, I asked for help in locating a wonderfully appropriate quote by Herbert Spencer. You guys have sent me quotes from Herbert, Edmund, Sarah, and Lady Diana Spencer. Greenbob40 even passed along a Spencer Tracy quote. Most of you got it right, though, and here it is. 'There is a principle which is a bar against all information, which is proof against all arguments, and cannot fail to keep a man in everlasting ignorance. That principle is contempt prior to investigation.'

"I intended the quote to be a caution for my audience, but, as it turns out, I was a little late.

"During correspondence with Asitr, prior to booking him on my show, he said to me, 'Facts can change, or swirl around chaotically. The reason they don't always cling to the constant, immovable truth is because we fail to interpret them correctly.'

"We've just taken our first few steps, and already we have one foot planted in misinterpretation, and the other foot is stuck in the ugly ooze of contempt prior to investigation.

"I had a telephone call on our last break. It was from a man with cold feet. He wasn't originally scheduled to be a guest on tonight's broadcast, but I think it's prudent to give him a little time. Later, he will join us to speak with Asitr. Because we need to do this, I have one request of our guest. Lockjaw?"

"Yes, sir?"

"I am going to take over the narrative. Don't go away. I'm still going to need you, but I have to give our surprise guest enough time to deal with his issues. Are you okay with that?"

"Relieved."

"Good. Let's buzz right by the obvious points. You recover and stay at the spring site for two days. The time is spent conversing with the boy you now embrace as your grandfather. You return to your base camp and attempt to explain things to Dave. How did that go?"

"He withdrew. He thought I was crazy."

"How did the Savant treat him?"

"They were polite, sweet, but distrustful. He wasn't mentioned in their prophecy. It's an uncomfortable time for them all until the re-arrival of the helicopter."

"I think it's fair to say that over the next three months an understanding was reached between the parties involved. You decided to stay with the tribe, and Dave decided to leave with the helicopter. Is that accurate?"

"Spot on."

"There were consequences. Dave told honorable lies. He threw his career under the bus by requesting compassionate discharge. Traumatic feelings he couldn't shake after seeing all his buddies die of snakebite was his story. I believe he did a difficult and honorable thing.

"As for the Savant? Not a pretty tale. It's sickening and shameful.

"Anybody want to see the only written record you will find of what happened to the Savant? You can find it in the February, 1966 issue of the Ford Foundation newsletter to the Rand Institute. The newsletter is what we call an 'industry rag.' It contains odd bits and pieces of news from around the world that don't find public print or airplay.

"This particular article is an interview with a Brazilian colonel named Frates. He's boasting about his unit's annihilation of a deadly band of communist-trained terrorists with western contacts. He claims it was a fierce battle to the death, and his unit suffered enormous casualties. Look at the picture of the colonel next to the story. I have it on my website. Look at his prizes. There is a pair of Beetle boots, Levis, a really ugly shirt, and a box of condoms. Sound familiar?

"Yes, it's evidence of western contact. Nothing else meets the standard of being called conclusions. He didn't have his facts straight and his conclusions wrong. He was lying, willfully and maliciously. Look at his smile. Nice white teeth hiding a coal black heart.

"I don't know which corporations benefited from this slaughter, but there was American complicity. The world is ripe with slaughter and some of it justified. But to slaughter the innocent for resources that benefit the almighty stockholder is a ..."

"Bill? Bill! Stop. I'm sorry, but you don't quite have it right."

"No? What is not right? My facts? I got those from you three."

"Good facts and bad conclusions, Bill. Don't feel bad. It's an epidemic."

"I'm not feeling bad, Lock. I'm feeling confused. What are you saying? Were the Savant slaughtered?"

"Yes, and slaughters of indigenous peoples still go on today. I appreciate your anger is justified, if not infectious. Like you, I feel like howling at the moon, but I can't set it right. I'll never accept it, and I can't stop it. We do think the Savant eradication was different, and maybe we can do something about that. It's on our list."

"Your list?"

"Yes, please respect why the list is private. We don't know why, after multiple lives, Asitr is here. Trying to figure out why he's here feels like another square-questions-round-holes moment for us. Narrowing our list of guesses is a difficult process. It's not all about Alazam, here we are. There's no magic involved."

"Okay, then. Let's do it like this. Tell my audience what happened to the Savant. Perhaps we can reach a different conclusion. You can explain it right after station identification."

7

"ALAZAM, HERE WE ARE," Otis repeated, while silencing the marble in his room. "Those aren't colorful, throw-away words, Doc. They caused a stir when they were broadcast. When the name Alazam ..."

Otis paused mid-sentence. He wasn't sure Dr. Milton was awake, so he quit speaking and waited. The doctor was slumped in his chair, one leg draped over the other, his hands folded on his lap, and his eyes at half-mast. Neither the sudden silence of the radio show or the words from Otis, speaking directly to him, changed the pose.

The silent pause continued until Doctor Milton lifted his left hand and waggled his fingers in Otis's direction, indicating he wanted him to continue.

"On the moon, when the name, Alazam, was spoken on the radio," Otis started again, "Kae'Lairy silenced the marble to bring the two watchers up to speed. His monologue was constructed with scraps of the clarity he felt upon entering the adventure and admissions of confusion at the end.

'Was this a coincidence?' Kae'Lairy asked the two watchers. 'Are you thinking a rebel angel under judgment couldn't surface? I need to tell you things you don't know and remind you of things you should already understand.'

"Barabajyl and Jederic leaned forward and rotated their head slightly left, indicating they were committed to listening and anxious to understand.

Otis tilted his head toward the ceiling and closed his eyes. The surface of his eyelids pulsed with movement, as if, underneath, he were speed-reading words on their surface. "I finally understood one of the burdens Kae'Lairy was under," he said after the pause. "The mighty often fall victim to believing power is an inoculation against traps of colliding ethical challenges."

Otis opened his eyes again and introduced a recording from the moon. "This is Kae'Lairy telling his brothers how he stepped into his trap."

*   *   *

KAE'LAIRY'S SOLILOQUY 1

From the time man learned to use the ethers for speaking to multitudes, my mind was set on monitoring radio broadcasts from earth. My motivation for undertaking the task was fear for the species. I was fearful necessary civic discourse would be smothered by hypnotic one-way messages intended to wither and kill the requirement for independent thoughtfulness. You can see and hear my fear is fulfilled. In modern cultures, human discourse, once born of observation and curiosity, is smothered by a monotonous shriek of angry parrots.

While listening to *The Bill Elliott Show,* I ended my intrusion of passive listening. The description of the lost world in the Amazon was a call to action. I shut down all monitoring not involved with the program and vowed to investigate.

It was I who designed and landscaped the world of the Savant. It was the Lord's wish to make it so. I never questioned why that world was made, but I was surprised to hear it talked about on the radio. Surprises were just beginning.

The second surprise was the involvement of Asitr. I knew him from before the flood. I enjoyed his gardens at the temple of the Adam. When his name was spoken, I summoned your brother, Olphrenjii. There was cause to include him. In Asitr's first life, Olphrenjii was his guardian.

Surprise number three caused my vibration rate to soar. The spark that caused the jump was the casual mention of the name Alazam. Baal Alazam was fallen. In the rebellion, he allied with the sect of Marduk. His involvement in Asitr's first life and the sly mention of his name couldn't be ignored.

As you should know, the co-existence of Alazam and Asitr, in the time of the big war, makes Asitr a legitimate judge for the fallen brother in this life. At the time of the broadcast, I believed Asitr would call for Alazam's destruction, and I would be the instrument to execute the conclusion.

In the clarity of conclusion-jumping, I didn't stop to rethink the pitfalls of human language, so radically evolutionary, never trustworthy, and easily manipulated.

When I left my sanctum to follow the mystery, I wasn't prepared for the tangling tongues. When last I spoke with man, we shared a common language, clean, clear, and married to the certainty of numbers. I especially underestimated the confounding nature of English, a language designed to understand engineering but misused to engineer misunderstanding.

Pardon the directly contradictory wording, but for the fallen, English is a God-send. They favor its use for expanding gradations of meaning in words. They craft words into alleys around truth, and they ride the maze of those alleys expertly, avoiding the highway that leads to the inevitable dead end. For them, every gradation between good and evil is one more step away from the inevitable.

Unlike the certainty in numbers, human languages measure meaning with untrustworthy scales. This and that can be blurred to appear that white is black, black is gray, gray is neither, and neither is any or all, regardless of what the definition of "is" is. Because the humans choose to be told what to think, they no longer reason. They prefer to parrot abstract conclusions and represent them as facts and truths.

Never has a human in the short life known the truth, but every human believes he knows a sufficient amount of facts. If challenged to rethink, they'll throw out the baby Jesus with the bath water rather than search for him in the dirty suds.

Because Loyals never lie, and every man is required to search for the truth, it's wise to avoid dialogue with humans.

Because the Fallen seldom lie, but enjoy tilting the facts away from light, they embrace the weapon of teaching. 'You can see why one side is weak in the usage, and the other is empowered.

Because I didn't respect the unfairness of our parameters, or foresee the frustration I would find in babbling languages, I acted unwisely. I went to earth because I thought I must. Uncalled by the Lord to action, I entangled myself, neck deep, in human nonsense and the English language.

*   *   *

After playing Kae'Lairy's deflective soliloquy, Otis touched the marble then massaged his temples before he continued speaking. "It was awkward," he said suddenly. "On the moon, I mean.

"While I watched the angels listening to Kae'Lairy, I saw the poses of his brothers slowly change. They understood. Kae'Lairy, brilliant among the brilliant, mighty among mighty, and loyal to the Lord, tried to do everything he thought to do. Still, here he was on the moon, twenty years later, resenting his role of choice, doubting his nerve, and most of all, weakening in his resolve to resist the temptation to rewrite everything in a language of his choosing.

"For the two angels studying the mighty Kae'Lairy's pose, it was fearful to observe his present faithlessness. When he activated the marble, and the radio show began again, the sound of Bill Elliott's voice was a soothing relief from Kae'Lairy's agitated rambling."

8

"WE ARE BACK. Back to the studio and back to the question. Lock, what do you want to say about the demise of the Savant people?"

"I want to say the Savant had a long and interesting life on this planet. They had something that must have been like the Garden of Eden had been. Faithfully, they kept their part in the cosmic dance of Asitr's coming and going for thousands of years.

"In his last life, when Asitr awoke to the process of downloading all his past memories., they calmed him. They knew their paradise would be destroyed. They were afraid, but they felt they were moving on to something better. The Savant tribe ended their days on earth as good stewards of a job well done. The crime that brought them suffering was a damnable burst of brief evil, not an existential tragedy.

"Those gentle people faced it the only way they knew how. They hid. Three helicopter loads of Brazilian rangers couldn't find them after a 24-hour search.

"Asitr and I hid near the spring to stay within earshot of the colonel's tent. After some drinking and swimming, the call was made by Col. Frates. 'Let's give 'em napalm, the eastern coordinates. That should flush them out." Remember, Bill, It's 1965. We were only testing napalm in 1965. We hadn't used it in Viet Nam yet."

"You knew about napalm? What it could do?"

"Yes. In 1964, I mapped an area for testing."

"I suppose hearing the colonel's order struck some fear in your heart?"

"I thought of the way Schellert died. Ever stand down wind of poison ivy smoke, Bill? I knew every person who came in contact with the smoke was going to die, never mind the Napalm. I told Asitr the same thing. He said, 'The tribe knows these are their last hours. They're happy to see the Lord. I wish I could go with them.' Then, he added, 'I suppose the time is now for the two of us to leave.'

"It felt silly to ask the question, but I did. 'There is a way out? We can just walk away?' I thought he might have been engaging in a little dark humor."

'Figuring that out is your job,' he said. 'Prophecy says you will take me out of here.'

"Does prophecy say how?" I asked.

"I proposed the idea that, maybe, I could hijack one of the copters. Asitr asked me if I could fly one. I had to admit I couldn't, adding, "'we would stand a better chance if we dove down the hole by the spring." Then he dropped one of his bombs. 'That's how Quetzalcoatl got out of here,' he said. 'I meant to tell you about him.'

"I accepted this with a matter-of-fact calm. At least it was a plan. I suppose I felt protected by prophecy. What I did next was a complete abandonment of caution. I picked Asitr up and began to walk toward the spring.

"The Colonel and some of his men were talking at its edge. Other soldiers were swimming. We were just ten yards away from the tree line when the men standing next to the pool became distracted. One of them let out a laugh. 'Look at this,' he shouted. All eyes turned to where he was pointing. Asitr's jaguar was draped over a branch of the oak that held the rope swing. Colonel Frates emptied his sidearm into the animal.

"Everyone who was not in the spring walked over to where the great cat slid to the ground. They chattered and laughed, drowning the voices of soldiers in the pool shouting warnings of a 'spirit' walking through their camp. Dressed only in gray limestone paste and patches of moss, I carried Asitr past the pool, slid down the little waterfalls, and without hesitation, I pushed him, feet first, into the hole that drained all the water flowing from the spring. I followed him head-first and didn't return to my senses until I saw the dim light at the entrance disappear, and realized we were being pushed along in a cold current of black ink.

"My calm turned to panic. I reached out to feel for walls. They found me. Consumed in a world without ups or downs, we banged and scraped, faster and harder as we went. I lost contact with Asitr, but bumped into him again in the dark. He was limp.

"I pulled him to my chest, then suddenly, I felt like a popped balloon. Flashes of light surged through my brain. Air expelled out of my mouth, and I began choking as water came back in. We were stuck in a narrow outlet. Water pushed so heavily against us I couldn't push back. I tried to force Asitr through, but I couldn't budge him. I gathered myself with the will to die trying. That's when Asitr put his palm in my face and pushed my head backward. I felt him slip away and through the hole. He'd saved his energy for that moment.

"Now, it was up to him to save me. I was in the latter stages of drowning, beyond helping anyone. My consciousness slipped into a comfortable zone of warmth and resignation. I wished Asitr well and blacked out.

"The next thing I recall was being dragged halfway out of a river and onto gravel. Asitr was pulling me to safety. After coughing water, I rolled myself over and blinked at a star lit sky. The deep sleep of exhaustion overcame us.

"In the morning, we woke up to the sun peaking from the other side of the poison ivy covered cliffs. We were still half in and half out of the river, covered from the waist down with leeches. Asitr summed our situation up neatly. 'We aren't in Eden anymore.'

"While we were still scraping leeches from our skin with sharp rocks, two American fighter jets shrieked overhead and dropped napalm into Eden. I held up my finger to test the wind. Judging from the location of the first bomb drops, and the direction of the wind, I made a bold prediction. "This Colonel will regret what he is doing as soon as the smoke gets to the spring." No sooner than the words left my mouth, a helicopter rose above the cliffs, taking the colonel safely away from the smoke that created such 'high casualties' among his troops. The innocent Savant people were on their way to becoming 'communist insurgents with western contacts.' In this case, history wasn't written by the winners. The winners were in a place where they couldn't be interviewed."

"Thank you for the perspective, Lock. Can I get one more brief description out of you to cover the next forty years?"

"Five years stomping around in the Amazon jungle, fifteen years of getting insanely wealthy in the antiquities market, and twenty more years of trying to figure out why this was happening."

"Well, I guess I couldn't ask for a more economical summation than that. We are going to forget about the survival lessons. We are going to skip past the wealth building years, and I'm going to admit to my audience that we still don't have an answer for my big question. Why is Asitr here?

"So, Lock, what does that leave us with? My audience is chomping at the bit for evidence. I want to start with your 78 RPM record. Without getting into the complete story of why it's going to be significant, give us a little background. How many people have you shared it with?"

"I used to play the recording at the orphanage. After our Victrola was replaced with a modern little phonograph our unit manager confiscated the record. He said it would ruin the needle on his new equipment. The letter from my father was tucked into the sleeve.

"I reminded him from time to time that I wanted the record and letter when I left the orphanage. On my eighteenth birthday, he gave me the 78 as a present. The letter was lost, but the message was retained in my mind. I was happy. Finally I possessed and owned a gift from grandfather to father, and passed on with hopes for my doing well in life."

"Did you ever play the record after leaving the orphanage?"

"I never intended to. People didn't want to hear the scratchy old thing. I did share it with a Montagnard boy in Viet Nam. His name was Gaipon. He spotted it in my hutch and became excited. His father had an old Victrola but no records.

"The first time I played it on his father's Victrola I was feeling particularly depressed about my Viet Nam mission, and I told him why I treasured it. He didn't understand me, but it was therapeutic for me to say it out loud. Gaipon didn't speak English, but his soprano, broken-language attempt to sing along was a delight for me. I considered him to be my best friend. That's why it was so hard to face up to the fact that I would shoot him to death in just two more days. Asitr can tell you more about that later."

"Okay, Lock. Let me make an appeal to my audience. I'm sorry we have to put these events out in such a spotty way. Sometimes there are just too many interconnected facts. When that happens, it requires some attention span and concentration. Be patient. Lock?"

"Yes, Bill?"

"I think this is the last time we speak to you on the air. If we need you again, I hope you make yourself available. Will you do that?"

"I am here to do what's needed, Bill."

"Thanks, man … Okay, let's move on to something I wasn't expecting.

"Listeners. You know I hate the unpredictable, but I love to be adaptable. Let's adapt to something unpredictable, shall we? I want to introduce a guest that wasn't even scheduled to speak this evening. He's our man with cold feet, Jack VanGrada. Tell our audience who you are Jack."

"Good evening Mr. Elliott. I also wish a good evening to all of your listeners."

"I'm sure the feeling is mutual. My audience loves everybody until they open their mouth."

"Ouch. I hope you aren't suggesting I will be boorish as well as having cold feet?"

"Not at all. I have a great deal of respect for you and your organization. I understand your cold feet as well, but you won't back out on our agreement."

"Bill, rescinding our agreement may be the prudent thing to do."

"Prudence is one thing, Jack, but your organization doesn't cultivate a culture of prudence. I believe you will keep your word about tomorrow's event.

"We'll see Bill. We maintain high standards."

"Okay. Let me invite my listeners who haven't heard of your organization to visit your website. You can get there by going to Explorersclub.com."

"Thank you, Mr. Elliott."

"Why don't you tell us a little about yourself and the Explorers Club?"

"Sure. I am proud to serve as the official historian of the finest international club in the world. Our flag has proudly flown over the men and women who have accomplished the greatest feats and firsts in the history of mankind."

"Name a few of those feats and firsts, will you?"

"I would be proud to. First, Bill, I would like to point out that if not for our earliest members having cold feet, we wouldn't have a club today."

"Very funny, Mr. VanGrada. You are, of course, referring to your club's role in assisting the expeditions who claim to be first to the north and south poles?"

"Yes, we also flagged the expeditions which were first to the Marianas Trench, the first to Everest, and first to the moon."

"First to the moon? That was a flagged Explorers Club expedition?"

"We collaborated with the effort. Armstrong, Aldrin, and Collins are all members. They carried our flag with them. Going to the moon was a perfect fit for our mission statement."

"Just what is your mission statement, Sir?"

"I suppose you want me to boil it down into a couple sentences?"

"Yes, good clock watching,"

"We bring a web of accomplished and exploration minded scientists, educational organizations, industrialists, and financiers to join in facilitating the exploration of land, sea, air, and space. We go where mans' curiosity takes him. We support the education of promising individuals who show an early aptitude, curiosity, and inclination to explore. In the shrinking world of untainted research, we stand alone. If I may be permitted to boast, we are the cat's pajamas."

"I suppose that's why you're nervous about being associated with tomorrow's media event?"

"Exactly, Bill. I don't want to participate in associating my club with a stunt."

"Well, Jack, here is a list of people who must have been afraid of failure but continued anyway. Tensig Norgay, Robert Henson, Ootah, Robert Peary, Roald Amundsen, Jacques Cousteau, Sir Edmund Hillary, Jacques Piccard, Don Walsh ..."

"Mr. Elliot, I understand your point. My point is, those men began their steps after much research and preparation. We acknowledge it is your guests who reminded us about a forgotten time capsule at our New York office. For that reason, we agreed to a public opening. We had no idea you were going to sensationalize the event with a wild, impossible story. In light of the late blind-side, we require some investigation and preparation of our own."

"Mr. VanGrada, I understand the caution. I do, but I certainly feel that if Asitr passes your test, you should put aside your contempt, prior to investigation."

"Regrettably, to be frank, I do have disdain for your presumptions. However, should Asitr answer my questions satisfactorily, I will honor our original agreement. The time capsule will be opened in front of any news media you can persuade to attend."

"Then let's bring Asitr on. Asitr."

"Good evening, gentlemen."

"Good evening, Asitr. Welcome to my show."

"Good evening, sir. Jack VanGrada at your service. I must say I'm surprised at your voice. It's good to finally hear the man I shared so much correspondence with."

"Surprised at his voice? What do you mean?"

"Asitr sounds larger than the three-foot Savant I heard about on the show tonight, Mr. Elliott. I think I expected a thinner voice. Asitr, you have a perfectly natural accent for a man who picked English up a short time ago."

"Time is a relative thing, Mr. VanGrada. When I first spoke English, Chaucer hadn't yet conceived his 'Canterbury Tales'. I have a natural accent in all the languages I've spoken, modern, ancient, and obsolete."

"Is that so? Perhaps you can translate this for me: *Naga bumpoppa jinshaw*."

"I beg your pardon?"

"I'm cutting to the chase, sir. I wouldn't expect you to recognize a word of that language."

"You surprised me. Are you related to Cyrus Affeldt?"

"Where did ... How do you know that?"

"I knew the man who taught that little jingle to his children. He had a few others he made up as well. I believe that one was done to tell the little ones they had to get ready for bed."

"Mr. Elliott?"

"Yes, sir ... Mr. VanGrada? Are you okay?"

"I'm sorry. I'm stunned."

"Yes, Jack, you've made that clear."

"Mr. Asitr ... Cyrus Affeldt was my great grandfather. He was proud to be a friend of Chief Buffalo Child Long Lance."

"Cyrus was a very funny man. A wonderful father. He once saved my life."

"Yes. That's not common knowledge. Tell me, where were you at the time?"

"We were at the battle of Vimy ridge, Jack. Historians say the battle was the beginning of Canadian military unity."

"That's correct, sir. My grandmother claimed you would never have gone on to win all your medals if G G Paw hadn't saved your life."

"Agnes is your grandmother?"

"Yes, she passed away in 1942."

"Too young. She was sweet as blueberry pie."

"Mother told us that's how G G Paw always described her."

"Gentlemen? Can I have my show back? I don't want to interrupt your little homecoming, but I think it's safe to assume Asitr passed your test?"

"I may have swallowed something hook, line, and sinker here, but I have no idea how Mr. Longlance ... Mr. Asitr, could possibly know my great grandfather's funny little patois, or come prepared to interpret a made up language that I, and only I, should know. I'm intrigued enough to welcome you at the opening tomorrow."

"Thank you, sir. I'll be seeing you at the club. Asitr can't be there, but Dave and I will see you tomorrow, noonish."

"I'll be looking forward to that. Gentlemen, I wish you both a good evening."

"And to you as well, sir, let's talk again about Cyrus. I have some good stories."

"Not tonight, guys. I feel left out, and we need to move on to my now-obvious announcement. Tomorrow, Dave and I, along with any news media we can convince to attend, will be at the Explorers Club for the opening of a forgotten time capsule. Why will that be important? Tomorrow we start to accumulate the promised proof. If you tune in to tomorrow night's show you'll hear Asitr tell us from memory about his life as Sylvester Long, a forgotten man in American history.

"Sylvester's story runs much deeper than simply being a good friend of Mr. VanGrada's G G Paw. Sylvester's story will be part of his explanation for the 78 RPM record that is Lockjaw's treasure. That story and our predictions for what will be found inside the time capsule will start our march toward proving we are not telling tall tales. So, Mr. Asitr."

"Yes, Bill."

"Look at the clock. I think the time has come for you to tell us what we are going to find in the capsule tomorrow. First, tell us how you know."

"I know because I put some items in the box. I can't tell you much about what others put in. When I placed my package into the capsule, I did notice one thing that was probably put in by Babe Ruth."

"What makes you think something was placed in there by the Babe?"

"I knew he was on the list of contributors. I noticed a baseball with his signature."

"Okay, sheesh. I guess everything doesn't have to be a big mystery."

"Everything and every thing is a mystery, Bill."

"Well then, let's get on to your contribution. What did you place in the vault?"

"I put in some recording technology history and a letter from my mother. Together, they highlight the false world of Chief Buffalo Child Long Lance."

"We will explore all of this tomorrow, but let's get specific. What is the item in the capsule?"

"A 78 RPM recording of an impromptu jam session with the likes of Larry 'Chin Feathers' McDonald, Johnny 'Go Man' Mohan, Daddy 'Long Legs' Spier, and a drummer whose name has been lost over time. It's the only known recording of Larry McDonald. Some say he is the bridge between hot jazz and R&B. The song, *Procrastination Blues*, was recorded in an after-hours club in New York by a man named Alan Blumlein. He was experimenting with, and trying to perfect, a binaural recording system."

"You mean stereo?"

"Yes, he achieved the patent for his invention in 1931."

"You believe this is the first ever recording successfully done in stereo?"

"I wouldn't say it was all that successful. It was ruined by a drunken Negro Indian named … well, you get the picture. I ruined the recording. You can hear a young patron named Louis Armstrong distinctly calling the song off in mid verse one. 'Hey, hey, hey,' he says. 'Move that mike away from our brother in moccasins over there. He's steppin' on the guitar lines.'

"He was right. You can hear my voice, but not many of my words. I sound like a fool. Blumlein moved the mike closer to the bass and achieved one edgy, but scratchy version of *Procrastination Blues*.

"After the second recording, old Satchmo approached me. He felt he'd been rude, so he convinced Mr. Blumlein to give me the aborted copy. Blumlein wasn't happy with the quality of the second take either, so he let me have them both. One, I put in the time capsule. The other was passed on to my son."

"Tomorrow, dear listeners, we will learn more about this. Right now, it's time to say goodnight. It's been wild, Asitr. Sleep well, my friend."

"Thank you, Bill. Goodnight."

"That's it for tonight, folks. Tomorrow we'll meet again. Same place, same station. This is Bill Elliott. Good night!"

9

HARBINGER INSTITUTE
April 1, 2025

OTIS BARELY GLANCED AT DR. MILTON as he reached across the bed to silence the marble, but after gathering his pillows and raising himself into a sitting position, he watched the doctor for evidence he was still awake. "It's getting a little creepy, Doc. I need to know you're listening."

Without changing the slump of his frame, or the droop of his eyes, Dr. Milton waggled fingers in Otis's direction.

Otis crossed his arms, narrowed his eyes, and stared in silence. After a loud sniff, he raised his thumb to his nose and waggled his fingers toward the laconic doctor.

Dr. Milton stiffened and sat up straight in his chair. "Mr. Beckley," he said, "I see you have concerns about my methods."

Otis shrugged. "I just want to be sure you're awake, Doc. You know what they say in some circles. *Humans got to sleep. Angels need to rest.* Which were you doing?"

The doctor lifted both feet off the floor and stiffened his legs. The stiffness traveled up his body until his arms spread and he let out a loud yawn. After a quick shoulder shimmy, he slowly folded back into his listening position. "You have your poses and body tells, Mr. Beckley. I have my attention to vocal tells. Let me assure you, your words are in good ears." Once again, Dr. Milton lifted his left hand and waggled his signal to continue.

Otis tried to stifle a yawn before he spoke, but the law of yawn contagion was in effect. "Oh, that felt good," he exclaimed. "I haven't yawned for twenty years. Angels don't know what they're missing."

Following the reunion of man and yawn, Otis ran his hands over his shoulders and biceps, re-exploring once-familiar territory. "Sorry, Doc, I've been all mind and no body for a long time. I'm coming around." Otis brushed his hand across his face and tugged on an ear before slumping into the pillows and getting back to his story.

"I'll play Tuesday's show for you, but I think you should understand the angelic activity between the *'good nights'* of Monday's show and the *'good evenings'* at the top of Tuesday's program.

"After the show signed off, Kae'Lairy made plans and Olphrenjii made moves

"Kae'Lairy's plan for himself was to put *ears* inside Bill's studio, trace the calls during the show, and find Asitr's location. He had tasks in mind for Olphrenjii and summoned him, but the Little Wing didn't come as called.

"After receiving Kae'Lairy's summons, Olphrenjii visited his sanctum in earth's asteroid belt and prayed. After prayer, he chose to answer Kae'Lairy by offering his own sanctum for the meeting place. In their world, Olphrenjii's resistance to authority and offer of hospitality was a message sent. *I'm on your side, but I'm not on your team.*

"You might think the mighty Kae'Lairy could force a little-wing like Olphrenjii to do his bidding, but like everything else they do, Kae'Lairy and Olphrenjii had rules to follow. Negotiations were in order, but before the sun rose on the Explorers Club in New York, both angels knew where they stood with each other.

"On the moon, Kae'Lairy explained the need for negotiations to Jederic and Barabajyl. This is the recording of his explanation."

Otis touched the marble on the cart and Kae'Lairy's voice, sounding more self-reflective than mighty, surprised the doctor when it filled the room.

*　　*　　*

KAE'LAIRY'S WORDS TO THE WATCHERS

I anticipated the prospect of Olphrenjii removing himself from my authority. We had differences in the big war, but I traveled to his sanctum and implored him to reason. I asked for assurances he wasn't interjecting old feelings into his refusal to enter into a pact.

In answer, Olphrenjii spread his arms, and light illuminated a string of asteroids from the rock he called his sanctum to the tiny shining ball that once was the core of planet Tiamat. "Here is the path of my disagreement with you," he said. "Does this new mystery have a connection with your destruction of the beloved planet? Is earth safe from your wrath? I have, foremost in my mind, the oath to protect humanity. Foremost, for you, is protection of the throne. I won't commit faithlessly to a pact."

I accepted and expected Olphrenjii's distrust, so I was prepared to offer him a pact of limited agreement. "Communicate?" I asked.

His reply was as terse as my question. "Yes."

Olphrenjii followed his agreement by moving into a pose of separation. "I ask you," he inquired in the formal manner, "Are you instructed by the Lord?" I understood the question was a required precaution before refusing a pact.

I responded, "I am not."

"Then, may I advise?" Olphrenjii continued the rite.

"You may," I answered.

"I see the possibility of this amnesia being purposeful and from the Lord," he offered. "I sense you see it as a danger for the Lord."

Despite Olphrenjii's distrust, I ended the ritual with the four *positives.* Friendly in posture, open in pose, respectful in facial attitude, and soothing in voice. "I have no argument, and so, my authority has ended," I told him. "Out of respect, I ask for foreknowledge of Asitr's plans and suggestions for my own path."

Olphrenjii told me he had already made contact with the Asitr and would soon take form. He pointed toward the core of the exploded planet, and his lighted path from core to sanctum retracted, leaving darkness in its place. "Look at what's been right in front of you," he said.

Olphrenjii's suggestion was a rebuke. I felt the jab and understood it was delivered because of past acts. Ignoring the message behind the answer, I asked, "Specifically, brother, in this mystery, where should I look?"

"Sing-songy and binary," he began. "This is the description of the Savant language. Is he here to speak to humans on the radio or to those of us, loyal or rebel, who speak the original language? Would you silence him because you don't know what he'll say?"

Olphrenjii was filtering his opinion through his perception that I was too eager to see danger and too quick to act violently. I didn't try to convince him differently. At the time, I didn't see a danger to the throne. I still believed my involvement would be as executioner in a sanctioned judgment. What I offered Olphrenjii was friendlier association in the form of agreement.

"I agree with independent cooperation," I said. "We can both see that traffic will be coming fast. I accept you will take form with the boys, but I ask you, is there any way, please, you can avoid taking form as that Ol' Frenchy, chute-packing guy, from Fort Huachuca?"

Olphrenjii didn't speak his answer. He leaned slightly backwards and smiled, signaling it was too late to change, the contact had been made, and he enjoyed my frustration.

10

HARBINGER INSTITUTE
April 1, 2025

O TIS OPENED HIS EYES and pinched the bridge of his nose between finger and thumb after silencing the marble. "Don't think of it as a grudge, in the human sense, Doc. For these two angels, the divide was an emotional sore spot, a difference of opinion from the big war, but it was a long way from subversive. Think of Olphrenjii's actions as more like a punitive act of grieving. They parted as allies with different paths toward a shared goal.

"Olphrenjii knew he could act independently, but still retain the protection of the mighty angel. When he took form with the boys, he felt free to focus on his primary concern, the protection of human existence.

"Kae'Lairy parted in full control of his own actions, stinging from Olphrenjii's distrust, but confident he could do what he might have to do. He was, first and foremost, empowered as a protector of the throne.

"Having to review the humbling meeting with Olphrenjii to Jederic and Barabajyl left Kae'Lairy feeling in need of delivering a reminder. The pride of his sect called for a demonstration. Just so there would be no mistaking humble for weak, Kae'Lairy lifted his chin and glowed. He held the light long enough to make his point. Right there, at the campfire, he was in no mood to be disrespected. The mighty one held his right to authority in a tight grip."

Satisfied he had no more to say, Otis activated the marble and unfamiliar bumper music introduced the beginning of Tuesday night's radio program.

*   *   *

THE BILL ELLIOTT SHOW
ON-AIR TUESDAY

"Good evening, friends. I am Bill Elliott, and here we are, together again.

"So what did you think? Did you notice the change in our bumper music? That scratchy piece of American recording history came out of a time capsule today. I think you know where it was found. Don't you love Ol' Satchmo sounding grumpy? I didn't think he was capable.

"How about that TV coverage? You missed it? So did I. There wasn't any. We are big mukluks in the tabloids, though. We'll get to that, read a couple of headlines, and begin getting to know Asitr. But first, I want to send out a big thank you to Mr. VanGrada for making a copy of the recording. Stay tuned. We'll be right back.

11

"EVERYBODY BACK? Listen to this headline in the *New York Cosmic Times*. Yup, that's the name of the newspaper. It says, and I quote, 'Pygmy Psychic Reads Letter Encased in Steel'. Beneath the headline, they have an artist's rendering of a man that looks like Hervé Villechaize in minstrel face.

"Here's another. This is from *Weird Globe*. 'Indian Prophet Predicts Contents of Forgotten Time Capsule'.

"My favorite is from the *New York Times*. Yes, we got a mention in the Times. Not a headline, but this, a half-page article on the *Amazing Illustro*. Look at the last sentence in the story. *Illustro pointed to the time capsule stunt at the usually staid Explorers Club as evidence that magic was more than the usual bag of tricks in the 21st century.* I find this all to be perplexing.

"Facts and conclusions. Facts and conclusions. Here are some facts: Dave went with me to the Explorers club this morning. We passed out sealed envelopes, and asked everyone in attendance to refrain from reading the contents until just before the opening of the time capsule. Nearly all of the news media members present opened their envelopes immediately. They might be corporate toadies, folks — but even the modern reporter will have some sense of curiosity. They compared one to the other, and then most of them left, grumbling about being used as stage props for a magic act. I suppose they may have lost that old pride in spreading the news, but they've retained a healthy sense of needing to be treated with deference and dignity.

"I want to be clear. Asitr warned us we would be perceived as performers, working a contrived stunt. I argued hard for the envelope strategy.

"The results of my incorrect assumptions are these: Mr. VanGrada is feeling every bit the odd boy down at the club. He's viewed as being part of a hoax. The club hierarchy has acknowledged our role in uncovering the time capsule, but they are so incensed by the taint of us they refuse to share access to the contents. They do acknowledge the Babe Ruth ball and the 78 RPM record. Those items were self-evident to all the witnesses at the opening.

"More importantly, Mr. VanGrada opened and read the letter inside the record's sleeve. As soon as Mr. VanGrada read it aloud, the box and all of its contents were taken from the room. A self-described officer of the club made a terse announcement to the effect that all the box's contents were Explorers Club property and they needed further investigation.

Dave proposed to him that Lockjaw would volunteer to take a DNA test to prove that he was the actual grandson of Sylvester Long. He requested, after the DNA test came back as proof of ancestry, the letter from the safe would be returned to Asitr.

"Their negative answer shines a light on just how much credibility VanGrada's people have given us. The response was: 'We have no doubt the inside knowledge used to perpetrate this hoax comes from one or more profligate offspring of Sylvester Long. Let us test Mr. Asitr's DNA against known samples of Mr. Long's and we will be happy to share the results with your public.' As a parting shot, he whispered in Dave's ear, 'Tell Mr. Asitr we will play the who's-your-daddy game under those conditions.'

"It's hard to understand folks, but it doesn't work that way. We're claiming DNA goes no deeper than the clay of our bodies. We certainly know there is *no* path between the clay of Sylvester Long's DNA and Asitr, grown from seed in the womb of a Savant woman.

"We've been asked to prove a claim of identical souls when we are claiming identical spirits. How do you display a spirit?

So whatcha gonna do? "How about this. We plug on. It's not our only card to play. Let's just pick up the sticks and keep building our case.

"Ready for some good news? I've arranged to have no local commercials tonight. We can't avoid our legal commitments to the network sponsors, and we can't get out of our station identification break, but we will have more time.

"This is how we are going to fill it: I have just a few questions to ask Asitr. Then, we will retell the story of a man once considered to be the best-known celebrity in America. No doubt he was the quickest to be forgotten. After we finish that part of Asitr's story, we're going to hear three more stories. Too ambitious for one night? Let's find out. Asitr? Are you with us?"

"I'm on the phone."

"Right now?"

"Yes ... with you."

"Oh! Of course. Sheesh. Okay, let's start out with some questions. I want to bring out some things you told me in our prior conversations."

"Of course. I'll try to be helpful."

"Okay, you told me, in this life, all the memories of your past lives are available to you. For the first time, you know your whole history."

"Yes. In the past, each time one life ended I'd awaken with the memory of only that life. I would tell the tribe one story from that life. The tribe would give the story a name. Every Savant was capable of retelling the story just as I spoke it, but one tribe member was chosen to adopt and recite the story."

"Is that why you call them Savants? Their ability to repeat exact detail?"

"No, like Lockjaw's name, it started as a joke and was eventually the only name they used.

"I told them a story about an autistic boy who was used as entertainment and espionage in the court of a Scottish Baron. The Baron used the popular term, *idiot savant,* to describe him. The tribe recognized the common bond of being able to mimic conversations. They dropped the 'idiot' portion after a later story defined that word as something negative."

"I was guessing they were an offshoot of the Xavant Indian race in Venezuela and Brazil."

"Given the length of the Savant confinement in that place we've been calling Eden, I would think it unlikely."

"You're not claiming that place to be the original Garden of Eden, are you?"

"I wouldn't know where that was. I came along seven to eight generations later. The people on earth in those days considered the entire earth to have been the garden."

"Asitr. How can I keep to a schedule with answers like that?"

"Don't try so hard to justify my being on your show, Bill. All this trying to prove I am truthful. Maybe we should just step out into the traffic and see what hits us?"

"You know what? I half-way think you're right. I am going to turn you loose very soon and let you walk in traffic. In the meantime, I'm going to put on my little orange vest and be your crossing guard."

"Okay, Bill. Be my guardian angel."

"I have a couple more questions. Questions about how you decided what to tell the Savant. In some stories you give a synopsis of a life, an overview. Other times you relive a moment or describe an event you witnessed. How does the decision come about? Is it a logical choice? An inspiration?"

"Each life was different. Think about your own life. If you could tell one story from your life to a stranger, where would you start? Would you do it the same way tomorrow? Can you select one memory and say that here, right here, is the kernel at the center of my life? In the story of Sylvester Long, I gave a synopsis. I believed at the center of that life was an unusually strong influence of the times I lived in. Society was the bigger story.

Today I might choose to tell the story of how I let my family down. I would choose that today because I have the hindsight to know the outcome of a happy ending. It would be a tale of second chances, a tale of a bittersweet life overcoming the bitterness."

"You are going to get the chance to tell us a little about both those story lines tonight. First, I want to understand something. Did you wake up knowing you were repeating a process? Did you know you were returning to your tribe?"

"Oh, no. I always woke with knowledge of my past life, but in the moment, I felt like I was in an odd dream. Savant faces were vaguely familiar, but tribal customs weren't. I knew the language. The Savant had to calm me and convince me the experience was routine."

"Asitr, how could they convince you to believe something like that could be routine?"

"They were just so naturally kind, and genuinely honest. Unpolluted in their own world. I wish you could have met them. Believing them was a natural impulse."

"Uncomplicated trust. Such a gift."

"They had no use for complications, Bill. A gray area to them was simply something they didn't understand."

"They would be very easy to mislead."

"They were simple people."

"The language was also simple?"

"I expanded their vocabulary every time I took on another life, but the language remained simple, I enjoyed the little nuances quite a bit."

"Asitr, I want you to help me out with something."

"I will try."

"I've heard you do this before. Tell our audience about the life of Sylvester Long. Not from memory as you would tell it today. I want my audience to hear it just as you told it the first time. In English, of course. I'll interrupt you when I think you've demonstrated something for us. Forget you are speaking into a phone, close your eyes, and picture your friends around you. Tell us that story the Savant called 'Tar and Feather'."

*   *   *

TAR AND FEATHER

"So, everyone is here? Is life not good? The blueberries are ripe and we swam today. Tonight, we are gathering together. Are we agreed that life is good?

"Who is to learn the story from my life? Come up, and sit with me ... Oh, I see. Totoca, are you ready to receive your new name? I'm sorry if I laugh. I am remembering last night when you entertained the parrots. You sing like a jaguar and dance like a mating lizard. Please, come. Sit, and receive the name of my teacher, Pop Warner.

Let everyone know that Pop Warner will remember my shameful tale of a man with two names, living in a country with three false hearts.

It is the European people in the land who have made this country. They call their land *America*. In spite of the excellent culture they brought with them, it is the way they have made their country that makes the rhythm of three hearts compete.

One heart has begun to glorify the culture of the early peoples. The European Americans call them Indians. The pale Europeans have conquered these peoples so quickly they don't even know the cultures of the conquered. The rhythm of any true Indian heart is nearly silent in my time.

Now, these pale people have convinced themselves they can be a better people if they would show admiration for these unknown cultures. Everywhere, people take time to proclaim they love what they don't know. They have decided to honor the Indian by absorbing them into their own culture.

Both Indian and pale Americans are lying to their hearts. Many told their hearts this was a good trade for the lost land.

From one end of this country to the other, for any Indian who is willing to trade cultures, it is advantageous to act American and have the face of an Indian.

The third heart beats with a rhythm of fear. This heart has decided it would be good to hate the newest peoples in the country.

66

They are the ones called negro, colored, darky, niggra, nigger, monkey, coon, tar, blue gum, sambo, yellow, boy, jigaboo, pickaninny, or black. They have a culture the conquerors will never accept. They've chosen not to share their own with them as well.

The hatred runs too deep. If provided a spark, the normally peaceful pale skinned can crawl out of their normal lives to become slathering murderers, hackers, burners, torturers, and dismemberers of negro men who have offended them. Until their madness subsides, they hang them from ropes for public display. Some become so gleeful at these ceremonies they round up their young children, dress them in their best clothes, and take pictures to remember the day. This ritual becomes too frequent in these days. From one end of the country to the other, it is disadvantageous to be Negro.

This is the country I was born into. I was born with the name of Sylvester Long. I was born into a negro family. My family's ancestors had the blood of African slaves, and the blood of an Indian woman. This Indian blood had marked my face.

It came to my father one day, while looking at my face, that I held a ticket to something no person in his family had ever had. My face gave me the opportunity to attain something that no member of my family could see themselves ever attaining. An education. The tools to achievement. That is how I was sent away from my family, and enrolled into a college for Indians. It is called the Carlisle school.

Indians needed no birth records. At Carlisle, I was accepted on face value as Buffalo Child Long Lance.

In this new world, I listened to the stories of the children who shared their years with me. I became the school's second-best athlete. My best friend was a man named Jim Thorpe. We were both to become famous in the world. Our teacher's name was Pop Warner. He, too, became known. It was Pop that encouraged me to find dreams that had nothing to do with sports. He said I could become great in many areas. In sports, I would always be second to my friend.

That is how the school and its teachers nurtured me. They encouraged me so well, I grew into a man who achieved every goal he set his heart to achieve. I was a vision of success, and yet the three hearts began to beat in such irregular rhythm I began to fear all would collapse around the lies at the core of my life. And they did.

Let me tell you the things I accomplished. Will you be proud to know me?

I learned to write so well that people paid to read what I had to say.

I learned to speak in a pleasing way and people would pay me to speak to them.

I could run so fast I was asked to travel the world. People would leave their homes to watch me run.

I clothed myself in such fanciful garments that people would praise my costumes.

I was accepted to be a military man in the highest college of military teaching in my country. The chief of the country, a man named Wilson, asked me to accept this honor.

I was given the highest military award the nation of France could give a foreign soldier.

I was given rewards and medals by the nation of Canada for my military experiences in their army.

I learned to fly a machine that can carry a man through the sky, and return him safely back to the ground.

A great man wanted to use a device that can capture and preserve movements of a play so it could be watched over and over again. He wanted to use his moving picture show to tell the true story of the Indian peoples in his land. He accepted me as a Blackfoot tribal chief who grew up in the old ways. He chose me to be a leading actor and adviser in his play.

As a result of these things I was given honors, praise, high paying jobs with no skills or duties required, and something called 'celebrity' — which is of sickly importance in the pale and negro culture.

The largest city in America closed its streets for me. They tore paper and threw it from high buildings onto me. I rode below them as they cheered, and shouted my false name. It is one of their highest tributes.

I was asked to join a club of explorers who are leading the world in the searches for truth and knowledge. They made me responsible for safekeeping the true understanding of the Indian culture.

Women admired me so much I had to hire a man to respond to their letters. They have sent me letters from more places than I had ever visited.

When the Americans sought out from whom to learn the culture of the conquered ones, they would come to me.

The tribes of the Indian nations would ask me to visit them. They wanted to see the mockingbird who pretended to know their dying culture. They never exposed me.

Are you now not proud to say you know me?

I know you are not. You can see the onrushing ironies. You can see the eyes behind the moss."

"Asitr?"

"Yes, Bill?"

"I'm sorry. It's time for station identification. We will be back in just one minute."

12

HARBINGER INSTITUTE
April 1, 2025

"EYES BEHIND THE MOSS," Otis repeated as he silenced his marble. "During the break, I think Kae'Lairy saw eyes behind the moss during a conversation between Bill and his secretary, Po. He thought it was important enough to play for his brothers on the moon.

Otis pulled the marble to his chest. "This is Kae'Lairy's recording. Listen."

> *"Check your email Bill. It's Albie Gentile. He's dead."*
> *"Dead? What happened?"*
> *"He drove into a sinkhole in Florida."*
> *"Sheesh. Those three are going to think something's up."*
> *"What do you mean? What could be up?"*
> *"Nothing. Call Dave. See if Asitr will take Albie's spot on Thursday. Ask him not to mention it to Asitr until tonight's show is over."*

"*Dave should be out of reach in that Eden place. You told me he was going there to recover some artifacts.*"

"*Right. Try him first. If you can't reach him, call Lockjaw. Got it?*"

"*Call Dave first. If he can't be reached, call Lockjaw. Ask him to wait until after tonight's show before he tells Asitr the news about Albie. Plug Asitr into the Thursday slot.*"

"*Close enough, babe. Remind me to give you a day off sometime. Go, go. There really is just one minute on the break.*"

Without further comment, Otis allowed Kae'Lairy's recording to play on. After the soft sound of the studio door being closed behind Po, Bill's voice was heard again.

"Sheesh Kamushka. I hate surprises."

Otis once again touched the marble. It was back to the show.

13

THE BILL ELLIOTT SHOW
On Air Tuesday

"WE ARE BACK. Didn't I promise you just one minute? Limited commercials can be a blessing or a curse. Most of you are probably still at the refrigerator. I'm not giving you time to get back. I want to plow ahead, so, Asitr?"

"Yes, Bill?"

"Do you know what I find to be unusual?"

"The ability of the human to dance like a mating lizard?"

"Ha! Stop that. Well, yes. More importantly though. It's my emails. Nobody has asked how you could know that Lockjaw was your grandson. At some point tonight, I want to know the answer to that. Can you fit it in?"

"I can."

"Great, but first, tell us about Sylvester's slide into shame and despair. His murder. The well-traveled 78. I don't want the recital. I want you to tell it from memory. Just fill us in on what happened to you."

*   *   *

PASSING FOR ACCEPTABLE

What happened was a predictable collapse of unsound structures, built upon falsehoods, and propped up with too many weak supports.

My image of the great chief was being held aloft on the backs of people who knew the truth.

Some of my editors sniffed out inconsistencies in my background, but they never followed up. They kept paying me for articles.

The Indian tribes I visited were laughing at me behind my back. I manufactured my clothing, claiming them to be the traditional dress of a Blackfoot chief. To the native people, they were gaudy and obviously inauthentic. The symbols were collections of a wide range of world cultures. Any Indian could see this was the dress of a gaudy poser.

I had only basic knowledge of the hand signals the tribes used to communicate with each other. It was only the most stoic of people who could sit without laughing while I fabricated their culture in my lectures to white audiences.

Every tribe I visited knew I would talk too loudly, laugh too loudly, and cross between my host and the fire. How could I be an Indian who knew the old ways? Yet, those people, who had reason to find me offensive, never gave me up.

There were others that chose not to expose me. The Hollywood studios wooed me until rumors began to circulate about my racial makeup. I began to find myself in a state of constant negotiations. It soon became clear they were becoming less and less interested as negotiations went along. Out of politeness, and the fear of being associated with me, they negotiated me away.

I knew the weight was going to be too much, someday.

The Explorers Club is where my spiral sped up, and spun out of control. That's where rumors stopped, and the truth began to

74

show itself. Where laughing behind my back, negotiating me away, and wishing I never existed, reached a point of impact and collapse.

As an explorer in my own unique and solitary world, I lost my way. My stealth failed. All of this in the building where I met the woman I would ask to marry me. I felt the only way things could get worse would be if my lover would turn on me. The only way things could get better would be if I could find the courage to be a truthful man. Things would get better and worse.

Sylvia was a girl from Missouri. My first impression of her was mixed. She seemed to be a bit frail. A little timid, unlike the starlets, socialites, and hookers I commonly reveled with. It was the smile that made people like her. Her smile and funny accent. Part southern belle, part Irish perk. She had a willingness to please. It was those attributes that landed her the job at the Explorers club. She cleaned the cigar room and ballroom three nights a week. The other four nights she tended bar at a speakeasy known for its late-night get-togethers. Musicians, who never leave the big town, and those just traveling through on tour, would gather there in the wee hours.

I began to frequent the joint four nights a week. One night, I made the mistake of asking her for a dance. It was on the dance floor where she crossed the line from being my conquest to being my target of adoration. She was liquid in her movements, daring in her display of passion, and unmistakably psychic in her ability to anticipate, join, and enhance her partner's moves. She was the same in romance.

Her magic was strong. I forgot my self-pity and sailed above the problems of the world. She made me feel I could become a man in the world. Like it or not.

To surprise her, I purchased two tickets to Niagara Falls. Secretly, I shipped her family in from Missouri. I told the club manager to start looking for another cleaning lady. I chose the ring. The surprise was about to be let loose.

I met her at the door of the Explorers club. It seemed such an innocent question. "Would you like to skip work and take a ride on the train?" Sylvia squealed with excitement. She was aglow, exuberant in her glee. Anticipating another eruption of joy, I reached in my pocket for the ring.

I wish I had spoken first. I wish she could have been restrained from asserting herself. "Can we go to Gary, Indiana?" She asked. "Daryl told me about Gary this morning."

I'd also received news from Gary Indiana that morning. Larry *Chin Feathers* McDonald had been a lynching victim in that town. *Why Gary?*

"Please?" she begged. "They lynched some niggra down there and they're going to leave him strung up for a couple days. I never seen a lynching, babe, can we go?"

My depression and self-pity returned immediately. It returned loudly. I verbally humiliated that woman with every bit of eloquence my rage could muster.

I watched the glow in her eyes begin to flicker, then turn flat. She couldn't understand why the man she loved would snap on her like that. The flat, death-like, look in her eyes suddenly gave way to wet, gushing tears. She would have walked through broken glass to please me, and suddenly, she was being called a mindless, black-spirited, blood-curdling waste of a human being. Without responding to her pleas for an explanation, I had her thrown out, vowing her job at the Explorers Club was gone to her.

It was apparent that the security guard was repelled by the need to do his duty. After showing her out, he looked at me like I was filth. I already knew I was. He left me alone to a cognac, and was probably still fuming when he returned just three minutes later with a message. "There is a negro at the back door who wants to speak to you. Shall I have him go away?"

It was my brother. He had gotten so old.

The security guard hovered at the door. Just curious, or protective, I didn't know. After an awkward silence, and a few glances between the three of us, my brother thrust his hand toward me. It contained an envelope.

"From mom," he said. He turned to walk away when I took it from his hand." Wait a minute." I called to him. "How are you all doing?" I suddenly needed to know. He answered in a low voice.

"You know. We get by." He gave the security man one long glance, and left me with these words: "We don't blame you ya know."

That was the last time I saw the person who taught me how to play craps, make a proper fist, shoot marbles, and identify the edible plants of the woodlands. I went back to my cognac, then lit a cigar before opening the letter. This wasn't going to be good.

> *My dear sweet Sylvester,*
>
> *Momma misses you. Clarence is in charge of the movie house in darktown. We saw you in your picture. We were all of us proud.*
>
> *Everyone stay fine but me. I am gotten so sickly and will never see you again. I write to tell you momma loves you. We all love you.*
>
> *Don't come down to see me. They are still lynching us down here and they would be mighty mad how we fooled 'em. We will laugh about this in glory.*
>
> *Love, momma*

I drank myself into tears, and then, into inspiration. I had something to put in the time capsule. The future would display my guilt and shame.

Next, I drank myself into a comatose state, safely senseless, until the club butler awakened me. He suggested I had better get cleaned up if I was to attend the ceremonies for the time capsule. I left the letter on the arm of the chair and went upstairs to bathe.

It was after my bath, two cups of coffee, and the selection of a clean suit, before I remembered to retrieve the letter. It was still on the arm of the chair. I may have been foggy, but I was certain of one thing. I had left the letter inside the envelope. When I returned, I found it open, outside the envelope. Someone had read the letter.

I went to my locker and grabbed the aborted 78 and placed the letter into its sleeve. I began to drink again, and don't remember much about the ceremony.

I remember even less about the next two weeks. I woke up filthy and broke. My watch was missing. My wallet was missing. The watch had been stolen, but my wallet was left in my other suit. My other suit was at the club. Simple enough, I told myself, just go back to the club and clean up.

When I arrived, I found something important had changed during my missing two weeks. I learned about it from the doorman. He said, "I don't want no trouble chief, but I can't let you in. You been voted out."

I didn't care. I wasn't returning to my old life. I was gonna go home. I was gonna go home and be with my family when my mamma was buried. I wasn't in the mood to explain it to the doorman.

"Sylvia give this to me," he said. "She says she need to see you." The doorman slipped a folded paper into my hands. I put it in my pocket as I turned sideways, and begin to push past him. He was thick around the middle, but he sucked it in a little to let me by, even as he was telling me to stop. "Please don't be trouble now, Chief," he said. "I gotta let you know you can't come in."

I promised him I just wanted my clothes from my locker. I got the words out, but it struck me quickly that he wasn't the one I needed to deal with. My forehead suddenly seemed to fly off my face and my head jerked back so fast I felt an electric shock run through me.

With my eyes still unfocused, I managed to make out a downward arc of a wooden billy club and ducked my head. Too slow, too late. I felt the top of my skull crack, and fell to my knees, struggling to remember how to work my legs.

I heard the security guard whisper my offense. "We don't have no niggers in here."

I blacked out.

When I started into consciousness again, I was in the hallway, halfway between the front door and the back. I was being dragged, a billy club against my throat, my feet dragging behind me. I was being pulled towards the servants and deliveries entrance.

I kicked and rolled. For a second I was free. Then the big white light, I thought I was dead. Oh, God. I wasn't. I was lying in the alley behind the club.

The doorman stood over me. He held out a pillowcase filled with the contents of my locker. My clothes, my wallet, and the second 78 RPM record that would be given to my son, all were in the sack.

"I'll just put it over here on the steps" the doorman said. "I'm real sorry, chief. A cab is coming to get you." He left me enough money to get to my hotel.

At the hotel I took off my wet clothes. It had rained while I was waiting for the cab. Shivering from the chill, I pulled the blanket off the bed and draped it over my shoulders.

I tried not to think of how I was going to feel in the morning. Maybe I hit rock bottom and the rest of the way was going to be sunny and bright. Sunny and bright. Sunny and bright. My old image of Sylvia.

"Oh, yes. The note Sylvia had given the doorman was still in my pocket. It was soaked in rainwater. The folded sheet of paper clung together. Ink smeared the page.

"Carefully, I lifted one section at a time with a butter knife. The news looked good. She had gone to San Diego to work for a socialite, a friend who helped me meet some of the right people in the movie business. It made me feel good to know that Sylvia was in good hands.

"I lifted another section and read, with both hope and dread, she wanted to forgive me. She needed to know what she had done to offend me. I remembered her pitiful look when I snapped on her. I knew she was hurt deeply and traumatically. I was torn. I didn't want to speak to her until I was sure of my feelings. I wanted her forgiveness, but I wasn't ready to forgive her. I needed time.

Another layer of paper was lifted:

... pregnant with your child.

The time I needed just dropped to the bottom of the hourglass. After sleeping for fourteen hours, and cleaning myself up, I boarded a train for San Diego, California. The pleasant motion of the ride rocked me into the notion that everything was going to turn out all right.

When I arrived, I told Sylvia my dark secret. She kept a smile on her face as she listened to my story. It began as something sweet, and hopeful. Soon, her smile changed into something cold, even frozen, chilling at the same rate her brain was flickering on to the concept that she was in love with a Negro. "I'll get us some lemonade," she said abruptly, and left the room.

I was preparing to give the speech of my life, this time, from the heart and truthful. I was going to make her proud to be in love with a man who would stand up for what is true.

I went to the sofa and removed a record from a box of gifts intended for the mother and child. "Ya know what I'm thinking?" I asked, loud enough to be heard in the kitchen. "I think we should start a scrap book. Something for the baby. We should start with this record. This is how it started for us. Remember that night? The baby may have been conceived that night."

While still rummaging around in the box, I heard her enter the room behind me. My mind was absorbed in my search for the engagement ring. I was still looking when something touched the side of my head.

It didn't really register. I heard her voice more clearly than I heard her words. It was a garbled, choking, halting and mournful sound. The tone caused me to stiffen. I started to turn, then ... *Bang!*

I floated above myself for an instant and watched my own eyes lose their light and go flat. I saw the blood trickle from the side of my head. I saw Sylvia standing over my body. I heard the gun drop to the floor as I whooshed off in a rush of movement.

Next, the stillness of sleep. Stillness turned into convulsive fear. When the light returned to my eyes, I saw my village around me.

I had a story to tell.

14

HARBINGER INSTITUTE
April 1, 2025

O TIS LEANED TOWARD DR. MILTON. "This is still running, Doc," he said, settling into his new position while placing the marble on the pill cart. "If you listen real close, you can hear the hiss of dead air. Soon you'll hear the sound of Bill's secretary, Po, shuffling around the studio, sliding her chair across the floor, walking to the door, the click of the doorknob turning, a soft bump as she closes the door behind her, then a muffled scream from the hallway. "Dead air! We have dead air!"

Otis let the sounds he described play, then he silenced the marble.

"You moved a little Doc. I saw you lean a little toward the sound. Gotcha."

Dr. Milton snorted very quietly, suppressing a chuckle, and returned to stillness.

"All of it, the hiss, the background sounds, the muffled scream from Po, is the result of Asitr going suddenly silent after telling his story.

"The unexpected silence left Po in a lurch. She tried to find a solution by searching an electronic plug-in device Bill called his *'bathroom buttons'*. In two years of broadcasting, Bill never once left his secretary in charge of the show, but suddenly, Po found herself in charge at a bad time.

"On the board are a dozen buttons. Each button has an identifying label. For example, if you hit the button labeled *Station Break,* a pre-recorded message will announce over the air, *'Thank you, it's time for a station break.'*

"Po, untrained in the use of the board, couldn't find the correct button to push for a guest who stopped talking. Bill wasn't in the room, and Po knew she had to do something. She considered prompting Asitr but froze.

"One button caught her attention. It was marked *'Silence'.* She pushed it impetuously, further frazzled when she realized continued silence was exactly what she got.

"None of that activity should mean much to you Doc, and for Kae'Lairy, it was only a curious development, but after he listened to an associated recording, he was shocked and embarrassed.

"The second recording is fruit gathered from Kae'Lairy's tracing Asitr's phone call from the studio to a fishing cabin in central Florida. This recording was made simultaneous with what you heard from Po in Bills studio."

Otis activated the recording and Lockjaw could be heard asking a question.

"Grampy? Are you okay?"

"Dramatic pause."

"It's turned into a mind-numbing vacuum."

"Bill isn't in the studio, Lock."

"Could be a potty break?"

"Look at the laptop. Alazam's light is on."

"Things are stirring, Grampy. Think Alazam found out Chaco Canyon is empty?"

"Maybe. He thought something was important enough to call Bill on the Telstar line. It might be time for Hayak. When you hear from Dave, fill him in."

Otis let his hand hover over the marble until the recording was finished. When it ended, he left questions raised by the two recordings go unanswered. The Bill Elliott show was back. Asitr was speaking.

*   *   *

CROSSBOWS AND POPPIES

I apologize. I didn't mean to leave everyone hanging in dead air. I hoped for a prompt from Bill before I begin my second story. I'll continue, but I want to explain something.

My own mouth is caught between two views. I promised I would tell you how I recognized my grandson when he stepped out of a helicopter in the Amazon. I know I have to do justice to the story of my grandson, but I need to give my own voice as a Montagnard child the same consideration.

My grandson, John '*Lockjaw*' Smith, wore a uniform in a war that never should have been. Perhaps you think he is a hero. Maybe you want to call him a '*baby killer*'.

"I just want to tell you the story of a friendship between a boy and a man, seemingly fleeting, but as deep as family.

When I was a boy named Gaipon, my people had just come out of a peaceful time in the highlands. That peaceful period for us is known as World War II.

Before that war, we were fighting the Vietnamese on the side of the French colonialists. It was an easy decision for us. The French didn't want our land and the Vietnamese did.

We were ethnically different from the lowlanders. We prayed to Jesus, but didn't accept the Pope. We sacrificed to the spirits of nature, but we rejected the philosopher of nature called The Buddha. These things made us unacceptable to the religious groups dominating the Vietnamese in the south. To make matters worse, we were told we stank and looked like monkeys.

World War hero, Ho Chi Minh of the north, and the carousel of military leaders in the south, agreed on one thing. The Montagnard must go. Allying with the French was an easy decision.

Easy decisions aren't always the safest. With weak support in the south, determined patriotism from a tough and experienced army in the north, and the clandestine campaign of undermining the French with acts of terrorism by America, the French withdrew, and we were on our own.

Chaos was swirling through foreign capitals. Madness became normal and normal, madness. The forces around us were as consistent as hyperactive chameleons. Our enemies were as principled as pirates.

My own people remained consistent. We were an independent people, with our own land, our own government, and our own culture. We would ally with anyone who would support us. Our Aria tribal leaders set out to find new allies after the French left us for the final time. We had one offer.

General Kuhn Sa of the KMT militia had an offer for us. General Sa was the leader of nationalist Chinese troops once loyal to Chiang-Kai-Shek. With Mao's victory, Kuhn Sa's army moved into the poppy growing regions of Laos, Cambodia, and Thailand. With the help of American aircraft and arms, they set up the money producing enterprise known as the 'Golden Triangle'. They controlled the supply for eighty five percent of the world's heroin trade. They wanted more. Their plan was to add one more area to their domain. The new acquisition target was the highlands of the Montagnard people.

Kuhn Sa offered to help fight the Vietnamese of the north and the south. For this he wanted our poppies, our women, and our culture. He said we could stay but we could not govern ourselves. Rejecting his offer meant that we were now at war with two governments of one country, and a militia with no country.

With the violence that erupted after the second world war, chaos blew upward from the lowlands and into the mountains. This was double, triple terror for a young boy wanting to be a man who could fight.

When I was ten years old, I picked up a pistol from the ground and executed a dying militia member so he wouldn't suffer. They wouldn't go away peacefully, so we killed them with our crossbows and buried them. They never returned.

Their American allies were the next to call. We were skeptical, but surprised.

The Americans didn't want to govern us. They wanted our poppies and enough land to build airstrips. They promised us our women would be safe and our culture would be acceptable. They promised to influence the Vietnamese of the south. That promise proved true. The southern Vietnamese withdrew from their battle lines.

The Americans promised to support us in our war against the Vietnamese of the north. They made steps in that direction. I was present when those first steps happened. They sent my tribe four impressive warriors. One of them was my grandson.

These four men lived with us and learned how to survive in our world. They were respectable and hard-working, learning our ways and sharing some of theirs as well.

After they built a small airstrip, more men came, different, not as impressive, and less likely to learn anything from us. They were introduced as the ground crew for *Air America*. They came to enlarge our small airstrip and fly our poppies.

During those days I saw a change in one of the four original warriors. Lockjaw, my grandson, began to spend more time away from his unit. He became a quieter, more introspective man.

From the time he arrived, he taught us the science of moving in units. All the Montagnard men enjoyed this training, especially the tribesmen of the Cheo Reo Banhar. These tough men already understood the power of fighting to protect their brothers in the field. The Cheo had the art of fighting in their ways. My grandson gave them the science. The Cheo were soon feared beyond the power of their numbers when the Vietnamese from the north came to claim our villages.

The Northern lowlanders sent too few, the first time. My grandson proved himself to us when he took the position most exposed in the first battle. The next time they came, they came in numbers large enough that we joined all our men from every tribe together with more and more warriors from America. We used the sciences we were taught and displayed the courage of a righteous cause. We prevailed, but the Vietnamese from the north left a trail of murdered village leaders.

I was no longer living in the central highlands when they returned with an army. I died in the defense of my people when I was that boy named Gaipon.

In my last days, I was proud to say that Lockjaw was my friend. I felt like he was family. Odd, because I would learn later, he truly was family.

We fished in the same fishing holes. He gave me the cookies from his rations. He talked to me and I would pretend to understand. It made him laugh. I would make up nonsense words, and speak them to him. He would smile and nod his head as if he understood. I laughed at him and his funny faces.

We both loved to watch the soaring birds glide in and out of the clouds as the clouds traveled up the mountains around us, and down the mountains below us. I often wished my world was like theirs. I wished we could move with the flow of a world suitable for soaring and not be affected by the hard, immovable facts set in stone. As things were, I was satisfied with small blessings and wishes.

I have to thank the French for one small blessing. My father claimed an item left behind when they abandoned us. It was an old Victrola. He treasured it but had no records to play. Lockjaw treasured his record even though he had no Victrola.

It is a testament to how much my father admired Lockjaw that he was willing to let me move the Victrola into Lockjaw's hut. With father's machine, and Lockjaw's record, we could hear the music my grandson brought with him from America. I was excited for the both of us.

It was so unexpected that the playing of the record would make him sad. He listened somberly, then let it continue to go around and around after the music stopped, and only the scratching continued. I wanted to hear the song again, but he was so still and serious looking, I wasn't sure if I should. After uncomfortable silence, he began speaking to me. Not our usual routine for laughs. He spoke distantly, then emotionally. I tried very hard to understand him. It felt important.

After going silent once again, he suddenly jumped to his feet. He restarted the record and began to dance and sing along. We played it so many times I began to emulate the lyrics. I made him laugh so hard he fell to the ground and rolled from side to side. We had fun.

Two nights later, I awakened to shouting in the night. Several North Vietnamese intruders tried to steal some dried fish as they fled their pursuers. I was about to pay the price for being too young to learn the science of pursuit.

I picked up a crossbow and gave chase across the airfield. To the Vietnamese running away, I was a silhouette against light. To the men guarding the airfield I was a shadow of retreating black. It was a tossup as to who would shoot me first. It was my grandson who was the surest of eye and the most quick to fire the shot.

I felt the impact, then the whoosh of movement, followed by the silence of sleep, and woke into a seizure so long lasting and violent it scared the Savant into prayer for my life.

I had just lived my last life outside this body. For the first time, all my lives' memories were downloaded. After an hour, my mind organized into a system that would allow me some control and sanity. One of the first things to astonish me as the memories meshed together was the remembering of events in different languages. I didn't have to struggle to understand what my grandson was telling me about his recording. I understood it, from memory, in the English words he used.

My eyes squeezed tight, trying to help me will myself back in time and back through space to be in the central highlands. I needed to explain it all to Lockjaw. He needed to hear me forgive him for his mistake of war. We needed to mourn together over a man neither of us had ever seen, my son from the seed of Sylvester Long, the man who was Lockjaw's father.

Eventually, but not finally, I resigned myself to knowing I had no control. I assembled all my facts, weighed them against the odds, and came to the conclusion I would never see my grandson again. Amazingly, two years later, I saw him step out of a helicopter again. This time it was to answer the call of prophecy.

15

THE BILL ELLIOTT SHOW
On Air Tuesday

"THANK YOU. Asitr, I think you handled that well."

"I'm glad to see you back, Bill. I felt lonely without my crossing guardian."

"Taking care of a little business. Speaking of that ... An executioner at the age of ten?"

"They were raping our women and killing our men. Their big guns made them feel more powerful than our many crossbows. They wouldn't leave. They shouldn't continue their deeds. They needn't suffer. I'm not ashamed."

"Understandable. I want to hear more from you, and more is just what we have coming up. We're going to hear three stories. I'm excited because I haven't heard these stories yet.

"I understand that the first story isn't one of your own, Asitr. It comes from the woman you call your mother. The first story you ever told to the Savant?"

"Yes. It's the story my mother told me after all the years she raised me. It's the story of how she came to adopt me and how she met a messenger of God."

"I will listen intently. Your second story is also from your first life?"

"Correct."

"And your third story?"

"I would like to surprise you with that one. We might not have the time tonight."

"Before I turn the show over to you, and you go walking alone in the traffic, we'll take a break and listen to our station's public service announcements"

"I'd like to make an announcement of my own, if it's okay, Bill. I heard some bad news this morning on my local radio station. Albie Gentile has been killed in an automobile accident. I want to send his family my condolences and suggest his book for all modern journalists. Fabricating lies and distractions composed of half-truths has a long history in their profession. Measuring the progress and regression of their craft is important. Reading Albie's book is helpful as a collection of cautionary tales well told."

"Thank you, Asitr. I intended to make that announcement later. Has Lockjaw extended my offer to fill the hole his death has left behind on Thursday?"

"He has, and I accept. If only the hole he leaves behind in his family's lives could be so easily healed."

"I, too, offer condolences, but life goes on and these messages need to be heard. We'll be right back with Asitr in one minute. Don't go away."

16

O TIS PULLED THE CORNER of his sheet away and reached to
silence the marble. Pivoting his body, he looked down at the
floor, then slid to the edge and draped his legs over the side. He
reached for the floor with one leg, but pulled it back before his foot
made contact. Scooting a little closer to the edge, he tried again
and stopped when his toe touched the tile. Before committing
fully, he turned his head to face Dr. Milton and smiled timidly. "So
many things get taken for granted, Doc."

"Don't try, Mr. Beckley." Dr. Milton unfurled and stood up,
leaning in Otis's direction like a shortstop expecting to charge a
bunted ball. "My ears tell me lunch is on the way. You can try
walking around after you eat."

Otis looked toward the door and listened. Impetuously, he
put one hand on the pill cart to steady himself and let his feet find
the floor. "I'll just stand up and get used to ..." As soon as he
detached his other hand from the bed he wobbled, and the pill cart

began to roll, crashing into the rolling display of equipment used for monitoring vital signs.

The crash was loud with collateral impacts. The water pitcher spilled its contents and splashed off the equipment cart and onto the floor. Dr. Milton's recorder skittered and bounced off the wall and into the puddle. Inside the monitoring cart, the neatly laid out emergency medical tools rattled around violently in the drawer. Loudly, the big blue marble rolled from cart to cart then plummeted to the floor. After impact, it bounced, and then dribbled out into the hallway, making tiny pinging sounds, like a tuning fork being struck repeatedly with drumsticks.

Dr. Milton jumped to steady his patient as quickly as a lightning strike, but just as thunder follows lightning, the crescendo lingered, the sharp noises blending into a roll of echoes in the tiny room.

After walking Otis gingerly backwards to the bed, Dr. Milton released his grip and retrieved his recorder from a puddle on the floor. "Quite a performance, Mr. Beckley. Very dramatic."

"Tada," Otis replied, blushing in embarrassment. "Thank you, thank you. I'll be appearing here nightly."

"It's best you follow doctor's orders," Doctor Milton said sternly, while wiping his recorder on his pant leg. "It's been twenty years since you've tried to walk. Is that right?"

A knocking sound came from the doorway before Otis answered the pointed question. Both doctor and patient turned toward the sound. Jarvis Douglas, surveying the damage, stood in the hallway, a blue orb in his hand.

"Everything dandy candy here Doc?"

"We had an accident, Jarvis." While answering his aide, the doctor reached under the monitoring cart and pulled the plug from its outlet. "We need some cleanup."

Jarvis sidestepped the puddle on the floor and set the marble on the bed. After the handoff, he furled his brow and scowled. "Sure, sure," he said. "You want I should give Mr. Beckley his lunch first, or clean up the mess?"

"Lunch first," Otis interjected.

We'll both take a break for lunch," Doctor Milton answered. "I'll have Rishard notify maintenance." While walking into the hallway, he turned and announced, "I'll be back in thirty minutes."

*   *   *

At the nurse's station, Dr. Milton checked the reports from his associates who were seeing his regular patients while he was on vacation. Nothing he read needed his immediate attention, so he scribbled a note, handed it to Nurse Rishard and walked away.

The nurse looked at the note and called after him, "Is this for the 'John Doe' room, Doctor Milton?"

"Stat," he answered over his shoulder.

Before going to his office, the doctor stopped at a restroom and pried open his recorder, dried the inside with a paper towel, closed it, and then he pressed replay. After pressing the *Play* button, he listened to *splash, clatter, clatter, ping, ping, ping.* When the recording cycled through the sounds of the scene, all the way to *"I'll be back in thirty minutes",* he hit Stop, placed the recorder in his shirt pocket, and continued to his office.

After entering, Dr. Milton took his briefcase from the closet and set it in front of him as he sat down at his desk. With hands on the latches, prepared to remove his lunch, he stopped and began thinking in streams of unrelated topics.

Wonder what lunch is today. Probably peanut butter. She's pissed I'm taking vacation time for that buffoon. Hmm, Abrams might have gotten his holy grail of a book out of this one. Odd duck, this Otis character. Very organized fantasy. Peanut butter. I'm not even hungry. Better bring flowers home tonight. He believes his own story. How did he get that way? Maybe we should go see her mom this weekend. We'll have to fly. Ha. It's not like the moon and back. Screw lunch, I need to get my mind organized.

Dr. Milton pushed his briefcase away and leaned back, staring at the clock on the wall. *I'll give him fifteen more minutes, then go hear what Asitr's mother has to say.*

After the clock made its quarter-hour journey, Dr. Milton left his office, walked back to what the staff had started calling the

John Doe room, and looked around. *Water mopped up, lunch tray already taken away, marble back on the pill cart.*

"How was lunch Mr. Beckley?"

"Fine, Doc. Ready to begin again?

Dr. Milton sat in his chair. "We left off with Asitr about to tell us a story he heard from his first mother?"

"Almost. First, I want to talk about Kae'Lairy and the off-air speed of events during Asitr's appearance on the show."

The doctor sat in his chair and morphed into his listening position. His eyes drooped and he exhaled. "Go ahead," he said. "I'm listening."

Otis ran his tongue over his teeth, brushed crumbs from his sheets, then began.

"Kae'Lairy was a fantastic multi-tasker. While Asitr was telling his mother's story, Kae'Lairy placed new *ears* outside Bill's studio. Outside the office, in Bill's large dwelling, he found a ham radio located in the basement. At the time, he assumed he'd found the 'Telstar line' referred to by Asitr.

"He traveled to Florida and hacked Asitr's laptop, copying its contents into the marble.

"What he found spurred him to contact Olphrenjii with a demand for information about 'Hayak' and the importance of Chaco Canyon. He sent the message as a command.

"Olphrenjii was puzzled by Kae'Lairy's change of tone but responded positively 'Where should we meet?' he asked.

Otis reached to the marble and said, "All this, in the time it took Asitr to tell this story. The story of Puth. The Savant were first to say it, so don't anticipate any context ahead of time. They called this story 'It Takes a Village'."

17

IT TAKES A VILLAGE

L ISTEN TO YOUR STORY and don't worry. This is what I know. You began life with no family and no tribe. The wisdom of custom said you should be left to die. Custom said a child should not be raised in a culture they are not born into. You were blessed enough to find the Bombag people. People who would change a culture to please their God. I want to tell you about us.

We are one of the old tribes. I am one of the old people. When I was a child I could speak to men and women who were alive the night we received our spirit from the creator. They all have said it was the first night they noticed the stars. I want you to appreciate this gift of a spirit.

Before we had spirits, we were empty souls. We were no more creative than the hare or the ibex. We only thought to achieve the things that would satisfy the needs of our body. We were neither grateful nor ungrateful. We never knew sad or happy. We knew only want and don't want, pain, pleasure, and indifference. We traveled in packs, leaving behind the weak, the infirm, and those young who were born to parents ignoring the instinct to raise children into strong and useful members of their band.

I am grateful I wasn't alive in those days. I grew up in the stability of knowing my land was secure and my tribe helpful to each other. Let me tell you how it was in our tribe the day we heard that an unknown people from afar had settled on our land.

On that day there were four tribal leaders. Each had different natures and abilities. There was Auth, who was my friend, Thosat, who was widely respected and admired, Foop, who was feared. Then there was I, myself. Puth.

Thosat was the great provider. With a good spear he could feed a family unit during any season. He could feed a village with just three wily and obedient helpers. Our tribe gave him those helpers. We gave him baskets, spears, food from the gatherers, and respect as well.

Auth was different. He had spent his youth gazing at the stars, observing the animals, and asking questions about the days before we received our spirit. In his youth it was known that he had received more beatings and ostracizing than anyone who had ever lived in our tribe. He was lazy, never successful at the hunt, or in completing projects. The campfire finally sent him into exile for the unheard period of five years. Nobody believed he would return.

Auth did return. He returned to us with stories never ending. Tales, incredible, about wonders, magic, and a culture so strange that Auth struggled to explain how it thrived. This culture could make and build things that Auth had no words for. He could only show us these structures by drawing pictures in the dirt.

He understood we didn't have the knowledge to grasp everything he had seen. The peoples Auth had met believed things that disturbed him. They had beliefs and rituals that Auth left out of the telling.

In time, we began to look forward to his tales while enjoying the merry drinks he learned to make in that strange land in the north. All enjoyed him but Foop.

Foop was very young to be looked on as a leader, but he was so skilled in the ways of the warrior that no one warrior would challenge his leadership. Foop was smart enough to recognize our fear and brash enough to act as the unchallenged leader of our warriors. When he would speak of himself he pronounced his own name as F-f-foop! He liked to remind us how he earned his name. It was the sound his spear made from flight to contact. No other warrior had the strength for such a dramatic sound.

Foop was secure within himself when displaying physical dominance. He was most incompetent when shaping the views of the tribe during campfire discussions, and hated the campfire presence of that lazy, lying, talk crazy Auth. He never challenged him at the campfire. He lacked the flexibility to espouse one idea only to be forced to accept another in the end. Sometimes I thought Foop may not have been given a complete spirit. Other times I was convinced he merely ignored its quiet voice.

I understood a terrible thing. If Auth were ever to disagree with Foop, and win the tribe's support, Foop knew he would kill him. Only the fear of banishment held him back. Murder meant a life of permanent banishment. A lonely life without respect is no life for the boastful in need of an audience.

Whatever his weaknesses, he could reason with canny coldness. He understood that, with patience, he would find a proper time to murder Auth. It was understood by everyone that no one person would be allowed to undermine the will of the tribe. One day, he reasoned, Auth would let his mouth put him between the will of the tribe and his own well being. That is when Foop could quickly murder him. He would be called decisive. Yes, Foop would wait. This is the pitiful depth to which Foop's mind could not delve beyond.

One other political force in the tribe was left out of his calculations. If there was one thing that Foop feared more than banishment it was I, myself, Puth. His fear of me stemmed from the same irrational reason I was the most influential leader in the tribe.

I wasn't born into a position of prominence in the tribe. I was old. Three hundred years in age. That alone was no challenge to the longevity of men and women who had gone before. Indeed, there was one older woman in the tribe. She earned her rations by helping at child births.

I had no skill that excelled others. I never swayed a council at the fire. There was no conquest in my past. No victory against an enemy either human or beast. I had no great beauty. I never had a child. Yet, I was a powerful leader. The source of my power was in my hair. My hair had turned from black to white. Such a thing was never seen.

The hairs turned one by one. The first hair turned white, and everyone remarked how unusual it was. Then, another hair turned white on the other side of my head. Then another. Another, and another, and another. Next, the tribe began to count the dark hairs remaining instead of the hairs turned white. Soon there were but five dark hairs, and a fire council was called. Every time another of my hairs turned white we would have yet another council fire. I would sit and listen to the same debates. We were determined to ascertain the purpose of my odd display.

Thosat was his sturdy, simple self in these debates. He was convinced that when my last hair turned white there would be an age of unparalleled hunting. One third of the tribe could be counted on to hold firmly to Thosat's opinion. This stubborn group was convinced that such a sign could only be an omen for the most fortuitous of events. Surely, they reasoned, Thosat was correct. What could be more fortuitous than great hunting?

The other two thirds of the tribe were firmly committed to whatever other idea the current speaker held. It was lost on all but a few of them that only time would tell. It was lost on all of them that maybe it meant nothing.

While the tribe waited and wondered, I was living a life of leisure. I retired from toiling, yet wanted for nothing. My nervous hope was that I would not be a disappointment on the day of the last dark hair.

The last full day when life was like this for me came with news. The news was exciting, and we held a fire council.

This time there was nothing much to debate. Thosat and his party had returned early from a hunt. Interlopers were beginning to build a structure at our lake. It was taken for granted that we had to kill them or make them leave.

Foop announced he would take two men and scout their camp. His party left immediately and returned before dusk. By the time he came back, nearly all the preparations were made. Thosat had set his gatherers into teams that would take up positions to prevent escape. He gathered food and water.

A proposal was made and passed. This would be an officially declared village event. The entire village would go with the warriors in the morning to watch the occasion. Auth selected boys old enough to make slings to carry Thosat's supplies. He fashioned three others to carry the slow and old.

It was left to Foop to choose the warriors he needed. We agreed on a strategy. We would attack with surprise. There would be no mercy. It was the usual strategy.

Best of all was the party that began the official village event. A village party meant we would bring out the merry drinks and gather the laughing weeds for the fire. We would howl with delight. It was best that way. Best we all enjoyed the night before battle. Things didn't always go well enough that we would feel like celebrating afterwards.

Usually, the outcome was successful, although we never achieved surprise. There was always one flaw in the planning for surprise. An entire village moving through dense growth, stumbling feet slow with lack of sleep and chattering heads still fuzzy with drink. It was a plan that worked the same almost every time. I was pleased that it gave our enemy a chance to run before they faced us. We would then reclaim the land without the necessity of burying the dead.

That night I went to sleep twirling my last dark hair in my finger. I had confidence in our warriors. I went to sleep light-headed and happy.

Thosat fell asleep thinking of the new baskets they would capture.

Auth stayed by the fire and stared at the stars. His mind raced free-form about the universe. He was the last to sleep.

Foop simply told himself to awaken before sunrise, closed his eyes, and slept. He woke up just before sunrise, threw water on the embers, kicked the sleeping body of Auth, announced the need for the space he lay in, and went to awaken twenty warriors.

Auth stood up, urinated on Foop's hut, and walked into the woods. He went to gather the padding for the sling he would use to carry me through the rough terrain.

I woke up to the sound of shuffling feet and the virile grunts of the warriors by the fire pit. They were seriously involved in attempting to menace Foop with dancing gestures. Only the ten most menacing would accompany him on the first strike. It was an honor to be chosen.

I saw that Thosat was leaving with his advance party. The supply caravan was well organized and ready to go as well. Auth was approaching with three older boys who were to help him carry me. "It's time to travel old mother," he called to me. Auth knew I had never given birth, but he also knew I liked the title.

"If I wind up in the lake it will be your fault." I answered. "I hope these three strong boys can make up for your uncertain feet this morning." He didn't respond, but I knew his head would clear as soon as we started walking. I was looking forward to this trip.

While on the well-traveled portions of our road I walked. When we approached the berry patches, I allowed myself the comfort of the ride. I fell asleep almost immediately and dreamed. I dreamed my hair had turned white just before the battle. The thought startled me awake. I needed to check myself. I twirled my finger around the hair and pulled it in front of my eyes. It was still black. I was comforted, yet I couldn't get back to sleep.

When the path narrowed, the branches started poking and slapping me as we pressed ahead. I looked on the face of my bearers. Auth was sweating. The boys were biting their tongues, holding the branches back as best they could, and walking gingerly down a steepening trail with ever looser and uneven footing.

"How much further?" I asked.

"A short time as the warrior walks. Much longer if burdened by the weight of a living legend," said Auth. It was good to hear him engage in wordplay. He was refreshed.

"Legends add weight with telling. Legends die when they are no longer discussed. This might be the first time a legend turns to dust because it was dragged through stickers and trees on a stony path," I said. "Stop, and let me walk. I can make it in warrior's time from here." It was a hollow boast, but they braced themselves and stopped for me to get out.

A soon as my feet hit the ground, I began to slide, but caught myself, bracing my foot against a mossy boulder and grabbing a sturdy tree branch. I stood a moment surveying the steps needed to get back on the steadier portion of the path.

Nervously, I twirled my dark lock with one hand. My other hand let go of the branch and reached for Auth. My weight shifted to my left foot, but a flat rock beneath the ball of my right foot shifted first. I caught the ground with my left hand and avoided dashing my face against the rocks. Sharp jolts in my palm from scraping flint gave way to growing waves of ache from a stone beneath my knee. The little pop at the side of my head was the pain that most concerned me

Thoughts were racing past me so fast I didn't have time to capture one. *Was it premature? Would it still turn white? Does anyone know? Can I put it back?*

A commotion interrupted my thoughts. More people were coming. Woman and children with a hunter carrying meat for the night's victory celebration gathered. *Oh, no. More eyes to see what I have done.* Next there was a bigger commotion from the other side of the path. Foop and two of his men pushed past a gatherer and spilled his grapes.

My mind kept going. *Maybe I could fool them all. Throw the black hair to the wind and announce the last turning? Announce a good omen for the battle? Could I lie that big? Should Auth know?*

Foop pushed his way up the path, excited and loud. He made an announcement. "We have them surrounded like sheep in the pen. If you want to tell your stories tomorrow, you will need to be there today. Hurry. They are preparing sacrifices to a god who is a cow, heating a shiny figure of cattle in fire for the burning. I won't wait. Hurry if you want to see."

Foop spoke quickly, then he was gone, back to the lake, as fast as he appeared. Everyone hurried and followed.

Only Auth and I stood still. I thought he must have noticed my crime. Something else was on his mind. "Cattle? Cattle? Shiny yellow figures of cattle on a fire? The bull of heaven?" He said this all quietly, as if to himself. He turned to me and said more loudly, "The people of the north have come."

I shared my news with him, holding my hand out to display the black strand wound around my finger. "Look what I've done."'

Auth ran down the path, shouting for Foop to stop. I ran as best I could to catch up. My balance was an old woman's balance. My speed was diminished with age. My determination was to ignore those handicaps, until I stumbled onto a battle zone. Right away, it was apparent. We had some strange players in this game now, and they weren't the Bombag.

Thosat ran to me and offered support. "What are you doing, Puth? You should come and sit. I will tell you what is going on."

"I see that Foop is trying to kill Auth," I said. They were both on the ground, and each was trying to choke the other. Thosat was excited, gesturing around the scene while babbling rapidly. "Yes, Auth has tried to stop the attack." he said. "Do you see? He can fight, but he has help. Foop tried to kill him with his spear but was unable to use his spear. There stands the tall man, and the shiny ones, and those baskets."'

I put my hand over Thosat's mouth. 'What? What are you saying?' I looked around and saw everyone eagerly watching Foop and Auth. What is going on?' I demanded.

"The tall man with the painted head scarf has snatched Foop's spears from the air with his hand. You should have been here. Amazing. Now Foop and Auth are fighting like lions." Thosat's eyes were wide. His excitement disturbed me. Thosat, the most steady among us, was in shock, his thoughts irrational.

"Who are the shiny people?" I demanded. 'Is that the shiny armor Auth has told us about?'

"Yes, shiny interlopers. What fine baskets they have." Thosat pointed to the baskets and smiled.

What else could I do? I couldn't admire the baskets. I needed to know what was happening. I needed time to think. My first thought was to scream. So, I screamed, "IS EVERYBODY CRAZY?"

Most of the Bombag people stood up and looked in my direction. Foop continued to dig a hole in the ground with Auth's face. He let up only to drive his knee deeper into Auth's backbone.

I screamed again. "MY HAIR HAS TURNED!" It was the only thing I could think to say. Even the interlopers stopped cheering on the fighters. Every head turned and watched me as I walked toward the tangled combatants.

Now, all but Foop and Auth were watching me walk toward them while they struggled in the dirt. On the way, I picked up one of Foop's spears. I measured the pole against my stride. I rocked it back and forth to find its balance. I was in full stride and swung. The spear came down on Foop's head. Foop's noggin made a sound like a drum. I didn't think I hit him hard enough, but when the spear bounced upward off his head, Foop's shoulders seemed to bounce up with it. He stiffened and half rose to his feet. Then he pitched forward and landed face-down on the ground.

I could see he was still breathing by the dust that he blew from his nose. Soon the blood ran down his face, and the dust became mud. All was quiet until the tall man spoke.

"Well done! I think we have a winner!" He approached me, arms outstretched, as if he wanted to embrace me. On the way, he loosed his head scarf and shook thick locks of white hair from under its restraints. "So decisive," he said. "You, old hag, have a flair for timing."

He smiled like an animal snarls, his voice filled with malice. I recoiled at his approach. This creature hated me. I could feel it. He hated us all. He would soon abandon his own men at the first sign things would go bad for him.

This is what I saw and heard. I would not lie to you. First I heard a voice. "Touch the woman and you will die." The words were spoken without emotion, as if all the speaker had to do was will it, and it would be done. The malicious one paused in his path and seemed to shrink in front of me before reversing his course. He turned and made fast work of the distance between me and his men by the fire.

I turned around to see the person who had spoken. Another tall man. He could have been a brother to the first. He smiled a different smile. He seemed more bored than concerned.

It was the malicious one who spoke next. "Baal Alazam, my brother. Have you any other mission from our lord?" He uttered the words greasily, like he hated to say them.

"I have business with the woman. I might make it my own business to expand the mission. Don't stir me to action, Baal Alayat."

The tall man, addressed by his brother as Baal Alayat, looked at a child in a basket next to the fire. I believe he was weighing odds against reward before addressing his men. "The interfering Alazam is given the woman. Will we let him have our sacrifice?" Alayat raised the child high and looked into its face.

"No!" The Shinies shouted it in unison, as if they meant it. All six of the shiny people drew short shiny weapons. Arrogantly fearless, faces set grim, and with menacing postures, all the Shinies seemed eager for the fight to begin.

Baal Alayat set the baby into its basket and took a step backwards. "Men," he said, "Enjoy the meat for the sword and flesh for the fire. I leave it to you."

Next, he disappeared. He disappeared before our eyes. Like a star blinks, he was gone. He left his men to fight for the dishonor of placing a living infant onto the altar bowl of a glowing hot golden calf. The smell of infant flesh, roasted over gold, was to be an offering to their mighty lord Baal Zebub.

For a quiet moment of frozen time it looked like the horror would be done. My tall protector stood and watched. Foop lay still on the ground. His warriors stared, dumbfounded. Thosat called for his men to come to him. His attempt to fill a military vacuum was going to be too late.

One of the interlopers took the baby from the basket and raised him into the air. His prayer made my stomach roll around. He called for the power of his lord to carry the battle. He held the baby to each corner of the earth and repeated his prayer. He didn't hear the other voice the first time it spoke up. It was Auth.

"I won't watch again." Auth pushed the words, barely audible, from his lungs, and he coughed dust. He got up on all fours and shouted, "I WON'T WATCH!" Auth's voice dropped again, but his challenge was strong. "You spiritless pig of a baby-burning whore! I'll fight you for that child!" He wobbled to a standing position and collapsed again to one knee. His effort seemed to inspire the tribe. Thosat and his men came all the quicker. They saw a man, who couldn't stand, become heroic.

The Shinies laughed aloud and touched swords together. One of them took a javelin of shiny metal and threw it in Auth's direction. It landed to his left and stuck into the hard ground with authority. It was a superior weapon.

I understood what I needed to do. I needed to go and get that baby. Who would harm me if the tall man was going to protect me? That is what I thought, and that is what I did.

Did the Shiny holding the baby see me coming? Yes. He guessed my plan and hurried to the hot bowl, stopping just before he was ready to drop the infant. He wanted to make eye contact with me as he did his deed. He enjoyed the dismay on my face when I realized I was going to arrive too slowly.

Something fast enough was on the way. A familiar sound zoomed past my ear. It was the sound of F-f-foop! He was returning a superior weapon to the Shinies. The javelin hit the man holding the infant so hard his shiny armor parted. His arms jerked violently toward his chest as he stumbled backwards into a stack of javelins. He died clutching at the air, still trying to hold on to his sacrifice.

That baby was you. It was you, Asitr, flying through the air, hitting the ground, skidding down the bank, and into the lake, away from the fire and into the water. I ran untouched through the Shinies, hurried to the lakes edge, and held you to my breast.

Behind me, the noise of violent struggle was just beginning. I'm glad it was behind me and out of my sight. It was an awful butchering of our people. The short spears they called swords cut our warriors to pieces. Our spears bounced off their armor. It was when we rushed in with everyone that it ended. We piled on top of them and held them like turtles on their backs, poking at them with sticks to find the killing spots beneath the armor. We pounded them with rocks. Finally, we pulled them down to the water and held them under. They were hard to kill.

In the final surge, the oldest woman in the tribe was trapped beneath a Shiny and drowned. That honor of age now fell to me.

We lost Foop. His legend will live as long as the story is told.

Thirty more Bombag died. Among them, the young boys who carried me to battle in the sling.

Thosat was wounded in the attack and lost a foot. He would have to turn to teaching.

Auth couldn't get to his feet until the battle was over. His body would mend, but soft foods would be his steady diet.

You and I were pulled from the lake by my tall protector just before the battle climaxed in the water.

We were wise to celebrate before the battle. Friends who wouldn't return left images of laughing faces and indelible memories etched on our minds. Gifts to us they were, from that night at the fire.

Every survivor suspected life would change. I was feeling like my voice would be needed at the next fire council. As a result of my hair, my new achievement of age and the presence of a supernatural protector, I began to feel I was best among us to chart our changes and recommend our new course, as I had signs, protection, and the longest history of seeing the changes creep up on us. I felt ready for what would be a curious council fire. A council forced to address unavoidable uncertainty.

The war of words around the fire that night became more important to us than the battle we had just barely survived. We made choices that we could live with. We defined our place in a world that promised a future of scary newness.

It was my protector who started the debate. He began to assert himself after our burials. During the night, when we returned to our camp, he followed alongside my sling and advised me of what was to come. He said he needed to stay and make sure my people fortified themselves against new Shinies who were certain to come. We should learn how to make the superior weapons, he said. We should build walls of stone. We should begin soon, allowing no other concern to delay us. He promised to show us how to accomplish these things and more. It made sense to me. I would carry the torch of his idea to the council. Who could disagree with his conclusions?

Thosat. It was Thosat who responded first. 'Give up the hunting? Stop the gathering? Act like we never needed our stores after a drought or storm?'

I could see the wisdom of eating and storing food. I had ideas to discuss but didn't speak them. My protector spoke over me and carried his case to the Bombag people directly. "Do the rest of you think it's wise to die on a full stomach when you can be lean and victorious instead?" His eyes were wide with incredulity, and he held a charming half smile on his face. He looked to be trying not to laugh at Thosat's simplicity and embarrass him.

I felt good he showed that much kindness to him. I forgot about my proposal and asked him the question that started Auth, once again, onto the path of heroism. "What would you have us to do?" I asked.

Auth spoke, unclearly at first, through his broken teeth and shattered nose, but he spoke forcefully. This was a new Auth who was sitting at the campfire. He wasn't engaging in word play. His demeanor was undoubtedly that of a man who was going to have his way.

"Shame on you, old mother, to ask him that. Ask us. We are the people here. We don't know who this is. Are there any here who need to be told what we should do with what we have learned? Without discussing it? Let this character who would tell us what to do identify who he is. What is his special interest and how does his power change our rightful ways?"

"Yes," added Thosat, "How is a stranger's agenda better than voices speaking for the common good?"

Both of these men spoke wisdoms that were crucial to governing wisely. I felt ashamed I had forgotten them in my excitement.

Once again, my strange protector spoke up. "I am the servant of a god who has no better above him. I have come to answer the prophecy of the white hairs. Can you miss the color of my own? Who is it that you thought I was? Your neighbor, the Banda? Do I look like a gatherer to you? Do you think I wouldn't have a plan? Do you think I wouldn't use the Banda to gather food for you? Do you think my habits rude or my mind so cluttered with the issues of survival I can't think straight? Who would refuse my assistance?"

He spread his arms and began to glow. His glow was beautiful to look at but just bright enough to make me turn my head away. It had a cowering effect on many of us — myself included. Auth seemed impervious.

"You appear to have the same skills as the cowardly Baal Alayat," he said. "You share the title of Baal." Auth was staring the stranger in his eyes and showing no signs of fear. It seemed to surprise our guest. He hesitated before speaking.

My protector spoke a little less arrogantly to Auth. "What is it you think you know, sir? I think we are not communicating well."

Auth responded in a voice not trying to feign respect. "I know from some travels that you look and act like a servant of the despicable Baal Zebub. Do you deny it?"

Now the stranger dropped his polite speech. "Didn't you hear that malicious spirit yesterday? I heard HIM claim that distinction. Who here didn't witness how a threat of my power ran him off. Are you attempting to do the same to me?"

Auth wasn't diverted from his question. "I can see the two of you cooperated in a deception. I'm trying to get an answer where you like to place questions. Will you give me an answer?'

The stranger stood and stepped toward Auth, pointing his finger in his face. "I have answered everything," he said, "but my patience with you is gone. It is best to listen to the inevitable and make the will of my god the will of your tribe." Baal Alazam spoke with a stern voice.

Auth answered him with a little less confidence in his own. "Our will is yet to be determined." he said.

Alazam pressed his momentum. "Your will should be with the will of the god who gave you the prophecy of the white hair. Would I be here tonight if the last hair had not turned? Who can dispute a clear sign from god?"

Auth wasn't ready to answer that question. I had his response wrapped around my finger.

"Hold all opinions until I have spoken," I said. I wanted to stop the nodding of heads. It looked as if the stranger's speech was winning the council. "I have seen the lessons of yesterday. I have seen the same ones you have seen. I have seen others as well. All of us will agree we must try to follow the will of God. What other path will take us to the end? Auth!"

"Yes, old mother?"

Auth looked at me, puzzlement in his face. I had never spoken to him so authoritatively.

Our tribe had terms of faith from before I was born. We repeated them in ritual form. I was going to lead him to the answer he needed with the questions and answers of our ritual.

"If we have hardship on the road set before us, what do we do?" I began.

"We overcome," he responded in the traditional way.

I continued. "And if we come across an enemy?"

"We defeat him."

"Is this the Bombag way?"

"Forever since the time of the Adam."

"Do we share the God of creation with the Adam?"

"We do."

"Is our God a liar?" I lifted my finger in front of his eyes, and Auth suddenly knew the reason for my reciting the Bombag terms of faith. He squeezed my hand before answering, then wheeled toward the stranger.

"Why would he need to?" Auth began adlibbing on our traditional answer. "No!" he said with finality. "Only inferior beings, humans, and fallen angels need to lie.' He stood up and circled the fire as he spoke. He was looking us all in our eyes, showing us he was speaking the truth. He ended his circle in front of the stranger. "Which of these do you represent?"

"I've told you who has sent me."

"If sent by the God of Adam why do you lie?" Auth's face was taking on a look of confident fury.

The stranger tried to recover. "You are putting words in my mouth."

"I was mining your words for meaning." Now it was Auth's turn to put his finger in the face of the stranger. What is your god's name?"

"Are you calling my god a liar?" Baal Alazam was attempting to deflect a direct challenge.

Auth was not diverted. He asked the question that could not be deflected. "You claim to do the will of our creator?"

"I do." It was the last lie left to be told.

"I call you and your pretender of a god a liar. Will you agree old mother?"

I lifted my hand into the light and let everyone watch me unravel a black hair from my finger. "This is the last hair, accidentally plucked by my own hand. It hasn't turned."

Auth drove home the spear of truth. "Would the creator NOT know that the hair has yet to turn? P-p-f-f-f-t!" Auth pointed away from the fire and into the forest before finishing. "Only your insipid, meddling, posturing, god would not know, yet seize upon speculation to fabricate lies. Go back north and never return. Follow your brother."

"I am obligated to respect the decision to rescind your offer of hospitality," Alazam said with an air of dignity.

Our guest, who tried to deceive us, was trying to recoup the dignity he'd lost. I guessed he wasn't often so unsuccessful with deceit. Unlike his brother, he didn't blink himself away. I guessed again that he had been drained of the power to do so. All our eyes were on him as he walked away from the campfire and faded into the darkness.

I was going to apologize to the tribe for my lack of principle, but the normal world wasn't ready to return. When we turned back to the fire, we saw we had a new guest, and he spoke.

"Don't be afraid," he said. "My name is Olphrenjii. I am a messenger from the one God." Surprisingly, we weren't afraid.

"Nicely done. You are, indeed, the winners." The way he said it sounded joyful.

I was amused. I didn't know why. "We've heard that one already," I giggled. I put my hand over my mouth because it felt inappropriate to be giddy.

"This time you hear it with sincerity from a messenger of the Creator who demands I speak the truth in its final distillation. I have seen you, and heard you, and you have made me believe in you. I believe you keep faith with the God who created you."

Auth was feeling giddy as well. 'Have you come to save us?' he asked. His voice sounded so childlike and hopeful. We all seemed like children at that moment. "Can we keep our lives as we know them?" he asked without waiting for an answer to his first question.

"None do," was the reply.

"What can we do?" Thosat spoke up and went straight to the heart of the tribe's concerns. "How is it our God will allow these men to ruin our world?"

"He allows them to tempt you. Why are you tempted?"

Auth gave him a straightforward answer. "I am tempted by the weapons that could make us all as powerful as Foop had been."

"Yes," he answered, "power is a strong temptation. What say you, Thosat? What is your temptation, as regards these spirits?"

"I want to learn how to blink off and become invisible," he said. We all laughed, especially the messenger. Thosat, who was embarrassed that his sincere answer sounded so silly, had to laugh at himself.

Then this stranger who had calmed us, and exposed us as children, reached out his hand toward me. I took it and trusted. "Don't let us down, please, sir," I pleaded. I lowered my eyes and knelt in front of him. I was surprised when he recoiled. I thought he was angry. I had turned my wondrous moment into a mistake of etiquette. Confused and contrite, I asked him to forgive me. I told him I had no talent for thinking straight around my superiors.

The messenger explained, "I am no more above you than are those servants of Baal Zebub," That is the will of my lord. He has made you to become more. Expect it to happen. Respect that it will happen. Act like you know it. Teach it to your children. Teach it to the child, Asitr."

This is when we knew your name.

Auth asked the question most of us were thinking. "Wouldn't we be more if we had those weapons?"

The messenger sighed with clear resignation and gathered himself to speak as if he were making a formal announcement. These were his words:

"I am here in regards to the child, Asitr, the courageous Auth, and the sometimes wise Puth. It is the will of the Lord God almighty they start a twelve-year journey of seed gathering. This journey will begin at the cave of the dry spring and it will end at the gates of the city to your north. There, after the time of wandering, the child Asitr will enter. Alone."

Olphrenjii broke his authoritative spell by softening his voice, adding gently, "That is what I have come to say. The journey will begin tomorrow, but for now, I would like approval to ask a question. This question is for the children."

We all leaned toward him in silent consent. Details of the journey didn't seem important at the moment. He asked the children to make a choice. "Which would you choose of these three choices?" he asked. Would you choose for me to walk away, blink out, or stay awhile, and walk you to your huts for the night?"

Thosat must have misunderstood the targeted audience. He jumped in the air with his one good leg and exclaimed, "Blink out! Blink out!" He was the only one to say it.

The children trusted the messenger from before he spoke. They all screamed for him to stay. "With your parent's permission?" He scanned the adults around the fire. None objected. Why were we all so relaxed?

Olphrenjii took each child by hand, each to his and her hut and called them by name. He had words for each of them that meant something in their lives. He assured some they would achieve their goals. He told some about strength they weren't aware they possessed. One young boy grasped the messenger's hand firmly when he heard he would be the next great warrior, but smarter than Foop. "I won't let us down,'" he said.

Causing tears, he told little Gaut that she would not be taken by Thant but another boy, a boy quite young and much more mysterious. He informed her that her wait for him would be long. The news didn't console her, but she kissed him goodnight anyway. He stayed to hear a prayer from young Autar, who asked the Lord to bless our messenger for "liking us folks who had rude habits and didn't always think straight." Olphrenjii certainly seemed to enjoy our children. Our children adored Olphrenjii.

That night he was a balm for us. We were unafraid and in concert with our spirit. The next day, Olphrenjii was more reserved. He wouldn't let his attention be diverted from his mission to start the three of us on our journey.

He began with a ceremony at the cave. One by one, we approached him and received a dusting of powder. He blew it on our hands from a plate. The powder was bright yellow and was far more vibrant than the yellow dyes we knew how to make. Each of us, one after the other, entered the cave and placed our hands on the wall in the pattern of a circle. We left behind bright yellow proofs that we had been there together, as a tribe.

I, myself, held you, Asitr. I lifted you up to the wall and pressed your hands into the design. To show that you were from somewhere else, yet accepted in our tribe, I placed one tiny hand inside the circle and the other on the outside.

I began to cry, and the effect was contagious. We all embraced each other at the mouth of the cave, and I told each one I would never forget them.

Then the messenger sealed it. He picked up the golden calf from the temple of Baal, etched numbers and symbols across its brow, and threw it into the cave. The ground rumbled. The roof of the cave door collapsed. It was dramatic and impressive. He turned to us and said, "This door is sealed and will be preserved in time through flood and progress. The Lord knows when the time is right for it to be reopened."

Finished with the ceremony, he turned to me and told us it was time for walking. Before he left us to wander, he made sure I knew the three lists I needed to pass on to you. The list of things to remember, the list of things to watch out for, and the list of numbers needed for a return to the cave. His final words were, "Never let Asitr forget that you all are made to become more."

These things you know, because I've told you they were so. This is the last time I will tell you. I myself, and old father Auth, now leave you here at the entrance to the city built by the fallen ones of heaven.

Child that you are, and as helpless as you look, I don't fear for you. Armed with what you know, sacks of seeds, and the love of your old mother, I tell you, with the approval of Heaven, you are not overmatched. God is with you. One more thing ... Always, remember to eat your garlic raw.

*   *   *

"These were my mother's words on the day she released me into the city of small gods. I never ate my garlic raw after that day. I hoped it wouldn't hurt her to know it.

"The second story I've promised begins when Mother Puth and Father Auth turned their back to me and disappeared into the forest. This story is not as I told it to the Savant. I'll tell it from the perspective of memory."

18

GARDENER OF THE GODS

I T SOUNDS CRUEL TO LET LOOSE A BOY OF TWELVE YEARS at the gates of a strange, dangerous world. I was expecting to walk through the arched entry and be handed greatness. Isn't that how it works for ... a chosen one? I strutted through the gates with confidence, but I staggered through the next two years in despair.

Think of my age. This is an age that still believes that goodness is what is expected in the world. It is the best age to recruit a true believer. It's an age too young for the burden of choosing a true belief.

Goodbye to the age of the delighted boy, preparing to become a man. I was stepping into that next age and there were problems. Lack of experience, chemical and hormonal changes, the craziness of finding out that goodness is both unexpected, and situationally relative. Endangered by that mix is the untested strength of belief in things taught.

Despite my mother's words, I felt over-matched. I cowered when no one stepped forward to show me my way. I prayed for an angel, for God himself, even for my parents to come and get me. All the prayers went unanswered.

After stealing food to stay alive, failing to sell seed, and being beaten for having nothing more valuable than seeds, I began to feel I didn't have the approval of Heaven.

It wasn't clear what exactly I was failing at, but I was failing. Tested, retested, and failing every day, until faith was gone.

Nothing replaced the lost belief in my mission. I tried to believe in people, but they wouldn't give me a reason to believe in them. People were either cruel to me or indifferent to my presence.

I saw people steal things for survival. I saw them steal things they didn't need. I watched big boys bully little boys. Big men bully little men. Powerful beings bully everyone. I saw murder for pleasure. murder for gain, and killing for survival and revenge. I saw the rape of children and the surrender of suicide. I watched as one of the bastard Anakim ate the blood of a man who offended him with an offer to share a goblet of beer. All before I turned fourteen.

Most of these things were viewed from my perch atop a grape arbor in the back yard of a fenced in butcher shop. Finding the butcher's shop saved me from a life in the alleys.

The shop shared an alley with an all-night beer hall and a gambling house. Whores who couldn't get jobs with the temple of Baal would frequent the alley because they were assured of the presence of drunken men with money. Thugs were attracted for the same reason.

It was under the light of the moon that I learned about the human capacity for depravity. I began to wonder why the God of creation who designed beginnings, endings, and limitations on all things didn't mandate brakes for such a horrible engine. Why was it so apparent that goodness had so many barriers and depravity such full license to run?

It was under the light of the sun that I tried to shake off my memories of those nights. I filled my head with the adventures of exploring. I was living in a city of such size, even after two years, I hadn't penetrated beyond its outer circle.

The owner of the butcher shop first brought to my attention the importance of this city being a series of circles. His observations became building blocks fitting squarely onto the foundation I received from my parents in our years of wandering. I was failing and falling when he saved me.

I was hiding from him for so long, it surprised me when he reached out to me. He made it obvious he was aware of the freeloader in the back of the shop.

First, I noticed that my ladder had been taken down. I spotted it leaning on a table under the arbor. I might have thought nothing of it if I didn't also notice that my sack of seeds was sitting on the table.

I kept my eyes on the bushes and the door to his shop while I inched my way toward the arbor. My heart sank with the fear of realizing I may have lost my safe bed. It dropped further after shuddering with memories of nights without comfort in the alleys.

Closer to the table I saw something that made me gasp. Next to my bag was a plate. It was stacked with beef and piled with grapes. A bowl lay next to it — a barley soup with floating islands of carrots, celery, and onion.

All my senses were on alert. The owner, I thought, was surely in hiding, waiting to catch me in his trap like a mouse. I finally acquiesced to the inevitable and approached the table. This looked like a fine last meal.

I attacked the plate like a ravenous animal, making guttural noises while violently waving my free hand to warn potential interlopers away. I was determined to force down as much as I could before my trapper seized me and punished me for squatting on his land.

Nobody materialized, but I soon learned what happens when a mouth full of stringy beef forms a mass of sinew in the throat of a glutton.

I remembered Auth dislodging a sprig of mint from Puth's throat. He had slapped her hard on the back while she hacked and coughed. The noise she made sounded like a dog with laryngitis. I was making that noise now. It seemed to echo off the gate. Barf! Arf! Barf! Arf!

The spasms grew more painful. The sound seemed to grow quieter. I couldn't reach my back with enough force to dislodge the meat, so I threw myself backward against the central pillar of the arbor. The pillar gave away and I fell down. I rolled to my feet and threw myself backward into the wall of the butcher shop. My head started to tingle at the scalp and the feeling spread down my face and began to center itself at the back of my neck. Still, the sinew held its ground.

My spasms stopped. I was no longer emitting sounds. My body had resigned itself to death by hysterical eating. I had just enough awareness to notice that something wasn't adding up.

I felt it odd that the sound of my choking should still be echoing off the gate. I found it even stranger that the gate was moving. It was moving like someone was throwing a weight against it. I made it across the yard, slipped the latch, and swung it inward.

Through tearing eyes and a clouding mind I saw something that terrified me more than the thought of choking. A beast, very dark, not shapeless, but nearly indistinguishable from the night.

The beast rose up in front of me and I discovered it had claws. I could feel them tearing at my solar plexus. The weight of the thing pushed me off my feet and air exploded from my lungs before I hit the ground. Meat erupted from my mouth. Once again, I felt claws dig into my body, then a wet tongue on my face

After removing the trailing scraps of meat from my face the beast sniffed the ground and found the larger pieces he had just forced from my esophagus.

I spent the rest of the night propping up the arbor, petting my new dog, and slowly enjoying the soup and grapes. A note on the table made the evening perfect. The butcher was offering me a job.

After two horrible years in the city, I finally had one good night. A night that began with the usual permeance of gloom turned into a hopeful evening filled with thoughts of a new companion, a surprise benefactor, and a job. I was feeling like the chosen one again. I fell asleep while scratching my new companion behind the ear, and wondering what kind of job a butcher would offer a chosen one.

When the butcher opened the back door. I jerked awake. The sun was rising. I could see the features of a dog resting his head on my lap. It was a forty-pound black dog with visible ribs, a white walrus mustache, and a brown mask. We were both looking at a round, red-faced man standing in the doorway. He stood still and silent. All three of us looked puzzled.

I jumped to my feet when the butcher turned to close the door. My new dog walked over to the butcher suspiciously and smelled a circle around his feet. Whatever the dog discerned from this made him bold enough to look up and sniff the air while he stared into the butcher's face. After sniffing the butcher's butt, his tail began to wag, and he ran back to my side. He had given the butcher his approval.

I didn't know what to think of the look on the butcher's face. It certainly wasn't the look of approval. I had cleaned up as much as I could. I fixed the arbor. Nothing was broken. Why did he look so concerned? So stern?

"Oh, sir! The food!" I said. "I just thought that ... I mean I thought ... the note said I could ... You didn't?" I was stammering and feeling foolish. The round red face in front of me opened its mouth and guffawed.

"The food was for you," he laughed. "I'm sorry about the soup. Good herbs are hard to find. I meant the meal to be a business dinner." He looked down at the dog. "Business that has no place for dogs. Have you been hiding this dog since you adopted my arbor last year?"

"Well, no sir. This isn't my dog. I mean ... not really ... yet." I was surprised he knew I was his tenant for the whole year. I wasn't sure I still had a dog.

The butcher stated the obvious. "He acts like he thinks he's your dog."

I was hoping I could gain the job and keep the dog, so I began negotiating for both. "Well, we just met, sir," I said. "He's a good dog."

"'Even good dogs have no place in a clean butcher shop. Even if they don't steal."

"I wasn't thinking, sir." It was true. I couldn't think of a reason for a dog in a butcher shop.

"They don't belong in my new restaurant either." Logic was the enemy again.

"I can see that, sir." I looked down and could tell from the ribs showing through the dog's coat that no food would be safe around him. "If only I could feed him well enough." My own attempt at logic sounded weak, but I was hoping the butcher could be generous to boy and dog.

"Why would you feed someone else's dog?" The relentless questions wore me down. I tried a question of my own.

"Well ... why would you feed me?" I didn't think it so funny a question, but the ample deposits of fat on my benefactor began to undulate rhythmically as he sat down, laughing.

"It's clear to me you have a dog." he said. "'I'm going to go into business with a boy and a dog. What are we going to call him?"

"I was thinking I would call him Barfarf, sir."

"Barfarf? Barfarf?" The rolling laughter came again. "Have you thought this through?"

"Well, there's a sort of story behind it, sir."

"I'll tell you what." The butcher said it suddenly as he rose to his feet, "I'm going to make us a pot of tea. You tell me the story behind that name, then we'll put our heads together to find a proper name."

"What's wrong with Barfarf?"

"Okay, let me put it to you like this ... Picture yourself in the street. The alley. The park. You are calling your dog. You put your hands to your mouth and scream out ... Barfarf! Barfarf! Barfarf! They have rules about people acting mad in public. Barking like a dog in public is usually construed as madness. There's also the problem of calling unwanted dogs to you."

I hadn't noticed anyone enforcing rules about acting out madness in public. The first argument didn't carry much weight with me. I had no trouble seeing the logic of the second argument. "Alright," I said. "We should find a proper name."

"Splendid," he said. "After we get that issue settled, we can discuss a business venture." After announcing those intentions, the butcher headed into his shop and returned a short while later with the worst tea I ever politely choked down.

I drank two cups of that bitter tea before I could finish telling him about the events of the night before. He kept asking questions about details, pouring more tea when my cup emptied. I didn't know a man could laugh so much. I didn't know that a man could be kindly, yet find such delight in hearing the story of a starving, scared, choking boy. His face, interactive with my story made me feel comfortable. I felt I had been listened to. When my story was completed, his face turned suddenly serious.

"I have an idea for a business,' he said abruptly, 'I think it's a good idea, worth pursuing. We have an immediate barrier to overcome, and I believe in the principle that immediate barriers be immediately removed. Are you in agreement?"

"I couldn't say, sir. What is the barrier?" I wanted my life to change, but I was cautious.

"We haven't introduced ourselves, and we can't go into business together without a proper introduction. I am Sami, Sami the butcher. With your help I expect, soon, people will know me as Sami the restaurateur — the finest restaurateur in all of Samyaza."

"And I am Asitr," I said. "The confused boy from atop your arbor."

"That is about to change," he promised. "You will soon be known as Asitr, the boy who grows the finest herbs, exclusively for Sami the restaurateur."

"I see. How did you know? How did you find out?"

"I've been watching you. I know about your little garden outside the city. Mighty fine herbs. They can make a top chef of me." Sami widened his eyes and spread his hands in front of his face. He looked like he believed he was talking about magic, or gold, or something equally wondrous.

"They are what they are. I've had little use for them since I came here. I'm sure they could be used to improve your tea-making skills." I was being honest. The seeds didn't open doors for me when I expected them to. Now, they were the reason Sami entered into his negotiations. We didn't need a written contract between us for what followed.

"Then what say we call our little business a 20/80 proposition?" Sami began.

"And the dog?" I was hoping the dog was negotiable.

"I'm afraid we still have an immediate barrier to a business relationship with the dog."

"He needs a name?" I was hoping that was going to be all there was to overcome.

"Yes, we can't be properly introduced without a name. Have you thought of something?"

"I think I will call him Sami, after his benefactor."

"Too confusing. It would be hard to tell us apart."

It was my turn to laugh. I was using muscles I hadn't used for two years. My face was getting stiff from smiling. I very much wanted to go into business with this man. "What should we call this dog?" I asked. "A good dog should have the proper name."

"Well then, I think we should give him a name that will reflect his role in our business." Sami rubbed his own walrus mustache and rolled his eyes in thought, but he wasn't offering any names or clues as to the role of the dog in the business.

I finally had to ask,"What role will he have?"

"I need a dog that will dispose of the larger bones in my shop. Does he like bones?"

"I think we should find out. Do you have any bones just lying about?" I relaxed. Negotiations were over.

I can tell you with certainty that the dog adapted to his new job as easily as his proper name became apparent. We anointed him with the name Mr. Bone. The name fit. He was born to the task of demolishing bones. Soon he was an eighty-five-pound partner in a business that grew as quickly as the herbs I planted in the back yard of the shop.

Mr. Bone didn't seem to mind that we didn't take him to the restaurant. After the unfortunate flatulence incident at the grand opening, he was barred from the premises. He was tail waggingly happy to be banished to the shop.

Sami was just as happy to spend most of his time at the restaurant. Soon after my first big harvest he learned to make a really good cup of tea. Customers began to give him gifts of teapots from all over the known world. He topped off his collection by purchasing one pot from every merchant in the city. His reputation heightened among the merchants when we hung the pots in the outdoor dining area where light illuminated the collection.

Sami, the jovial entrepreneur, was truly in his element when mingling with the lunch and dinner crowd. His customers came from all circles of the city. I, also, settled into my job with delight.

We hired a serious and talented young butcher named Vanpandikuladezan to run the butcher's side of the business. We called him Vandi. Vandi treated Mr. Bone like an equal in the business. He took care never to give him more bones than were healthy to eat. The excess, he ground up to fertilize my gardens. All was well. As Sami would say, "All is well and getting weller!" It kept getting weller and weller for two more years.

Sami congratulated himself on many a night for placing his restaurant in the second circle from the gate. "Too dirty for the temple bunch and too established for the criminals in the first circle," he would say. It was that same safe, but not staid, atmosphere that lured the artists and musicians into the second circle. Many of them were regulars at Sami's.

One of those musicians got lucky. He received a garden apartment and an expense account when he accepted an offer to play during morning offerings at the Azazel complex.

I began an exciting project of my own. I had just turned sixteen and was starting my own business. It was Sami's idea. He set me up with enough equipment to begin my own landscaping business. The lucky musician was my first customer. With my first job being in the temple district, I was getting good word of mouth in all the right circles.

Word of mouth cost me everything, friends, companions, business, sanity ... everything.

The momentum for that little ball of events began rolling when my client referred me to his patrons in the temple of Azazel. He gave them two locations for places where I could be contacted. He mentioned a butcher named Vanpandikuladezan and a restaurateur named Sami.

Vanpandikuladezan was a name known to an infamous bastard Anakim named Herakles. I never met an Anakim that wasn't dangerous. All of them are bastards born as an unblessed creation and every one dangerous. Nonetheless, you can't help but pity them their existence. I pity them all but Herakles. He is a lover of monstrous acts, and lovers of monstrous acts are so damned hard to pity.

The malign focus Herakles leveled at Vandi is difficult to understand. The proportion was so off. In Herakles' mind, a seed of disappointment grew into a living rage, was fed by hate, unconstrained by compassion, and bore the rotten fruit of a plan for casual violence. He set his mind to taking Vandi's soul, and he was going to have fun doing it. We never saw it coming.

They came with the noon crowd. I was at the restaurant with a batch of newly dried lemon verbena. Things were getting busy, so I strapped on an apron and began to take food orders.

Sami was in the back, negotiating with his friend Baddar. Baddar was delivering fresh fish for the evening meals. Those negotiations came to a halt when, to the sound of breaking pottery, the birthday boy entered the restaurant, shouting for service.

Sami knew the source of the shouting and understood the sound of breaking pottery was from his prized teapot collection, but he acted calmly and quickly. His first impulse was to protect his customers and his staff. He chugged toward the dining area.

I bumped into Sami at the kitchen door. He pushed me, hard, into the kitchen, and hissed for me to stay put. He was much quicker than a man his size should be. At the sound of a bellowing voice, he spun and zipped away, dancing and dodging through the aisles between tables.

Louder than the din of the entry, the bellowing voice cut through the restaurant, shouting repeatedly, "owner, owner, owner."

"Yes, sir. Yes, sir. Coming!" Sami knew the urgency of the situation. He knew Herakles was the strongest, meanest, and dumbest of the Anakim. Familiarity with the monster made him anxious and eager to grant every request the brute would make. I, myself, was frozen when I saw his face. I remembered him as the blood eater from the alley.

"I'll have a table away from the street stench." Herakles's first demand was no surprise. He was known to hate the smell of unwashed people.

"If only I had known you were coming." Sami was thinking quickly. "I would have reserved the patio for you. I have the perfect table, near the smoker. The way the wind is blowing, you will smell only the chicken roasting in sage butter."

People were already edging toward the exits. Stories went around about Herakles and his penchant to become violent if he perceived people were fleeing him in social situations. Sami didn't know which way the beast was thinking today, but Herakles gave him the opening he was looking for to clear the room.

"It's my birthday," he said. "I'll need your best."

"Did you hear that?" Sami said it loud enough to be heard. "We are having a private celebration for a man of renown." Herakles nodded in approval. "Everyone out," commanded Sami. "No need to pay for your meal. See you soon. Out, out, out."

The diners rushed out eagerly. The last to pass Herakles on the way out was Sami's friend Baddar. The fisherman's exit brought some comments from Herakles.

"Hooga Mushka, man. What are you? Some kind of fisherman? Take a bath. Sheesh and Sheeshka Mushka!" Herakles was shouting terms of disrespect. Then he laughed as Baddar scooted off. Taking out his short sword, he smashed another pot in celebration.

I could hear Sami's anger as he entered the kitchen. "Impotent freak." he whispered. Much more loudly he added, "Asitr will seat you, and I will bring you everything I have for your sampling. Please, be comfortable ... Asitr!"

I knew Sami was worried. I could see his face was grim. He put a finger over his lips, looked into my face, and bellowed, "When you have seated the gentleman you can take your clumsy fool of a self home. I will entertain these luminaries myself." His attempt to get me out of harm's way didn't have the desired effect.

"He stays," Herakles shouted from his table. "He will be my wine bearer for the evening. I will train the fool for you, teach him some focus." I hurried to his side, and he grabbed my tunic, pulling my face close to his. Up close to him, I thought he smelled like a toad.

"Got ears boy?" He asked. "Spill a drop, you lose an ear. Drop a goblet, you lose your head. Fair enough?"

I answered with a steady voice. "I'm equal to the task, sir." I meant it in a different way than Herakles heard it. Hatred had overcome my fear, and I felt my moment was coming.

The feeling washed over me casually at first but developed into a certainty. As surely as I'm chosen for greatness, I knew this thing didn't need to live. I was going to find a way to destroy the monster. Reasonably sure I was under the protection of Heaven, I asked. "Allow me to choose you a wine?"

Taking a detour past the wine rack, I ran to the shed. Inside, I had some hemlock, dried dragon berries, and datura seed soaking in a jar of alcohol. They had been soaking for two weeks, and the potion was ready.

I knew I had one bottle of stout wine with a flavor heavy enough to hide the poisonous content of the brew. It was going to need a minute of breathing before the flavors could blend, so I grabbed a weak offering of melon rind wine to buy some time. I was sure he would demand something more powerful.

Time was on my side. I was certain he would remain until the cupboard was bare. Complete immersion in overindulgence was his reputation in the days he was unconstrained.

This is what I have done in every life I have lived. I have gathered good facts and reached bad conclusions. Herakles and his party stayed less than ten minutes. He ignored the weak wine.

Sami served him potatoes and roasted beef within two minutes of his arrival. Herakles finished his plate and once again bellowed for the owner. He was beginning to show his intentions.

"Where did you get this beef?" he demanded. Sami ran to the table. Herakles asked the opinion of his friends. "Do you recognize the source of this beef?" It appeared they did. They all agreed they couldn't be mistaken. They were certain they recognized from where this beef had been attained.

"What is the problem, sirs?" Sami was clearly in the dark. "Is there a problem with the beef? I have lamb and chicken. Let me clear your plates and bring you something suitable."

Herakles gave a surprise answer. "I want to see your butcher. The beef is delicious. Bring me the butcher."

Sami was visibly shaken. He wasn't on the same page as Herakles, but he knew the book. "The butcher's not here." he said. "He only delivers. Please, let me get you some mutton, maybe?"

"From what address? I have to tell the man how much I appreciated his cut." Everyone at the table weakly suppressed a laugh into their hands. They were sharing some mysterious enjoyment of Herakles's declaration of appreciation.

Sami was suspicious of any polite reason for Herakles to want to see Vandi, so he lied. "I would have to look it up sir. I don't have a head for remembering addresses or names or ..."

Herakles cut him off. "Get the address." he demanded.

Sami jumped. "Yes, sir, I'll find it right now." He sped away back to the kitchen, grabbing my arm on the way. Loudly, he shouted, "Come here fool, get the good wine." Quietly he whispered, "Run to the butcher shop and tell Vandi who it is that wants to see him. Tell him to run to the bridge grove, and we'll try to find out what he wants. Make sure he hangs the closed sign ... go!"

I ran as fast as I could. I used all the shortcuts I knew. It wouldn't have mattered. Herakles had stopped by the butcher shop before he went to the restaurant.

Why the little head game? He didn't stay to watch our pain. He didn't linger to enjoy the public reaction to his crime at the butcher shop.

The public reaction. My fellow human beings. I saw them milling around the shop from two blocks away. I turned the corner, lost my balance, and dropped to the ground when I focused on the object decorating our sign pole. It was the head of our friend Vandi.

I stood up and stumbled through the excited crowd, stopping at the front door. The rest of Vandi's body was in our display window. He was hanging up-side down, wearing a garish note of explanation that explained nothing.

You took my cow. I killed your pig. Ledger even.

There was nothing in the note I could understand. The only thing standing in that vacuum where I searched for reason was my own rage.

In shock, my body wracked with a sickly shiver, interrupted by an arm on my shoulder. It was a man I had come to recognize as a regular at the gambling hall.

"Hey look, it's the seed kid!" he said. The crowd pressed in on me. "Sorry 'bout your dog, kid. He was a good dog."

"My dog?"

"Squashed his head flat with one foot," he grinned. "Go see. Brains all over the alley."

I didn't know if I was more shocked at the gleefulness of the delivery or because he didn't express regret about Vandi. It didn't matter. I had no time for paralyzing outrage. Sami was alone with a monster.

After one step toward the restaurant, I changed my mind and ran down the alley, letting out a primal scream of rage when I ran past the body of Mr. Bone. I was still screaming when I leaped over the fence, ran through the yard, and into the shop. Vandi's sharp cleaver was still there, coagulating blood cooling on its surface.

I picked up the bloody blade and ran toward the ogling crowd. It gave me pleasure that they mistook my intentions. Some of them screamed. I couldn't help but notice how abruptly their attitude changed when they thought it might be their own head about to be taken. My path cleared in front of me as I ran past them and back to the restaurant.

In hindsight, I could have come up with a better plan than running and screaming through the streets with a bloody cleaver. I was rushing headlong into the worst of it. Soon, I would feel like a fool with a butterfly net, trying to catch a mammoth jumping off a cliff.

"Asitr?"

"Yes Bill?"

"We have station identification and national news. We'll be right back to our madman with a cleaver in just three minutes."

19

"OKAY. WE ARE BACK. I don't know about you guys listening at home, but I am getting a serious case of tingling neck hair. I didn't expect so dark a tale in your first life, Asitr. What type of artifact are you going to produce from this story?

"Artifact?"

"Evidence. You know, the promised proof of your tales?"

"From this story? No, but listen to the BBC Asian report tonight. They are going to air a segment mentioning your show. I believe what they talk about will be another proof of my truthfulness. You will be surprised."

"My show, mentioned on the BBC? Why? Never mind, I'll check it out. Everybody else keep your dial tuned right here."

"You needn't worry Bill. I think the Asian report will air just after your show ends."

"Okay, Astir. I'm sure I have the more exciting guest, so let's get back to your story. How does your mission with a bloody meat cleaver become a fool's errand with a butterfly net?"

"I get arrested for madness in public and murder. Madness and murder."

"Take a breath Asitr. Tell us the rest of your story."

*   *   *

STONED IN A LONELY HOLE

Madness is a word with too many meanings. I was consumed by madness when I ran to the restaurant. When I turned the corner racing to the butcher shop, I went weak and buckled. On the way back, when I turned the corner by the restaurant, I felt powerful. I saw Shinies milling around the building, but I thought I could run right through them. It was madness.

The feeling dissipated as soon as they tackled me. I didn't resist after they had me down. I regained my senses and tried to tell them about the danger to Sami.

Finally, when I gave up trying to explain myself the beating stopped. I could see the restaurant when they stood me up. It was a relief to see Sami, talking and smiling, shaking hands with their captain. Herakles was nowhere in sight. I learned later he had left almost as soon as I took off for the butcher shop.

The Shinies, who had been drawn to the sound of the breaking tea pots, were on hand to restore order, but they waited for Herakles to leave the area before asserting their authority. They demanded I explain the bloody cleaver. Before I caught my breath enough to explain, a witness came forward.

The witness was a priest from the temple of Azazel. He identified me as the young vandal who had done the damage at the restaurant. He pointed to the cleaver on the ground and expressed fear at the idea of seeing so vandalous a ruffian with such a dangerous and bloody instrument.

I was confident witnesses would discredit him. I thought Baddar would step forward. I knew Sami would tell them the real

130

story. I was about to learn confidence can be the weakest, most vulnerable feeling ever to take over a mind. My confidence vanished, and my madness returned like a hammer blow when I pointed to Sami and their Captain Asyut, touching goblets in the act of a toast.

If you were one of the Shinies, what would you think? They knew I had been running like a madman, weapon in hand, through the streets. They had a witness who identified me as the vandal in the restaurant.

They subdued and calmed me once, but once again, I erupted violently and suddenly. When my eyes locked in on the table between Sami and their captain, I began screaming, "Sami, Sami, Sami." How were they to know I was trying to warn him?

I could see him with his arm around their captain, both holding wine goblets, an open bottle of the stoutest wine sat on the table in front of them, containing enough poison to kill a demigod.

Blows to the head rendered me unconscious. Every time I revived, I began to scream again. Finally, I was tossed into the twenty-foot-deep pit the Baal temple used to hold the worst of criminals. The only way out of that pit, customarily, was after the brief interval between sentencing and execution.

I nearly died in the first ten minutes. I hit bottom, repeatedly barking the words, Barf! Arf! Barf! Arf! My pit mates kicked and threw stones to silence me. I didn't care how painfully I died. In my madness I judged myself too reckless to live.

Death would have come if not for the sudden thump of a new prisoner dropped into the hole. The new man in the hole bounced to his feet like he was made of rubber and stopped the attack with a swift move, grabbing two stone throwers and shaking them like small trees. When the rest of them backed away, I went silent.

Hooga Mushka, I thought. What kind of madness is this? I didn't perceive the events to be real, even when the rubber man approached and introduced himself to me. "I am Olphrenjii. Have peace and shut your reckless howler of a mouth. Be patient."

Olphrenjii put his hand on my forehead and I fell into the sanctuary of sleep. When I woke up I was sure it had been a dream.

Olphrenjii wasn't there, and nobody seemed to remember the event. I asked about him, but got back only empty eyes and requests to "shut up".

Shut up is what I did. For the next two years I didn't utter a word outside the complexity of guttural grunts. I was waiting to die, indifferent to the thought of it, and relaxed in my new state of madness. My physical condition grew even more unhealthy than my broken mind. Suddenly, it was my birthday.

That's what I was told by the men who pulled me out of the hole. My age at arrest was put down as sixteen years. Two years in the pit meant I was now eighteen and old enough to execute. I was going to have a trial in the courthouse of the Baal complex. Herakles, son of Baal Zebub, was listed as a witness for the court. The temple was asking that, in the name of justice, I be trampled by bulls, the properties once operated as a butcher shop and restaurant be seized, and an auction be held to disperse the properties.

I didn't need to see the son of a temple deity on the witness list to know I was going to be trampled. That's how it was in those days. There were super interests such as the men of renown. There were creatures, not really human, but much like today's corporations. They ruled as entities given standing in the courts above men. There was the system of justice that could be bought by wealthy men. There was the system of justice for the rest of us.

It didn't matter to me. I had given up all hope in achieving justice for Vandi and Mr. Bone. I accepted responsibility for the death of Sami, the only man I loved and trusted in a cruel world.

A trampled body would be a fit ending for the misery of my trampled mind.

The charges were read. I was accused of the poisoning of Captain Asyut and Sami the restaurateur. A second charge, the decapitation murder of the butcher, Vanpandikuladazen, was also read. For good measure, I was also charged with vandalism.

There was one other name on the witness list. A man named Enoch. Enoch signed the witness list on the day after I was arrested. When he signed the list, he was a very important man. He was the chief priest in the original temple of the Adam. He was the seventh chief priest in the bloodline to hold that position. This position gave him the security to tell the truth. No temple wanted yet another war between gods.

I believed there was nothing he could say, however, to free me from the inevitable. I regarded my witness as an odd piece, dropped into the wrong puzzle box, curious, but inevitably not part of the solution. This time, I had both fact and conclusion wrong.

Herakles didn't show up for court. Enoch asked the judge to release me into his custody. In return for the property rights, his request was granted. It just goes to show you how things can surprise you when you don't keep up with current events. In the two years I spent in the pit, changes had taken place in Samyaza. It all started when my witness, the great prophet Enoch, started taking walks with God. The big G God. The God of creation.

When word spread of Enoch's walks, the former inhabitants of heaven lost some swagger. Some of them, like Baal Zebub, got out of town. They left the operation of their temples to lesser gods. It became apparent over time that all of the temples were squabbling to gain favor with Enoch. He, in turn, mystified them by treating all of them with respect. It was easier on the little godly ego that he didn't flaunt his all-powerful protector. Enoch showed he recognized a picture bigger than himself when he saw it.

It was my impressions of this man that I tried to share with the Savant. I told them very little of my early problems in Samyaza. I was embarrassed by my foolishness, madness, and failures. I understand now, how those embarrassments, and all the other embarrassments in all of my lives have created wisdom in me. I hope to use my new wisdom for the purpose I am meant for.

I still don't know what that purpose is. I trust I will know when the moment comes and if I have to wield a cleaver for that end, I will do it with faith I am not acting out of madness. I know I haven't lived all my lives to simply entertain you with stories.

I have a list. Telling you about Enoch is on that list. Perhaps it is why I'm here. Are you at all familiar with his name, or the hysteria of so many people who try to define him?

I will tell you what I can about him. What I know comes from the years I gardened for him, how he was before he visited Heaven, how he was when he returned. Reach your own conclusions as to why he was special in God's eyes. I only want to tell you what I know.

I know he was a friend of a butcher with a funny name. It was this butcher who told him of a spotless bull with a healthy appearance. The best kind of bull for a worthy sacrifice to God in Heaven.

A pouch of carnelian and sapphire exchanged hands twice, and the bull was purchased. It was taken to the temple where Enoch accepted delivery. A pouch of gems was a very high price to pay for a bull. It was a fine animal.

The Baal temple thought they would gain possession of the animal. Herakles heard of the bull's attributes. He decided to go hunting and bring the cattleman a corpse of a lion to purchase the bull. He wanted the animal for the terrible ritual of the Apis.

Herakles arrived too late. The bull had been given to the butcher Vandipandikuladazen, for transfer to Enoch's temple,

In his anger at having missed acquiring the animal, Herakles demanded to be told the name of the butcher and the location of his shop. He decided he would visit both the man with a funny name and his employer. The reasoning behind making those visits show both the flaws of his design and the horrible consequences possible when the creation of life becomes a toy in the hands of inferior beings. Here is the four-point plan of Herakles as told to his father Baal Zebub:

First. Gain respect from the merchants.

Second. Have some fun.

Third. Drink the blood of a crafty man.

This was a mixed bag of emotions for his father. He knew better than to show his son that a four-point plan needs more than three steps. His son was gifted in craftiness and strength, but could never be taught logic or math.

Zebub was pleased his son was having fun at the expense of the race he hated, but overriding his initial approval of his son's acts was an angry taste of sourness. What soured him was the thought of having given life to a being that felt he needed something his father couldn't give him. He couldn't give him a spirit with the will to be creative. The fount of life, the blood wherein the soul resides, was all he could give him from union with humans. The spirit wasn't contagious from man to manufactured being. Baal Zebub learned it was a mistake to have created a being of mixed species. A being who inherited the basest of gifts from the stupid, smelly, spineless, greedy, gullible children of the earth, but was immune to its greatest gift.

Herakles resented being confused as to whether he had a spirit or a soul. He wasn't sure if he had either. He believed the act of blood-eating would elevate his stature. In his mind, the act was no different than taking the soul, or the spirit, he didn't know which. It didn't matter, it was fun. His proof was in the terror of witnesses.

Zebub's shame at his son's compulsion to honor men in this way deepened his hatred of our race. It also gave root to an idea that he would propose to all the other fallen who had fathered Anakim. He proposed the assignment of impossible labors. Labors designed to spread them over the face of the globe, dispersed into a world full of stupid, smelly, spineless, greedy, gullible children of the earth, and out of the city where Enoch resided.

I first heard of these events when I was pulled from my pit and taken to my new home in the inner circle of the city. It was a comfortable home with a couch, a garden, a cooking area, and a view of the temple of the Adam. In this place, I would heal, work, watch the comings and goings of fallen ones, and have conversations with Enoch.

*   *   *

STONY HOLES

My first conversation with Enoch took place after I had been nursed back to physical health. He took me to a sitting area near a vineyard that grew at the edge of the Adam temple wall. The location, next to the entrance, was a popular place for people to sit while waiting for an audience with a priest.

Grass no longer grew where the people walked. Common native bushes dominated the area. They were sickly looking and devoid of flowers. Enoch told me it had been a beautiful grove when the benches were first put in place. In those days, priests were often told by visitors how the sight caused many of the pilgrims to meditate on the thoughtfulness of a creator who chose to weave beauty into his design. It was my job, he told me, to return that area into such a place again.

To do the job I was given a sack of seed. It was the same sack of seed that Enoch had retrieved from Sami's restaurant.

By fall, I had made paths for walking and beds for planting. I made one bed for varieties that people knew and had learned to love. The next bed was for varieties that people loved but displaying colors they didn't expect. Another bed was for varieties that nobody from the local area had seen unless they had traveled to the region of the Bombag

All of these beds were viewed on the walk to the benches. I designed the sight lines from where people sat to display my favorite varieties. Towering stalks of Lion's Ear bent over the benches and dangled their odd flower clusters. Gardenias I had moved from my secret garden scented the area. Creeping carpets of a forgiving variety of thyme covered the ground, adding additional aroma to the walkway when stepped on. They thrived in their use as a cushion for bare feet.

The priests proclaimed the project to be successful. Enoch came alone to visit the garden and wept. It was on that day he first shared some of his secrets with me. Before he trusted me with those secrets he first asked about my life.

I told him about Puth, Auth, and the principles of the Bombag people. I told him the story my mother told me. The same story I would one day share with the Savant. Then the man who walked with God surprised me with his response. "I wish I could have met your mother."

"I wish I could have met your God," I responded, "Perhaps I could have learned to trust him."

"Your mother didn't tell you to trust the God of the Adam?"

I told him, "Yes, she did."

"Oh, I see." he said. "Yet you don't."

"I do. I'm not sure that just because your God has the same name, he is the same God." I hoped I wouldn't offend him after all his kindness, but we were discussing an issue that could only be settled by wielding the hammer of honesty.

"What is it that keeps you doubting, son?" He looked at me as if he had found an unusual bug in the bushes. His eyes narrowed, but they sparkled, looking younger than the rest of the man. I could see something in my answer had surprised him.

"I don't think the creator built your temple. I don't think he designed the city. I don't think that your son, Methuselah, teaches the pilgrims the truth about the creator's supreme reign in the universe. I don't believe the creator shares sovereignty with the beings that created the bastard Anakim. I'm not even sure that you walk with him. I still harbor suspicions that you use his name to achieve your own earthly ascendancy, sir."

Enoch cocked his head to one side and smiled at one corner of his mouth. It was an uncomfortable smile. He finally broke into a full grin and embraced me. He shook me and pounded my back.

"Yes, Yes," he said with exuberance. "You are one that will understand. I can talk to you if you will listen. Will you hear me tell how I discarded the little gods and embraced the creator?"

I feared he was making an attempt to convert me, but I gave him permission. I paid close attention to the craftiness in his wording. Auth had warned me, I must protect myself from the lies hidden inside the platitudes. It was his turn to surprise me.

"Come with me, he said. "I have something to show you. Do you want to see the evidence of the lies this temple was built on?" He didn't wait for an answer. He was excited. I had to trot to keep up with him. He called back to me without breaking stride, "You will appreciate this more than any man I know."

It was the first time I had been called a man. I rubbed my hand over my chin to see if I had sprouted hair. I felt the same old fuzz. The great Enoch called me a man and I wanted to think of his judgment as proof of my manhood. I had to catch myself. He had told me something I wanted to hear, and I understood he may be slyly breaking the ground for any seed he wanted to plant in my mind.

I followed him through the first gate and then through the second. I balked at entering through the third. He recognized my fears when I held back, but he calmed me with another surprise. "This area is for high priests and the temple gardener only. Congratulations on your new job."

Enoch went through the gate and straight to the door of the inner sanctum. "I don't need to warn you about entering this building, do I?" Enoch, not waiting for an answer, asked the question while disappearing through the doorway.

He didn't have to ask. All inner sanctums in Samyaza were restricted to everyone but the high priest and visitors from Heaven. The penalty for anyone foolish enough to ignore the rule was death.

I was afraid to even look into the interior of the sanctum. I turned my back to the doorway and familiarized myself with the layout of the inner temple circle. One structure dominated the area. A round ziggurat stood at the circle's center. A field of grass surrounded the tower.

"Take a look at the field around the tower," Enoch shouted from inside the sanctum. "It's a field of holes."

It didn't take long to find holes. The area was full of them. Holes as deep as a man's arm from finger to elbow, and as wide as my own fist. I know, because I got on my hands and knees to examine them.

The holes, all of equal size, were kept uniform with brass inserts. I put my eyeball to one and tried to see into it. Every time I tried, my shadow darkened the bottom. I scratched at the dirt around the hole. I found it went only inches deep before the dirt ended and stone began. These holes had been drilled into solid rock and sheathed in brass. Somebody wanted them to last a long time.

When Enoch exited his inner sanctum, he was burdened with an armload of items. He balanced an oil lamp, a short wooden stick with a carved auger at the end, some sticky clay in a jar, and a parchment resembling a calendar. It looked like a calendar, yet there were no dates. Squares with multiple symbols and numbers filled the rows and columns. Each square encased two symbols and three numbers.

As soon as Enoch set these items on the lawn, he dashed back into his sanctum, reappearing seconds later with three long poles. Each wooden pole was very long, equal in length, and surprisingly light in weight.

A single brass ring sat atop one end of each pole. The three rings were of descending sizes. The largest ring was as big as a man's head. The smallest ring was half that size. At the opposite end of the poles were brass casements. Each casement was as long as the holes were deep.

Enoch stepped from the shadow of the ziggurat and held up the calendar to catch the light. He gave me a test before we went farther. After I identified the most commonly known stars and constellations, he made sure I knew my numbers, letters, and symbols. I had Sami to thank for my passing grade. Enoch told me Sami had taught me everything I would need to know to become a god.

The comment scared me, but I soon understood what he meant. Under his instructions, we began applying his tools to the ferreting out of great cosmic liars.

Enoch asked me to select one square on the calendar. After I chose one, he pointed out the two symbols and three numbers in the square. Next, we applied the sticky clay to the auger end of the short wooden stick. With preparations complete, we searched for the holes with the same three numbers as the selected square.

We did this by inserting our auger with sticky clay into the holes closest to the base of the ziggurat. Raised copper numbers were affixed to the bottom of each hole. When the auger was withdrawn, we could see the number of the hole indented into the clay.

Starting at the base of the ziggurat, we probed hole after hole until we found the first number in the square I selected. We inserted the long pole with the largest ring easily into the copper sheath.

The other two holes were easier to find. Enoch told me they would be in a straight line, and each farther from the wall of the ziggurat. We placed the pole with the smallest ring into the hole farthest away, then turned the poles until each circle was facing the center of the tower.

Gathering the oil lamp and calendar, Enoch motioned for me to follow him to the top. When I caught up with him, I saw the view and gasped.

Twilight had come. From my high perch atop the tower on the highest hill in Samyaza, I witnessed the lighting of the lamps in all the sections of the city. As if someone was using a dimmer switch, the city slowly grew brighter in every circle at the same time. I walked around the top of the tower several times, marveling at the best view of the city I had witnessed since my time inside the walls. I was beginning to feel safe.

Enoch lit the lamp and called me to his side. He was holding the calendar. "Do you see the large symbol in the square we've chosen?"

I saw it, but the symbol was unfamiliar to me. Enoch told me it was the symbol for the shem. He asked me to find the same symbol depicted on the floor. I found it in a sea of other strange runes and symbols.

"Stand with your toes touching the symbol," he instructed. "Look straight ahead. "Do you see the circles atop the poles?"

I didn't.

"Try again, he said. "Keep your toes on the symbol and turn your body until you face the rings. Align your eyes until you see the smallest ring in the center of the two larger rings."

I was grateful he was sharing a process with me instead of just telling me his conclusions. I stood on my toes until I saw the three rings were properly aligned with my eyes. They fit together so well they formed a tunnel. If I moved my eye too much in any direction, I could only see a blur. With eyes perfectly aligned, I was focused on one steady point of view in a movable sky.

"What is this?" I inquired.

"This is an instrument of deception enabled by the measuring of the heavens. This is how you can predict when a priest will block the light of the moon or darken the sun."

Confused, I had to ask. "How does this predict the behavior of the enlightened?"

"You have to know their game," he said. "Are you ready to know the hour of the next eclipse of the sun?"

I had always been afraid of the loss of the sun or moon. I witnessed many angry priests threaten to throw the earth into darkness. I saw the creeping blackness begin to spread across the face of our heavenly torches. People always relented in time, and the curse was always reversed. Wisely, I believed, the people always donated more freely for the priestly compassion. I had to ask Enoch if I understood him correctly.

He didn't answer. He watched my eyes for the moment I grasped the importance of what he was showing me.

When I understood, I slapped myself in the forehead. Sami always said the priests would never deliver on their threat. He said they understood the darkness needed the light to survive. Sami's belief was the exact opposite of the teaching in the temples. They preached how light was in need of the darkness. I never understood the difference. Now, I guessed both theories were a parsing of irrelevant mushka.

I asked Enoch to make sure I understood. "Are you saying the fallen ones use a foreknowledge of predictable events to fake powers they don't have?"

"I am. Let me show you." He held out the *calendar*. "What symbol is this?" he asked, pointing to the last and smallest symbol in our selected square. It was the symbol for the star Antares.

There were no more symbols in our chosen square left to be identified. Enoch turned the calendar around to display its backside, then, he held it in front of the lantern. With the light showing through the thin leather, I saw them immediately. Vertical columns and horizontal rows of symbols, invisible in direct light, visible when the light passed through the parchment.

Enoch told me to find the first symbol in our square on the front and show him where it was depicted on the left vertical column on the back side of the calendar. Next, I found the second symbol in the horizontal row at the top. I followed the lines from each of them to where they intersected. They intersected at a depiction of a blackened sun.

"How is this going to tell us when the next eclipse occurs?" I thought it was an obvious question.

"It won't," he said. "You have to wait for Antares. You have to wait for her to sit in the center of your tunnel of circles. When Antares sits in her spot, then you can count down the time to the event."

How simple. How complicated. So impressive. You would have to start with a survey of the solar system. You would have to drill your holes at just the right locations on earth to compensate for its wobble. You would have to measure and predict the wobble. Enoch was correct. With this knowledge, I could pass myself off as a god.

What a feat of science and determination. Understanding the difficulty in carrying out the project illuminated an inescapable conclusion. This much thought and preparation for the sole purpose of deceit was scary. The brilliant and determined designer could never be trusted.

I was afraid to ask who the designer was. Instead, I asked about the method for counting down the time to the event. The clever man who had solved the puzzle of the holes had the answer.

"Inside the inner sanctum there are two water clocks," he said. "One of them has a lever decorated with stages of the moon. This lever is pulled when the triggering star centers itself inside the rings, and the back chart indicates an event with the moon.

The second water clock is used to measure the time for an event of the sun. On this clock is a lever decorated with an image of the sun. I have measured the length of time in them and can duplicate their function with sand. There are thirty-six hours between the trigger of the star within the rings and an event of the sun. Twenty-four hours between the trigger and an event of the moon."

I couldn't refrain from asking the question any longer. "Who designed this system and who built the field of holes?"

The answer was Marduk. Marduk was the ancient name. I knew him as Baal Zebub. Enoch told me all of his names.

"*Baal Zebub: One who flits or flies about.*"

"*Baal Bamoth: Lord of high places.*"

"*Baal Hazor: Lord of fortresses.*"

"*Baal Halastor: Lord of those who quickly fly.*"

My most enigmatic favorite: *"Lady Beer: She who makes wells."*

Enigmatic is the best word to choose when describing Marduk. His temple claims he is a god, opposed to light, yet propping light up in the name of peace between gods. He is the least often seen and the most often sought. He's sought by man because his temple offers ease of worship. His temple practices appeal to the portion of the soul that doesn't want to listen to the spirit.

He appeals to the fallen ones and rebel watchers for different reasons. They have a saying amongst themselves that illustrates his appeal. "With Marduk, you can't maintain peace. Without him, you can't win a war." The closest Marduk had ever come to making a permanent alliance with any of the others was in his promise of sanctuary at his fortress on Tiamat.

I told Enoch I thought the hour was late, and already, I had taken in more than I could digest. Announcing my weariness, I begged his leave by asking him to save more room in my head for thought the next time we talked. He promised he would, and the very next day he showed me he hadn't understood his own pledge, or perhaps, the capacity within my head.

The following day began with a sense of purpose. Somehow, I understood everything Enoch told me a little better after a night's sleep. I felt compelled to take a walk to the field of holes. I was hoping to find Enoch. What I found was surprises."

*   *   *

"Surprises must wait, Asitr. We have to cut away, so we can be told about products we can't live without. We'll be back in three minutes."

20

"THIS IS GETTING REDUNDANT," Otis said, while reaching for the marble. "Marble on, marble off, I wish this thing came with a Clapper."

Otis stretched forward, touching his toes several times, keeping his eyes on Dr. Milton while he rocked. "I'm getting back to normal, Doc. I don't think I'll have any more balance issues. My muscles don't show any sign of attrition. I'll be good to go by tomorrow."

Waiting for a response to his self-diagnosis, Otis readjusted his pillows and pulled his knees to his chin, wrapping his arms around his legs, stalling before changing the subject.

"How are you at astronomy, Doc?"

When the doctor waggled his fingers, Otis knew no answer was forthcoming. "Okay," he said. "I was hoping to skip the Tiamat lecture."

When Dr. Milton let the comment pass without response, Otis sighed and began. "You may doubt it, but at one time, Tiamat was a planet in our solar system. Now, only the tiny core and debris field remain.

"The ancients had maps indicating a planet between Mars and Jupiter. I suspect their information came from Enoch, but I'm guessing. The Greeks called the planet, Phaeton. Twenty years ago, the moderns called it unscientific twaddle. Okay, just the stuffy guys who didn't want their books out of print, but proofs were piling up.

"An astronomer named VanFlandren put forward a theory he calls "The Exploded Planet Theory". To prove his thesis, he submits a connection between mysterious dark debris areas on planets and moons in earth's solar system as evidence of its demise.

"In modeling the rate of spin on each moon and planet, he predicted the likely outcome of how wide an area, and in which areas, debris from a planetary explosion would impact if the explosion were to emanate from Tiamat's location. The modeling agrees with where you find each dark spot on every surface.

"Additionally, a formula called the Titus-Bode equation shows a predictable pattern in the spacing of our planets. If you use the equation, you find one anomaly. There is nothing in the space between Mars and Jupiter where the equation says a planet should exist. If you assume something was once there, and use the equation, you'll find Tiamat's inclusion erases the anomaly.

"Kae'Lairy didn't need to use the Titus-Bode equation, the maps of the ancients, or the modeling of the debris impacts. He didn't need the information from the spaceship *Voyager*, indicating the materials in the asteroid belt were once subjected to a single extreme heat event.

"Kae'Lairy once walked the planet. He visited the watchers who were stationed there. He blew the living daylights out of the damned thing when it became a threat to the loyal angels in the big war.

"Olphrenjii, the lone watcher from the planet to remain loyal in the big war, never got over the destruction. He believed the trigger was pulled too soon. His grieving was colored by his love of his sect's unique ability to perform their style of music. Without a throng of voices singing in the tones of his sect, mixed in the atmosphere of his planet, no duplication is possible. Even in his own mind, it could no longer be heard.

"After the war, when other sects celebrated victory with song, Olphrenjii traveled alone in the debris field, moping and wailing over the loss.

"When Kae'Lairy summoned Olphrenjii a second time, he chose Olphrenjii's own sanctuary for the meeting. In angel protocol, to enter the sanctum of another angel, without permission, is a serious offense. To make a summons to appear in one's own sanctum is a warning of probable confrontation. To demand Olphrenjii's obedience in the location of his anguish was close to intolerable disrespect.

"When Olphrenjii approached his sanctum, listening to Asitr's story of his early years in Samyaza, he paused to ponder before reporting. Nothing he could think of explained Kae'Lairy's attitude of disrespect and warning. When Bill interrupted for the news break, Olphrenjii gave Kae'Lairy those three minutes to explain himself.

"No explanation was forthcoming. Immediately on Olphrenjii's arrival, Kae'Lairy, without greeting, was abrupt with a stream of questions. 'Who is Hayak and what's going on in Chaco Canyon?' he asked. "How do they know secrets from the mind of Baal Zebub?'

"Remember, Doc, they're still under the requirements of a pact to cooperate in trading information. Olphrenjii replied with what he knew. 'I'm accepted into the team, not into the inner circle,' he explained. 'My function within the team is to arrange transportation for a group of men chosen to explore the cave where the golden calf of Puth's story is entombed. What is troubling you, brother? What information do you have for me?'

In his bed at Harbinger, Otis tensed, and then went limp, his legs returning to their prone position. From the corner of his eye, he noticed movement. His pigeon returned, strutting back and forth on the ledge. Otis snorted and smiled.

After a loud exhale, he began again, his voice low and solemn. "I know how Olphrenjii felt when Kae'Lairy responded to his questions. He got the old *need-to-know* dismissal. The *I-have-a-secret* and *I'm-not-going-to-tell-you* treatment.

"Kae'Lairy wasn't going to be helpful. He announced his withdrawal from their limited pact. 'I will accept judgment,' he said, 'but I'm releasing myself from our binds. I'm removing myself from my intent to support Asitr. I believe he's a reckless baboon, likely to misplay his hand.'

"Olphrenjii didn't object to the news. He showed no outer sign he was fazed by the announcement. 'I'm confident Asitr is part of a chain made by the Lord,' he responded. 'Who can be against His will?'

"Kae'Lairy was equally unfazed. Despite acknowledging he was in violation of the rules of his pact, he answered firmly, 'Do what you must, you have your responsibilities. I have one duty for you. Send an arc of video games from earth, to this location.'

"Olphrenjii posed to display he was now fazed. He showed Kae'Lairy the *what-the-...* pose. 'For what purpose?' he asked.

"Kae'Lairy met Olphrenjii's posture by displaying the *get-over-it* pose, and answered his question with a chilling response. 'I want to give earth one chance to avoid being the next debris field.'

"Olphrenjii froze, but finally calmed himself enough to offer advice. Purposely choosing the Greek word, Olphrenjii admonished his superior, '*Repent* your decision.'

"Kae'Lairy rejected the message by replying in the English, 'I don't need to *rethink*,' he said. 'What I need is video games.'

"Glowing in tones of anger, Olphrenjii raised his arm and let loose a beam, illuminating a large chunk of debris near Tiamat's core. 'There is where I will deliver your games. Flee from my abode and never enter again.'

"On the moon, Kae'Lairy made it clear to Jederic and Barabajyl; he wasn't going to be any less mysterious with them than he was with Olphrenjii twenty years ago. Whatever he was thinking, whatever secret he knew, Kae'Lairy wasn't going to share it.

"When Kae'Lairy reactivated the marble at the campfire, and Bill Elliott could be heard greeting his audience after the break, Jederic and Barabajyl were in poses of confused horror."

21

THE BILL ELLIOTT SHOW
On Air Tuesday

"AND JUST LIKE THAT, we're back. Asitr?"
"Yes, Bill?"
"You say you were surprised on the way to talk to Enoch."
"Yes."
"Continue your story."

*   *   *

HOLY STONE

The gateway to the inner circle of the complex was blocked by a strange mix of Shinies, a company of archers from the Azazel complex, an Anakim named Satan-El, priests from every temple and a worried-looking man I knew to be Methuselah.

Above the temple, a silvery shape that looked like the symbol for a shem was hovering. Now, I felt, I truly needed to see Enoch.

Believing I could find him within the center circle of the complex, I reviewed my options, took a deep breath, and walked forward.

I had a new understanding about the superiority of the masters these men served. It gave me courage to know they were inferior to those who served Heaven. Every step closer I had to remind myself, *I have the promise given by my mother and the access offered by Enoch. I have official business to attend to in a place I've been given permission to walk. When will be a better time to test the protection of Heaven?*

Growing closer to the strange crowd, courage diminishing with every step, and praying the cloak of invisibility could somehow be part of my protection, I continued to advance.

Obviously, a very important gathering was taking place, and I planned on crashing the gathering by announcing I had some grass to trim.

Methuselah ran to intercept me, placing his hand on my chest.

The nearby Satan-El seemed amused. "Let him go in," he said, laughing. "He should meet my father."

"I agree," said Methuselah, "Take him to your father and explain the interruption."

Satan-El withdrew to the gates and I addressed Methuselah with bluster. "I have grass to trim. Take me to your father and explain your own interference."

Methuselah took my tunic in his hand and shook me. Enoch's son seemed to read my mind, and he gave me good advice. "Having the protection of heaven doesn't mean you can call upon it like you would a trained dog. Consult your brain for some linkage between the facetious use of power and the wise faith of an informed soul. You will find there isn't any. Sheesh Kamushka!" He made a sweep of his hands toward the crowded gate. "Recognize the exceptional and make an exception. Today is not the day for getting underfoot."

I felt foolish but tried to maintain some pride. "I just don't think they can harm me," I explained. "They don't scare me anymore." It was a lie.

Methuselah added fuel to my fear. "They can make war on Heaven when they unite. Surely they wouldn't do it without

150

reason to believe they could win. Go home. I'll tell my father you came to see him."

Methuselah kept his promise, and Enoch came to my house after the meeting ended. It was early afternoon. He began his visit by announcing he wouldn't answer questions about his busy morning.

I had to honor his request. A long silence between us helped me clear my mind of the questions that still pressed me for attention.

Looking tired, Enoch took a seat on my patio wall and twirled a milky white stone between his fingers. At last, he broke the uncomfortable silence by asking me what I thought of his son.

"He's a large man with leadership qualities," I said. After more silence, I asked him a question leading to another day of packing too much into a small head.

"Does he serve the fallen ones?"

"He sees them as gods above us in the creator's tapestry. I think he shares a fault with his eighth grandfather, Adam. They are both deceived by the same lies.

"Have you shown him you've deciphered the method of the holes?" I asked.

"Yes, I have," Enoch said with sadness in his voice. "It wasn't a moment of inspiration for him. He feels he is fortunate to be a priest in a temple. He is convinced he is among the illuminated ones, serving the god of light."

Once again, Enoch anticipated my next question, "My son's uncompleted beliefs are sincerely held," he stated, "and waiting for an unknown moment to inspire the next steps he takes. Methuselah believes that his god walks the earth, and where he touches it, he brings warmth. It's a beautiful image in the heart of my beautiful son. The image has the ugly side-effect of continuing to diminish creation with the splintering of its true glory. He's a good son. He respects my own beliefs, he tries to listen for truth, but he doesn't have enough disrespect for the liars."

Enoch's answer was straightforward and right to the heart of what I wanted to know. He answered almost all my questions before I had to ask them. I had one question left. "Do you walk with God?"

"Yes," he said. "He leaves no footprints. He takes no form. I haven't seen his face."

"And how is this walking?" I didn't understand walking without form.

"This is me, walking with God in his full spirit. Powerfully louder than the portion of his spirit I was born with. This is not God slipping on sandals and putting on the body of a man. He is postponing that gift for us. Our walks are not visual, but they are lucid and clear. When I leave the city to walk alone, he is literally with me as surely as you are now. You can be sure the fallen ones know it."

"Why has he chosen you to walk with?" It was a rhetorical question, really. A puzzlement. Unanswerable.

Enoch answered by telling me a story from his youth. He called it his special moment of inspiration.

Enoch's story began when he was twelve years old and left his temple complex, without escort, for the first time. My story in Samyaza also began at the age of twelve. I, also, was leaving the comfort of familiar surroundings and venturing into the city alone.

Enoch was a chosen one. He knew, by tradition, he would be the next in line to become chief priest in the temple of the Adam. I was assured, from stories my mother told me, I was also a chosen one.

All similarities in our lives ended there. I was hiding in the alleys of Samyaza in my twelfth year of life, eating garbage and failing at selling seeds. Enoch was studying the artificers' crafts at the temple of Azazel. He went home to servants after a day of making jewelry from precious stones. At this point, it seemed, tradition was a better prognosticator of success than a mother's tale.

Enoch's classes were taught by Azazel himself. Although better known for his classes in weaponry, Azazel's true passion lay in crafting adornments for the body. In the beginning, Enoch was inspired by Azazel's passion. He wanted to become an artist.

As time went on, disenchantment with the teachings of the school set in. Enoch had a different opinion than Azazel on the definition of what constituted art. For Azazel, art was in volume, rarity, and flash. "You can never use too many jewels," he preached. "The harder to find the better. The more of your body reflecting light, the more prestigious the adornment."

Azazel's insistence on adhering to these standards was reflected in a phrase he often used to inspire his class. "If your creation is less than the beauty of Lucifer, you have created nothing." His students, having never seen Lucifer, felt they had no measurable standard to go by. None of them ever pleased their teacher.

It was the same message day in and day out. More and bigger, more and bigger. Every student in the class wondered if Azazel's school of adornment was teaching the love of artistry, the lust for more, or jealousy of Lucifer's beauty.

Enoch lost interest but held his tongue. His father advised him, before he went to the first class, "Learn what you can, but don't risk offending other temples."

Axel, a student from Azazel's own temple, finally asked Azazel a question Enoch wanted to ask, but was afraid might offend. "Could a single ring, of exquisite design, hold as much beauty as the angel Lucifer?"

Azazel didn't bother to answer. He turned his back to the class, placed a large ruby to his eye, and changed the subject.

"My favorite of crystals," he began. "Do you know the source of the beauty in this gem?" He didn't wait for an answer. "There are enrichments within this stone that reject all light in the red spectrum. They cast it out and back into your eye. All other spectrum passes through the crystal. This is why you see the stone as clear and red. You can't find such beauty in perfection.

"In heaven, they have a lens that can see through the enrichments. It gives the stone the look of a common diamond. Imagine. If you follow Heaven, you follow a master of the common. A master who considers enrichments to be pollutants."

Seemingly dumbstruck, Axel tried to make sense of Azazel's irrelevant answer. "Who made the crystals that offend Heaven?" He blurted the question without thought of offending his master.

Azazel, again, ignored him but continued speaking.

"There are lenses in my shem. When used at night, they can make the fire-born body of gods become invisible. They can make the bodies of warm-blooded animals glow an eerie green. There is another lens in my sanctum with the ability to see inside you. I use it to strip away the flesh and lay bare the skeleton. Just toys. Playthings." His voice dropped so low he seemed to be speaking only to himself.

Some students leaned in to hear him better.

Enoch recoiled in fear.

Azazel picked up an emerald, held it side by side with the ruby, then wheeled around, facing the class again.

The students, who had been leaning forward, jerked backward at the sudden move.

Azazel laughed at their reaction, and then resumed teaching in his normal voice.

"With perfect eyes, you can see everything in any mode you choose. You can see into, or through, anything. Simply control your mind and set your eyes to do it. You need only know the spectrum and frequency of light and choose the corresponding attributes of the viewed object."

"Don't ask me to teach you," he continued. "You could never be so high in the order of intelligent beings." Elevating his voice, Azazel boomed his final thought, filling the classroom with echo, "Do you think I'm lying? Axel. Am I telling the truth?"

As Enoch told me his story, I sensed he was approaching his moment of inspiration. I can say, without reservation, he was approaching a moment where he was struck with a lightning bolt of aspiration. He watched Axel's eyes blink in panic while the student's mouth ran through the stops and starts of trying to speak. No words beyond uh, uh, uh, passed his lips. Enoch knew his classmate was in trouble.

Before the stuttering stopped, Enoch pieced together the issues of a bigger picture. His mind ran through a gauntlet of answers to the questions this moment conjured. He flipped the switches in his electric mind and sorted the black and white, good and bad, yes's and no's of the dilemma Axel was facing. As quickly as the questions came to him, he arranged his answers into the code he would live by the rest of his life.

The way he explained the code sounded, to me, like a foolish quest. "Liars are everywhere and easy to spot. Challenging each lie, as they unfold, would be like stomping on a locust swarm to save crops. I will look for all the truth I can understand."

For now, Axel wasn't going to have Enoch to pull him out of his pit, but an interruption would give him a chance to breathe.

As Axel panicked like a mouse racing back and forth between two plugged holes, the sound of a visitor caused the playful cat Azazel to refocus his attention. A messenger from the Baal complex was standing in the doorway with a box of rocks. "From my master, Baal Alazam," he announced.

Without invitation to enter, the messenger walked to the front of the class and set the box on Enoch's worktable. "It's for your class," he said crisply, then turned to leave. He wasn't to the door yet when Azazel stopped him.

"Wait, what can I do with this?"

The rocks didn't look like anything special. They were a milky white, small and rounded like tumbled river rocks, pitted, like stone too soft to polish. Enoch picked one up and held it to his eye, wondering if some light might filter through sparingly, in the manner of milky quartz. He saw no evidence of light penetrating to any depth.

Azazel attempted the same test. His *perfect* eyes couldn't find the life of light in them either. Removing a leather buffer from Enoch's table, he strenuously rubbed a corner of the stone, dropped it back into the box, and pronounced it too soft to polish.

Enoch removed the same stone from the box, inspected the rubbed corner of the rock, and came to the same conclusion. When Azazel ordered the messenger to return the box, Enoch stepped aside. He glanced at Axel's face and could see the fear reduced to sporadic twitches around his mouth. Relief lasted as long as it took for the messenger to reach the door.

"Stop! I have a gift for your master. Something he can actually use." Azazel looked at Axel and gave him his playful cat smile. "I understand the temple whores are asking for new adornments. I am gifting your master a talented artist to make them. Axel? Would you enjoy working with the finest whores in Samyaza? What do you say to a change of scenery?"

Enoch saw the twitching fear on Axel's face wash away. His is eyes widened and sparkled, the quiver disappeared from his lips, but his once stuttering lips betrayed him again. He gushed a thoughtless response. "I would enjoy that very much, master. I would never be able to repay you."

"I'm certain you won't, no matter how much you might try." Azazel was beaming, almost laughing, from the fun he was having.

Enoch felt sick in anticipation.

Axel was still smiling when he heard there would be a price, if not the ability to repay.

Addressing the messenger, Azazel delivered some conditions on his gift of an artificer. "I must make sure my prized student will be safe in your master's temple. Inform Alazam he must remove his tongue to keep him safe from his penchant for stupid questions. He must remove his testicles to keep him safe from seduction. After his imperfections are removed, change his name. He will be called, Diamond. No other improvements will be necessary."

Enoch had confirmation of his decision to forgo challenging every lie he faced. He didn't know it in that moment, but he was holding in his hand the source of the inspiration for succeeding in his quest to find all the truth he could understand.

On my patio, while he told me his story, I watched him rub a corner of the stone in his hand with his thumb. I guessed this was the milky stone of his story. I had no guess as to how he found inspiration from something so plain.

"Do you know what is needed when searching for the whole truth?" Enoch was fond of priming the mind with an unanswerable question before he gave the answer. I shrugged my shoulders and waited. He gave me a list.

"You need to know you will never find it.

You need to understand the creator has made us to try, in spite of the futility.

You need an anchor to hold your place while sorting facts from conclusions.

When you wander too far in searching, you need a beacon to mark the spot where your anchor is set.

You need to find an inspirational moment to define your anchor and beacon.

"You need the proper lens to see."

Enoch tossed me his stone and continued. "You have my inspiration in your hand. You have the lens in your well, go fetch some water."

I brought a bucket of water to the patio, and Enoch told me to drop the stone into the bucket. I may have dropped a common river rock into the bucket but what I pulled out would make Lucifer jealous of the beauty. The lens of water revealed colors in the brightest hues and most reflective sheen I had never imagined. I burst out a description that probably summed it up sufficiently. "Holy stones of fire!"

Enoch didn't need to prompt me for more descriptive detail. I was spewing it as fast as I could think of it … ribbons of fire … blues that burn … impossible greens … more lustrous than gold … more reflective than quicksilver … reflective depth with palpable dimensions … I could have gone on, but the stone began to grow cloudy again. Another dip into the bucket once again exposed the secret identity.

"What is it?" I asked.

"An opal," he said. "The trigger of my moment of inspiration, my special moment of wonderment. Look what the Lord has hidden here! Why? What an unnecessary thing to create. Why would one so high want to take time out to surprise and delight me? I began to see the same pattern in all of his creation."

"Whoa!" I blurted. I knew my reaction had been intense, but I surely didn't look into the stone and see God. I dipped the stone again, hoping I could find my own anchor and beacon.

I realized any design was, by definition, purposeful. Intellectually, I understood a design like this was the product of a beautiful and loving mind. I recognized comforting differences between the design of the holes in stone and the holy stone of design, but … was it really a design? Could it be … natural? Does *natural* have to be a random accident?

Enoch interrupted my thoughts. "I came by to give you my stone. Call it a reminder, a reminder not to look for liars without also looking for the truth."

I meant to ask him why he didn't give it to his son. I didn't have the opportunity. He jumped to his feet and spoke his goodbyes as he was walking away. "I need to see my family," he said, "before I leave on a long journey."

He didn't tell me he was being taken to Heaven. He didn't tell me I would be without my teacher for decades to come.

That night, dreaming dreams of colorful hues not yet seen, I slept.

In the morning, I woke up wanting to believe there was a creator who could see into anything and see through everything. I felt disdainful of philosophical distractions that insinuate ugliness in the creator's intent. I decided those distractions should be chopped away like trees that block the sun. I was hopeful, but not without doubt.

I put the stone in my tunic and headed for the city gate. I had some plants I wanted to find in the hills.

On my way out of the city, I avoided the buildings Sami and I once called our business. I preferred my good memories of Sami, Vandi, and Mr. Bone to the ghastly images the locations inspired. The path I chose led me to the square of public auctions.

Anything could be found at the auctions. A large crowd gathered that day. I joined the crowd to see what the attraction was. The Baal temple was selling off some whores.

I couldn't avoid looking. I was at the age of stirring in my loins while contemplating the mysteries of the divine geometry. Here in front of me were the most geometrically divine of all the whores in Samyaza.

In lust for these women, fathers gave up their sucklings for one hour of pleasure. I once came close to sharing the fate of those unfortunate children, but the thought didn't enter my head at the moment.

On the very same day that Enoch horrified me with a story about the fate of his classmate, mutilated for work in the whore's harem of Baal Zebub, I lusted over the whores. I didn't give Axel a thought until later.

Repeat customers, who often cursed the portions of money, goods, or labors the temple required, but never objected to the price of one hour, packed the square. I didn't detest them. We bonded in enjoying the state of mind that goes along with the blood draining from the brain and down to the lower regions.

These women, always sold before their youth faded, still had their full allure. I gave strong consideration to buying myself a woman, but I had only one thing of value. It was the stone in my pocket. Enoch's opal. A treasure I couldn't trade for something fleeting. Blood returned to its usual places, and I felt shame for being tempted.

Only ten steps later, I overcame my shame and stopped for another look. If I hadn't, I would never have seen them. The white-haired Baal Alazam and a disheveled young girl he was dragging to the stage.

From the dress and the hair, I knew she was Bombag. Alazam was begging the auctioneer to halt for just as long as it took to sell a girl who was, "only good for beating and drowning". His sales points brought howls of laughter from the crowd. Sales were slow. He was warming up the crowd with a little lightness.

"What will you give me?" he asked the crowd. "What would you give for the opportunity of owning a girl whose idea of body paint is the blood of her troublesome tribe? Is she trainable? Yes, of course she is. They all are. Who will give me something worthless for this worthless girl?"

The woman he was humiliating was filthy with mud and blood. She looked like me on the day I was taken from the pit. Her eyes were rolled back into her head, and her legs were shaking. Alazam kept her standing by supporting her weight with a rope behind her back, wrapped around her elbows, and held tightly in his hand.

I felt the urge to charge the stage. It was the example of Enoch that restrained me. Surely, there was a way I could rescue this girl and neither of us would have to die for my effort.

I had only one thing in my pocket to offer for her. I took it out and held it above my head. "I offer one magic stone."

The crowd looked and laughed.

"Don't laugh!" Boomed the white-haired Alazam. The crowd hushed, and Alazam held onto the silence of the crowd, letting it linger, as if he were playing a musical instrument. When he held the silent note long enough, he finally laughed, and the crowd joined him.

"He's offering more than she's worth. Maybe we can talk the price down."

Alazam pointed in my direction and invited me onto the stage. "Come up here, young man, and tell me what you plan on doing with her. If it pleases me, she is yours, and you can keep your rock."

I vaulted onto the stage and offered him the stone.

Alazam held it up for the crowd to see and encouraged the crowd to join in the humiliation of the woman. "Do I want this rock?" he shouted.

"No!" they shouted back in unison. A carnival atmosphere was growing.

I was fighting off memories of the atmosphere around the butcher shop when Vandi was killed.

"Do I want the girl?" Azazel lifted her rope until her toes just dragged the ground.

"No!" the crowd responded.

Alazam almost let me walk away easy. "I believe we..."

I thought I was going to hear the words, greasily spoken, my mother heard from Baal Alayat on the day the Bombag fought the Shinies. I believed he was going to say, "I believe we have a winner."

He didn't say it. Stopping in mid-sentence, he sniffed the air.

Alazam's eyes narrowed, and he stepped toward me as he let go of the girl. She fell like a sheep, struck in the head for slaughter.

I reached for her, to claim her, but he grabbed my arm.

"Do I know you?" He whispered the question as he put his face to mine. Our noses touched. His tone was menacing, and his grip was painful.

"I only know you from stories," I replied, honestly. I hoped my voice sounded sure and steady.

He held my arm tight and studied my eyes for what felt to be a long time.

The sounds from the crowd were changing. A murmur started to ripple through.

Alazam noticed and he let go of my arm.

"Tell us what your plans are for this female animal." He was talking to me but addressing the crowd again. "If we approve, then she is yours to take home."

Getting into the spirit of the negotiations, someone in the crowd shouted, "Pass her around, then stone her for infidelity."

I was sure, now, what path I needed to travel for gaining crowd approval. With a deep exaggerated bow to Alazam, I reached for my stone, pleadingly. When he gave it to me, I held it above my head. "I have given the stone a name." I said. "I call it the rock of humiliation. With the powers of magic within this stone, I can remind the wench all her living days of her value in the world. Plain to look at. Stone stupid."

I got a few chuckles. Alazam also seemed amused, so I pressed forward. "I will make her wear it around her neck as a challenge to rise to its level. If she can't match within herself the beauty in this rock, I will toss both rock and woman into the quarry."

Some in the crowd seemed to think I had been clever and shouted for Alazam to give me the girl. My pitch wasn't good enough for Alazam, however.

"Clever, but too good for her, he said. "I don't want anyone to say they have been cheated in a deal with the temple of Baal. Come on now! Someone make me an offer that will match the worthlessness of … that."

He pointed to her body, limp on the stage. I couldn't tell if she still breathed.

"Old fish!" I heard someone shout. It was Sami's old friend Baddar. "I have a wagon of fish that no one will buy. I was hoping to sell it to a gardener for plant food. It's been drawing some attention on the way, if you know what I mean," he said, waving the air under his nose. I would like to deliver her atop my smelly load. I get paid by the pound. you know."

The crowd approved. One brave soul shouted out, "For the sake of Baal Zebub, give him the girl and sell us some whores!"

Alazam knew his moment on stage was over. He declared the fisherman the winner and returned the crowd to the auctioneer.

Baddar pushed an empty cart to the stage and, with a wink, commandeered my services. We loaded her on his cart, and she remained unconscious for the entire bumpy ride to my house.

Baddar stayed the night and helped me nurse her. When she started to breathe comfortably, we relaxed and drank to Sami,

Vandi, and Mr. Bone. We cursed the bastard Anakim. We celebrated our successful deception over a pipe of the laughing weed, drank some more, and by morning we were friends.

Before the sun rose, Methuselah came to my house with the same woman who had nursed me to health. He also brought shocking news.

Enoch had been "taken up" in the night to intercede before God, in the name of mercy, for all the rebel watchers and fallen angels. Methuselah told us they sensed an approaching judgment against them.

I was offended the devils thought they could replace sincere repentance of their acts with the intercession of a good lawyer.

Baddar felt the same. "Aznevet gawnawuck?" he managed. Our night of drinking had taken his tongue. "Washa mushkabush pucky!"

Methuselah wisely suggested we both get some sleep, and he put his nurse in charge of the girl.

My new life without Enoch commenced with youthful excess, but it wasn't really going to be my life. My life started when my days were enhanced by love for the Bombag girl.

She told me her name was Gaut. I remembered her name from my mother's story. I had questions to ask her. She requested I hold them until after she could speak without tears.

Gaut was tough and responded well to care. As soon as she was healthy enough, she began to find work around the house. Soon she showed a talent for all things creative. I admired her.

She became my friend and helpmate. Truly, she was like the stone. The deeper I saw into her, the more beautiful she became. After a long wait, she finally shared her knowledge of the Bombag.

The Bombag were a tribe no more. She believed she was the only one to live after a war that pressed the Shinies to reinforce their efforts with mercenaries from the Banda tribe. Finally, inevitably, they wore them down and destroyed them. "We had a good leader," she said. "We just didn't have enough people."

I didn't want to hear the details, but I did ask about Puth and Auth.

She had no news of them, but she shared a memory of the night the tribe was visited by a messenger of the Lord. "I held a baby that night, at the campfire. I know it was you. I know you are the mystery man I was promised."

I accepted her statement as a proposal of marriage.

At home, she scolded me for being lazy. In public, she showed respect. She was a very good wife.

As each year ran up to greet us, we left it behind us. We had three children by the time the rings showed us the hour of Antares's eclipse. At the ages of three, four, and five, the children remained as unimpressed with my ability to predict an eclipse occurrence as they did with my impersonations of the monster Herakles.

It seemed to me, as time went on, the stories about him softened his horror. Every telling of a story ripples out from the center of the event, adds wrinkles, and spins away from its truth. I, myself, began to use the name of Herakles to provoke giggles from my own children.

I was free-falling in a sappy descent into softness, far too happy for a man my age. My reputation in landscaping allowed me to hire young men to do most of the labor. In time, I walked away from all of the work offers outside the temple.

I set up my sons, Sami and Auth, in a new landscape business in the third circle, and they rewarded me with a sound sense of fair business and the skill to make it successful. Their industrious passion exaggerated my own lapse into a permanent state of laziness. It seemed the more laughing weed I smoked, the lazier I became.

Gaut eventually gave up chiding me for my sloth, but never stopped showing me love. When we bathed together, she wore Enoch's stone. The short life we shared was happy.

Baddar died from drinking when the children were aged twenty-three, twenty-four, and twenty-five. He had been a good uncle figure, teaching them the recreational method of fishing. Baddar loved his time on the river until the day he died.

I helped carry his body to the river. My memories of younger days were rekindled as the funeral procession wove its way through the streets we used to walk. Too many were the horrible memories, burning as hot as the pyre where Baddar returned to ash.

With the opal in my hand, I prayed to the Lord for the lens of death to help Baddar see the way to Heaven. I sincerely felt he heard me, but a part of me wondered if he cared about men who lived life without renown. I hadn't yet had my moment.

Later, with my daughter at the age of marriage, I had nobody in mind within her station who would be good enough to claim her. It didn't occur to me to look for him just a few homes away.

Methuselah proposed it. He told me his son was smitten with a girl beneath his station. It was my daughter Puthal. Puthal let me know that she was also smitten with his son, Lamech.

We had the feast of our lives, enhanced, because Methuselah rejected offers of attendance he received from the other temples. It was a bold move, made in tribute to his father. We had a fine, intimate wedding at the temple.

I reveled in my happy, unremarkable life until the day remarkable returned to the mix. Enoch was back from his journey. Methuselah brought me the news.

A gathering was scheduled for the temple leaders at the field of holes. Once again, I was uninvited.

Once again, Enoch came to visit me when the meeting ended. Once again, he asked me to refrain from asking the details of the meeting.

I thought I knew the basic outcome. The wailing of angels, even the wailing of the fallen, is a terrible thing to listen to. It could be heard throughout all sections of the city. The indescribable sound causes the organs of the body to cramp, the eyes to shut tight, and the ears to feel pierced with needles. I sensed the wailing affirmed their judgment was appropriately more painful for them, than was the pain to those who heard them wail.

By contrast, in the home of Methuselah that night, there was the sound of joy and dancing. Musicians tried hard to live up to the description Enoch had given us about the purity of sound distilled into melodious emotion in Heaven. I, myself, felt the band was successful in their attempted emulation. I was transported on their sound back to my memory of the city view from the ziggurat on the night the lamps were being lit. I was having a good time. Two announcements were going to make it even better.

Lamech and Puthal announced the coming of a baby. They blessed the Lord for having Enoch with them for the announcement. I danced without shame of my clumsiness, overcome with joy.

Enoch elated me further with a second announcement. He told us he already knew he would celebrate a baby born to his grandson and my daughter. The Lord said his name would be Noah and the name would be known until the end of earth. God's word and blessing guaranteed it would be so.

Like Sami always said, "All is well and getting weller."

I called for the band to play my favorite song. Gaut sang with them. I was feeling rapturous.

In keeping with my record for good facts and bad conclusions, I felt I had just made a breakthrough. I felt I was having my moment. It was an aneurysm of the brain made painless by my immersion in feelings of pure joy.

The sudden sensation of movement overcame me. I was whooshing off to have my first talk with the Savant. I told my new tribe, the biggest regret in my first life was spoiling the party by falling over dead.

*   *   *

"Oh boy, Asitr. You cut it close. What a life you had. There is certainly no time left for your third story."

"I'm sorry Bill, perhaps tomorrow we can begin with that story."

"We're expecting some artifacts from Dave in the Amazon tomorrow. I'm excited to get on with the evidence portion of your tales. I also want to get around to interviewing you about some personal things."

"Personal things?"

"Yes. Philosophies, religious beliefs, the items still on your list. I have a list of my own. My audience and I have questions piling up."

"A lot can happen between now and then, Bill. I wouldn't make a list of questions for me just yet. I think I need to tell my third story."

"I'll find time for your story if you allow me a good interview."

"A promise from a host to his guest?"

"Asitr, we do share a love of the old ways don't we?"

"Not to over-hype the good old ways, but there is comfort in protection."

"Before we go, I want to ask, did you notice something missing tonight?"

"Yes, You didn't give us your traditional post-news rant."

"Bigger things have come to an end, eh?"

"Amen. Something is always biting the dust."

"On that note, it's time to say goodnight. Let's hope for a good night's rest."

"Fat chance, Bill"

"We'll see. It's midnight. Everyone, don't forget to look up your local BBC station before you turn in. If Asitr is correct, we're going to get a mention. I'll be listening. This is Bill Elliott saying goodnight until tomorrow."

22

HARBINGER INSTITUTE
April 1, 2025

O TIS PULLED THE MARBLE from the table and placed it in the crook of his left arm, rolling each of the fingers on his right hand across the surface like he was fingerprinting himself. "No fingerprints stick to this thing, Doc. Weird, huh." Next, he held it up to his face and scanned the room, stopping when he came to Dr. Milton. "Do you know what I see?"

Dr. Milton's finger waggled.

"I see you sitting in your chair, head on top, feet on bottom. The images are supposed to be up-side down and they're not. How do you explain that? If you look through a round, transparent ball, the image is supposed to be inverted."

Otis waited for a sign the doctor was interested in his observation but didn't even get a waggle, so he set the marble back on the cart and closed his eyes, waiting for almost a minute before speaking again.

"I think this. The dynamics that transform events into a story aren't linear progressions like a Rube Goldberg device," he said after his quiet moment of reflection. "It isn't one event followed by another and another until the motion stops, any more than a song becomes music by playing a series of notes, or time can be understood by glancing at your watch.

"As time glided across the distance between the Tuesday show and Wednesday night's broadcast, that big mess of events was ... well, I don't have a word for it, but everything that happened wasn't a case of walking in traffic to see what hits us. Long before the events of Wednesday were initiated, teams were built, plans were made, and traps were set. Those twenty four hours were the product of forty years' work. Focus, coincidence, knowledge of the past, and skills for the future came together in ways unpredictable. To understand how those twenty four hours came about, you should know more about the team, especially David Blank.

*   *   *

DAVE

On the moon, Kae'Lairy told his listeners he thought Dave was an orangutan. "A glorious orangutan," he called him, "gracing a pack of chimpanzees led by a baboon."

No slander was insinuated in Kae'Lairy's description of Asitr's team. Jederic and Barabajyl understood the wording and the respectful pose used to deliver the words.

I've heard humans use a similar simian comparison for highlighting differences in the problem-solving skills of men. In both cultures, Orangutans are the most respected of the problem solvers, and chimpanzees, for their willingness to try anything, are the most entertaining.

In the human version, a gorilla is a punchline. If unable to resolve a problem immediately, the gorilla makes fearful noises, uproots bushes, shows his teeth, and beats his fists into the dirt, railing at the world for his own limitations. Using this method, the gorilla almost never finds a resolution to his problem.

There is no gorilla in Kae'Lairy's version of Asitr's team. Kae'Lairy would have preferred some useless noise and bluster to what Asitr represented. The choice of a baboon to describe Asitr was a reference to the old kingdom hieroglyphs of the Egyptians.

Baboons, imported from lands south of Nubia, began their life in Egypt, defanged and clawless, as pets for the wealthy. They were common sights in the temples of Horus, because of their odd habit of gathering together at sunrise and chattering toward the rising sun.

Their image as pampered pet and worshipful servant of Horus had a short run. The lasting image of the baboon was in the hieroglyph. The image of a baboon was the symbol for anger. If his tail was raised, it was the symbol for enraged fury. If the baboon held a knife, he became the symbol for extreme danger.

Given what he had seen on Asitr's computer, Kae'Lairy knew Asitr was still in possession of his teeth and claws. Indeed, he had weapons much more worrisome than a knife.

The angels on the moon understood conceptualizing Asitr's team as monkeys, but Kae'Lairy didn't want them to dwell on the baboon. He wanted to make a point about Dave in particular.

"While problem solving," he began, "an orangutan maintains a peaceful, even vacant, outer appearance. On the inside, great thoughts are bubbling through his gray matter at erratic intervals, like swamp gas in a lily pond, or slowly, like lava in a lava lamp. Eventually, something gels, and the orangutan will stand up and unceremoniously solve the problem."

Jederic and Barabajyl could sense a eulogy of respect in Kae'Lairy's voice, and in his pose, an attitude of sadness. Kae'Lairy's respect for both Dave and the orangutan was obvious.

"If success after hard thinking is any measure of an orangutan," Kae'Lairy continued, "Among those '*old men of the forest*', Dave can walk proud."

I can testify that Kae'Lairy was correct. Dave sat for three months in the Amazon, while his bubbling brain and vacant appearance hid a determination to find answers to the question first asked while staring at fruit and dead birds by a campfire.

Curiosity ratcheted into an obsession after losing friends to poison ivy. By the time he flew home from Eden, it became a quest.

He vowed to one day figure out the answer to his persistent question, "What the hell is going on?" He decided the surest way to achieve his goal would be to begin with a different question. "Who sent us here?"

Dave began his search in earnest when, three months after landing in a lost world, the very same helicopter pilot who dropped them off, returned to pick them up.

Captain Avery Arrington was a very friendly fellow. When he flew Dave from the Amazon to Panama, he answered every question Dave threw his way.

For a man with Dave's intellect, even the "I don't know" answers were helpful. Answers to questions about the advanced electronics were even more helpful.

By any measure, an offhand comment at the end of their flight provided the most important words from Arrington's lips. "You should look into that Telstar thing, son. It's a lot more than just trading live pictures of Lady Liberty for live shots of the Eiffel Tower. A lot of this new stuff is coming from that project."

Dave, needing to understand as much as he could about the Telstar project, worked nights so he could catch lectures during the day. He sat in on classes at every university in New York City. Books on math theory, electronics, political science, business administration, tax law, the binary theories of Sister Mary Keller, and the works of Nicholas Tesla littered his home.

In 1974, Dave felt he was making progress. The irregular swamp gas inspirations and the slow, slow process of lava lamp ideas started to take form with his growing understanding of Telstar. If only he could get access to an IBM 360, he could gain access to Telstar data storage.

Dave called in sick and percolated. For three straight nights, he sat and stared vacantly. When the sun hit his window after the third night, Dave stood up and walked to NYU. He turned in a bid for the job of maintaining the punch card operation on the school's 360.

Dave's winning bid was ridiculously low. The job was ridiculously easy. He replaced balloons.

When a punch card is read by the big binary brain of the 360, a balloon rapidly expands at just the right moment to trap the card against a lighted window. The light, shining through the pattern of punches, triggers sensors. Those sensors, activated by the light, send information to a storage area inside the brain.

The weakest link in the lightning-fast process was the balloon. Somebody had to regularly replace the tired balloons. If a balloon popped, the big brain wouldn't know what to think.

Dave kept the balloons fresh, and he managed to keep the big brain refreshed with new punch cards, storage discs, wireless applications, and memory retrieval software, all of Dave's own coding. Dave was gathering and storing a lot of information he didn't know how to use. He had a need for a good chimpanzee to conduct trial and error testing.

A chimpanzee arrived one day while Dave was replacing balloons. It was early in the morning, the night-janitor had already clocked out, and a sudden greeting startled him.

"Hey, guy. Does this big puppy have Asteroids?"

Dave turned, and I remember he suppressed a grin when he saw me, a young disco nerd wearing white bowling shoes, white belt, red bell bottom pants, and a silky wide-collared shirt with a faded depiction of pineapples and palm trees. Clashing with my snazzy ensemble was a neon pocket protector, Lone Ranger lunch box, and a mouth full of braces.

"Asteroids?" he asked. "Nope. I keep her lubed up with preparation A."

"Obtuse humor. Rare. I'm Otis Beckley."

"Not so rare, just dull and barely recognizable. I'm Dave Blank."

With introductions out of the way, we started our friendship.

I noticed Dave watching me as I walked around the room, taking in the magnificent giant-sized computer. The intensity of his gaze made me uncomfortable, so I returned to light banter before I told him the bad news. "Oh, I see, hard to notice because it's obtuse. Hmm ... Gotta be a word for that. Anyway ... I'm here to replace you."

"Yes, the word is obtuse ... what?"

171

"Bad choice of words, sorry," I apologized. "IBM has all the rights for maintaining the computer. I'm their guy. You can keep doing what you're doing, with a raise, even. I'm going to cut your floating point section off into an independently functioning unit, jazz up the binary-coded devices, jam some hard drive, shrink your eight-inch floppy to five and a quarter, lay a heavy dose of new multiplexor, and hide it all with the interruption mask so you can get down with some big endian byte ordering and I can riff some heavy shit with my slut mods. Clear?"

Dave, with a blank look hiding a sudden eruption of swamp gas bubbles, made the decision to see what I could teach him. "What's this about asteroids?" Dave asked the perfect question.

The arcade game boom was still five years away, but the games of the future were already here. They were being passed around on discs, along with information-sharing on the breakthroughs in storage capacity, miniaturization, power supply, and integrated circuitry technologies.

To the army of pimply chimpanzees, those isolated breakthroughs were engineering problems waiting to be solved. Somebody needed to put all the parts together and make something usable. Networking through the magic of floppy discs, working information was shared along a grapevine of whiz kids. Along with the information, came games, games, games. They were the bananas in the care packages of knowledge that kept the army of chimps on task.

My personal focus was on creating a universal language all binary electronic devices could understand. I was attracted to the 360 at NYU because it was equipped with a rare "backward compatibility" feature. The compatibility feature allowed the computer to operate with any one of the eight most commonly used operating systems. You simply had to shut the whole thing down, replace the system being used with one other system in the menu, then isolate tasks, preventing spillover that could cause the computer to freeze between the yes and no answers. Nothing good ever came of a binary computer getting trapped in the land of "*I don't know.*"

I believed those eight programs could be taught the same language, advancing the quest for a universal link between all binary devices. It was some darned hard thinking for a chimpanzee. When I needed to refresh my mind, I played *Asteroids.*

Within the year, Dave and I became fast friends, rivals in the world of electronic gaming, and the accidental discoverers of the world's first Internet.

The net we found was conceived from the teachings of Baal Zebub. It was constructed by Baal Alayat, and piggy-backed onto the Arpanet and Telstar programs. It would be almost thirty more years before we knew we had found it.

As Kae'Lairy told the two angels on the moon, "A three-legged beast got its first two legs on the day those two met. Most unforeseeable was the third leg. Asitr had the key to unlock, back-engineer, and hijack the mother of internets.

It was true, Doc. Without Dave's preparation, my ability to talk to machines, and Asitr's knowledge of the first language, the three of us would still be like those three famous monkeys, *See no secrets. Hear no answers. Speak dead languages.*

23

HARBINGER INSTITUTE
April 1, 2025

O TIS PULLED HIMSELF UP and rearranged his pillows so he could sit higher in his bed. When he was comfortable, he reached past the marble and poured a glass of water from the fresh pitcher on the cart. Between sips, he opened his mouth, as if he was about to speak, but words didn't form.

After draining the glass, he found his voice. "Nothing better than water when you're thirsty," he said. "Where was I?"

Before answering his own question, Otis put his empty glass back onto the cart and lifted the marble, placing it in the crook of his left elbow. "I was at Dave's when the reunion happened," he said abruptly.

In an incredulous voice, Otis admitted he didn't have a good analogy for his reaction to meeting Lock and Asitr. "It was like seeing *Gumby* shopping at Wal-Mart," he said. "Can you believe it? Nearly forty years gone since Eden, Lock knocks on Dave's door in New York with the greeting, *Hi, Dave. It's been awhile, remember us?*"

Otis reached toward the orb with his right hand and paused, his index finger hovering over its surface. "I figured to make a little polite conversation then leave them alone to reminisce. I told them a story about a computer glitch, a man with a dog, and an *Asteroids* tournament at NYU.

Because of that story, we became a team with access to travel, weapons, and secrets. In short, we had everything we needed to make Tuesday night's show the cheese for luring monsters to judgment. Listen to the first nibble. This is from Kae'Lairy's ears in Bill's studio." Otis's hovering finger touched the marble and Po's voice whispered.

✳   ✳   ✳

"Bill? Telephone. It's your friend Stanley. Sorry, he insists you take it."

"Yeah, thanks babe, put it on the headphones and close the door behind you ... Mister ... Alazam, is it? Why are you calling me here?"

"Yeah, Listen. I found the fools. They said they heard about Gentile on a morning radio show in Florida. Only one radio program mentioned Albie in the morning. Tell them I'll have them by sunrise. Earlier, if they try to skitter away"

"They've been to Chaco canyon."

"Chaco? Freak of nature is over his head. He's monkeying with the wrong crowd."

"They found gold."

"How?"

"Remember when you used some Anasazi slaves to bury the small chunks?"

"Sure, get to it."

"Do you remember a slave at Chaco you said smelled funny? You told him he reminded you of old Samyaza. That was Asitr."

"No. I cooked that whiner and ate him myself."

"And now he's back. I think tomorrow he's going to tell that story on-air."

"Skarrar. I've got to fix this, right now. Guess who else is back."

"Who?"

"I'm going to take the shem and check out Chaco. Tell Asitr I remember him. He started to scream before I even lit the fire."

"Who's back?"

"Watch you don't get brave. I have work to do."

"Who's back?"

Asitr was right, Doc. A good night's rest? Fat chance. Even Bill's secretary is in for a bad time. Listen to this. Once again, this is from Bill's studio, after Asitr told him he was going to be mentioned on the BBC.

"Bill, do you want me to pipe the BBC into the studio after you sign off?"

"No, Po. I want you to leave right now. I'm firing you for your own protection."

"What? Why?"

"I'll send your things. You have to go right now. Go home. Get out and lock the gate behind you."

"What is going on?"

"You're fired. Get out and don't forget to lock the gates."

"Last week you ask me to marry you, and now I'm fired?"

Otis touched the marble again and began talking as soon as the marble silenced.

"Po stomped the two blocks from Bill's one-block compound to the front door of her second-floor apartment. Fumbling for her keys, she began crying when she realized she forgot to lock the gate on the way out.

"Running back to carry out Bill's request, she noticed a half-dozen men standing under an advertising sign across the street from the gate. They broke up their conference when she approached, but they raised her level of alertness. She glanced around the street and noticed several more men walking the sidewalks around Bill's block. To her, it seemed like a lot of traffic for that time of night. This neighborhood was usually very quiet. An eerie similarity in the way they were dressed caught her attention. Her nerves, once again, caused her to fumble with her keys.

"After locking the gate, Po made it back to her house in time to hear the BBC Asian report. Her tea kettle began to whistle. The kettle, together with her own loud sobbing, forced her to turn the volume up on the radio. As interested as she was to hear a mention of her former radio station on a BBC program, her mind kept drifting away from listening to the radio. She wanted to know what was wrong with Bill. Who are those men on the street?

"She walked to her window and peeked toward Bill's block. Nothing caught her attention Aside from the blue flashing laundry sign in the window across from Bill's gate. After a moment of hypnotic staring, she spun from the window and turned off the radio. 'Damn you, Bill Elliott.' She spit his name out angrily, and marched to the kitchen where her whistling tea kettle was growing insistent on attention.

"In a shadow, halfway between Bill's gate and Po's door, a man named Hayak stared at her window until she let go of her drapes and marched off to tend to her noisy home.

Hayak, an Armenian smuggler, was a friend and business partner during Asitr's wealth building years in the antiquities market. The men on the street were his crew. After Po turned away from the window, he returned to where his men were strolling the neighborhood around Bill's block. He had a heavy responsibility for ensuring that Bill's compound would be a no-fly zone for the little wing sects of angels, but a nagging question kept popping up in his mind. Was Po an innocent?

*   *   *

GOOGS

"Sorry, Doc, I'm almost finished burying you in digressions. I'll get to a timeline of events soon, but there is one more piece of the Asitr team I want you to know. He's the newest member and the reporter who mentions the Bill Elliott show on the BBC.

"Guglielmo Singh's friends called him Googs. His reputation for relishing a good adventure, and his circle of friends, led Asitr to choose him to be the man to report a news tip. A Montagnard group in Viet Nam, he told him, was attempting to buy back their old homeland with the largest gold nugget in the world.

"As a reporter for the BBC, Guglielmo was interested. His favorite type of assignment was reporting on wild rumors with very little chance of reaching fruition as fact.

"For this assignment, Guglielmo traveled to Hanoi, hoping he was about to assay the record-breaking nugget. Realistically, he expected the more common result, a large gold matrix. A matrix of this size was rare, but a solid nugget of this size could be priceless. In his excitement, on his way out the door for the meeting with the Montagnard elders, he almost let the phone go unanswered.

"I'm too curious," Guglielmo said out loud as he walked back into his room to answer the phone. 'This better not be more paperwork,' he bellowed at the persistent ringing.

It wasn't more paperwork. It was his friend, Jack VanGrada, calling *en route* from a time capsule opening in New York, to a hotel in Phoenix, Arizona.

After the debacle at the Explorers Club, Dave recruited VanGrada into Asitr's team. With information Jack learned from Dave, he filled Googs in on some background of the nugget. In the process, Googs agreed to help document two other upcoming projects.

In spite of a new schedule that didn't allow time for sleep, the information Jack gave Googs on the telephone made Guglielmo feel like a kid at Christmas.

At the elevator, on his way to the interview, Singh looked up and down the hallway. Nobody was around, so he cut loose in a four-second version of his happy dance. His theatrical, silly, waving of feet and wild finger pointing came with lyrics. "Two. Two. Two myths in one. Chicka bobba, chicka bobba, chicka bobba loony pants, chicka bobba loony pants, chicka chicka pow!"

Calming himself when he heard the elevator door ding, a suddenly dignified looking Mr. Singh smiled at the gentleman in the elevator. On the way to the lobby, the two of them chatted about monsoon season mosquitoes until the doors opened. "You have a nice day now, young man," said the old chap.

"Sir, I assure you, my recent bouts of crushing boredom are about to end," Googs called over his shoulder as he hustled to meet his limo. "Legends, and treasures, and watchers, oh my. Chicka pow!"

*   *   *

THE BBC REPORT

"... Yes, Roger. That is indeed an interesting change of heart. I'm sure you will have more information after the close of the summit. Now off to Viet Nam and my favorite geologist here at the BBC, Guglielmo Singh. Mr. Singh, I understand you're in Viet Nam to inspect a mysterious gold nugget?"

"I am, Margot. Good to talk to you again."

"Now, tell us something about this. It's big, I understand."

"I tested it myself earlier today. It is the genuine article, and it is large. A little more than 76 Kilograms. Richly luminescent and pure I might add. It's quite an exciting find."

"And who is taking credit for finding this nugget? I'm not at all clear on that part of your story."

"The Montagnard organization who possess the nugget is saying it is a gift from the spirit of a boy named Gaipon.

"That's exactly the reason I'm still unclear, Googs. The part about the boy not being alive rather muddles up the chain of custody possibilities don't you think?"

"One of many mysteries around this nugget, Margot. So far, the nugget is holding on to its secrets."

"Well, then. Googs, what do we know?"

"Here's what is clear at the moment. The tribal organization attempted to put it up for bid on an on-line auction site. They want to purchase the lands they were expelled from in Viet Nam's ethnic disbanding campaign of 2002."

"Hmmm. Interesting. Tell me, would the value of the nugget be enough to purchase those lands? Have you figured out just how valuable it is?"

"By weight, three quarters of a million dollars American, or a little more than five hundred and thirty thousand pounds British.

Certainly not enough to return the quantity of land that's been seized. The true value lies in its appeal to collectors."

"I had no idea there was such a group. Gold nugget collectors?"

"Collectors in general, Margot. It may be too late, however. The government is said to be threatening to seize the nugget."

"I suppose that should encourage the current owner to step up and be recognized?"

"The owner is certainly stepping up, Margot. Being recognized? That's a bit more murky. The picture I'm getting is one of a three-foot-tall South American linguist, magician, baffle-gamer sort of chap. He claims he once was a Montagnard boy named Gaipon. His is a convoluted story of ... well ... life jumping, I suppose you would say. Currently, he's trying to explain things on an American radio talk show in New York City."

"And how's he doing? Do we know what he's been saying?"

"I've yet to hear him. If our listeners would like to find out what he's saying, they can search for 'The Bill Elliott Show' on station WNGS in New York."

"Well, Googs, I'm curious to know what this is about. Would you keep us informed?"

"I will, Margot."

"For goodness sake, a gigantic gold nugget, gifted from the grave. Thank you for your report. A world-record gold nugget. How about that. Now off to Malaysia and a chat with ..."

24

"OFF TO MALAYSIA," Otis repeated, "without ever leaving the studio. The magic of radio ventriloquism."

Otis set the marble back onto the tray and, despite his promise, reverted again into digression. "I heard the secret to traveling faster than light could be described as an upside-down ice cream cone. Did you ever hear that one, Doc?"

Otis didn't expect an answer, but he went silent while trying several positions to get comfortable in the bed. He finally settled on sitting awkwardly cross-legged, like a yoga newbie. "That's how one of the chief architects of the MX missile system described it. He was probably better known as a bass player for the band *Iron Butterfly*. They found his van at Yellowstone Park a week after he posted that description to his colleagues. They've never found him. Have they? I mean, I've been away awhile."

Knowing he wouldn't receive a response, Otis continued. "I read another description of how to manipulate time. This one is just as mysterious and unenlightening. *Time travel is possible by using the process of radio ventriloquism and the perfectly attuned voice.* That, Doc, was lifted from the Telstar web.

"We found a wealth of information on that platform, all of it attributed to the science of Baal Zebub, but that little nugget about time came without the science. Luckily, we didn't need to time travel, we needed a weapon, and the weapon we needed was on the secret web, complete with construction manual, under the heading: S.I.Z.M.O.

Sonic Interference Zone Manipulating Orchestrator

"Even before I manufactured the first prototype, everybody started calling it a gizmo. I liked the original name. Sizzz. The name promised a danger. In the end, I couldn't fight it. I could discover the design, I could build it, I could be the first to use one in anger, but I couldn't stop the name change. Gizmo it was.

"That brings me to this: I'm going to let the back story go. What's important to know is everyone was in place, trained, and prepared when the BBC report aired, and the clock was ticking. Okay. Midnight to midnight, it's the rapid-fire round, Doc. Keep up."

* * *

ONE MINUTE AFTER MIDNIGHT

Sitting in his studio after signing off the air, Bill shivered when a low buzzing sound, inaudible to human ears, came through the window. Like the first wave of nausea that lets you know you have the flu, the shiver demanded to be taken seriously.

The feeling washed away, but a sense of dread remained. He'd heard the buzz and felt the initial chill once before, a long time ago and far away from earth.

Bill rolled his chair to the right of his desk and unplugged his bathroom board with its twelve buttons. He removed a different board from its storage drawer and plugged it in to the same port. His new board was adorned with only one button. Beneath the button was written three letters. *DDD.* "Die, Dirtwing, Die," he said to himself after pushing the jack into the port.

Satisfied he had done all he could do to protect himself from the worst, he sat calmly, waiting for the BBC report, his fingers tapping rhythmically next to the button, and trying to ignore the buzzing sound coming through his window.

At the end of the BBC broadcast, Bill took a globe of the world from his desk and threw it against a wall. The base separated and shattered, but the globe stayed intact, bouncing from furniture to furniture before settling in the center of the room, spinning like a cue ball. "It's going to be a long night," he said out loud. "It's always been just a matter of time."

*   *   *

TWELVE PAST TWELVE

Po rushed to her whistling tea kettle after turning off her radio. Unnerved by the whistling sound, she hurried while pouring the water angrily into her cup. The splash of water onto her wrist caused her hand to jerk, spilling a wave of scalding water onto her hand. Hopping up and down, she held her hand under cold water, cursing Bill. "Damn you Bill Elliott. I am going to punch your face. You wait. It's just a matter of time."

*   *   *

TIME ZONES

Before the pre-recorded report aired, Guglielmo Singh was flying backward through time zones. As promised, a Halliburton corporate jet was fueled and waiting for him at the airport in Saigon. When the jet landed in Phoenix, Arizona, a stretch limo, with a magnetic sign advertising *Fast Eddy's Rentals,* whisked Singh away to a helicopter pad where Jack VanGrada waited by a vintage tour chopper. Painted on the side of the helicopter was a sign. The lettering was faded, but clear enough to read.

Whirly Bird Tours
Hike the canyon from the sky!

"Are you good to go, Googs? Get any sleep on the flight?" he asked.

"Sleep? Who can sleep?" Singh mumbled.

"I'll fill you in as we fly. We're less than an hour away."

"I must say, Jack, your travel arrangements are unique and sometimes impressive. Is Halliburton part of this adventure?"

"No. Using the proper channels, correct passwords, and codes, we secured a no-bid contract. It's the way they like to do business."

"Let's hope for better results, shall we? Will we arrive on time?"

"Your interview on BBC just ended, we have to wait for word, but everything's just a matter of time."

*   *   *

12:49 AM, WEDNESDAY

In the Amazon, Dave couldn't tune in the BBC. When the program aired, he and his pilot were already asleep.

Only his cameraman was still awake, fascinated, snapping pictures of the millions of twinkling stars he had never seen before. "It's been heaven," he sighed to the night sky, before shuffling off to his sleeping bag. "Good night, stars. In the morning, I have a sunrise to film."

Three feet away from where the photographer admired the stars, a Laberria serpent felt it was now safe to slide away and enjoy a night of feasting. He'd waited for the big heat source to move on. He was patient, knowing instinctively it would be just a matter of time.

25

ALL DAY – ALL NIGHT

H AYAK AND HIS CREW began loitering on all four sides of Bill's compound one hour before midnight. When midnight arrived, gizmos were fired up.

After Hayak returned from following Po to her home, he made the rounds of his crew, encouraging them to stay focused on the sequencing of on-off, walk-stand operations orchestrated during training with Lockjaw.

He was satisfied Bill's entire block of buildings was being painted with what Hayak's crew called *gizmo vibes*. "Remember your relief schedule, don't zone out, no drops," he told them, "This could take a while. It's just a matter of timing."

2:08 AM

Inside a cave tucked under a lip atop the wall in the federal area of the Grand Canyon, I noticed a change in lighting. The moon stopped casting light into the mouth of the cave.

We were trained for this. Neither I nor my two companions from Hayak's crew moved to see the reason for the sudden, but expected, shade. Seconds of tense silence were rewarded when the cavern lit up with the glow of light emanating from the head beams of Alazam's shem.

After the soft thump of shem touching ground, I stepped into the golden glow and froze for an instant. For the first time since I built our first gizmo, I paused to rethink. Am I really going to dissipate an angel?

Yes. Yes, I was. My instant of doubt gone, I pointed toward the clear dome of the craft, held my arm out straight, and pushed the trigger.

On the moon, when Kae'Lairy relived the moment, he spoke like someone resigned to an unpleasant outcome.

"So it was," he said. "Weak-minded, enraged, and consumed with malice enough to fill up his pages in the book of life, Baal Alazam, under the light of the moon, and under judgment, flew his shem into a hole beneath a lip overhanging the Grand Canyon.

"Expecting to see gold or punish the fools who took it, Alazam came in confident, but after Otis pushed his button, every element in Baal Alazam's body vibrated into smaller and smaller pieces. With the energy released from the rupture of each ever-partitioning piece, the shrinking fragments propelled deeper and deeper, farther and farther, until movement stopped. Baal Alazam was so dissipated and small, no piece was left capable of measured movement. No space was required to hold any part of him, and he had no mind, weak or strong, to think with. Therefore, he was no more. All he left behind was a man just awakened from the forced unconsciousness of spiritual possession."

After a pause, Kae'Lairy shocked the two watchers further. "The instrument of Baal Alazam's destruction was designed by his own master. The very high frequency of sound it generates is deadly to Anakim, familiars, and watchers. Deadly to Little-Wings, like you."

Kae'Lairy paused and waited. These watchers were quick-minded, but they had to flip quite a few mental levers to fully appreciate what they were being told. Breaking the lengthy silence, Kae'Lairy put it into words for them. "Monkeys with guns. We have monkeys with guns. This will matter, over time."

2:27 AM

Jack VanGrada nudged the nodding Guglielmo Singh. "We just got the word," he yelled over the copter's engine, "We can go straight in. The shem has landed."

Singh wiped a little dribble from his five o'clock shadow, pushed one reluctant eyelid a little higher, and asked, "And the pilot? Has your gizmo been effective?"

"I'm not sure. They say they have a really hysterical man named Stanley Goodhope. That's all I know."

It took a second, but Guglielmo suddenly realized what he was being told. The idea of it found some of the spark he felt at the elevator and a sudden energy burst out of him. "Chika pow! We have a shem."

2:50 AM

Kae'Lairy spent an hour in the asteroid belt studying the program loops in video games. None of the games Olphrenjii left for him helped to find what he was looking for, a real-world equation for a *reload saved game* button. He was, admittedly, desperate.

"I repent my decision to never again set foot on earth," he wailed. "I pray that Asitr will do the right thing." At 2:50 A.M., he touched down in New York.

3:00 AM

Guglielmo and Jack reached the mouth of the cave with tools for assaying and shipping prep, but they didn't have the tools they needed for the problem they found inside.

Stanley Goodhope, a hysterical man with the stamina of the insane, was stuck, screaming, in the cockpit of a tiny flying device of unknown origin and technology. It was clear the man was probably going to exert himself to death if they couldn't figure a way to get him out. The sun was going to rise directly across from the cave in less than four hours. If they didn't think of something, Stanley Goodhope was going to suffocate or bake.

When Googs and Jack arrived, I told them Hayak's men were preparing to cover the shem, Goodhope and all, then secure a sling for the big copter to grab onto for the ride to its new home.

"Aren't you being a bit cold to the poor gentleman inside? "Googs asked sharply. "Isn't he a victim as well?"

I knew enough about Goodhope to answer … "I'm not confusing him with Alazam," I said. "Take a look at him. All of his convictions took place before he was possessed. This is no victim. The crimes he's suspected of are unspeakable. I give less than a damn about Stanley Goodhope. Let's get this puppy out of here and worry about the maniac later."

Along with my opinion, I passed Jack and Googs a printout of information on their man in the flying machine.

Guglielmo read down to the crimes Mr. Goodhope had been convicted of and stopped reading halfway through the paragraphs of unspeakable suspicions. Looking up, he saw VanGrada had also ceased reading.

All our heads turned together, staring at the man in the cockpit. For the first time since I pointed my gizmo and pushed the button, Stanley Goodhope fell silent. Wiping a circle through the cloudy film of moisture growing inside the cockpit, Goodhope put his eye to the clear spot and looked outward at the circle of grim-faced men staring back. "He told me I would fly," moaned the voice trapped inside. "He promised me I would fly."

VanGrada was the first to speak up. "I'm not very proud to say this," he said. "I just want everyone to know my priorities are no longer centered on freeing Goodhope. Let the machine be his coffin. I have kids myself, but you don't have to be a parent to … damn. I say we work on keeping the shem in one piece and getting it to the lab. If we happen to figure out the cockpit along the way, well, there's a really nice jumping off perch for him to attempt flight." Everyone's eyes followed Jack's hand as he pointed to the edge of the cave floor.

I walked to the edge of the cave and looked down into the dark canyon. "I'm not presiding over an execution, boys," I said, while tossing a stone over the side. "Once we get this flying contraption squared away, he's our burden. If he lives, he needs to be interrogated."

"Well and good, well and good." Singh spoke his approval. "I am going to supervise the packing up of the nuggets, please. We have jobs enough to go around. It appears we have two nuggets larger than the one causing the hubbub in Viet Nam, and we have some graffiti to preserve, both Mesoamerican and English."

"English?" VanGrada asked.

"On the ceiling, above the big nugget, there's a name scratched in limestone: *Jacob Waltz.*"

"I'll be damned." VanGrada clapped his hands together. "We have an ancient flying device inside the *Lost Dutchman's Mine.* We could use the services of the Explorers Club."

"We have better," I said. "This puppy is going to a place where secrets are a way of life. We have the proper codes, channels, and passwords to access all the tools available at Area 51."

6:00 AM

Po made a pot of coffee, drank two cups, and called Bill. He didn't answer the phone. Hanging up, she whispered through clenched teeth. "Damn you, Bill Elliot."

6:18 AM

Dave rolled out of his sleeping bag and covered his face when he noticed the camera. "It's too early, Grayson. Wait until I've had coffee."

The photographer, Grayson, continued to shoot, asking questions as he filmed. "What news would you like to hear today, boss?"

"Got it. Come home," Dave replied, while briskly rubbing his face awake.

"What do you want to tell the guys back home?"

"Having a wonderful time. Wish you were here."

"Is that all you want to say, Mr. Blank?

"Sun's coming up. Who's making coffee?"

6:19 AM

As the sky began to lighten, a message to the nervous system of a laberria serpent told him his hunting was over for the night. Spotting an entrance in a pile of stacked stones, the serpent entered and took possession of a comfortable cavity.

In the dark and out of sight, the thickly muscled predator nestled against neatly folded army-issue uniforms and digested his evening prizes as he slept.

6:40 AM

With the sun rising just over his left shoulder, Baal Zebub decided his vacation was over. His favorite things on earth, movies and coffee, would be put aside. From his perch opposite the cave where his gold was being stolen, he witnessed the execution of his most loyal lieutenant, and the capture of his shem. He was angry and motivated.

"I'm not here for a cup of coffee and a movie," Baal Zebub said into the swirling canyon winds. Before exiting, he grinned toward the cave and used his best Arnold Schwarzenegger voice. "I'll be back," he said. Then he flew off to round up a posse.

8:00 AM

Inside a little fishing cabin on Lake Stumpknocker in Florida, an alarm beeped. Asitr sat up in bed and shut it off. "Lock?" he called.

Lockjaw came in from the kitchen where he was making coffee. "Get your sleep?"

"Like a baby with colic," Asitr answered. You?"

"Like a baby waiting for news." Lockjaw chuckled as he set a cup of coffee on the nightstand next to Asitr. The phone on the stand caught his attention. "Look, we got a message."

"What's it say?"

Lockjaw punched the *Play* button, and VanGrada's voice barked two words. "Got it."

"That's the way to start a morning," Asitr said, after his first sip. "Dave should be checking in as soon as he gets back to Panama."

8:40 AM

A very tired Guglielmo Singh glanced at his watch and frowned. The assay was finished, but the gathering of weighted bundles for shipping was going slow. Concentration was difficult. Knowing both he and VanGrada had to be in Illinois in just ten more hours added to the pressure.

VanGrada also glanced at his watch and worried. The shem wasn't ready for its helicopter ride, the big copter was on its way, and time was up for extracting Goodhope. "I'm calling Dave to let him know what we have to do," he announced.

"Call Asitr," I told him. "Dave hasn't checked in, might not be back."

Guglielmo barely heard the conversation. He was zoning out, his mind distracted. Again and again, he caught himself staring into the center of the circle where Goodhope wiped the inside of the cockpit clear of condensation. Goodhope's eye, weirdly magnified due to his cheek being pressed tight against the glass, darted rapidly around the cave, never seeming to focus on one thing until it stopped and focused on Googs.

When Stanley caught Guglielmo's trance-like stare, he began to scream again. "I'm a pheromone for the angels, it's true. When I do what I like to do the angels come. I'm a pheromone for angels. Let me out. I can prove it. I can fly. I'm a pheromone, I'm a pheromone." Goodhope punctuated his words by banging his head on the dashboard.

Guglielmo charged the cockpit, panicked, afraid of the damage being done inside. He relaxed when Goodhope quickly knocked himself unconscious. "There, that's better," Singh whispered, while briefly envying him his sleep. Shaking his head vigorously to avoid giving in to a need to close his eyes, he shouted out to nobody in particular, "Say, fellahs, who's made coffee?"

8:59 AM

Po was on her second pot of coffee and her fifth attempt to get Bill on the phone. He didn't answer. Hanging up, she screamed her anger, "Damn you, Bill Elliot!"

9:00 AM

VanGrada gave Asitr his progress update from the Grand Canyon. He reported most of the gold was ready to move, but the big copter was going to arrive in one hour, and Stanley Goodhope was still stuck inside the shem. "Any advice?" the message asked.

Asitr responded to the request. "Stick to schedule. Secure and disguise the shem. We need you in Illinois. I'll let Ol' Frenchy know you're going to be late. Tell Otis, good luck at X-filesville."

9:07 AM

After Lockjaw sent him a description of the difficulties in the Grand Canyon, Olphrenjii went into action. First, he wrote names on slips of paper and placed them in front of three coffee cups on the counter of an abandoned coffee house at the outskirts of Carbondale, Illinois. He tacked a note to the front door of the building, leaving the door unlocked. One last note he stuck to the door of his bus with bubblegum. After driving the short yellow bus into a patch of weeds behind the building, he locked its doors.

Three men were supposed to meet him at the coffee house at noon, but duty called elsewhere. The notes would have to suffice.

He arrived at the canyon without form. Invisibly, he directed a pulse from his own body to a panel of the flying device, and with a quiet *fweep,* the cockpit sprung open.

Nobody heard the cockpit open, but no one could avoid hearing the whoop of Stanley Goodhope as he sprang from the craft, paused at the ledge overlooking the canyon, and with arms spread straight out and wide, he launched himself into the wind with the farewell message, "Good bye, bitches."

"Accommodating fellow," deadpanned Singh.

Jack VanGrada delivered the eulogy. "Well boys, I give the approach a seven, the late flailing about a one, and the scream before splatter a decisive ten."

Olphrenjii stayed at the cave until the shem was packed and hooked to the giant Sikorsky helicopter. With the removal from the cave complete, Olphrenjii followed Otis and his cargo all the way to Area 51. He observed the shem off-loaded into an isolated hangar at the edge of the main complex and considered his job there complete. With Goodhope succumbing to a self-inflicted attack of free will, and the shem delivered safely, he flew back to Carbondale and slipped back into the character of Ol' Frenchy.

11:09 AM

Lock opened his laptop and smiled. He saw files, sent from Panama, with attachments waiting to be opened. He chuckled at the video of a cranky Dave being harassed by his cameraman.

He opened the second attachment and lost his smile. The transformation of his face started when his brow wrinkled, followed by his eyes narrowing, and finally, the total collapse of the upturned corners of his mouth heralded bad news.

Lock's voice choked when he passed the computer to Asitr. "I'm sorry, Grampy. You need to see this. It's from Grayson. It's bad."

Without further warning of what was to come, the video rolled again. Asitr watched Dave remove a stone from a rock ledge. Looking away from the hole and directly at the camera, Dave reaches into the hole and removes a pile of olive drab clothing from the cavity. In a blur of movement, a short, muscular snake launches itself out of the hole, burying fat fangs into Dave's neck. The rest of the image shakes violently when the snake drops to the ground and the panicked, unsteady cameraman dances away from the ledge.

There is a brief black blink between shots, followed by a close-up of a sweating, white-faced Dave, sitting with his back to a rock, giving his final report as the flora and fauna expert on the mapping team.

"Lots of things different here, boys. The poison ivy is trying to make a comeback but there's no spring. No magic forest.

I found some new stuff. Kapok and Capirona are starting to take over.

I just met a Laberria serpent. They're shy creatures.

Some folks call them the neo-tropical rattlesnake. One of a few snakes in the world with two toxic venoms. One to kill the nervous system, the other to break the flesh down into a hemorrhagic goo. They didn't have those when we were here did they?

Listen, I have just a few minutes. This was nothing nefarious. I just got lazy and forgot my training. Don't you make my mistake. Go get 'em, but don't forget the danger of a deadly creature, trapped and surprised.

You're the last survivor of the mapping team, Lock. See you in the uncharted realms."

After giving a light-hearted imitation of the Queen Elizabeth wave to end the video, the screen goes to black.

Asitr stared at the dark screen until his voice steadied. "Did you see Grayson's CCs?" he asked Lock. "I think he sent it out to everyone on Dave's call list."

"Everyone?"

"Jack, Otis, and Bill... us."

"What are we going to do, Grampy?"

"Call Jack," The words came out of his mouth like they were released from a popped bubble. Stopping again to hold back an insistent sob that hung stubbornly in his throat, he finished his thought. "Tell him he's in charge of the cave opening in Illinois."

11:52

As soon as the wheels were up on the charter from Phoenix, Guglielmo Singh announced his intention to sleep through the entire flight. Before he got his wish, VanGrada pulled him away from dreamland with an ominous sounding, "Oh, God. Poor Dave."

Googs rubbed his eyes and focused on the screen as Jack played the video again. Watching Dave's last moments in the short life had different effects on the two men.

"Dave was supposed to take charge of the Illinois cave project when he returned," VanGrada said, in a voice made monotone by shock. "He's the man. What are we going to do?"

Shocked by the video, and speechless, Singh began to rethink his involvement with Asitr. He passed the laptop back to Jack without comment, and told himself he would figure it all out after some good sleep. Turbulence, legends, watchers, devils, and serpents invaded his rest in ways he no longer thought of as exciting. A lot had happened in the two days he had gone without real sleep. Now, he was afraid to close his eyes.

NOONISH

Starting at ten minutes before noon, in Carbondale, a series of limos pulled into the parking lot of an abandoned building. A heavy forest of black-barked trees encroached on the building from three sides. They cast shade onto the parking area where the limo passengers emerged.

On the other side of the road, spindly trees, with the same dark bark, grew in a bog-like depression covered in yellow moss. The dark irregular angles of the tree branches were highlighted all the more by the bright beams of sun that penetrated through them and marched across the wet, moss covered floor. If a person had the time to watch, he would see the tufts of illuminated moss give the appearance of creeping eastward while the sun ambled west above them.

The grayed wooden building across the road from the marching moss was battling a march of another kind. From sagging roof to crumbling foundation, the structure looked resigned to being corrected by the creep of nature, and comfortable with having its memories swallowed by the forest. A partially obscured sign at the road's edge, facing north, shared one memory of what the building was last used for. It read:

JavaJive

Last good cup until Memphis

On the ground, in front of a wide, wooden porch, a *sold* sign lay face up.

On the door, a scribbled note read:

Somthins gone aft aglay. I'll be late but right on time. Set yoursef to home.

Coffee on the counter, microwave in back.

Your gider,

Ol' Frenchy

A coffee house in its last life, a house with coffee at the end of its life; the empty building awaited. Soon, three men would rendezvous under its roof to join a quest for a golden calf in a sealed cave.

The first to arrive was the kid from Kirksville. With two cameras draped around his neck, and a large suitcase in his right hand, he managed to contort in front of the Java Jive sign and take a selfie with his cell phone. He stopped after looking across the road and took time to remove a camera from around his neck and photograph the glowing yellow moss beneath the twisted, gothic black limbs in the bog. He snapped off more pictures after turning and seeing the old house with noon sun baking into its gray wrinkles.

When he entered the building, he walked straight to the counter and selected one of three cups of lukewarm coffee with a note underneath. It read,

Kid from Kirksville.

"Yum. Caramel almond," he said out loud. "My favorite,"

Next to be dropped off was an older man struggling with two suitcases and a backpack. After taking in the parking lot, he walked to the side of the driveway. He thought it was odd to have just one sign advertising the coffee house to people leaving the area. After kicking around in the weeds, he found another sign lying on the ground. It read:

JavaJive

Best Cup in Carbondale

Walking around back, he spotted a short school bus. A sign on the door read,

Don't Touch the Frog Horn or Flame Dispencer

Peeking in the window, he spotted blankets, sleeping bags, and a large liquid-nitrogen tank with an air horn attached. Lying next to the tank was a vintage WWII flame thrower. After first checking the tree line, he looked deeper into the woods. Returning to the front of the building, he peered through the door window, walking in.

With a nod of the head to the young man texting at a corner table, he walked to the counter and selected the thick, dark, cowboy coffee with floating grounds on top before he read the note.

CSI

"Not hot enough," he said to the kid from Kirksville on his way to the back room to find the microwave.

Last to arrive was the oldest of the three. Looking dressed for colder weather, but not looking uncomfortable, the newcomer pulled his laptop over his shoulder, glanced at the standing sign, adjusted his bow tie, then walked straight to the front door. After reading the note on the door, he chuckled. The note under the last cup of coffee, *Old Words Professor,* gave him another laugh.

"Ooh. A little coffee with my cream," he said. "Just the way I like it. Ahh, room temperature."

Addressing the other two men in the room he asked," Who is this Ol' Frenchy, Scottish, hillbilly? Have you seen him?" Shrugs from the two occupied tables greeted his question.

The kid never lifted his eyes from his cell phone. The other man never removed his eyes from the man at the counter. Finally, the older gentleman answered the stare with an introduction.

"Ancient language specialist."

"Kid from Kirksville."

"CSI, retired."

With the introductions finished, the old language expert sat down at the counter, opened his laptop and began trying to figure out the speech patterns displayed on the notes from Ol' Frenchy.

2:03 PM

Po spent the daylight hours sitting in her rocker at the window, watching men wander like ants around Bill's block. Now and then, she'd pick the phone up off the floor and call him. He didn't answer.

Twice, she got out of her chair to make coffee; many more times to finish the two pots, one cup at a time.

Shortly after two o'clock, she made lunch. While spilling chips onto a plate and smearing tuna salad on toast, she tried to organize question marks into a list. What she came up with was two whys and a who, and no path to a what. Without a what, she knew, the how, as in how is-this- fixed, would be elusive. Normally, her lists were a first step toward organizing, but a series of question marks proved resistant to the process.

Po wiped questions from her mental blackboard and came up with a new list:

Eat lunch at the window.
Call Bill one more time.
Set the alarm for six o'clock.
Get some sleep.

Po's chips rattled on her plate when she lifted it off the counter. She paused until the little tremor in her hand subsided, then she snagged the last cup from her second pot of morning coffee and headed for the rocking chair by the front window.

Before sitting, she looked through the gap between the curtain and the window frame. The *ant-men* still loitered around Bill's compound.

Through the viewing slit, Po focused on the street while lowering herself onto her rocking chair. Upon sitting, she balanced the lunch plate on one knee and leaned over with the intention of picking her telephone off the floor. As she leaned, coffee slopped over the edge of her cup and wet the bread on her tuna sandwich.

Overcompensating for the spill, Po took her attention away from balancing the plate on her knee and focused on calming the sloshing coffee in her cup.

The plate tilted. Potato chips slid to the edge. When the soggy sandwich started to slide, Po reacted quickly. Her hand snapped back to her plate in an attempt to slap it tight against her knee.

The plate, struck on one corner, reacted to the hurried slap like a flipped coin. As it tumbled through the air, chips flew like a covey of startled quail. The wet sandwich performed a one-and-a-half twist, ending its flight with a belly-flop on top of the phone.

Po squeezed her eyes and, without looking, pulled her cup toward her mouth and drained what was left of her twelfth cup of the day.

She sat like that, eyes shut tight, lips sucked in between her teeth, one foot tapping so fast it was almost a twitch, until she made a new mental list.

Clean the rug.
Call Bill one more time.
Set the alarm for six o'clock
Get some sleep

With the list finalized, she opened her eyes, averting her gaze away from the mess on the floor and toward her narrow view of the street.

Before her eyes focused, the phone rang. Under the sandwich, the normally shrill ring tone clanged soft and muffled, like PVC wind chimes, but it startled Po. She jumped out of her chair at the sound, then immediately sat back down and grabbed for the phone beneath the sandwich.

It was Bill. "Don't call again," he said, as soon as Po put the phone to her ear. "I'm not obnubulating. Take a trip or stay home. I'll call you if I need you." With that, he hung up.

Po listened to the click from Bill's phone and walked to the window, silently staring down the street to his compound until the dial tone brought her attention back into the room. Scowling at the mess on the floor, she revised her list again, mumble-moaning between each item as she mentally locked them in.

Wash soggy bread and tuna out of my ear.

Clean the floor.
Look up the word, obnubulating.
Set the alarm for six o'clock.
Go to sleep.

Robotically, Po forced her way silently through the list, stymied when she couldn't find a definition for any form of obnubulate. After exhausting her resources, she surrendered and moved on to the next item on the list. With her alarm set, she crawled into bed. While slipping her satin mask of darkness over her eyes, she sighed, "Obnubulate. Damn you, Bill Elliott. What kind of trouble are you in?"

26

O TIS STOPPED RUMINATING the timeline of events when a soft tapping of knuckles on the door broke his concentration.

Jarvis Douglas entered the room carrying a clipboard and speaking apologies. "Sorry, gentlemen. We need to get Dr. Milton's signature."

Dr. Milton took a yellow Post-it note off the clipboard, read it, and put it in his shirt pocket. After reading and signing the single page document, he returned the board to his aide. "Thank you, Jarvis," he said. "Is there fresh coffee at the nurse's station?"

"Just now, Doc. The smell get to you?"

"That and some subliminal advertising. Would you get us a couple cups and some fresh water for Mr. Doe."

"Right away, if the nurses ain't drank it up already."

Dr. Milton put his hand to his chest and tapped on his shirt pocket. "Thanks for this, Jarvis. I appreciate it."

Otis watched Dr. Milton curl his body back into his listening position, remaining silent until the doctor waggled his fingers to signal he was ready to listen. "I think I needed that break, Doc. I was getting to the tumultuous three o'clock hour. I'll start in Carbondale.

3:00 PM

Back in character, Ol' Frenchy slipped into the front door of the coffee house with the intention of establishing a team dynamic, while avoiding membership into the team.

Everyone looked up from their electronic devices when he closed the door behind him, so he made his presence felt as someone with answers who shouldn't be approached with questions

"Catty-cornered, dissociable, and snobby-like, to set apart from one to each another when you might all be deceased to death by sunrise." He stared at each of them through squinting eyes, one at a time, until he felt they were sufficiently uncomfortable.

"Get you each some acquaintin' momentums before the other two shows themselves up. They've been made delayed, so let's chat us up some. Sittin' disjointed apart don't acclimate teams building,

Ol' Frenchy pointed his forefingers toward the floor and made circles in the air. "Mingle's what I mean," he said suddenly. "Mingle like loose fragments, searchin' for purpose. One needs bein' the clean, dry surface, another needs bein' the glue. Next one gotta mash 'em together 'til the three come to knowin' you make one whole piece outta two because it takes three. Ponder internally on that together. Any more questions? Good. Dinner in three hours."

Satisfied he struck the right balance, Olphrenjii walked back through the front door, across the porch, past the front window, and out of sight.

Inside the coffee house, amused snickering followed his footsteps across the porch. On the heels of their shared moment, the Kid-from-Kirksville and the language scholar were asking questions.

"How long did he say we were going to be stranded here?"

"That wasn't Jack VanGrada, was it?"

"Anybody bring a radio?"

"The show starts in five hours. Is it daylight savings time here?"

CSI withheld his questions but proposed a theory. "Smells like something has gone aft aglay, boys."

3:33 PM

Jack VanGrada and Guglielmo Singh arrived in Memphis, Tennessee, to a major surprise. The car they expected was not reserved. "Never was," they were told. They were already three hours late for their noon appointment in Carbondale. Another hour went wasted while phone tag went on between them and Asitr.

Originally, Ol' Frenchy was the guy responsible for all the travel arrangements. Once he revealed his identity to Asitr, those duties fell to me. I believed the job would be as easy as pressing buttons on my computer, but ... well, I'm getting ahead of myself.

In Memphis, Googs made the transportation issue moot. Mission cautions and common sense aside, he took his credit card from his wallet and walked to a rent-a-car counter. "I need a vehicle with a USB port for operating my laptop and a back seat big enough to sleep on."

"We had computer blackouts today," said the man behind the counter, "We have what you're looking, for but they say it will be another fifteen minutes to run an operations check."

I don't know the comp today, but twenty years ago, fifteen minutes in IT time was an hour of real time.

At quarter to five, Jack slid into the driver seat, and Googs forced his drooping eyes to find his port and connect to the radio band carrying WNGS radio.

"How long to destination?" asked Googs.

"Less than three hours," Jack answered. "If we get the breaks on the road, we'll get there before showtime"

I can't say Googs didn't get any sleep, but just over the Illinois border was a trooper with piercing lights, an aversion to being called constable, and plenty of time for whole-car drug searches and sobriety testing. I will say the quality of the sleep experience was low.

"Next time we get pulled over, don't engage the Smoky in arguments over whether a BBC reporter is entitled to be called a journalist and American reporters are not. Certainly don't insult the man ..."

"She was a woman, Jack."

"You don't tell man or woman they need counseling in human relations before they can stick a cowboy hat on their head and call themselves an officer of the law."

"I was utilizing the freedom of speech you blokes fought us for."

"You need to get some sleep."

The bickering went on until they arrived at their destination on the outskirts of Cairo, Illinois.

3:43

Just before Jack called Asitr to report his transportation issue, a rolling computer blackout shut down Asitr's computer. After the phone discussions with Jack, it came back online with a message.

> The Telstar connections are deleted. Mentioning the destruction on the radio has consequences. I have the power and license to blow up the planet.
>
> If you judge timidly, I have the power and license to judge you harshly.

Asitr was stunned by the message. The questions he couldn't answer turned to doubts.

Lockjaw gave him the reasons for continuing the course they were on.

"Grampy, I've grown old without paying attention to the process. From the moment I picked you up and shoved you down that hole in Eden, I've been infected by you. I caught that step-out-into-traffic-and see-what-hits-us bug. You're God's wunderkind, living your last life. It's your last chance to fire. Are you still that twelve-year-old kid, doubting the protection of Heaven?

"If we're a link in a long, long chain, let's not be the weak one. God doesn't play dice. We can bet the planet on that."

Asitr, renewed, nodded agreement. "You're right. It's pre-show jitters."

27

O TIS ROLLED TO HIS RIGHT and retrieved the marble from the cart. "That leaves only me, Doc. I'm not the best one to tell my three o'clock story. This is Kae'Lairy explaining himself on the moon. Listen. He'll answer one of the questions you asked me this morning. Why are you here?"

Otis touched the marble and Kae'Lairy's voice took over the narration.

*   *   *

KAE'LAIRY WELCOMES OTIS ABOARD

When I arrived in New York, I noticed Olphrenjii had placed air runes around Bill's compound, to warn Little-Wings away. The precaution was prudent.

Their presence at that location told me this is where judgment was going to take place. Why a trap for Alayat and an ambush for Alazam?

The difference between the ambush of Alazam and the trapping of Alayat puzzled me, but an eruption of messages, caught on my monitoring band, redirected my attention to Nevada, where the shem was taken.

When I arrived, the shem, still wrapped under a shroud of tarps, sat alone inside the hangar door, dwarfed by the giant, nearly empty, high-roofed building.

Otis Beckley sat at a desk in the center of the building. Atop the desk, next to a laptop, his feet were in motion, continually bumping into each other like two metronomes in combat. An arm's length away, an open *Lone Ranger* lunchbox held the weapon used to dissipate a fallen son of Heaven.

I approached the desk and stood silent behind the chair, observing. When the feet stopped their movement, Otis spoke a word, "Omlar," and the computer screen glowed to life. He followed with commands, all spoken in the language of the Adam. I watched his screen cycle through pages faster than a human eye could follow. At each page, his computer burst through requirements for code compatibility, payment platforms, passwords, and antivirus software. At the end of the process, travel arrangements were secured for Asitr and Lockjaw to arrive in New York on Thursday morning.

Why? Why wait until after the Wednesday show to arrive for judgment? Did Asitr want to set another trap by announcing the cave opening while on-air? Surely Alayat knew he was cornered, yet he is going to go on with the show?

I waited until the travel arrangements were completed before I spoke. "It would be singularly unwise to allow these technologies to remain in the hands of man; don't you think so, Mr. Beckley?"

He stiffened at the sound of my voice, but his response was calm. Without hurry or delay, he spoke, "Dut," and the computer screen darkened. He removed the gizmo from his lunchbox and stood to face me

210

I ask him again. "It would be singularly unwise to allow these technologies to remain in the hands of man; don't you think so, Mr. Beckley?"

Showing he was schooled in the old ways, he questioned my intentions. "What is your name and why are you here?"

"I am the mighty Kae'Lairy, messenger of the Lord, hero of the big war, bondsman without peer, and above all things, protector of the throne. Should I ask again?" I glowed to introduce the thought into his mind I might not be so easily dissipated.

His reaction, an unsteady balance, a drain of color in the face, betrayed a slippage of confidence. His pale pallor turned blue in my light, and he responded in a voice pushed thin and breathless by fear. "Are you here as a messenger?"

I told him I was the attending angel of judgment, here to execute a sentence. With my obligations to answer name and purpose fulfilled, I waited for an answer to my question, twice asked, and again, he answered with more questions of his own.

"Can we keep the gizmos? You want the shem? Is it ... I mean ... Did I do wrong to dissipate Alazam?"

He continued blurting, adding answers to his questions. "Alazam needed dissipating. Don't let Alayat escape. Take the shem. Take the shem. I mean, he really did ... really ... and we needed ... he needed dissipating." His stomach muscles lurched as he attempted to control its contents, then he regained enough courage to declare, "I'm not afraid. I would do it again."

I repented my intention to communicate with the nervous chimpanzee when he retreated into babble. He ceased speaking when I waved the gizmo from his grasp and crushed it into a stream of elemental dust, staining the concrete floor.

Following my demonstration, a long, low-volume squeal, like a flatulent whistle of air escaping from a pinched balloon valve, leaked from his mouth. The words he intended to carry on the stream of air were unable to form in his clenched diaphragm. The one body function operating at full capacity was production in the sweat glands. When his legs lost their will to support him, he tottered awkwardly and slumped backward into his chair, fainting, due to the shock of his own misunderstandings.

While he was out, I began the process of speaking the Telstar web from the entirety of the Internet. *"Omlar sanaptu, sesame sanaptu fwu."* I secured the laptop, sealing all but myself from access to its applications. Once in command, I separated content and function into three categories.

First, I built a fence around the code written in the binary long form.

Next, I rounded up all of the Telstar data from inside the fence and boxed it together with all the code written in the language of the Adam.

I could have spoken away the entire box at that moment, but my choice was to be thorough. The Telstar operating system was the first to be erased, resulting in a rolling blackout of internet access across the world

Item by item, I viewed each file, deleting as I went along. Each deletion sent shivers of Internet blinks. At last, the last. One file remained to be viewed, the rumored collection of Baal Zebub's scrolls of science, *Silver Book.*

I read it.

The file's deletion sent one last hiccup across the Internet. Electronically and forensically, Telstar and *Silver Book* were scrubbed.

Deleting the file wasn't good enough. Having read it I became a threat to the throne, too loyal to be mistrusted but too infected to be welcome in Heaven.

All of my decisions, since that moment, have been made without conviction, ad-libbed as fast as time moves. In the next few hours leading up to the radio show, I made good decisions and bad ones.

I cancelled the travel reservations for Jack VanGrada and Guglielmo Singh because I couldn't be in two places at one time. Asitr's right to judgment couldn't be interfered with, but the Illinois cave opening, scheduled for the same day, was better off delayed

Otis Beckley needed to be calmed before I did what I had to do. "I'm not here to execute a judgment against you," I told him in soothing tones. "You have delivered a true end for a creature who let jealousy turn to hatred, mistrust metastasize into faithlessness, and faithlessness become rebellion. Alazam was a creature with his foot on the neck of humanity. Be comforted."

Once I felt his fears were calmed, and with no offer of peace or explanation, I set my bondsman's box on the table, opened it, boxed Otis Beckley's spirit, and reconstituted his body for cryogenic storage. "You know too much," I told him. "I must protect the throne."

Brothers, I imprisoned a spirit not under judgment. Woe for me, I can't tell you why.

28

HARBINGER INSTITUTE
April 1, 2025

"THERE YOU HAVE IT, DOC. One of the reasons I'm here." Otis laughed as he silenced the marble.

"I was boxed because I'm a nervous, pale-pallored, chattering chimpanzee who is a danger to the throne of God, on account of knowing too much."

Otis massaged his temples and asked for a moment to re-gather his thoughts. He pulled himself back into a full sitting position against his pillows, fussed with the matted sheets around his feet, and briskly mussed his hair before continuing.

"I don't want to give the impression I didn't have issues with my new out-of-body experience, but confusion was minimal. Four of my five senses worked. I could smell the hangar. I could see it. I felt the boundaries of the void inside the box. I heard Kae'Lairy giving commands to the computer.

"When I heard him send his threatening message to Asitr, I discovered a spirit can shudder without the connective neurons the organic body requires.

"I learned anger lives outside the clay, undiminished in the spirit. Helplessness and hopefulness live there together as well.

"Helpless, but hopeful, I watched Kae'Lairy finish his work at Area 51. He had a shem to hide, and he chose plain sight as the best cloak.

"At the Pahrump-side entrance of Area 51, near to the food delivery elevator, is a smoking-approved zone where the underground restaurant workers take breaks. For the last twenty years, they've had a shem to contemplate. It's doubtful any of them has contemplated on the shem as the actual holy grail of the installation they work for. To them, it's been an attractive sculpture, with a granite base and a bronze plaque. The plaque reads:

```
Ancient One-Pilot Flying Device
Disabled 2005
```

"Kae'Lairy was done. With only four hours to go before the Wednesday show aired, he rested while I began my twenty years of life in a time-warped limbo by probing for cracks in my prison.

"Leading up to the eight o'clock hour, time warping seemed to be the theme of the hour.

"In New York, Po spent the time leading up to the show tossing around restlessly in bed, waiting for her alarm to go off.

"On the road, Jack VanGrada and Guglielmo Singh slogged toward the coffee house at legal speeds.

"In Illinois, the boys at the coffee house shared a Burger Doodle dinner and a lengthy Ol' Frenchy diatribe about the inequality of ice distribution in the nineteenth century as compared to the equality of Burger Doodle availability in the modern era. His perspective on the "lesser computed and compulsively under-thought-of angles to view the "computable disorderliness of proportion" effectively spurred a migration of listeners from the dinner table. The three men gathered together, staring at the parking lot, whispering their hopes for the quick arrival of Jack VanGrada, and sharing in the comradeship of men enduring a shared prison sentence in the crawling time zone of annoyed boredom.

"None of them had long to wait for showtime. It just felt like it."

*   *   *

UP ON THE ROOF

Just before dark, Kae'Lairy set down on a rooftop, two blocks away from Bill's compound. I still had enough sunlight to see Hayak's men patrolling the streets around his block. Minutes went by, maybe just seconds, and the cityscape in front of me changed in slow motion.

Hayak's ant-men melted into the dark borders where dim streetlights drew circles on the ground. In the distance, beyond the neighborhood, pockets of sharp, intrusive light sprouted like radiation in colors made dull in the sun, but vibrant under the moon.

I looked upward. Nearly cloudless, only Venus and a toenail moon competed for the sky.

I tried to picture what Asitr felt in Samyaza, watching the city brighten in the soft tones of lamps being lit around him, like little campfires for the family circle.

A blue neon sign, across from the gate in the wall around Bill's compound, mesmerized me with its tireless blinking. My mind was just too frayed to think, so I stared at the light until Kae'Lairy broke my trance by placing the marble next to the box and spoke.

"What can you tell me about Po?" he asked.

"I didn't know much about her. She's Bill's secretary. Hayak was given the responsibility of tailing her, monitoring her phone, and protecting her if we put her into harm's way."

"Po is in trouble," he said. He kneeled and placed his hand to the rooftop. "She's two floors beneath us." After he stood again, he gave a play-by-play of her evening.

"When her alarm went off, she sprung from her bed, tore off her blindfold, and slapped at her bedside radio so hard it flew off the end table. I don't think she slept well.

"She made coffee, but she didn't put on her nicotine patch. She took her vitamins but didn't brush her teeth or change clothes. She's shredded her routine. She's under too much stress right now. What's she going to do when she learns her predicament?"

I didn't know what to say, so I asked, "What is she doing now?"

"She's sitting at her window, clutching a warm cup of coffee to her breast. Her cracked bedroom radio is next to her. It still works. There's a notepad on her lap, but she has nothing to write with. She's calming down, staring at a blinking blue light. I think it comforts her. Good, it's show-time."

Bill's old bumper music started to play on the marble. It was the song Po liked. The sweet and melancholy strains of the JED song, *Dancing on the Edge of Time*, mingled together with my surreal feelings of helplessness and hopefulness.

Here it is, Doc. Wednesday night, and almost everyone but Bill's regular audience and Po, can see the eyes behind the moss.

29

"GOOD EVENING, FRIENDS. I am Bill Elliott, welcome to another evening of something different.

"Tonight, is another bare-bone, minimum-commercials night. Settle in.

"We begin with some sad news. Last night, I told you Albie Gentile died in a sinkhole on a Florida highway. The earth, literally, opened up and swallowed him down. I'm sorry we didn't get to know him better. He was two days short of being our featured guest.

"Tonight, again, more sad news. This news hits close to home for a lot of us. David Blank, the man we opened the show with Monday evening, has been killed in the Amazon while retrieving artifacts from the home of the Savant tribe.

"Dave perished in a crazy, improbable manner. He was slain by a serpent in a place called Eden. It seems Death is stalking my show, and he has a sick sense of humor.

"Asitr."

"Yes, Bill?"

"Did Dave ever tell you how we met?"

"Yes. You were a student at NYU, finalizing a thesis on integrated computer technologies for radio. You wanted to develop a technology for a network of home-studio radio broadcasts. An independent radio press, I believe you called it."

"That's right. Today, because of that work, I have a network of one to my credit. Dave was very helpful. He and a friend who worked for IBM supplied many missing pieces for my thesis."

"Dave and Mr. Beckley were very good at supplying missing pieces.

"Yes, Beckley was the name. The three of us had some fun with a computer game."

"Asteroids, Bill. They say you kicked their butts."

"You've talked to Beckley? How is he? How did you run into Otis Beckley?"

"Dinner at Dave's. Lock and I picked up some Chinese carryout and knocked on his door. His friend, Otis, was there."

"How nice. Those were fun days. Do you have his number? I'd like to give him a call."

"I believe he plans to knock at your door soon. Could be those Asteroid butt-kickings still bother him. Watch for him to walk through the crowd gathering outside your gate."

"I wouldn't call it a crowd, Asitr, but there is a buzz around the old homestead, ever since you mentioned that big gold nugget."

"Yes, we thought the nugget could present problems for you. We kept it quiet for a while."

"Okay, Asitr, we should get back to your story. I want to interview you tonight, but if you would like to say anything to memorialize our friend, do it now, we have that short station identification coming up soon."

"Just a funny story about you and your dog, Bill. Remember Herk?"

"My goodness, old Herk. He was a mess. Dumbest dog ever. Dave must have told you about the flash incident."

"Yes. Did you ever teach him to sit?"

"No, he ran away the same night as the flashing malfunction. Go ahead and tell my audience, just so they know what we're talking about."

"I should leave that up to you. I wasn't there."

"It wasn't really a funny story. It was just a weird computer glitch with a newly installed speech recognition device."

"Yes, not really funny, but much more than a glitch, am I right?"

"I don't know what you mean, Asitr. During an Asteroids challenge, the screen flashed a solid bright white. When the screen returned to normal it was game over. The spaceship, flying blind, was dust on the screen. When we figured out what triggered the flash, we had a little fun with it."

"The trigger was telling the dog to sit. Am I right, Bill?"

"Well, Asitr, the funny part was after we figured it out. Otis and Dave kept erasing my best starts by telling Herk to sit. It was in good fun, but I wasn't going to let them beat me on my last night in town. I fixed the problem by deleting the voice recognition program."

"Along with the Asteroids game, right?"

"Everything on the disc, actually. I gave them a new disc. The games went on."

"When they told me the story, I was intrigued. You wouldn't happen to know the word for 'flash' in the language of the Adam, would you, Bill?"

"Why ask?"

"The word for glimmer is a soft spoken, *zt*. The word *flash* is the same, but nuanced differently. Say the word commandingly, as in how people train dogs, it sounds like 'SIT!'"

"Asitr, that's interesting, but we have a lot on our plate, and you have fifteen seconds until commercial. Any final thoughts on our friend, Dave?"

"Dave knew this was the short life. I have forever to come up with thoughts. None of them final. He and I will talk again."

Okay, then. Let's do the mandatory identifying and move on. This is Bill Elliott.

30

HARBINGER INSTITUTE
April 1, 2025

"W ERE YOU SURPRISED BY ..." Otis paused mid-sentence while he quieted the marble. "Did you expect fireworks to start the show?"

Otis talked past the question without waiting for an answer he knew wouldn't come. "I knew what to expect from Asitr. He was eager to eliminate Baal Alazam, but he wanted time and distance between himself and the moment he would have to decide the fate of Baal Alayat. Lockjaw characterized the long-distance approach as 'the grand jury phase'.

"Alayat was a surprise. Why was he staying in character as Bill Elliott? What was he expecting to gain? I asked Kae'Lairy for his opinion.

"Everything," he answered. "He's profiling his judge."

Otis reached again to touch the marble. "I listened for it, the profiling, when Bill returned after the break."

31

"OKAY, WE ARE BACK. Let's move forward. Still with us, Asitr?"

"All the way to the end, Bill."

"Evidence, Asitr. Let's recap for my audience."

"Okay."

"There is the time capsule, the letter, and the 78. Most of my emails are leaning toward the explanation given by the officers at the Explorers Club. They believe a hoax is being perpetrated with foreknowledge by someone from Sylvester Long's family."

"A fair suspicion, Bill."

"You have the artifacts Dave died to retrieve?"

"They are on the way."

"Do you believe they will be accepted for what they are? Some of my listeners are already touting them as planted evidence. Forensic examination will need to be done before ..."

"Bill. Why bother?"

"Why bother?"

"Do your listeners believe we've faked a gold nugget?"

"I haven't received a single doubter's email on the nugget, Asitr. Those who mention the nugget believe the BBC report. The predominant issue with most of them is how you are using it. Let me read a representative sample ..."

"Bill, please. Let's stop dancing. Can I fill in some blanks for you?"

"Please do."

"Scratch the *Lost Dutchman Mine* off the list of unsolved mysteries. I can tell you it was never a mine in the first place. Poor old Jacob Waltz found a stash of gold collected by Baal Zebub and hidden by his lieutenants. We've removed the entire collection to a safe location."

"Hold up, Asitr. You're dancing way too fast. How about letting your old dancing partner catch up to these new steps. I'm breathless."

"The gold is not going to be negotiable, even as 'evidence'. Neither is the shem."

"The shem? What are you saying?"

"Baal Alazam flew his shem to us last night. The shem is safe, Alazam has been written from the book of life."

"Impossible."

"There's more. Irrefutable proof of my lives is coming very soon. A few short weeks, I hope."

"I'm afraid to ask, Asitr. I'm still trying to wrap my head around what you've already told me. Is Alazam the man you've ..."

"Creature, Bill."

"Beg your pardon?"

"Alazam was not a man. He was a creature. Demon, devil, genie, if you prefer."

"Okay, Asitr. Alazam was the creature you had been hiding from?"

"He was the one we felt could be the most easily lured."

"There are others?"

"We'll know soon, Bill."

"Soon, as in very soon? Like the irrefutable proof you promised?"

"Perhaps sooner. The irrefutable evidence comes in the form of fingerprints."

"Fingerprints?"

"I know I have the same prints as Gaipon and Sylvester Long. I don't have prints from any other lives to compare. I'll have some soon."

"How soon? Where are they coming from?"

"The 78, wrapped in Lockjaw's military uniform has been dusted. The napalm smoke actually helped preserve the prints on the record."

"How do we know they aren't your own prints, from this life?"

"Larger fingers, same prints. We also have Gaipon's prints on an antique Victrola. I'm convinced we will find my infant prints inside the *Cave of the Dried Spring* mentioned in my mother's story.

"Okay, First thing, Asitr. You are implying you've maintained the same fingerprints in all your lives. Secondly, what makes you think they will still be on the cave wall after all these thousands of years?"

"I'm relying on intuition here, Bill. I don't think the ritual of the angel Olphrenjii was purposeless. Nothing on his list of things I should be taught has been purposeless. The numbers he gave Auth and Puth for finding the cave were GPS coordinates. I was always supposed to go back. The cave was sealed through flood and progress. It won't be sealed against my return."

"How soon will you know, for sure?"

"I have a team there as of today. There is pre-Columbian graffiti on the stones around the entrance. It needs to be preserved. Our team should open the entrance within the week."

"Very exciting, Asitr. So much news. I didn't take any of this into account when I prepared my interview for tonight."

"Can you feel it, Bill? Things are moving fast."

"Asitr, we have time enough. You fascinate me, and I don't want to let you go without trying to plumb your depths. Your experiences are unique. How you have been shaped by them needs to be examined. I want your insight. Share it with me and my listeners."

"I have issues with being set up as someone who can teach. I think that is what you have in mind isn't it, Bill?"

"I'm unclear what you mean, Asitr. I want to explore your personal philosophy, your politics, and your religion. I want to know what your lives have done to you."

"Politics and religion. Very divisive. Topped with a sprinkle of philosophy? Divisive and boring, Bill. I'm trying to narrow down why I'm here, and you are trying to stir the waters with divisive and boring. Like you said, I'm unique. So are your listeners. Like you and me, they each have their own path to follow. My path would be more helpful if it were laid out in stories. Each person could take what they need and process it into their own lives. I don't want to be like an on-line university."

"Now, what does that mean? Like an on-line university?"

"You know, here is your list of questions. If you give us enough correct answers you get a degree. No fussy discussions, challenging professors, comparing theories, testing ideas on other students, you know, those exercises that build the ability to think for yourself. Just memorize what we say is correct. They are like the FCAT in high school. You receive a stamp of approval, at best, and bypass the chance to understand how to learn, at worst."

"Look at what you just did, Asitr. You gave an opinion. Was that so hard? All I want is a little more opinion from you, and then we can get back to story-telling. For the sake of my audience, let's get inside your head."

"Okay, Bill. I hope you have an exit strategy."

"I don't go anywhere without it."

"I'll consider myself forewarned."

"Ha. *En Garde!* You're a funny man, Asitr. Let's get serious."

"I'll try."

"Let's start light. Favorite author?"

"Anonymous."

"I thought we were going to get serious."

"I am, Bill. There is a piece of poetry I've read over and over again for centuries. I'm fascinated by its endurance. I think I'm just now understanding its universal appeal. Nobody knows the author. I first read the poem in Minos, more than six thousand years ago. I've seen it in nearly all my lives."

"Sounds fascinating. Can you recite it?"

"The English version goes like this:
Here I sit, all broken hearted.
Came to shit and only farted.
I repeat, Asitr. I thought we were going to get serious."

"I'm quite serious, Bill. As a matter of fact, I see linkage between what we are doing now and the universal message of the poem. I don't want to exit my last life without leaving behind something of substance, as opposed to a temporary cloud."

"Asitr, stay out of advertising. Whatever it is you want to sell just became unmarketable."

"I'm not selling, Bill. I just want to narrow my list."

"If this were a court of law, I would ask to treat you as a hostile witness. My audience has some excellent questions they want asked. Will you respect them as my guests?"

"I'll try to be more patient, Bill. I got lost in our moment together. It must have been the dancing. Certainly, I'll push back our moment of inevitability for some polite time with your other guests. My apologies."

"Thank you, Asitr. You can be like an unruly child. You do understand, I don't believe in the inevitable."

"I know what you're saying, Bill. Forget what they say about death and taxes. I've lived many lives without paying taxes. Death and regret. In my experience, those are the inevitables. Death and regret."

"You have a dark philosophy, Asitr. What is the biggest regret you have in this life?"

"I regret I don't know why I'm here. My list is getting shorter, but I still have unrealistic hopes. Not everyone can be Frank Sinatra."

"You want to be Frank Sinatra? I expected more."

"The song, Bill. I'm referring to his song. You know, *I've had regrets, but too few to mention.*

I have too many regrets to mention and I don't want to chase rainbows into more regrets."

"Confession is good for the soul, Asitr. What is your greatest regret?"

"Lockjaw is collecting my stories to the Savant in a book. There are seventy stories. I've lived more than seventy lives. You may wonder how many more, but I will never tell you. I regret I'm too ashamed of those lives to share them with my grandson. Would you share your greatest regret with me, Bill?"

"I see. How about sharing more opinion? Which philosophers have had the biggest effect on your belief system?

"Quite a few, but it's all about that elephant thing."

"Elephant thing?"

"The old tale of the blind wise men and the elephant. Each wise man holding a different part of the animal in his hand. Each one describing a clear picture of the piece he is holding, but he holds just one piece, not the true design."

"Do you see all of that big truth?"

"Absolutely not, Bill. I don't think any man ever will. I've gathered enough experience to notice that all of those brainy guys are simply straining and squinting. I don't want to end up with a handful of elephant and proclaim I've found wisdom, but I can learn something by stitching together the descriptions of the other blind men, and imagine some good engineering possibilities for the separate parts to come together."

"You could wind up putting the ears on the elephant's back and declaring he has wings. How is that helpful?"

"I'm content to let the complete elephant remain invisible to me. I think it's God's will that we earnestly look while respecting there's too much to see."

"What an interestingly futile philosophy. I hope your views on religion have more potential to satiate a thirsty spirit."

"I'm not a very good source to talk to if you want to hear respect for religion, Bill."

"No? I'm a little surprised to hear you say that."

"I lived my first life in a city of religions. None of them were created by God. I found his temple in my gardens, the ecology of his creation, and in communion with people who search for truth. I listen for the voice of the spirit when it whispers warnings and inspiration. Organized religion has always left me with a dissonant spirit."

"That's pretty harsh, Asitr. You trust your own search is better off self-guided than following the lead of some of the greatest minds the world has ever produced?"

"Which one would you recommend I outsource my obligation to, Bill? Great minds don't really think alike.

"Are you saying you believe religion is like paint-by-number art? An inferior replacement for a sincere search?"

"Yes. It doesn't matter if they teach you to give your fortune to charity, amass fortunes as evidence God loves you, donate your money to the church, confess to another human, count beads, splash water on your head, memorize words, decapitate infidels, only eat foods without faces, eat mushrooms that make you see faces, eat fish on Fridays, meditate yourself into an alpha state, dance yourself into a frenzy, refuse to dance altogether, tease snakes, or beat yourself with whips. If you accept dogma as truth, then you have left the road, pulled up anchor, and darkened your beacon."

"Okay, I have a question one of my listeners wants me to ask you. This question is from SquareBobSpongePants13. I think it's a good post. He wants to know if you agree that more bad comes from religion than from philosophy?"

"I'm guessing what he means by bad is bloodshed and violence. I don't know the cumulative answer, Bill. If someone is forcing you to worship their choice of God, fight like hell. Is someone telling you their economic philosophy is better than yours? So what? If they attack, defend yourself. If your leaders attack them over philosophical differences, get new leaders. Pick a side as if you understand you will be judged for your decision. If you're an American, use your ballot but don't let them take your bullets. Find a prosecutor who understands the Ricco act. It's conspiracy when your leaders vote proposals into law without even reading them. You're a nation of laws. They're important. Stop riding the coattails of your better generations' accomplishments and protect what they handed down to you. Rethink everything, and then step up."

"Was there an answer to the question there?"

"Yeah, right ... Philosophy or religion, which is the bloodiest. Neither, they are tools, used to inflame. The vast majority of bloodshed is over love of money. It's not the reason your boys fight. It's the reason they're sent."

"So is this why you're here: to end the reign of demolicans and republicrats?"

"No, Bill. I can't vote. You pressed some buttons. Good profiling, I'm hoping the next batch of Americans get it right."

"Okay, this is a redundant question. Why are you here?"

"When I tell my next story, my list could narrow. Being an authority on ancient history and religion, you might enjoy it. The story involves my happy life as a scribe and ends with the most unpleasant death I ever suffered in all of my lives."

"Yes, I would enjoy that. Another tale from the era of prehistory?"

"No. My story begins in Babylon, at the very dawn of history."

"Were you someone we would all recognize? Alexander perhaps? Herodotus?"

"Both are dead by the time of my story but important in the telling. I was a scribe for Berossus. It begins in the period often called the twilight between history and myth."

"Berossus. The Bel-Re Satummu in the Esagila of Babylon? Leader of all organized Baal worship in the civilized world? Keeper of the largest library in all of mankind? Author of the *Babyloniaka*. You worked for him as a scribe?"

"Yes."

"Berossus and Herodotus? There are few faster downward spirals of presenting ideas, then flashing credentials, and finally, hurling insults, than trying to fix points of academic agreement when discussing those two."

"Yes, Bill. You can throw Manetho into the mix and you have the three authors responsible for shattering the time-lines of history, as taught in the western world."

"Manetho. Author of the classic work *Egyptica*, present in your story?"

"Indeed."

"What other names would I recognize?"

"The story is driven by the orders of the dead conqueror, Alexander. A secret plan to end the influence of the prophet

Zarathustra is revealed. Important in the story are the Egyptian, Manetho, who is possessed by the spirit of Baal Alayat, the Babylonian, Berossus, who is possessed by Baal Alazam, a phalanx of historians, traveling with the Greek ambassador, Megathenes, a powerful angel called Samayel, and the presence of a very aged librarian named Mazgabar. I, myself, was the venerable Mazgabar ... Bill?"

"Yes, I see. I was trying to total up the potential for a chaotic tale. The great Alexander, three world class historians, an ancient prophet, a renowned diplomat, a feeble librarian, two possessing spirits, and an angel we all know better as Satan? It sounds like a story of unverifiable confusion. Do you have the archaeological evidence to back this up?"

"Not exactly."

"You have no corroborating artifacts?"

"I agree human history in this period is entrenched in myth, resurrected only by archaeology, unless, like me, you were there at the time."

"But, you have no artifact? What do you mean when you say, 'not exactly'?"

"There is a book, not in my possession. I'm hoping the story will help me find it."

"Is that why you're here? To find a book? You lived all those lives to find this book?"

"No. I think of it as a family heirloom. The presence or absence of the mark of Alexander on the leather binding can help me narrow my list. The story, itself, centers on a confrontation that took place inside the Esagila hallways when Samayel announced a plan to replace Marduk's doctrines with his own strategy of malign neglect."

"Well I have to hear this story. You can tell it right after we do our FCC commitment to announce the obvious. It's time for station identification. Don't go away. We will be right back with a story of men and devils after this.

32

"**P**O WAS SO OVERLOOKED by the Asitr team." Otis silenced the marble and took it off the cart absentmindedly. He stared out the window without watching the transition between cart and bed. After setting the device down next to his leg, he wagged his head slowly and shrugged his shoulders before he continued.

"We should have given her some thought beyond assigning Hayak to protect her. In hindsight, not making contingency plans for the boy-girl possibilities was just dumb. It was kind of embarrassing to learn her back-story from Kae'Lairy on the moon."

A tap of the finger from the hand holding the marble in place activated Kae'Lairy's voice as he gave his brethren the account of Po's reaction to the mention of a book in her boss's collection.

*   *   *

AT A CAMPFIRE ON THE MOON

Po found a direction to expend her pent-up anger. She understood Asitr was looking for a book she had seen on Bill's desk earlier in the week. She knew it wasn't something he kept in his library. He said it was precious and priceless. Blaming Asitr for her world being turned inside-out, she pounced on an idea to make him go away.

Roiling around in her spirit were the dark temptations of a jilted lover, victimized by her own expectations. She was stuck in the muck of that funny human love.

Because these humans root their love in each other's imperfect natures, we are incapable of understanding the emotions that make the muck powerful. We can only shrug off the behaviors as sanctioned insanity. Only bad spirits would exploit the weakness.

Po's sanctioned insanity began when she first heard Bill Elliott on the radio in his inaugural season. She thought he ranted too much. Clearly, he was a little disorganized. His rants, she felt, were cries of pain from a genius who struggled to be properly understood. His disorganization, however, she felt was manageable.

Po, a Mensa member herself, sized up her love of organizing and capacity for patience then came to a conclusion. Bill Elliott needed her. She went to his office and told him so.

Bill gave her a job, and it turned into a life. She sensed the pressure he felt in his solitary world, and understood venting in on-air tirades was therapy for his diminished spirit.

When Po took the duties of contracts, bills, and fans off his shoulders, he told her she freed him. After he grew more comfortable with her, they often relaxed together as Bill read to her from ancient manuscripts.

For her duties, Po received a good check and a sense of basking in the glow of a sad genius who spent his off-air hours slumping under the weight of a mysterious past. She felt like the two of them were living in a gothic novel.

At times, she thought, Bill seemed to be two very different people sharing a single body. One was the recluse she believed knew so much, and cared for the world so much, it had crushed him. The other was an oddly shy man who had a boyish way of making her want to mother him. She was comfortable accommodating both of them.

In her diary, she wrote "I would do anything for Bill."

On the next page is written "... anything except roll over and play dead after the ungrateful, self-absorbed, pansy son of a bitch up and fires me!"

Now, she thought she knew the reason Bill wanted her out of the way. "Give him the damn decomposing old pile of precious, priceless crap!" she screamed at the radio, bringing her fist down on top of it for emphasis. The radio ceased to function.

Empowered after teaching her radio a lesson it would never forget, she charged out of her house and marched the two blocks to Bill's. For the second time in her life, she was going to tell Bill he needed her.

The crowd stopped her. The small group of men who circled his compound was still there. Added to the mysterious mess was a new group of people milling about the gate.

After a television studio truck pulled up to the small crowd, she paused long enough to hear the pretty reporter lady request that somebody in the knot around the gate should make some signs before she could put them on television.

Po didn't have to be a genius to understand her best option was to turn around and go home. She had another radio in the kitchen. She arrived just in time to hear Bill's voice say ..."

33

THE BILL ELLIOTT SHOW
On-air Wednesday

"AND WE ARE BACK. Let's get right to it. Asitr?"
"Yes, Bill?"
"You're going to tell this story just as you told the Savant?"
"Yes."
"Let's hear it."

*   *   *

FINALLY, THE TEAM ASSEMBLES

Otis tapped the marble to allow Dr. Milton to hear the Babylonian story introduced, then he tapped it again.

"I don't want interrupt the story to give you more information, Doc, so I'll tell you now. VanGrada and Googs pull into the coffee house parking lot a little late for the beginning of the show. Before they got out of the car, the two older men inside the coffee house came out to greet them. Both begged to ride with Jack and Googs.

'The kid from Kirksville drew the short straw,' they explained. 'He's got Ol' Frenchy 'til morning.'

"As they scrambled into the vehicle, the little yellow bus slid next to them, throwing gravel onto the rental. The garbled words, 'Be appeased,' blared from the torn woofer, jacked up to the volume usually reserved for a teenager showing off his first radio.

"Above the din, Ol' Frenchy screamed, 'You're late. You change plans like dirty underwear, not intuating dirty underwear changes plans. Don't repent on following.'

"He gave a circular motion with one finger, pointed to the road, kicked up more gravel and led the caravan to an overgrown gap in the trees just two miles down the road.

"The vehicles bounced and slid down a cratered, rocky, long-abandoned driveway until they had to stop at a solid treeline.

"Ol' Frenchy sprinted from the bus, flamethrower over his shoulder, and approached the car. 'Fifty yards to go, straight ahead through bumptious twists and turns. Sleepin' bags tonight and tents tomorrow. Follow up when you see the campsite is ready,' he said. 'You can call yourselves bein' in the danger zone, so watch your step, brothers. Get it? Stepbrothers? No? Good.'

"Without pausing to answer questions, he bounced, illuminated by headlights, through tall grass and large rocks until he disappeared into the trees.

"Wait for it," CSI said. Seconds later, an orange ball of flame showed through the gaps between trees.

"Got us a campfire," Ol' Frenchy shouted from the forest.

Led by the beacon of the flame, reduced into a manageable campfire, and the sound of Asitr's voice on the radio, the five men found the clearing where they would await the uncertain events of the night. Choosing sleeping bags from a stack near the fire, they settled in just in time to hear Mazgabar describe the power of Samayel's voice."

Otis tapped the marble again. "Okay, here's the story."

*   *   *

Paul Moore

RECKLESS ABANDON IN BABYLON

Ignore the shaking of my hands. I am here and safe. I wish you could see the place I have come from. It is the center of the world. The campfire of powerful men. Everyone says it is the place to be and the place to go.

This was true for me. I did well. My walls were trimmed in polished gold. My food was rich, served to me on plates of decorated stone. Labors, I had. They were labors of love.

Life was good, yet my hands still shake. An echo of a condition of my age or an echo of my last days of torture, I don't know. I suspect the memory of torture, as I remember my hands as old but steady. I choose to tell you about my last days.

I was an old man, who spent his life copying manuscripts and filing them into places where they could be found. I did the best I could, but it seemed no one but myself could follow my system for finding them. There were so many. Forty thousand. The copying scribes could renew and copy just so many. With my ancient hands, I was copying so few. While on my own time, I copied the older, less desired manuscripts.

From youth, the old scrolls fascinated my imagination because I wasn't yet allowed to see them. Curious, I was. Now I was old, I've seen them, and thought of them as my own. Covetous, I was.

Retired, I would have been. If only my master Berossus could have found someone to learn my filing system. I didn't like the idea of being separated from the obscure manuscripts. What loss, if they missed a turn at being copied. They, the roots of knowledge, were the ones most likely to fall into oblivion. In my system, they were the ones only I could find.

I especially was protective of the few written in languages that could no longer be read. Fascinated, I was, with the scraps of words so different and similar to the languages I did understand. They were my purpose. I had just a few not yet copied. In the end they cost me my happy life.

The New Year in Babylon, it was. Ceremonies are what we had. It was a time to serve at one of my ceremonial duties. This year, I was especially anxious to do well. We had two exceptional guests. One was a Greek named Megasthenes, the other an angel of mystery.

Both arrived the night before the ceremony. Megasthenes arrived on horseback with a caravan of librarians and scribes. The angel, Samayel, arrived atop the Etamananki in a flash of blue light. Both were given places of honor at the New Year's ritual.

I enjoyed the ritual. Front of the stage, I was, an imposing figure of wisdom. As dignitaries and kings of all the large cities and temples watched, we scribes laid flowers at the foot of the stairs leading to the Etemenanki.

The highest, it was, of all the high places in my city of Babylon. At the top of this ziggurat was the woman who awaited the return of Baal Marduk. Each New Year a different woman was honored. This year's woman was not at the ceremony. I was told she died from fright when Samayel appeared.

Berossus chastised me for fretting. 'She is only a decoration atop the structure' he said.

The Etemenanki. Below its base, and buried, was the brick of the famous Nimrod. A tower it is, built atop Nimrod's ancient structure.

Nimrod's old structure imprinted all the way to the beginning of mankind's survival of the flood. Our new lofty abode, above Nimrod's crumbled and buried tower was symbolic of our hand outstretched to our god, supplicating him to return. I believed we were enticing him with a female. I never considered her to be a decoration of flesh. What did my god want?

I was proud to be a part of the ritual. I had participated in eighty-five of them. Due to my long service and slowness of foot, I had the honor of placing the first bouquet. There I did stand, with all eyes on me, as my younger scribes would parade in front of me and leave their offerings as the litany was read, and the chorus of pilgrims would honor Marduk in many of his fifty names:

"Oh Lord, at thy going into the temple," Berossus did say.

"Be appeased," answered the chorus.

"Oh Prince, Lord Marduk, at thy going into the temple."

"Be appeased."

"Oh great hero, Enbilulu, at thy going into the temple."

"Be appeased."
"Be appeased Oh Lord, be appeased, Oh Lord."
"May thy house say to thee, be appeased."
"Be appeased, Oh Lord of Babylon."
"Be appeased."

This litany would continue until all the representatives of every temple and every city would ask that Marduk, in many of his names, would "be appeased". Then, it would start again. This time the gods who once claimed to be his superior would beg his appeasement and ask him to return to Earth. Berossus would say, "May Anu, the great father of the gods, say to thee ..."

The chorus answered. "How long will you remain in your present state? Is it not time for a change? Be appeased."

"May the great mountain, father Enlil, say to thee ..."

"How long? Be appeased."

The list of supplicant gods and great heroes went on and on. The great mother Ninlil, Ninurta, Shamash, Ea, Damkina, Nabu, Urash, Tashmetum, Nana, Madana, Baba, Adad, all were called by Berossus and all would plead, through the voices of the chorus, "Be appeased."

At the end of the ritual they proclaimed together, *"Oh, Lord, mighty one who dwells in Ekur let thine own divine spirit bring thee rest. Oh, thou who art the hero of the gods, may the gods of heaven and earth cause thine anger to be appeased."*

Finally, Berossus would speak with forcefulness for all of us in the Esagila. "Do not neglect Babylon, the city of thy rejoicing, Oh, Lord be appeased. Look favorably on Babylon and Esagila. Oh, Lord, be appeased, may they say to thee. The bolt of Babylon, the lock of Esagila, the bricks of Ezida restore thou to their places. Oh Lord, be appeased, may the gods of heaven and earth say to thee."

This is how it was done. As it was done in Sumeria, in the first language, it was done that way. I, myself, have copied these words from the time of Sumeria, and they never changed, until Samayel gained his ascendance.

I, Mazgabar, saw the change come while sitting in the dark. Hear how I became witness, participant, and victim of the events that spun out of a parade of dignitaries, the angel Samayel, Megasthenes, and the late arriving Manetho.

The rush of change started in the dark hours of the morning after the New Year's ceremonies. I was asleep in the library but made wake by visits to my master Berossus. I didn't know upon awakening that it was the day I would lose faith in the gods of the earth.

The visits started with Megasthenes. He came as the leader of the Greek commission of preservation. This commission was sent to carry on the work of a pilgrim who had visited our city. The first Greek I had ever seen. His name was Herodotus. In the time he visited, we withheld from him our library. It was our right, because it was ours to say.

Then the Greeks returned in a different way. They came as warriors. Their leader was a great and terrible conqueror, Alexander of the west, King of the cities who had defeated the mighty Persians when the Persians ruled Babylon.

I saw him enter our great city when he was victorious, and I was fearful. Soon, I was grateful to see he loved the Esagila. I gave thanks when he spared the books. Next, I was puzzled to see him change. Our city conquered him.

Alexander's dress and manners became nearer our own. My people were comforted, but his Greek warriors were displeased. They were so displeased, they did something unthinkable. They plotted against him.

Some of his most trusted units came together to decide they would return home and leave Alexander to wear dresses, drink eastern wines, dally with eunuchs, and worship Marduk. These men, so far away from home and so deserving of returning in glory, were now willing to return in disgust. Alexander did not let this happen. His loyal generals made war on the mutineers.

A warrior of high intellect was sent to guard the Esagila on the night Alexander broke the rebellion. His name was Megasthenes. The same Megasthenes who has now returned as the leader of the commission of preservation.

My lord Berossus talked with him long into the night of rebellion. They shared stories and theories. Berossus allowed him into the library. I was called to show him our collection of books in the Greek language. Likable, he was. A complex thinker who grasped things quickly and theorized too fast for my mind to follow. Berossus not only kept up with him, he plotted ahead of him. Berossus planted a seed into his head that night. When Megasthenes returned, I saw the seed bore fruit.

Sleeping, I was, on a couch in the library. When I awoke, I could see a shadow in the moonlight. Fear, it was, that kept me silent. I had been told not to fall asleep in the library. I had been caught before, and beaten, but was too curious not to sneak forward and peek. I saw my master. Why would Berossus stand in the great hallway at the dark part of the morning?

The answer came as a tail upon the question. Greetings were exchanged, and then two shadows embraced. Berossus spoke the name, Megasthenes. Megasthenes spoke the name, Berossus. At first, they conferred quietly. I couldn't hear the words. They spoke in the whispers of men discussing a secret. Then, one word enlivened Megasthenes. Suddenly excited, he no longer whispered.

"Magi? How goes it with them?" He asked.

"The rules are in place. We have reached an agreement," answered my master, Berossus.

"An agreement?" Megasthenes spoke as if surprised. "Not what I expected. Where did your hatred go?"

"I hate them more than ever. I'm watching them."

"Then, after I arrive in Seleucia, you can watch them being slaughtered."

"The Persians have had enough of them?" My master's question showed it was now his turn to be surprised.

"It is we who have had enough. As soon as I inform the Persians of the Greek opinion, the Persians will also feel so disposed."

"Excellent," agreed Berossus. "It will be welcomed in all the civilized world as a blessing."

"Who will be next?" Megasthenes again surprised Berossus. "Don't you wonder, good man, that your own belief will be next?"

This, thought I, was too bold a question to ask. It sounded as a threat.

"The world will always deal with a religion that has but one voice," answered my master. "The Magi allow everyone's spirit to choose. You can't negotiate with a religion of one million voices. We will be here forever."

Footsteps, I heard, and another shadow stepped into the moonlight. He was Manetho, the most powerful priest in the land of Egypt, famous even in our land.

"Greetings to the great Megasthenes," he said. "I have news from home. Good evening to our host."

Berossus, thought I, waxed angry as soon as the voice spoke. He spun and faced the man who spoke the words. "Where have you been, and why have you missed the ceremony? Why do you greet my guest first and myself last?"

"We will blame it on my memory. I forgot I was in a sovereign country. In Egypt you wouldn't be addressed at all unless you were needed. You wouldn't speak unless asked."

Manetho angered me with his disrespect. How could he be so unafraid of his host? Had the Egyptian Greeks aligned themselves with the western Greeks? Was there going to be a united front from Alexander's splintered parts? Again, the answer was tail to the question.

"Ha! Ever the snippy little Dirtwing, aren't you?" My master turned his expression around and approached Manetho with his arms outstretched. They embraced and kissed each other on the cheeks. Now, I thought, they might be brothers.

I was walking the wrong path of facts. It took long moments of eavesdropping and then, finally, the coming of Samayel to teach me where to find a fresh path. I'll tell you what I learned before the angel Samayel joined everyone in the hallway.

Megasthenes and the two priests were here to make a pact. Several pacts. The first was to do what they could to wipe out the corrupting ideas of the Magi.

The second was a quickly agreed upon system for turning over all the documents in the Esagila to the Greeks, the Persians, and the Egyptians. Berossus organized a plan where they would first turn over all the documents of which we possessed four copies or more. On a return trip, the commission would pick up the rest. This plan would give enough time to have copies made for Babylon, Greece, Egypt, and Persia.

The third pact was more complicated and became more divisive than cooperative. Each leader insisted on changes within the spheres over which the other two had influence.

Megasthenes wanted Manetho to stop his drive toward turning the pantheon of Egyptian gods into a monotheistic religion. Berossus agreed. "It is no different than the magi corruption," he argued.

Berossus wanted Megasthenes to promote Baal worship in the land of India. Manetho disagreed. "The dust from Tiamat darkens that future."

Manetho wanted Megasthenes to tell his people how their gods had traveled from the ark, to Egypt, through Babylon, and came thrice-corrupted to Greece. Berossus was livid to be considered a third-place corrupter. "We were the first to corrupt," he boasted. "Soon you would reduce us to alien life forms, out of place in the matters of creation."

Megasthenes foresaw the disagreement and came prepared to offer a compromise. He proposed that a new religion should manifest itself. It should contain the obvious truths of all three beliefs and present itself to the world at a future time when any of their three systems should start to disintegrate.

This is the moment they stopped conferring. This is the moment I was hit with ugly truth. A blue light flickered and the angel Samayel stood among them without the warning of footsteps, and without the substance of shadow.

"What do you mean? *Start* to disintegrate?" He bellowed. "Define that. I hear the death rattle of two civilizations and the birth pangs of another. Two of you have already collapsed, and the other will become a spoiled child." His voice, I felt through my skin. It felt powerful.

All three heads bowed. Nobody spoke. I was certain he could hear me breathe. Afraid, I was, already, from realizing my religion was being negotiated. I was disturbed to see that truth was not in the negotiation.

I quickly added a wall to the darkness between us, fearing Samayel's eyes could penetrate both wall and darkness. He seemed larger than he did at the ceremony. The other three seemed much smaller. This is what the angel told the three:

"I'm here to assist you. You try too hard to make plans, but the truth is a turtle cannot decide to hibernate in summer and roam through winter. A plan must come with realistic expectations. Listen to what I expect from you."

"Berossus," he said. "You tread water. Your beloved Marduk is never going to have power in heaven. He is losing his influence on earth. Your devotion is a cry for guidance."

"He will return," Berossus insisted. "Remember how you need him."

"Will you be here to greet him, or be dissipated with words from my mouth?"

"What must I do to appease you Lord?" Berossus bowed, he sounded unsure of his loyalties.

"Listen. Then act." Samayel's response was a command, not advice.

"Manetho." Samayel spoke the name crisply, and Manetho took a step forward, standing stiff, unbowed.

After studying the Egyptian through narrowed eyes, Samyayel spoke. "For you, I have different concerns but the same instructions. Listen. Then act."

"I acknowledge your superiority," answered Manetho. "Propose to me what you will. I will consider everything but commit to nothing. I am free of Marduk."

"You will bow again." My master hissed at Manetho.

"Great cats of Cambyses! Fools!" Samayel made his voice to be as large as his stature. "Succinctly implied within my instructions to listen is the inference that you *must* prevent your own mouths from blurting noises, while your ears are thirsting for words of reason. Even the Greek has learned to listen without speaking, and he's weighted down with the impairment of being fully human."

The angel had made his point. The growl of the word *"human"* bounced out of the hallway and into the open air.

Samayel, now in control, bowed to the frightened Megasthenes and asked him, politely, if he would excuse himself, so the three "brothers from heaven" could solve their differences in a matter suited to their own "species." Consent and exit were quick.

After promising to return that evening for dinner, the future ambassador of Greece to Persia and India hurried to his quarters and immediately pursued the goal of becoming dream-smashing drunk.

As Megasthenes left the building, Manetho and Berossus stood with heads bowed. Samayel let them linger in their pose for nearly a minute. Finally, he said, "Speak."

In unison, Berossus and Manetho spoke, "Our respect, Lord Samayel. What do you wish?"

The angel addressed them, telling each how he saw them.

"Berossus and Manetho.

"Alazam and Alayat.

"Symbolized by the moon. Symbolized by the sun.

"Power behind the kings of Babylon. Power behind the pharaohs of Egypt.

"One who grovels before a missing god. The other a pretender to godhood.

"Lover of red. Lover of blue.

"Astrologer. Astronomer.

"Enlightener of Megasthenes. Confounder of Ptolemy.

"Immovable object. Bender to the winds.

"I am here to be recognized as your irresistible force. I have a new focus for you."

Again, the silence. Again, I had to cover my mouth to quiet my breathing. When silence enough passed for Samayel to accept submission, he promoted new plans for their future.

"Do you recognize something different about the Greeks? Don't answer. I know you don't. There is a difference we should embrace. They are becoming more. I know the idea is bitter. Soon, the flavor will sweeten. You forget the strategy. Never give up the strategy because you embrace a tactic. What is the strategy? Don't answer as Berossus. Answer as Alazam. What is the strategy?"

"Put off the inevitable, lord."

"Manetho? Answer as Alayat."

"I agree with Alazam. The strategy will always be to defy the inevitable."

"Alazam. What tactics have you chosen for forwarding the strategy?"

"I keep the voice of Marduk alive, to seduce the world away from the pathway of the inevitable."

"Alayat? Do you have a tactic?"

"Avoid the leadership of Marduk, but embrace his knowledge."

"Oblivious and more oblivious. I wish I could explain this to Marduk, himself. Try to understand." Samayel glowed. It wasn't bright, it didn't cast shadow, but he glowed while he educated Alazam and Alayat.

"The Greeks are an evolved tribe," he began. "They enjoy a speaker with ideas and logical designs of communication. They enjoy art as gifts of inspiration. Mathematics is naked before them.

"Most importantly, the least of them is encouraged to be a worthy individual. This belief will lead to them stepping into our dreams ... our dreams. Did you expect me to say nightmares?

"This is the twilight hour, my little brothers. Look into the gray, then find what will step in with the light. What I see is an idea of personal freedom. This freedom will grow until there is chaos. Each man will be his own emperor, and each man will squander the common good for his own ends. The human will become repugnant in Heaven.

"Alayat. Tell me what you are thinking."

"I'm thinking you are mistaken. The rare enlightened person is believable. Clusters of enlightenment, possible. An entire tribe? Unthinkable. If it were true ..."

"Alazam. You have plans with the Greek, Megasthenes. Tell me about them."

"He will allow himself to be possessed. I promoted the idea when he came with Alexander. I had decided to possess him myself, but I no longer wish to follow through."

"Follow through."

"I have a renewed influence here," my master protested. "If the Greeks are becoming dangerous to our strategy, I have to stay."

"Don't fear the Greeks. Embrace them. They will do our work for us if we leave them alone. Fear the Magi."

My master, Berossus, sputtered a laugh, but caught himself, asking, "What's dangerous about those fortune tellers?"

"Dangerous?" Samayel glowed brighter and glided toward my master. "They have the ability to turn the Greek attitude into a spiritual movement. We can't let this Greek revolution embrace the idea of humility. Ideas cross borders and infect the ones they touch. The Magi influence has to end."

"But lord Samayel, Megasthenes is going to convince the Persians to destroy the Magi. He doesn't need a new spirit to accomplish the mission."

"I don't want them destroyed. I want them discounted."

"In what manner?" asked Manetho, stepping toward Samayel's light.

"Add to their books. Divert their path. Offer them too many branches, and scoff at their roots. It is already begun."

"Already begun?" My master was surprised. "Under my nose and within my territory?"

Ignoring the question, Samayel continued. "Their prophet, Zarathustra, is being corrected. His very name is changed. I have convinced his priests there has been a mistranslation. He has lost his tribal name."

"No longer known as *One Who Owns Feeble Old Camels*?" Manetho sounded amused.

"He has a name to go along with the new books. He is now, 'Bringer of the Golden Dawn'."

"And what of the new books?" Berossus asked the question with impatience.

"You will see them soon. Once again we have to share equal importance with the Creator."

Manetho sounded unconvinced. "The Magi will accept all of this?"

"Most," answered Samayel. "It's not the flock I am concerned with. They are illiterate. They believe what they're told. There are some priests we need to find."

"Why so important?" Manetho let his doubts show in the tone of his voice.

"There's a new field of holes."

The answer silenced Manetho, but enlivened Berossus. "Marduk has returned?" Berossus turned his face to the ceiling and spread his palms as he asked the question.

"If only he were here," Samayel answered, "I would not have to educate you."

"But lord Samayel..."

"Listen first, fool. There is a field of holes. There are but three holes, but they will predict the place and time for the coming of a king. He won't be someone we will welcome. Use this foreknowledge. We have an opportunity, through Megasthenes, to dismantle a prophecy. Are you sure Megasthenes will be possessed?"

"He affirmed it just before you arrived. I have a different spirit in mind for him."

"Your brother, Manetho?" Samayel scoffed.

"Herakles," was the quiet reply my master gave, as if he were embarrassed to say it.

The name must have been a complete surprise to Samayel and Manetho. Manetho tried to bury a sound coming from his throat. It came out choked, then exploded into laughter. Next, Samayel joined, and the laughter raced through the hallways like the rattle of cranes in rolling thunder. The echoes made me clasp my ears and drop to my knees. Before the laughter stopped, I pulled myself into a corner.

I knew the name from many sources. There was the Herakles who terrified the world before the flood. There was the Herakles of the Greeks. Father a god, mother a human. I believed they were the same, but softened by time. Then, there was the Herakles in the animal games.

Each Saturday there were games in the pavilion. Tradition, it was, for animals to fight. A popular game was battle between a pack of dogs and a baboon.

Old, I was, before I witnessed a baboon win. Dogs would die. Some were crippled and put to death for the sake of mercy. The fierce baboon's long teeth would score him victories, but in the end, he would be torn apart. Every time, until the great baboon Herakles arrived.

I, myself, knew things about the baboon and my master Berossus. I knew things that caused me moments of curiosity, but never a guess as to what these things could mean. These pieces fell together with words overheard, and my moment of understanding was melting my fear.

My fear was a candle, standing cold and horrified, until anger, like a red-hot poker thrust into its center, melted my inhibitions from the inside, and only hot anger stood where the candle had been. Can you see how the pieces fit? Let me tell you before imagination lead you to other dark thoughts, cursing you twice.

"Berossus bought the great ape from a caravan. He gave it to trainers who begged for the privilege of training him. "He is a prize. The biggest baboon ever on earth," is what they said. In the end, they all agreed he could never be trained.

Berossus trained him in the time it takes to make a camel kneel for mounting. Without leash, and obedient to my master's voice, Herakles reintroduced himself to the trainers by bowing in front of them, walking into his cage, and closing the door behind him. Impressive, it was.

Each of the trainers began making plans for the big baboon to perform in the great circus. Berossus forbade their plans. "He is my beast," he said, "and he will fight the dogs."

In his first exhibition, he made the crowd gasp. The first charging dog was plucked out of the air by the mouth of Herakles. The second dog was seized by his back legs and swung like a club. This contest ended with whimpering dogs cowering at the walls, awaiting their turn for execution. Herakles seized each by their faces and shook them until their necks did snap.

More terrifying than the performance, was the joke of Berossus when I asked him how such a thing was possible. "The beast is big," he said. "His thirst for bloody fun was small. I've given him a more entertaining spirit. A perfect match. Would you like to get in the game? I can find a new spirit for you as well. Imagine ... Mazgabar! Wild man! Fighting scribe of the Esagila!"

Terrifying was the joke. Worse, were the facts. My master wasn't really Berossus. He was Baal Alazam, a possessor of man and facilitator for a possessor of beasts.

Now I knew, and now I knew I had to listen, then act. Mushka on me, I had been serving a lie. Now, to honor my own human spirit, I would meddle. To confound a plan to defy the inevitable, I listened intently and learned.

"Let me see if I follow your plan." said Samayel. "You have convinced an important man to surrender his body and spirit. He is, no doubt, expecting an improvement in abilities?"

"He wants to enhance his position for a reach into the Athenian inner circle."

"You were going to reward him with a mad and dysfunctional Anakim?"

I could feel embarrassment in Berrossus' response. "I have rethought, Lord Samayel."

"Did you desire his own guards to murder him before he arrived in the Seleucid court?"

"At the time, I didn't see his importance. I had no other to offer him."

"I see. I too have done some rethinking. Alayat, you are about to become a Greek.'

"Not I, Lord Samayel. I have my own plans."

"I think your plans are complete. You have finished your history?"

"I have."

"You have taken the pharaohs of your cities, strung them in a line as pharaohs of the nation, destroyed the monuments that betray the deception, and added centuries to the civilization of Egypt. The soul you possess has no idea you have done so?"

"He hasn't seen the world since he agreed to be possessed."

"Awake him. Convince him he has suffered amnesia, and then tell him what he needs to believe. You have two days. Then, you will take the Greek."

"I will show respect, Samayel, but I recognize that you can't make me do this."

"Are you going to test me?"

"I know you sit in Heaven and prosecute the humans before the Creator, but you don't have his protection. Has your rebellion cost you the right to judge freely?"

"Don't misstep here, Alayat."

"Dissipate me, and the Lord of Heaven will judge you, immediately. Am I correct?"

"You think too much and go forward with your thoughts too boldly, Alayat. For the sake of Marduk, I will spare you, but I leave you without my protection."

He was there, and then he was gone. Between there and gone was a blue flash, followed by silence. Berossus broke the silence with an admonishment I felt were equal parts of respect and relief. "I think you played him too hard, brother. He may have taken both of us out of life."

Manetho surprised me. "Don't you ever welcome the world of nothing? To dwell among the missing? Often, I welcome the idea of dissipation. Do not to try to be my master."

"You needn't have a master to be cooperative. Honor our pact, and don't chase allies away."

"I will not possess the Greek."

"No need, brother. I will. Tonight at dinner. Today, I will have Mazgabar bring me the old books. None of them will reach the libraries. They will burn before the sun sets."

Relieved, I was, to hear their steps trail down the hall and out of the building. The weight of what I heard set on me all at once. I had until sunset to save my books and a foolish Greek.

The sun was not risen, but there was a ribbon I couldn't call light or dark. Like the twilight mentioned by Samayel, I recognized the fleeting ribbon as the crucible where the old is no more, and the new is undefined. Like Samayel, I decided to make an impact on what the new would bring with it from the old.

Run around the library, I did. Ran to meet Berossus and Manetho before they could leave the area. I knew if I bumped into them now, I could get an early start on my day.

Manetho congratulated me for my love of duty and my will to start my work with the rising of the sun. Berossus grunted a welcome, then instructed me to organize the scribes so the necessary books could be separated and delivered.

"I will be happy to do so." I said, with truth in my heart.

Taking time to plan before I started my tasks, I realized I was going to do something special. In the twilight moment, I recognized what was to come. With a forward-thinking vision and knowledge of the plots of others, I felt confident. What could go wrong?

Before my assistants arrived, I gathered the scrolls, parchments, and books Berossus wanted burned. Of those with four or more copies, I made piles. One pile to be sent to Egypt with Manetho for the new library of Alexander, another for the Greek ambassador, a third pile to be taken to Greece with the preservation commission, and the fourth pile for the fire.

After separating, I gathered the old manuscripts which had less than four copies. Happy, I was, to see there were few. Confident, I was, I had time to finish my plan.

I started with the books of Enoch. Three manuscripts were copied and ready. One, only, did I need to transcribe. Nearly finished, I was, when my scribes began to enter the Esagila. As they entered, I gave them instructions.

All the books my master allowed to be sent away were placed into three piles. Leather pouches were prepared and labeled. Each library was to receive an equal set. I promised a reward for an early finish, then told them to inform me when they were done. I myself, would check each collection before they were dispersed.

After the instructions were given, I went to my office to copy the last book to be saved. I called this set of engravings on goat skin, the *Nameless Book*.

This collection was rumored to have stories which had been read on the ark, when the temptation to curse God for the bobbing loneliness of endless water needed to be appeased by distraction.

I often wondered what distractions lay in the curious script. I believed I may never learn the language, but held hopes that someone in Persia, Greece, or Egypt could bring those stories alive again.

The thick leather covering also added to the mystique. There was an engraved gold depiction of a circle, made with many hands. One set of tiny hands intersected the circle. One hand on the inside, one hand on the outside. The symbolism was something I never saw in any other culture we had preserved, and it drew me in. Strong, was my feeling. Protective, I was.

I let the thought enter my head that maybe something could go wrong and gave in to my doubts. This book needed extra protection, is what I told myself. The mark of Alexander would be what I would use as a ward against Berossus.

Putting away my quill and picking up my engraver's tools, I set myself to finish the leather coverings. First, I duplicated the circle of hands. After finishing the fourth covering, I began to engrave the mark of Alexander onto the back cover. I finished only one cover before being summoned to visit the commander of the Esagila guard.

I made plans with the guard for where and when we would meet for the book burning. On the way back to the library, I took time to sit and think about my plans. I found them flawless. What could go wrong?

From my own purse, I arranged for an afternoon feast. Figs, lamb, rice, and wine were the rewards I presented to my workers. "When all the pouches are filled," I told them, "we will celebrate good work done quickly."

The celebration gave me the distraction I needed to slip the outlawed words into the traveling pouches. Of the four nameless books, I chose the one with the mark of Alexander for traveling to Egypt. The library they were building was to have the name of Alexander, and the choice seemed appropriate. I had time left over for figs and wine. Puffed, I was, with pride in my cunning. All was going well.

Even the whim of illness seemed to smile on me. Manetho took sick. He sent me notice he would not be at the dinner with Berossus and Megasthenes. I was to be in charge of loading his library for travel. When I finished the task, there was still time before dinner.

My scribes delivered the books for burning to the guard. Berossus, I knew, would be at the river for his ritual bathing. Manetho was ill in bed. All were busy, save myself and Megasthenes. Opportunity, I had, to be alone with him.

Megasthenes greeted me with respect, and he had questions for me concerning the packing of the books. The thought behind the questions revealed he had more than a dutiful attention to their safety. Comforted, I was. Yet suddenly, a thought. I wasn't prepared to warn him about his bad decision to enslave his spirit.

I had taken this part of my design for granted. I too easily assumed I could rearrange his thinking as simply as I could rearrange a shelf of parchment. Realizing this was the un-thought thing that could go wrong, I pushed recklessly ahead. There was nothing to do but overextend myself.

"Your spirit", I started, "is a good one. Only a fine spirit can love the history of time and the paths we choose while following time's walk."

"Thank you, and well-put, venerable scribe," he said. "Berossus is lucky to have you."

"Why would a wise man surrender his spirit?" I jumped in with abandon. Recklessness was ruling my mind.

Megasthenes was reaching for wine, but stopped and eyed me like I was a frog who jumped on his table. Softening the look, he smiled and asked, "Share this wine with me?"

I could see he was cautious. Perhaps he suspected a coincidental conversation.

Reckless to the point of blunt and in-artful, I was. Sweating and devoid of sense, I broke courtesy again and snatched the first glass of wine he poured and drank it straight down, without even waiting for him to pour his own. I recognized I was doing these things, but I seemed unable to stop myself. Never had I been this nervous.

Out of a sack I brought with me, I removed his copy of the nameless book.

"This book," I said. "Our steps through time. Stories from those who lived before the flood, and traveled aboard the ark. Tales from people who told stories that echo, still, in all the corners of the world. Those stories are in here. I can't read the words. There are people in India and Persia who might. Our very first steps through time. Would you trade the eye-witness report of their current events for the lies of Ginjiis, bad spirits, or false gods? Could anything be more foolish? Perhaps, good sir, to surrender your spirit, give your mind to slavery, and allow another to use your position and intellect."

Megasthenes sat silently and closed his eyes. I, myself, was unsure if he was going to allow me to continue in life. Had my point been accepted? I stumbled on. "There is no difference between the two in principle. To make a lie of the past or make a lie of your life. Why allow your name to be a hiding spot for a liar with no regard for what makes you the man you really are. Would a wise Greek scholar be fooled so thoroughly he could follow through with such a dark deal? Honorable Megasthenes ... make your mark in time with your own steps."

It was the turn of Megasthenes to drain his glass of wine. He couldn't consider my meaning to be coincidental conversation any longer. Nervous, he was, and he looked toward the doorway to his parlor and then toward the entry to the kitchen. "Outside," he said forcefully. "Servants have ears. I want to show you something."

For the second time since I lay in the dark and found the courage to meddle, I was unsure that nothing would go wrong. I lost more confidence when I saw where I was being led. We were going into the compound where the performing animals were caged. He was walking with foreknowledge of the area.

I followed, as Megasthenes turned to enter the aisle where one special animal was kept. Yes, he was, and I followed like a possessed man with no will to escape destruction. We stopped before the dispassionate gaze of the great baboon Herakles.

"What do you see in the face of this creature," asked Megasthenes.

Afraid, I was, struck mute and trembling. My jaw quivered. My hands trembled.

Megasthenes saved me the embarrassment of a weak reply. "Let me tell you a secret, recently revealed to me. Do you know that this creature is the greatest of all the killing beasts in Babylon because he is possessed by a spirit not his own? I, too, have wanted more than could be mustered from my own abilities. On my first trip to Babylon, I suspected the truly great people of my country would outperform me in the duties of higher public service. I did not accept this. My people honor great achievements. I truly do want my actions to bring great achievement in the time I live in. Therein resides the temptation."

Speech tried to find my mouth, but Megasthenes put his hand to my lips. "Please let me finish," he said. "I drank myself into unconsciousness this morning. When I awoke, I passed by this cage and stopped to watch him. He doesn't have the instincts he was brought here with. This is no great beast. He is a consumed beast, with another's will, and another's thoughts. Understanding this, my friend, is a temptation-breaking realization. You come too late to save me. I am proud to have saved myself. I suggest you focus on your true mission."

Earlier, I had lost my faith in Marduk in the span of one conversation. In listening to Megasthenes, I began to believe that somewhere, somehow, an unseen hand was making things right. Feeling confidence again, I happily informed Megasthenes I believed my true mission was finished. "Let us be proud to be men of ability and integrity." That is how I put it. Puffed up, I was, with pride.

"Please be careful." he warned me. "The price for removing items from the Esagila without permission is severe."

"Stretched and burned," I said, "But I am finished without being suspected. What could go wrong?"

The stretching started the next morning. Slowly done, it was. Berossus was there through it all. "Greek mercenary." Those are the words he used, when he spit on my face.

Somehow, forbidden books were found in the bags intended for Athens. He didn't say how. He seemed satisfied there were no more with the Egyptian or Persian collections.

I remember a sunrise and many more hours. I felt my spine dislodge from my hip. Shaking my body, like Herakles would shake a dog, I fought the pain with more pain. I tried to make my own neck snap, but my mind no longer ruled my body, and I could only manage to increase the shaking in my hands. The sight of me made Berossus laugh. Helpless, I was. Helpless to stop his entertainment.

When the coals were brought into the room, I no longer cared. As they shoveled them below where I hung, I felt oddly cold. Finally, a welcome whoosh. Movement carried me away to be here with you and safe."

34

"Y OU'VE LIVED in interesting times, Asitr."

"Don't you know it."

"So, it's safe to say Megasthenes never found the field of holes?"

"My guess is the prophecy was never disrupted."

"We are talking about the Star of Bethlehem, am I right?"

"I wouldn't preach it as fact, Bill, but yes. I believe three hundred years after Megasthenes arrived in Persia, the three Magis began their journey after stars lined up in the new field of holes."

"So, you truly were at a crossroads with multiple detours. Jesus is announced in the east, Satan replaces Marduk, western philosophy begins its ascent, and the brothers Baal, Alazam, and Alayat go their separate ways."

"I couldn't say your last statement was accurate, Bill. They had differences."

"Well, I think it's safe to say, with Alazam dissipated, they're no longer a pact."

"Perhaps, Bill, but I can't rule out the possibility that Alayat could soon join Alazam 'among the missing' in the 'world of nothing'."

"So, another revelation of what still remains on your list. You want to find a book, or perhaps you want to dissipate Baal Alayat. Anything else?

"What to do with Alayat is a hard call to make, but I believe he knows he's a trapped spirit."

"A hard call? What do you mean?"

"Alazam was an easy judgment. Alayat is more complicated. How would you profile him, Bill? The Alayat from my mother's story was ready to roast me on a golden calf, but he blinked out at the first sign of trouble. Would you say he was a coward?"

"He didn't sound fearful of Samayel at the library in Babylon. He, literally, stood up to Satan."

"Okay, Bill, let's say he's not a coward. Was he playing a role with Alazam in a plan to recruit the Bombag?"

"Just playing devil's advocate, Asitr, let's say he was. Why would a tribe of less than one hundred people be important?"

"They wouldn't be, today, unless there were coveted resources in their home. Back then? We're talking about a time when one hundred people of faith and principle were a prize. The temples of the fallen ones would compete for their allegiance."

"Keeping faith didn't do them much good."

"Not in the short life, Bill. At least they weren't looking over their shoulders for the inevitable to come."

"Alright, Asitr, let's say a tribe with the Bombag's principled nature exists today. You know, I mean a country, or culture. Who would that tribe be? In your opinion."

"You're very clever, Bill. You ask purposeful questions. What is the purpose of that question?"

"I don't know what you mean. I thought maybe you could say something nice about the country you are in. I set you up pretty well. Go ahead, wax poetic."

"Poetry again?" Are you are trying to turn your audience against me? This is bad dancing, Bill, but I'll play. I call this poem,

Not So New World Order.
You are the very model of a modern major funeral.
Digging holes and throwing dirt, assisting your own burial.
Letting go the future, parting eco from the nomical.
And all the while declaring you are just so darn phenomenal.

"There, you have it, with apologies to *Pirates of Penzance,* I've waxed poetic. I dedicate the poem to all the great civilizations who buried themselves. I don't see the benefit to you. Let's get back to why I'm here."

"I'm just helping you with your list, Asitr. Why so impatient?"

"I know you're desperate, Bill. I'm not dancing anymore. My traps are set and my purpose is at hand. You know what's going on. Ask me something pertinent."

"I decide which questions to ask on my show."

"If I am a poor guest, under the rules of hospitality, you have the right to toss me out."

"You're an arrogant little man, Asitr."

"I humbly agree, Bill. I claim the protection of Heaven. I can stand up straight and make eye contact with your navel. I have a penis. Arrogant. Little. Man. You nailed it."

"Sheesh. You win. I have a proposal. I want you in my studio for tomorrow's show."

"I accept. I've already made arrangements."

"Is that right?"

"I propose the rules of the campfire, Bill. The rules of hospitality just won't do anymore."

"So, you want to be fair. I get my say, and you get a vote. You haven't thought everything through, Asitr."

"I will be serious. Judgment is a terrible and holy responsibility."

"How soon can you be here?"

"Very soon. We've blue-toothed tonight's show while traveling. We're very close."

"I'll have accommodations ready for you. I strongly suggest you read the book before the show tomorrow."

"The book. You have it?"

"Think of it as my gift to you."

"Perhaps your trap for me?"

"People. Dear listeners. I can see your emails. I don't have answers tonight. We still have an hour and a half left in the show, but I'm done. For the rest of the night, you are going to hear music, not answers. So ... you have my apologies, enjoy the music, have a very good evening, and tune in tomorrow.

"To my disingenuous guest, I say *'Skarrar'* and *'sheesh kamushka'.*"

"Disingenuous? *Hooga mushka, dipnot. Skamoosh.* Remember the requirement for honesty at the campfire, Bill."

35

HARBINGER INSTITUTE
April 1, 2025

A TAP OF THE FINGER silenced the marble seconds into Bill's first musical selection. Otis hummed a piece of the melody before he addressed Dr. Milton. "Do you recognize the tune, Doc? That's Po's favorite bumper music, the JED song, 'Dancing on the Edge of Time'. It's a sweet melody with overtones of melancholy. Because of timing and mood, Po heard it as martial music as she marched toward Bill's house.

"During Asitr's story of his life as a Babylonian scribe, Po began connecting memories of living with the two Bills and meshed them with fragments from Asitr's story. At first, she thought she may be swallowed up by insanity, but soon, an eye blinked behind a curtain of moss. She listened, trying to believe any other possible conclusions for what she was thinking, but conceded to reality.

"For Po, the fall from ridiculous heights of worshipful love to unpalatable depths of anger over sudden, unexpected rejection, was only warm-up. The moss had fallen, and she could see Bill for the first time. An image of her future wedding invitations came to mind and she laughed at the good fortune of finding out in time.

The Nguyen family would like the pleasure of your company
Come help us celebrate a wedding
Our daughter, Po Nguyen, and Baal Alayat
will bind themselves together
At blankety blank PM
On the umpteenth day of NEVER! NEVER! NEVER!
In the rites of Holy matrimony

"Another shock jolted her as she realized she was not so lucky. Raging hormones didn't help her think. She tried, but all of it, twisted and moshed together, made her crazy. I was in position to witness her metamorphosis from victim-in-the-dark to advocate.

"I was startled when the stairway door on the roof flew open and Po sprinted past the box. She ran to the ledge and stopped. Directing her rage skyward, she raised a fist and screamed, 'I didn't ask for this. Why are you doing this to me? Is inter species mating still a capital crime for the planet?"

"Po looked at the street below, then jumped on top of the ledge, shouting toward the toe-nail moon. 'I'm not jumping. You're going to have to push me. Go ahead. Push me.'

A small gust of wind caught her off-guard. Fighting too hard against the gentle puff, she almost fell into the street. After catching herself, sweaty and shivering, she growled in a whisper. "You passive aggressive excuse for a God. Is that all you've got?'

"When the gust died down, she slouched, teetering on the edge until she jumped back onto the roof top, feeling better. 'Bill was right,' she said aloud, 'It's very therapeutic to rant.'

The rant relief was short-lived. Despair returned after realizing she was still unable to work out a puzzle with impossible intangibles. Stroking her stomach, Po looked out over the crazy, seamless, patternless, knot of lights in the city and moaned, "What about my baby?"

She put her hands to her mouth like a megaphone and screamed with ferocious passion, "Damn you Bill Elliott!"

After her bugle call, she went back to her apartment and dug her old Walkman out of the closet so she could listen to the show on her way to lay down the law.

"Briefly, she celebrated her first good news in two days. The batteries were still working. So were her primal instincts. Whatever confusion was in her mind, the animal nature aroused inside of her could eat it alive. Trouble was coming for everyone."

10:34 PM

Otis paused before he spoke again. His mouth moved, as if more words were going to come, but each time, he stifled himself. Finally he snorted and shrugged. "Sorry, Doc, I was thinking about a what-if ... anyway, meanwhile, back at the studio ..."

"After Alayat signed off, and put an hour and a half of music on queue, he tried to access his surveillance app on the computer. It was just a shot in the dark. He understood the Telstar web was gone.

"Next, he reached for his *Die, Dirtwings* board. Upon rethinking his situation, Bill was so sure of what was coming, he pulled the plug and put it away. Self-dissipation was no longer plan B.

"Alayat knew he had no escape from the building, and no bargaining chip to offer. He was dealing with men who wouldn't accept one. With nothing to lose, fully exposed, outflanked, and with true conviction, he reaffirmed his decision. He would use the campfire as his vehicle to jump into traffic and hit something before it hit him.

"In a fit of self-amusement, and in full theatrical voice, he boomed to his empty room, 'In the far corner, from the far distant past, almost four feet tall, champion of the Bombag, the last Savant, and the last opportunity for escaping the inevitable. Asitr-r-r. And in this corner, the last Dirtwing and his host, Robert McKinney.'

"Aware he needed the help of the man he possessed, Alayat released Robert McKinney and explained the situation.

"On the moon, when Kae'Lairy commented about the on-air confrontation, and Alayat's reaction, he summed up by saying, 'Alayat succeeded in getting himself thrown into the briar patch.'

10:41 PM

Across the street from Bill's gate is the only business on the block, a laundry. At night, the brightest light on the street shines from its big front window. All night long, the big blue neon sign flashes, off and on, off and on, hard wired to be indecisive.

Po stood with her back to the gate and watched the crowd in the reflection of the window where the blue light was hung. Light off, she saw the crowd. Light on, she saw herself. Light off, the image of the crowd pops onto the window. Light on, she is frozen in blue ice, undecided, but not indecisive. Her skill for organizing was being tested. Thought ribbons dominated her mind.

He loves me not, he loves me so.
Should I stay or should I go.
Yes? No!
Scary crowd, or froze in ice.
I don't really have a choice.

Pulling the gate-key from her pocket, she took a half-turn, slipped her headphones off her ears, and stopped. Out loud, Po choked out the words, "I don't have a choice either way."

Turning back around, she saw the crowd again, then she saw herself. Then the crowd.

Baby safe. Baby in danger.
Baby in danger. Baby safe.
Baby unsafe. Baby in danger.
Baby in danger. Baby in danger.
Baby in danger.
Should we stay, where can we go?
Have our say or hit the road?

10:50 PM

Ol' Frenchy monopolized the conversation at a campfire near the *Cave of the Dry Spring*. Already in his sleeping bag, Jack VanGrada, made no attempt to get involved in an Ol' Frenchy verbal romp.

Guglielmo Singh, utterly deprived of sleep, passed out as soon as he lay down. He missed hearing Asitr's loss of patience and Bill's decision to end the show early.

The Memphis CSI man sat next to the fire, headphones on, listening to Bill's musical selections. He, too, would be asleep soon.

The language expert from FSU also retreated to his sleeping bag after failed efforts to spot the source of Ol' Frenchy's speech patterns. He took his headache with him.

The kid from Kirksville was awake and filming everything. Occasionally, he would interject sounds that punctuated the gaps between Ol' Frenchy's words. He said things like, hmmm, or uh-huh, or yessir. At the moment, the kid was filming Ol' Frenchy cautioning his camp-mates.

"The difference between the polite way of sayin' howdy that first night and later on measurin' up each other's wanna-fight has me somewhat ponderous."

"Uhuh"

"What about our boy! Traded him straight hoogas for his mushka didn't he?"

"Yessir."

"Still ... It's like the time the airplane hit me in the head ... sorta sudden, but in slow motion. The duck warning didn't keep up with the whomp sensation. Not intuiatin' there was a duck. That cleared away, if the plane had been a train, I'd have never made it. A shorter drop, sure, but I never would have known."

"Hmmm."

"Maybe it's more like when you go flyin' on a kite. That first time you feel the crosswind. If you live through it, you get warned the next time. That's what it's like. I never been through it, but it feels like that first time. The warning."

"Uhuh."

"Strange how we can't let 'em know our names. Had a mule I called Carmelita. Big, big eyelashes. Was a four-legged woman, that one. Made eye contact like a lawyer. Lockjaw took her prospecting and came back with rocks. I took her out and lost her every time. She always beat me back home, so the next time I went with her, I just opened the gate and stayed home. Took care of that problem. That's what we need to figure now. How to take care of this here problem. Get ahead of it, and wrestle it down to the ground 'til it 'splodes into spent up energy dissipated all over the universe and never with even the remotest chance of ever reforming two pieces together 'cause it won't even have pieces cause it's dissipated. That's the plan. Now, how do you think we oughta go on about doin' that?"

"Hmmm"

The soliloquy went on until midnight.

10:55 PM

Po watched in the window as a figure broke from the crowd and walked in her direction. Every time the blue neon went dark, the figure seemed to jump closer to her.

She recognized he was one of the men she had been spying on since Tuesday. Their wardrobe of black cargo pants, dark shirts, fedoras, berets, and cabby hats, although not identical, were clearly meant to be uniforms

Letting go of the gate key in her pocket, she moved her hand to her purse and removed a canister of pepper spray.

When the man was almost to the sidewalk behind her, she spun around and faced him, eyes narrow, mouth held humorless and silent.

"Beg your pardon, Ms. Po. My name is Hayak." The man had a soft voice with an unfamiliar accent. "We know who you are and mean you no harm. We're working with Asitr."

"Asitr?"

"Yes, miss. Asitr. Can I be of any assistance?"

Po didn't respond verbally, but she flipped the cap on her pepper spray.

After giving her a chance to speak, the man offered advice. "I think it's safer you go somewhere, please. Could we offer you a ride?"

"I'm thinking." Po made the statement as if nothing else needed to be said. The look on the man's face let her know she needed to add clarification. "I don't know," she added.

"That's fine, Miss. If you want to leave, we're here for you. If you feel you need to stay, we will help you through the gate. It's a small but unpredictable crowd."

"Thank you. I see that. It looks like they've assigned an officer to this party." Po pointed to a patrol car stopping near the crowd at the gate. Asitr's man nodded his head in Po's direction and trotted to where the policeman was getting out of his car.

Po turned back to the window and, off and on, she watched.

11:10 PM

After the policeman left, Po marched to the gate and unlocked it. Behind her, a scuffle broke out when two men tried to press their way past her and through the gate. Both were jerked off their feet by men wearing dark clothing and out-of-style hats.

Po walked through the courtyard and sat on a bench with a view of both house and gate. Being invisible, under the dark shadow of her favorite oak, was comforting. She knew she wasn't ready to enter the house.

After a few minutes, while stroking her belly, she regained enough calm to find some common ground with God. "This is the only way to carry a spirit within a spirit," she prayed. "Don't blame the innocent. We need your strength."

By 11:40, they slumbered.

MIDNIGHT

By midnight, everyone but the kid from Kirksville and Ol' Frenchy were in their sleeping bags. Very little moon light filtered through the twisted black branches around the entrance to the sinkhole. No wind stirred the leaves. A click, snap, click sound from batteries being replaced in the camera was barely audible above the sound of a seemingly endless tale of hair-raising encounters with Arizona Gila monsters. Eventually, Ol' Frenchy inhaled.

The pause was notable. The sudden quiet made Guglielmo stir in his sleeping bag. The FSU guy actually woke up. Then, the light.

At first, the light was a Tinkerbell blue kind of glow. Then it whitened, widened, and pointed in their direction. The source was just high enough to make the men tilt their heads upward to watch it become a beam, focused on the campfire, edging nearer, getting ever so much brighter as it got ever so much closer.

Ol' Frenchy moved away from the campfire and into the shadows. "Hmmm," he said.

The FSU guy answered, "uhuh".

In unison, the CSI man and the kid from Kirksville whispered, "Yessir."

VanGrada lay awake in his sleeping bag. Taking his cue from the sleeping Guglielmo Singh, he lay still. His heart pounded. He knew his little machine had worked on Alazam, but he couldn't be sure what would show up tonight. Nervously, he pressed the power button and gripped the machine tightly.

"Hello!" A strong voice called from the direction of the light. "Hello! Who's there?"

VanGrada sat up and returned the question. "Who goes there?"

There was a rush of movement down the path, followed by angry swearing, and a dog's yelp of pain. The light dropped and rolled into the forest as two figures slid down the last, suddenly steep, slope in the trail. When they skidded to a stop, they were just ten yards away from the campfire.

The kid from Kirksville raised a flashlight in one hand and continued filming with the other. In the light, and through the lens, the view revealed the new arrivals.

Helping himself back to his feet was a forty-ish looking man in blue jeans, boots, a flannel shirt with the sleeves rolled up over the elbows, and a *Why not Ethanol?* cap hanging cockeyed on his head. A muscular pit bull was on his left side. A rifle hung over the man's right shoulder.

"Are you OK?" asked VanGrada. He held his ground in his sleeping bag. Nobody went to offer the stranger a hand, or invite him into the camp. They were following Asitr's rules. No offers of hospitality and no names.

Paul Moore

The intruder adjusted his hat, walked over to his flashlight, picked it up, and shined it around the camp. His face showed he wasn't in a very good mood. "I asked y'all who was here? What are you doin' out here?"

VanGrada, lying on the ground, his hand shaking, was answering for everyone. "We know why we're here. Who are you and what do you want?"

Everyone but the sleeping Singh waited for a name. None came and the tension grew tauter. Was this a fallen one refusing to give his name or a suspicious neighbor?

"I'm asking again," the stranger said while un-shouldering his rifle, "who are you and what are you doin' at this ungodly hour, in this unsafe forest?" His Pit stared at the snoring Singh and wagged his tail. The click of the rifle's safety felt like a tightening ratchet.

VanGrada, again, answered for them all. "Mister, we are here with the permission of the owner. I suggest you lower that barrel and tell us who you are before we call the police." The stranger paused, then propped the rifle against a tree. "I live next farm over. Wilson don't ever let people camp here."

His statement was simply said. His gesture with the rifle was reassuring. He gave the appearance of being who he claimed to be, but he didn't offer a name.

VanGrada sat up, cradled his electronic gizmo, and used a different approach. Without offering hospitality he tried to lighten things up. "Glad to meet you and your dog. Does your dog have a name?"

"I call him when I need him. He's a 'specially good dog."

"His name is ... *WhenIneedhim*?

"Taught him every trick in the book and then some."

"I didn't catch your name." As Jack asked the question, he raised his sonic weapon out of the bedroll and into plain sight.

The stranger continued on about his dog while scanning the faces around him. "Dang dog has more spirit than your usual pit. He's my faithful, good ol' fun-lovin' companion. Check this out. Here's a little trick you'll like."

Herakles tensed and dropped into a leaping position. His cold, emotionless eyes were looking straight into the lens of the video

275

camera as it continued to run. Suddenly, the dog and every human being in the camp, not named Guglielmo Singh, recoiled at the sound of a quick, crisp blast from Ol' Frenchy's air horn.

The stranger jerked his head toward a brief flash of blue light in the trees. When he saw Ol' Frenchy striding out of the dark, he snarled one word. "Mushka."

Herakles paused, growled, then showed his teeth.

Striding slowly, but talking fast, Ol' Frenchy closed closer to the fire. "You've got a windy wind-up, but where's your pitch? Did I hear you say dangerous? This here woods? You're walkin' it with a killin' machine, dipnot ... Don't you know about pit bulls? Look to me like you're in your child bearin' years. You don't want to have this guy around your younguns do you? Jack? Play that dog a note. These bad boys are less than one percent of the dog population and they do forty percent of people mangling, sixty five percent of people killin'. Most of 'em younguns 'cause youguns like to twitch, you know. Think it's the forest that's dangerous? Jack? Point your gizmo thingy at this here dog and see what happens."

Jack didn't have to hear it twice. He was attacking backwards. His shaking hands accidentally turned the power off while fumbling for the trigger.

While Ol' Frenchy was striding, Jack was fumbling, Herakles was growling, Singh was sleeping, FSU was praying, CSI was freezing up, and the kid was filming, the intruder was giving a slow and deliberate command. "Have some fun Herakles."

As if shot from the same cannon, Marduk and his one-dog posse shot forward.

Marduk launched himself with a trail of blue light into Ol' Frenchy.

Herakles did the same thing, without the glow, at a weaker target. He charged into the camera with such force the lens pushed deeply into the kid's right eye socket, but Herakles didn't linger to finish him. He caromed toward the sleeping face of Guglielmo Singh.

With the timely recovering of his faculties, Jack VanGrada pushed the right buttons, aimed well, and dissipated the spirit that was never meant to romp through God's creation.

Instantly, the driver was gone, but the vehicle was still flying to bite the face off a sleeping man.

Googs was saved when a sudden burst of extremely bright light emitted from the spot where Ol' Frenchy and the stranger collided. The dog's charge halted. Every man and animal in the area who wasn't sleeping was blinded. The intense flash jolted Guglielmo Singh awake.

The adventurous Mr. Singh opened his eyes to the open mouth, bad breath, and dripping foam of a blinded and confused animal. "Good boy," he squeaked. "Good dog ... Fellahs? Fellahs? What's the story here?"

The dog rolled his eyes, looked embarrassed, sniffed, then slowly backed away before he bolted into the woods. Singh jumped to his feet and watched the dog disappear into the black.

"Did you see that?" How the devil did that bloody thing ... fellahs?" Singh finally took heed of the swirl of arcing lights and flailing limbs battling atop the campfire. Ol' Frenchy was trying to 'wrestle the problem to the ground and *splode* it into dissipated energy.'

Singh was the only one of the group able to see one set of lights go screaming into the night sky and the other light bind itself to the ground and begin to take the form of a weak apparition of Ol' Frenchy.

Slowly, like an old man with a bad back, Ol Frenchy stood up in the middle of the campfire and moaned, "Dang, he was a big wing." Then, in a much louder voice, "Hey! Cut the buzz, I ain't the dog, man. Shut that gizmo thingy off 'fore I 'splodes!" The blinded VanGrada was waving his gizmo in the direction of the campfire.

Only Googs had vision, so only he saw the result of focused energy intersecting Ol' Frenchy, shattering him into the oblivion of dissipation. This time, unlike at the canyon, there was no human being standing in his place.

Herakles was written from the book of life, a confused dog was somewhere in the forest, a surprised and angry Baal Zebub was off into the stratosphere, and Olphrenjii was among the missing, in the land of nothing.

Left behind, temporarily blinded men were demanding answers from the member of their party who knew the least about what had just happened. "There was a fearsome dog," Singh said, "then I think we killed that bloody Ol' Frenchy."

While driving the kid to the hospital, they called Asitr and emailed the video of the confrontation. The clear sound and images were intercepted by Kae'Lairy, who told the watchers on the moon, "It had to happen sometime. Monkeys with guns. Skarrar."

When Asitr received the news of Olphrenjii's dissipation, he reacted physically. A feeling of nausea grabbed him at the solar plexus and twisted a moan from his mouth. Lockjaw thought his Grampy was having a stroke.

"Regrets, always regrets," Asitr told his grandson. "This is so familiar. Dave didn't need to go back to the Amazon. Where's Otis? What happened to his web connections? Why did I have to stir things up before we went to the cave? What about our Armenian friends? Do they have Alayat trapped in his house, or do we have them trapped with nothing more than gizmos for protection? Why am I either too scared or too reckless? I'm good at being the victim. Why did I think I could be a leader?"

"We knew it was dangerous, Grampy. It's the short life. Remember. It's the short life."

"Not for Olphrenjii, Lock. He was supposed to live forever. I managed to get a guardian angel killed."

1:08 AM

Robert McKinney walked the halls inside the building while he listened to the last broadcast on his headphones. Occasionally, he would pause at a window.

From the second floor, he could see over the walls of the compound to the opposite side of the street. He didn't like looking out the window overlooking the gate. People stood at the gate and stared at the building. He felt like they could see him, and he was sure they would disapprove if they knew what they were looking at.

On this trip up the hallway, a red flashing light caught his attention, so he parted the curtain and looked toward the gate. At the end of the block, another light was flashing. The yellow lights of the city's street sweeper competed for attention.

Robert figured the sweeper was waiting for the policeman to finish with directing the loiterers to pick up the discarded signs lying around the gate.

The news lady had made a second trip to find something newsworthy in the crowd, but even after suggesting signs, she didn't see anything that fit into her wheelhouse.

Curious, Robert went down to the courtyard to get a better look. Hiding in the black shade of the garden area, he began ticking off the messages on the signs being tossed into a pile by the police car. With a mix of amusement and embarrassment for the human race, he pondered each message and wondered if the sign makers and he were listening to the same radio program.

```
ISA
Illegal Space Aliens
GO HOME!
*
SHARE THE GOLD!
Gimme Mines
NOW!
*
H.O.A.X
Heavenly Order of
Ancient X-men
*
W.A.G.G.L.E.I.T.
Women Against Godless Gold Loving
Entertainers Instigating Tyranny
*
The World is EXPLODING!
Boomdyada Boom! Boom!
Out of the pile, one sign stood out as being sensible.
*
REPENT=RETHINK
```

Robert reached to turn up the volume on his headphones and bent his body to sit on the garden bench behind him. Before he reached the volume knob, his headphones flew off into the bushes and his head jerked sideways from the force of a heavy purse, connecting with the right side of his face. Po was awake again.

"Damn you Bill Elliott." He heard the words and raised his hand to defend against another blow. The blow landed on the other side of his face, and he stumbled as he turned, then lurched toward his attacker.

After grabbing at the sound in the dark, his ears were jolted by another scream. "Damn you Baal Alayat."

They both bounced off the bench and onto the ground. Robert had to wrap Po up with his arms and legs before she quit her attack.

Robert had a lot of explaining to do. After Po quit struggling to reach her pepper spray, he introduced himself. "Hi, Po. I'm Robert McKinney. We need to talk."

4 AM

Alayat saw the flicker of blue as Baal Zebub entered his studio. He wasn't surprised, and he wasn't afraid. He was ready.

"My last disciple." Zebub didn't speak the words with pride. He didn't offer peace. "My least reliable. Alayat, you are a betrayer."

"You are mistaken, Lord Marduk, I have surprises for you."

"I am already surprised by you. I've been listening. Will not bow before me? Allow your brother to fly into a trap? You defy and insult our strongest ally? What is your surprise for me?"

"My plan, master, is to present you with the ripened fruit from your mind. I've saved your writings, perfected your science, and made ready the foundation for your rule in Heaven."

"Interesting. Speak. Impress me. Make me want to reward you."

"I built your wireless web in space. I archived all of your scientific work in its database. Yesterday, it was destroyed."

"So far, I'm not impressed."

"It can easily be rebuilt, better and safer. What you may find impressive is the reason we won't have to rebuild."

"Don't pander to me, Alayat. I see how the humans have built us hundreds of platforms to spy, steal, and misinform. Impress me quickly, or surrender hope."

"Your big theoretical project. I can make it happen."

"Go on."

"Follow me."

Leaving the studio, both spirits passed by the room where Po and Robert were in animated discussion. Without form, they paused in the doorway, unseen. Robert was telling Po his life story. "Bill Elliott is my guardian angel," is what they overheard, "I wouldn't be alive without him."

Pleased with what he heard, Alayat continued down the hall, down the stairs, and into the basement, stopping at a wall between the washing machine and the tool bench. "Your safe room," he said, as he slid apart two large panels, revealing the lustrous shine of pure gold.

Zebub said nothing, but the rise in his vibration rate was apparent to Alayat.

Knowing he was riding a crest of approval, Alayat made his move to advance from the safety of his master's new attitude, and move directly to securing his trust. With all the necessary postures of submission, Alayat bowed while touching the golden wall. Thick golden doors parted at his touch, revealing a ten foot by ten-foot room with a single table, a bookcase, and chair. One massive book occupied the bookcase. "For you, master."

Baal Zebub stroked the door and stared into the room. "How thick?"

"Four feet of solid gold all the way around. Ceiling, floor, walls, and doors. Supremely conductive, impenetrably anti-magnetic. I've sealed it against all things but my own touch."

"You will transfer the door to my touch."

"Of course, master. Did you see the prize on the bookshelf?"

"My *Silver Book*?"

"Turned black with time, but with all of your science still intact."

Walking into the golden room to retrieve his book, Zebub asked, "What about my theoretical project? What have you been doing?"

"I've figured it all out. The solution came to me while constructing my big-wing catcher."

"Your what?"

"Big-wing catcher, enjoy it." With those words, Baal Alayat slid the two golden doors into the closed position, sealed them, using his own touch, and replaced the outer wall to its original position. Inside, a horror monger wasted his angry wail on walls that echoed inwardly, while outwardly, snuffing out any sign of his presence.

On the moon, Kae'Lairy told the two watchers he observed the whole thing, from the moment Zebub blinked into the studio, until he walked into his golden trap. "I was disheartened," he said. "Asitr is over-matched. Alayat has battlefield options. He has maneuvered into a position where he can clash on a field filled with loopholes in the rules of Heaven. I regret not being able to take the field. I felt to do so would entangle myself in free will and abandon my protection of the throne."

5:30 AM

The more frightening the news from Robert, the calmer Po felt. Still, she worried she was experiencing the calm of the crazy, where illogical thoughts are acceptable and welcome.

Finally, she tired enough to suggest some rest for herself, and for Robert, some alone-time to finish listening to the broadcast.

Robert stopped at the window while putting his headphones back on. It would be daylight soon. The police car was gone. The crowd was gone. The streets looked shiny with water from the cleaning. Across the street, a tall, gray haired black man stood in front of the laundry. A child stood next to him ... or was it a little old man? Lockjaw and Asitr had arrived.

Robert sprinted to his room and grabbed a book with the mark of Alexander and a circle of hands. Not slowing down, he raced to the gate and unlocked it. "Welcome," he said, "First you read, then we talk."

Asitr took the book from Robert's outstretched hand and said, "Thank you. Show us to our room?"

For Asitr, the rest of the morning was filled with reading, thinking, and re-thinking.

Po slept late. When she woke up at noon, she prepared a brunch for everyone.

1 PM

The food was good, but the atmosphere was uncomfortable. It was the first time all the human participants awaiting the campfire were together in the same room.

Asitr and Robert sat in a corner sharing hushed conversations about the book.

Nervously, everyone else in the room ate, drank, and spoke in polite, inconsequential terms.

Kae'Lairy summed up the atmosphere as, "paranoia, mingled with more paranoia."

4 PM

Alayat could sense a sleep come over his house. All humans were napping. Just four more hours before show time.

At the cave site, the mood was somber. They returned from the hospital with bad news. The Kid from Kirksville was going to lose an eye. Googs boiled water for coffee. Nobody expected it to be near as good as yesterday's coffee, but it was coffee. After returning to the cave, the crew didn't care about the quality of the cup. They needed to give their hands a warm, familiar friend to hold while thinking. A little steam on the face while contemplating. Something to sip on while waiting. Just four more hours before showtime.

36

"GOOD EVENING. I am not Bill Elliott, but you remain his guests. Answers are on the way, buckle up.

"Let me tell you what is going on in the studio this evening. We are having a smokeless campfire tonight. No s'mores, no burned hot dogs, no cowboy coffee. We're being very civilized, munching on sugary cantaloupes from Florida and bagels from down the street. I don't expect the civility to last, but there's no civility requirement in the rules.

"My name is Robert McKinney. Don't let my voice fool you. I'm not your old faithful night-ranter. I am not now, never have been, and never played him on radio. I will introduce you to all the guests in the studio and start explaining things right after these announcements."

*   *   *

"We are back, and I have some things to tell you.

"Tonight, you are going to catch a glimpse of a world gone by. I'm not talking about Victorian days, the Roman era, or even the ice age. You are about to listen in to a time when the world was so small, and human existence was so fragile, rules with unbreakable bonds were enforced by the angels themselves.

"Tonight, we are conducting the show under the ancient rules of the campfire. You at home may think we are telling ghost stories, but you should think of this as a court trial. The big rule? We are required to respond, to any question asked, with honest answers.

"I am warned by Asitr, avoiding honesty is the fastest way to realize you don't like the attending angel. Think of him as the bailiff. I don't need convincing. I'm scared through and through, so let's get on with telling you who is here.

"Lockjaw, Mr. John Smith, good evening."

"I'm hoping for a good evening for you as well, Robert."

"Thank you. Is it fair to say you will be an active participant in the campfire?"

"Without reservation."

"Could you tell us what you are holding in your hand, Lock?"

"Left hand, a bagel. Right hand, a gizmo."

"Sustenance and destruction. Very balanced."

"A man's gotta do ..."

"Asitr. Good evening. I don't need to ask you to accept the campfire rules. Have you brought an attending angel?"

"I hope you're not trying to rub salt in a fresh wound, Robert. I lost my guardian angel, but I have faith in the protection of Heaven."

"You've lost your guardian angel? I'm sorry. I know how tragic that could be. My own guardian is in danger."

"Robert, give some consideration to understanding Alayat isn't your guardian angel."

"Asitr, I'm going to introduce everyone, and then I can tell you why I know he is my guardian."

"Okay."

"My beloved, Po, is here tonight."

"I'm not taking part in the campfire, Robert. Leave me out of this."

"Po, Robert doesn't have the authority to give you special treatment. If you are going to interact, you're bound by the rules."

"Stick it, Asitr. You're not in Samyaza now, you're in the good ol' USA. Robert can play your game, but I'm not waiving my rights. I have a guardian responsibility, myself."

"I see. I respect that. You may have no recourse but to jump in later."

"Asitr, I don't think Po will be necessary. You didn't bring a gizmo for her, did you?"

"You know why we're here, Robert. How are you going to introduce him? How do you know he's in the room?"

"I'm going to introduce him by telling you a story from my life. Are you willing to listen?"

"With interest. Please, go on."

"Dear listeners, members of the campfire, Po. My story."

*   *   *

THE SECRET LIFE OF LITTLE BOBBY MCKINNEY

I should have prepared something. I prepared my opening statement. Bill always told me I should know what I'm going to say the first time I open my mouth, and then go with the flow after that. Nobody knows what's next. I mean, nobody knows what will happen after the part that was prepared. Let me start again …

I'm Robert McKinney. I'm a little bit like a Savant, a little like Asitr, and scared I'm gonna mess up. It's what I do, normally. Not really, not all the time, just normally, if it's important. I don't mean to … oh, boy … and I don't like to be laughed at. You couldn't tell it, but I'm really smart and really stupid, too. I'm stupid because I think I'm so smart.

Nobody ever told me it was stupid to believe you were smart. By the time of my fourth birthday, I thought being smart was everything.

It made my parents happy to show off how smart I was. They told everyone I was gifted. They said I had a large vocabulary, I was good with jigsaw puzzles, and I could read like a high school kid.

It was all effortless. My father taught me the alphabet when I was in my terrible twos. It didn't mean anything to me, but, when I recited it, people smiled and said I was smart.

Then, at three years old, the Three Stooges taught me the alphabet was pieces of a code. Each letter had its own sound. Each sound connected to the sounds of other letters and, they made words. With knowledge of the code, I could read about other people's thoughts. I could write down my own thoughts. It all started with the song:

B A Bay
B E Bee
B I Biggy Bi
B O Bo
Biggy Bi Bo B U Bu Biggy Bi Bo Bu.

With silly, simple phonics, the Three Stooges set me on the road to reading. I wasn't memorizing a list of words that will be on a reading test. I was actually reading.

People were amused, sometimes too amused. I was very sensitive to being made sport of. My aversion to being laughed at led to giving my parents an ultimatum on the night of the duck.

We were at the dinner table and they were arguing. I was immunized to my parent's fights. It was business as usual with adults. I interrupted them on this particular night with a question I felt was more important than who had forgotten the electric bill. I just asked it straight out. "Does *duck* start with *W*?"

They stopped arguing and took time out for me. They loved me. I was the reason they stayed together. "What do you mean?" asked my mother.

"Listen ... Duh-Duh-Duck ... Duh-Duh-W," I said. They laughed and laughed. It didn't matter to me that they weren't being angry with each other anymore. They were laughing at me.

I told them if they laughed at me again, I would cry. It was the most serious ultimatum I could muster at the age of three.

I should have learned a lesson from the night of the duck. I should have learned either humility or the lesson that Asitr took so many lives to learn. Knowing facts didn't always lead to a correct conclusion. I didn't learn that little tool of reasoning until I was almost five. It started with a car ride and a stop light.

While waiting for the light to change, I was practicing my words by reading the signs on the window of a store. I found what I always searched for. A word I hadn't learned. I sounded it out aloud. "Kuh- Ko-Kotex! What's a Kotex?"

My parents began to laugh at me again, but it was short-lived. They were learning not to make me cry. "It's something special, just for women," my mom answered.

It was an incomplete answer, but it satisfied me. It was just a big setup for the next night.

We were home. My father was discussing the Christmas party at the machine shop where he worked. "Christmas bonuses, a free turkey, and a dance band," my father said.

"It sounds like fun," said my mother, "I wish I had something special to wear."

I made a suggestion. "Why don't you go to the store and get that Kotex?"

There was no stopping them. They laughed like hyenas. They couldn't stop. They both held their stomachs, sputtering and howling. I thought I hated them with their ugly convulsing faces and their cruel laughing games.

Eventually, I forgave them. It was February, and we finally got the snow I prayed for at Christmas. Stupid God. Two months late.

While making snow angels in the vegetable garden, it became apparent that my old snow suit was a little too binding. I couldn't get the full extension I needed for the really big wings. When I thought about the problem, I came to a solid conclusion, based on facts. I really did need my parents. Who else would get me a new snow suit?

On the way to the back door I could hear my father shouting at my mother. He was louder than I had ever heard him. It was something about his boss, my mom, and the Christmas dance.

All the noise ended with a loud bang ... Then, for just one heartbeat, all was extra quiet. In that suddenly silent moment, I wondered if my mother lit a firecracker to make my dad shut up.

When I got to the door, my father opened it, and I let him know what I needed. He looked through me like I wasn't there. Then, without a word, he walked past me toward the garage. Okay. If that's the way he wanted to be, that was fine with me. I would get the snow suit from my mother.

After watching my dad walk into the garage, I went in the back door of the house, remembering to remove my snow boots. My mother called from the kitchen with a funny, pinched voice. "Go next door and get Linda, baby. Go get Linda, now."

While I started re-snapping the buckles on my boots, I thought I would let her know what I wanted, too. "I need a new snow suit, mom."

"Yes, dear ... get Linda." she said.

"This one's too small. I can't make the big wings."

"Ohhhh ... hurry ... Linda."

Mom sounded very different. Grown up but small like me. I needed to see why, so I went up the stairs to the kitchen and found her. She was sitting against the far wall, her eyes fixed on the stove. I looked at the stove and didn't see anything interesting. Then I saw the pistol on the floor. "Mom?" I crossed the room to ask her about it.

Standing over her, I saw the blood seeping through her fingers where she was holding her stomach. Both her hands, spread out over her belly, reminded me of when she told me something strange. "This is where I carried you when you were a baby."

I put together everything, the gunfights in the cowboy shows I watched every Saturday morning, the sound of the firecracker, and an additional piece of information I picked up from reading. People bled when shot. My mom was shot. She was bleeding. Didn't I tell you I was a genius?

I went a step further. Linda's daughter, Regina, informed me I hadn't had the correct idea of when a woman wears a kotex. "They only need it if they were bleeding," she said. "Bleeding from where babies come from." Knowing those facts made it obvious. I didn't need to be a genius to figure out my mother needed one right now.

I ran to Linda's house and didn't bother to knock. I burst in, shouting, "I need a Kotex! Give me your Kotex, quick!"

Linda made a face at me, raised her hands to her mouth and started spitting into them. No, no she wasn't spitting! She was laughing at me! What was wrong with her? I shouted in anger, "Give me your damn Kotex!" She sat down and howled like a crazy animal.

Linda was making me mad and wasting my time. I ran back to my house and into the garage to get my father. Then I recognized another part of my Saturday morning education come to life. Someone had strung up my father. He was hanging from the rafters like a horse thief.

In all my thinking, I never thought about my parents dying. My dad's lifeless body made me feel helpless. I knew I couldn't save him, but I was sure my mother really needed a kotex, and I had to find one fast.

I retraced the route to the store in my mind and took off running. I was about to stop from breathlessness when I saw the stop light and pushed on.

You know what happened next. I announced what I needed and strangers made sport of me. I did the only thing I could think of. I ran up and down the aisles in search of the one thing that could save my mom.

A lady ran after me and tried to stop me. She said she wanted to help, but at the time, I just wanted her to stop grabbing at me, so I threw cans at her and started my search again. Finally, there they were.

I grabbed a box, and after seeing the clerk standing at the front, I changed directions and pushed through swinging doors to the back room and out the open door to the parking lot. I was free. Free, and out of breath, so I ran to hide behind the dumpster.

The cashier ran by me twice, but he didn't see me. Like Asitr, hiding in the library, I was sure he would hear me breathing, but he didn't. I waited until I heard his footsteps run back inside, then I began to creep out and look around.

That's when I saw the man, sitting in his car, holding one finger over his mouth. His other hand was pointing to my right, warning me the cashier was there. I froze until my new friend pulled his car out of its parking space, drove it over to the dumpster, swung the passenger door open, and whispered, "Hurry. Get in."

When I did, he pushed my head down and drove off.

"I've got to get these to my mom," I said, when he let me lift my head. "Right now." He made me tell him the problem, then offered to help.

"Tell me where you live. I know what to do."

He followed directions real well. He stopped once, and pulled the car over to let an ambulance whiz by. There were more sirens. Then a police car. When we turned up my street, we could see there were more police cars at my house.

"It looks like they are after you for stealing that box from the store," he said. "I'm going to take you somewhere safe."

That's what the man told me. He said the police could fix my father, and they were sure to have plenty of Kotex on-hand. I went with him quietly, worried, but thankful.

A question needed to be asked. "Are you my guardian angel?" Regina told me they weren't real. I never believed her. It was my little test. He passed. He didn't laugh at me.

"I am your guardian angel, son. I'm here to love you." He said the words ... I ... I believed him."

"He said he was here to love me. Intellectually, he understood the word was a magical charm, but he didn't understand it like someone who feels it. Asitr tells me that love is understood by the soul but embraced by the spirit. I say some people carry the definition around only in their heads, free of understanding and never embraced. My false protector didn't embrace it. He enjoyed the snare of it. I lost my self-confidence when he took me to his home, shut the door, slapped my face, pulled down his pants, and chose the words, "I love you."

I fought him with the arsenal of a child. "I don't want to," I said. He picked me up by my hair and carried me to a small room in the basement. I had just one more idea for stopping him. I managed to get it out between sobs ... "I'm only little," I begged.

"That's why I love you," he said. My last defense crumbled. He made sure I feared the love word for years.

That same night, the voices started. So many of them calling out to me from every direction. Each voice shouted to be heard over other shouting voices. I knew the word to describe it. It was cacophony. In the cacophony, one word kept emerging. Love.

Between my abductor's physical torture and the legions of voices shouting for my attention, I didn't have many sleeping moments for two weeks. Every second of my life was misery. I worried fear would kill me, and at the same time, I was afraid to be alive.

As Mazgabar would say, "Desperate, I was." Desperate enough to call for magical help. I thought about calling to God, but he showed me with his snow that he was slow to come. I didn't want to spend another moment alive like this, so I crossed my fingers and asked for a real guardian angel.

The voices hushed right away. One voice spoke clearly. It told me to look up above the bed. I did.

It was nighttime, and the room was black. My room stayed dark during the day, but I could tell it was nighttime. A little light from the laundry room was leaking under my door. It was much more yellow than the real day light when it shined through the basement windows. The artificial light mixed with the blackness of my room, making an ugly shade of black-brown, like the color of an old water moccasin.

Did you ever try really hard to look into blackness? You start to see things. Formless things from out of your imagination. I saw a formless blob, blacker than the heavy brownness, and I knew for certain it was real. I could feel pressure on my chest when it dipped down low. It had a sense of controlled movement about it. It was the source of the clear voice in my head. He whispered his name to me. "I am Baal Alayat," he said. "Tell me your name, and ask me to come and help you."

At first, I was too afraid. I tried an old, failed, request. "I don't want to."

Thankfully, he persisted. "I am Baal Alayat. Tell me your name."

"I'm Bobby. Bobby McKinney. Can you help me?"

"I want to help you," the voice said. "Ask me, by name, to come and save you."

This time I asked him. 'Bill Elliott, come help me.' I had mispronounced his name, but he came. The joy! I felt immediately at rest and laughed aloud.

The sound of my laughter brought in my abductor. He turned on the lights and checked the locks on the door. "What the hell is so funny, love bug? Having a dream?"

At first, I was afraid, but as he closed the door I shouted, "You're going to be sorry now, mister!"

He came back in and raised his hand to strike me. I don't remember the attack. I had a guardian angel, and he took it all for me. All the abuse and all of the guilt. He would return my self-awareness only when it was safe. I would have died without him.

One of my happiest memories is how I felt when I learned, after four years of captivity, my monster was burned to death in a *suspicious* fire.

The police interviewed me. Most of their questions were about possible motives and enemies. They called the monster "my dad." They told me my name was Alvin Chomuk. They made fun of me. They called me 'Alvin the chipmunk', so I shut down and shut up when the rest of their questions centered on suspicions it was I, who set the fire.

God bless me if I did. God bless my angel if he did it for me. I know what it's like to need revenge. It made sense to keep my guardian a secret. Everything was better if I kept my mouth shut. My life became a victory of teamwork. Like Asitr in the hole, I served my time in a building used for the warehousing of human flotsam. Asitr's angel came to calm him and give him protection from predators while he was in his hole. I had an angel who took my abuse and left me without the memories of how I was bruised and bloodied while in the warehouse of human degenerates. God bless my angel.

*   *   *

A DIFFERENCE IN EXPERIENCE

"Asitr. Is destroying this angel the reason you've jetted through your lives? Do-over after do-over? To be here with murder on your mind? You can't convince me to stand by while you try to dissipate my protector."

"Can I call you Robert, or do you prefer Bobby?"

"Call me Robert."

"Robert, I know from your story, you started your life as more than your years. You had gifts, and you tried to use them. Horrible experiences, terrible consequences, they've twisted your life around. I think, today, you are different than the little man in a child's body. You are now a child in a man's body, are you not?"

"Don't try to diminish me that way. Where has all your life experience gotten you?"

"I don't mean to diminish you, Robert. You're so impressive. Much better balanced than I would have suspected. You were a remarkable toddler. The things you did to save your mother, and so young. The important thing is the effort you showed to make things better. Unbelievable at so young an age. What were you? Four and a half?"

"Almost five."

"Not four and a half?"

"I'm not lying. I know it would hurt Bill if you think I'm lying."

"Thank you for that, Robert. I'm glad you know only the truth is acceptable."

"I feel the same way, Asitr."

"I know you are a deep thinking and serious child. You are a child, though, aren't you? How many years have you actually been in control of your thoughts? How many years of experiencing the world do you actually have? You know what I mean. In those terms: how old are you?"

"Bill and I figured it out last month. We decided I was twelve."

"Twelve? How strong you are for twelve. I was twelve when I entered the city of Samyaza. You are doing a much better job of staying strong than I did."

"I have a guardian angel."

"I had my Sami. He taught me. I had Enoch. He rescued me from men and myself. He showed me that looking for the truth was more important than looking for liars. I had a guardian angel when I was thrown into the Samyaza hole. He calmed me without possessing me. Sami and Enoch encouraged me to learn from my experiences. What has Bill taught you?"

"He's read to me. I know more about history and man than professors who teach it."

"Reading? Is that what consumes Bill's time when he is outside your body?"

"Po tells me I am always in the library, reading. I know that means we both are consumed by it. It's safe for me. He speaks to me when I read. He helps me to understand."

"Tell me something you understand."

"I understand all of mankind is heading to an inevitable downfall because we are greedy and easily misled."

"Is that something Bill told you? I thought he was one to avoid the inevitable."

"It's a part of his makeup. If you listen to his show you would know that."

"Do you listen to his show?"

"I've heard them all."

"What do you feel like you've missed, from skipping over so much of your childhood?"

"Playmates. Playmates and baseball."

"Of course. Childhood friends and the freedom to play, before the years of responsibility. Has Alayat helped you fill the void?"

"He tried. I told him how, before I lost everything, I used to watch the older kids in the neighborhood. In the summer, they left their houses with baseball gloves, balls, and bats. They never even planned anything; they just ate breakfast and met at the school for games. I told Bill I was more impatient for having baseball buddies than I was for starting school."

"How did Bill try to help you?"

"He gave me a surprise. We went to a school away from the city. He said all the city schools had policemen to keep kids away. When he stepped out of me, I was sitting on a bench. I had a glove on my hand. A real leather, six finger, baseball glove, all broken in and soft. There were lots of real baseballs at my feet and a Stan Musial bat leaning against the bench. I felt happy."

"Were there other kids around?"

"No, I thought maybe I was early, so I started practicing. First, I tossed the ball into the air and tried different ways to catch it. I was pretty good, I thought. One-handed catches and a real good sliding dive. I hoped some kids saw me and wanted to play, but I got wise real soon."

"Did something bad happen?"

"Yeah. Pretty bad."

"Take a breath, Bobby ..."

"Robert."

"I'm sorry, Robert. Tell us what happened."

"I was tossing the balls straight up, and trying to hit them with the bat. I wasn't very good, I kept missing, but I got into one like Mickey Mantle. I felt it all the way to my shoulders, and the ball shot out of the infield, over the outfield, and stuck in the big chain link fence so hard the whole fence rattled.

"I never saw a neighborhood kid hit one so far. That's when I started thinking. I looked at my shadow, rolled up my sleeve, and felt my muscles. Then, I understood. I dropped to the ground, rolled onto my back in front of home plate, and scraped my fully extended arms, hard, against the rough orange dust. I was making a snow angel in the dirt, crying like a baby girl, scraping and bleeding. I was so angry. When I stood up to see my big dirt-winged monstrosity, I knew. I was a freak. When I heard laughing, I knew I was a freak who needed to be feared. Thank God Bill took over. I don't know what might have happened."

"Bill didn't tell you how he handled the cop?"

"What cop?"

"The man laughing at you. He was a policeman."

"How do you know."

"Research, Robert. We didn't know about you, but we have records for Alvin Chomuk. Knowing about Bill's host was important to us."

"What happened with the policeman. What do you know about me? I'm not Alvin Chomuk."

"The policeman didn't know you, Robert. His records said you were Alvin Chomuk. He put you in his little municipal jail and issued you tickets for public drunkenness, loitering, and trespassing. When he looked up your record, he saw you had been in the nut house for ten years, and tried to get the judge to send you back. In his report, he says you were a violent pervert and a danger to the children."

"See, Bill saved me again. I never went back."

"Bill kept you weak by not letting you learn anything."

"I'm not weak."

"You're so fragile, I have to tip-toe around anything you can't handle like an adult, but you're such a smart child. I believe you have the potential to grow out of your problems, but not with Bill's guidance."

"Bill told me you wouldn't understand."

"How about you, Robert. Do you understand anything that Bill hasn't influenced? Tell me a conclusion you've reached on your own. Something you've thought about but haven't discussed with him."

"I can't think of any ... Do you mean anything at all?"

"Yes."

"I think I know what went wrong in Babylon. How you got caught."

"Really! I would like to hear what you think about that."

"Bill says he didn't have anything to do with you being punished for saving those books. I believe him."

"What do you think happened?"

"I don't know why you can't see it. Even Bill didn't see it. You talked about your plans with Megasthenes while standing right in front of Herakles. I think Herakles told Berossus about your plans, but he messed up. I think he told Berossus you were giving the books to the Greeks. When he found the books going to Athens, he asked Bill to check his own bags going to Egypt. Bill volunteered to check Megasthenes' bags as well. He found the books, but he lied to Berossus."

"Why did he do that?"

"He still wants to be a guardian angel. He does what he can. He is so alone without the protection of Heaven … he does what he can."

"I should thank him for saving my book. Will you tell us why he's not here?"

"He is here. You know why he can't speak, yet. It's in your book."

"Yes, Robert. There are a lot of things to think about in those stories."

"That's right Asitr. You have to think of the disadvantages Bill has to live with."

"Disadvantages. Do you mean the loss of abilities?"

"Yes. He used to have powers like a superhero. Now, he needs humans to function in the world."

"Wasn't he functioning the night you let him in?"

"He was alive, but he needed my help, and I needed his."

"He needed your help for what?"

"To take form. To exercise his will on the world around him."

"Exercise his will? By usurping yours?"

"No, Asitr. Exercising his will, physically. Pick up a pencil, talk into a microphone, absorb the tortures of a cruel abuser … that sort of thing. Do you believe God's judgment was wrong? I believe God taught a lesson to those rebels that only Bill took to heart."

"What lesson was that, Bobby?"

"Robert!"

"Sorry, Robert. What was the lesson God taught the rebels?"

"If you're through with me, Bill wants to tell you about that."

"I'm not finished. I have very important questions for you."

"Go ahead, I'll tell you the truth."

"You love him don't you."

"I love him like you must have loved Sami and Enoch."

"Sami and Enoch never robbed me of the spirit God gave me."

"Bill has been giving me mine back as I get strong enough to deserve it."

"Deserve it? I have so many problems with that. I think you're shrinking, not growing. Do you know what brainwashing is?"

"Do you know what undeserving is? I don't think you deserve to judge him."

"Tell me about your child."

"Don't you dare, Robert, stop right now! That's off limits, Asitr! If you want to talk about my baby talk to me. I'm the mother. I say you don't have permission to talk about my baby on the air! I mean it. Both of you. Change the subject."

"Po, I understand why you don't want to do this, but nothing is off limits. I need to know who the father is."

"You need to know crap. Campfire my ass. We are on the radio! If you try to make our baby a hunted thing, I'll knock you all the way back to Babylon for more stretching."

"Robert, please tell me Alayat isn't possessing Po right now."

"He's not. I swear."

"Then one of you, tell me who the father is."

"She's right, Asitr. Talking about our child is off limits."

"Then shut down the show. This campfire will continue without the audience."

"Bill wants the world to hear his judgment."

"Then answer the question, Robert. Rules of the campfire. An answer is required for a question directly asked."

"Don't answer, Robert. It's not your decision…either of you. Nobody can change my mind. And you, Asitr…You go to hell!"

"Okay, Po. Fair enough. Robert, we should finish this off the air."

"No, wait! Asitr, Po, let the truth come out. Bill says we don't need to be afraid of the truth."

"That's it, Robert. This show is over. Neither of you are going to turn my baby into the Antichrist."

"They can't do that babe, stay calm. Bill needs us … Po? … Po! STOP!"

37

T HE LAST WORDS of Bill's final broadcast were followed by the hissing sound of dead air. When Kae'Lairy replayed the show's last moments on the moon, he let the hissing linger, then silenced the blue marble and held it to his eye. "Wouldn't it be grand if we could gaze into the ball and see the future?" he said. "See how things turn out before we act?"

When he removed the sphere from his eye, he spun it on his index finger while imitating the practiced excitement of a bored carnival barker.

> *"Round and round she goes.*
> *Never stopping, out of reach, yet forever close.*
> *See what's coming? Nobody knows.*
> *Where are the corners where the mysteries grow?*
> *The big blue marble is caught in the throes*
> *of the chaos of people on the tips of their toes,*
> *eyes full of fire, blowing steam out their nose.*
> *The human is trouble, since before he wore clothes."*

That's a Kae'Lairy original poem, Doc. On the moon, it's how he followed the dead air at the end of the show. He let silence punctuate his odd departure into poetry, and moved into a pose neither angel recognized.

Speaking for the first time since Kae'Lairy approached them, Jederic moved into an aggressive pose and challenged the mighty one. "So, you are saying Asitr's tale is over, time is up, end of show, end of story? We are to listen to an empty hiss like Gaipon trying to fathom meaning in the scratching of Lockjaw's record? You are not Lockjaw, following deceitful leaders, and we are not Gaipon, listening to an incomprehensible language. You are a mighty angel of God's construction, tempting yourself with deception. We are listening to a language we understand. Why do you engage us, then keep a secret that will undo you?"

No answer was given. Instead, Kae 'Lairy tapped his box and told the chronology of what happened in Bill's studio after the show went silent. He dotted his I's and crossed his T's. He gave the federal judge version. All letter of the law and no spirit of the law for balance. To Kae'Lairy, the moments that followed the end of the broadcast was as frustrating as trying to organize quarks in a blender.

I was a captive audience, body frozen through, but mind fully alert. My seat was the best in the house. I saw, heard, and understood everything that was happening. Kae'Lairy's box seat put me in position to give you the play-by-play. account of what happened in Bill's studio.

I think you would appreciate the human version. Kae'Lairy's version was only a conclusion about chaos in the numbers, all summed up with a final score of spirits jailed in his penalty box. I believe the game was more than the score, so I'm going to give you the play-by-play.

*   *   *

BOPPING BOBBY

Bill's broadcasting studio didn't have the old-world feel of the rest of his house and bore even less resemblance to the old familiar studio images seen on TV and movies. The set-up was modern and uncluttered. The big desk, piled with scripts, disorganized sheets of paper, and a single microphone, never existed. The wall, with the big glass window between the host and engineer, was never part of the set-up. Neither was the engineer.

Bill did have a big desk. Nine feet wide. Three feet across. From the time of his first show, the surface stayed uncluttered with papers and devoid of microphone. Sculptures and curios from around the world replaced them.

The desk curved on the right side. The curved wing held a wireless computer system. Next to the computer was a board, with an array of electronic ports of all configurations, and a series of plug-ins for jacks of all sizes.

Bill's rolling chair was positioned for speed and laziness. If he pushed the chair back to the shelf-wall behind him, he could reach all his plug-in boards. If he slid the chair away from his computer and to the left, there was a small refrigerator, a smaller bar, and a tube attached to a cylinder filled with laughing weed and heated with a ceramic coil, digitally set at two hundred degrees. The tube could be pulled out far enough to allow Bill to inhale the vapors from the cylinder while seated anywhere at the desk.

If he pulled the lever on his chair, he could recline and enjoy the ceiling. Suspended from the ceiling, was his array of microphones, nearly unnoticeable alongside mobiles and sculptures of fictional winged creatures who have famously intruded into the history of flight. There are pink pigs, a single golden carp, fez-headed monkeys, and a falling Icarus.

Poor Icarus, hanging lower than the rest, wings blackened, face frozen in the moment of understanding. His eyes are up-cast, his arms spread in prayer. Clearly, Icarus was a focal point among smiling, flying pigs, a gasping fish, and an army of angry, evil primates.

Bill appreciated his fine art and curios atop his desk. The ceiling, a gift from Bobby McKinney after Bill challenged him to get involved in a creative project, he cherished as a masterpiece.

One step down from the desk was the guest area. A very large, semi-circular couch faced Bill's desk. Five matching footrests were spaced evenly in front of the couch, but there was comfortable seating for nine adults.

Behind the couch was a faux fireplace. One of the plug-ins at Bill's desk had a library of fifty distinct fires to display in the fireplace, but Bill chose to darken it for the evening.

One comfortable chair, at the left of the couch, sat next to a small table. On the table was a Bible and an ashtray. Just past the table was the doorway for entering Bill's unusual studio.

Entering the room, the control panel on the wall directly ahead of you would be the first thing you noticed. Stepping through the door, Bill's elevated desk was visible on the left, and the couch was welcoming on the right, but the dominant view, unless you looked up, was the lighted control panel on the far wall.

On the evening of Bill's last show, something had been added to the room. Between the door and the control panel, and between the couch and Bill's desk, was a rolling catering cart, large enough to display dozens of cantaloupe slices and a variety of bagels.

The cart was centered in the room, but the quadrant between Bill's desk and the table, and the control panel and the table, is where the bloodshed happened.

Po sat on the couch with Asitr and Lockjaw. While everyone else was willing to sort through issues and rethink, Po was squarely planted on the corner of unequivocal and immovable. She was immovable in purpose, but she moved like lightning when conversation turned to her child.

While the show was still live, after suggesting a visit to hell for Asitr, she stood up from the couch, rolled the caterer's table out of the way, and approached Bill's desk. Reaching the desk, she didn't hesitate. She knew what she wanted. The best battering tool she could find, a bowling-trophy-sized lead glass sculpture of a praying angel.

The audience heard Bill raise his voice with the command, 'Po, wait!' His pleas for her to let the truth come out were ignored. Asitr and Lockjaw tried to approach her. She responded by dumping the cantaloupes on the marble floor between them, then rushing to the control panel. Bill rolled his chair to his left and jumped to his feet in a mad dash to stop her. He was too late. Po used her forearm to swipe at rows of switches. As her arm came down, you can hear Bill's last words on the radio. 'Po? ... Po! STOP!'

She wasn't sure her maneuver worked. Many of the lights went dark, but other lights remained on, so she used the angel, bringing it down hard enough to see sparks behind the panel's brand-new gaping hole. Still not satisfied, she raised the battering angel above her head once more, but changed the target as she felt Lockjaw grab at her feet.

Lockjaw wasn't actually grabbing at her feet. He was sliding across the floor on a surface of sugary, aromatic, cantaloupe juice. Asitr fell on his backside when his feet slipped from under him and Lock tried to jump over him when he realized the slick floor wasn't going to allow him to stop. The effort turned into a gliding ride, ending at Po's feet. The only man not down and still rushing to Po's location was Robert McKinney.

Robert was at the edge of the step on his desk platform when he became the recipient of Po's rash decision to fling her glass battering ram at the man coming toward her. The angel's flight was anything but graceful. The glass angel rolled, bowed head over bent knees, like a circus tumbler, and ended her journey with glass feet making contact with Bill's forehead, between the eyes and just below the hairline.

Two sounds, on contact, melded together into a whimsical tone. Buhping-g-g. The thud of heavy impact, and a high-pitched echo, like a ballpeen hammer bouncing from an anvil, froze movement and ended all the noise in the room except the occasional spark from the control panel.

The sparking could have been soundtrack for what was going on inside Robert's brain. He stood straight from head to toe when the leaded angel found its mark. Robert's eyes rolled toward the ceiling. Both his arms jumped to trauma position, elbows at the sides, fingers spread wide, forearms straight out. If the moment were captured in a snapshot, Robert would look like a zombie trying to dog-paddle.

Lock noticed the impact area begin to swell immediately. Pressure built so fast, the seam opened, at first with white edges, then with red. Slipping once more, Lockjaw managed the distance to the injured man in time to see the seam on Robert's head begin to gush. At the same time the gushing began, Lockjaw reached for him, but like a frozen string standing on its end, Robert suddenly thawed and dropped straight down onto his own feet. He looked formless, without bones, before he rolled down the step, stiffened like he was being electrocuted, then lifted his arms back into dog-paddle position.

38

"**M**R. BECKLEY?"
"Yes, doctor?"

"Time for a comfort break. Do you need anything? I can call an orderly."

"I could use some coffee, if you're willing to finish up tonight."

"I have as long as it takes, Mr. Beckley, You tell an interesting story."

"Especially the way the show ended, right?"

"What do you mean?"

"You have a tell. Angels pose to inform each other how to gauge the words they speak. We do it too, but for us, it's involuntary. We call them tells."

"Is this something I need to hear? It can wait."

"When I was reciting the end of the show, your eyelids raised. You shifted into a distant stare. Lines deepened above your nose. Tiny dimples showed up at each corner of your mouth because your jaw tightened. You shifted in your chair. It all happened when you heard the last words of the live broadcast. Those last words meant something to you. Want to share?"

"Ha. I'm going to get a book out of meeting you, Otis Beckley. Two coffees, black, coming up. I'll send Jarvis in to assist you to the restroom."

After Dr. Milton turned the corner and walked into the hallway, Otis hopped from his bed, checking his balance before walking to his bathroom. When he returned to his bed, he noticed the pigeon was back at the window. "He still thinks I'm making it up," he complained to the bird, "but I see progress."

A knock on the door took his attention away from the window. It was Jarvis. "Doc says you need assistance to the toilet?"

"Took care of it, thanks Jarvis. I'll tell him you came by."

At the nurse's station, Jarvis grabbed his coffee cup but set it back down when he saw Dr. Milton drain the last of the pot into two cups. "That John Doe's a talker, Doc,' Jarvis called out to him. 'He's gabbin' at that bird on his window. I guess he's gonna need a dinner menu?"

"Give him the dietician special. I don't want to coddle him with the good stuff."

"Good stuff? You funny, Doc."

*   *   *

"Okay, Mr. Beckley, watch the coffee, it's hot. Anything else before we begin again? "

"No, thank you. Jarvis stopped by. Let's get this marathon over with."

"Great. What happened in the studio after Bobby got clobbered?"

*   *   *

QUARKS IN A BLENDER

Things moved fast. Po spoke first. "Is he hurt bad?" she asked. The absurd question went unanswered.

Lockjaw dropped to his knees and began putting pressure on the gushing wound.

Asitr, in a suddenly raspy voice, asked Lock if Robert needed to go to the hospital.

"Right now," Lock answered. "We should gizmo him first. Alayat could be hiding in him."

The debate brought about by the comment was passionate, but short.

Po was no longer concerned about her child being discussed on the radio. She staked a claim to a position at the campfire by offering observations and opinions. "Bill still hasn't been given the chance to defend himself. We don't even know if he is possessing Bobby. Hospital now, we can talk about Alayat later." She followed her opinion with a question. "What will happen to Bobby if you gizmo Alayat? How did it go with Alazam's host?"

Lock didn't have concerns for Bill. He had a hard time finding sympathy for the devil who tried to roast his Grampy. "Gizmo now," he said, "we can't let Alayat escape."

Asitr, who was having a difficult time standing, pulled himself onto the couch, clutched a numb left arm, and thought about Stanley Goodhope. *Was his madness at the canyon due to the gizmo? Was it all just Stanley's virulent insanity?* On top of those questions was the mystery of Alayat's location.

Asitr asked himself the only question left that mattered. "*Which decision would be wrong?*" With all other options swept away by the question, Asitr focused on saving Bobby. He asked Lockjaw, "Will he make it to the hospital?"

Lockjaw's answer sent Po into a loud mournful fit. "Less than 50/50 Grampy. We don't have time for an ambulance, we have to drive him. Let's gizmo and go."

Po felt appropriately responsible for Bobby's condition and wailed loud apologies to Baal, Bill, Robert, Bobby, Lockjaw, and Asitr. "I did it. I did it. It's my fault," she screamed. She was loud enough to mask, from everyone, the quiet rattling of the doorknob. Nobody missed the startling crash when the door burst inward.

Hayak arrived from the street. A locked door couldn't stop him from finding the reason for the show's abrupt ending. The door hung crookedly on one hinge. Hayak leaned on the other side of the door frame and glanced around the room, looking twice at the ceiling, before he spoke.

His questions came out in an excited stream. "Is everything right? What happened? Oh, Ms. Po, you are all right? I heard you scream. Who's hurt? Where's Bill? Is that blood? What are you doing, Lock? What is Lock doing? Asitr? Do we need an ambulance?"

Nobody attempted answers, because a different voice, speaking strongly, took command. The words came, calmly spoken, from the lips of Robert McKinney. "It's me. Alayat. Robert will be fine, his brain still functions, but we need to stop the bleeding. I have what we need to cauterize." The sense of spinning panic in the room subsided with Alayat's focus, and under his guidance, everyone worked to save Bobby.

Po supplied the towels and ice for the head wrap. She also chipped in with the constant reminder to, "Oh, hurry, hurry."

Asitr, under Alayat's directions, ran to the library and retrieved a ceramic rod with a cord and digital temperature control. It was right where he said it would be, bottom desk drawer, next to Bill's pipe.

Lock provided the benefit of previous wound-cauterizing experience.

Hayak contributed by squeezing the split edges of Robert's forehead tightly together while Lock used the glowing ceramic rod to seal the blood flow.

Alayat provided them with the perfect patient. He remained motionless during the process of prodding, searing, and sealing the wound.

When the bleeding stopped, and the ice wrap was secured, the patient broke into a wide grin. "He won't even know it happened," said Alayat. "Do you suppose he'll notice the big scar?"

The mood was briefly celebratory. Very briefly. Hayak was not amused. "Where is the fun for you Baal?" he asked. "You offend me. Why you use this screwed up kid? Look, look at him ... yourself ... look at yourself. You have wetted his pants, and laugh to see his big-ass scar. Does this boy have all the bad luck, or do you torture him for the jollies?"

Opposition to Baal was at the heart of Armenian history from the day of its birth, and Hayak was a true son of his people. In Hayak's first meeting with Asitr, at the beginning of the wealth building years, he made two things clear. "I am a smuggler, not a thief," he proclaimed. "I have love for everyone but Turks, Satans, Kurds, and Baal."

Coolly, calmly, Alayat stood, took a small item from his desk-top, and spoke to Hayak directly and by name. "Hayak Asmudi," he said, "Welcome to the campfire, I have a precious gift for you." Alayat extended his hand to offer an ornate, three-sided arrowhead.

The tight lines across Hayak's face altered slowly, as recognition and doubt put a dent in his single-minded attitude. The, *I dare you* look slid slowly down his face. The subtly softer *don't mess with me* pose replaced it, but he made no move to accept the offer.

Alayat set the arrowhead back on his desk. "We'll keep it here until later. I have a box for it."

Hayak responded dryly. "It's an elegant replica."

Alayat smiled like someone confidently amused. With his bandaged head, he looked like Mona Lisa in a turban. "Replica?" he said. "I crafted the three cutting edges from a bracelet given to me by Nimrod, the hunter. I made the longbow with wood from the wahdi at Shubat Tepli, I made the shaft thick and heavy from the heart of cedar. I fired the arrow into the air. You know the legend, but I can tell you the truth. Armenia would never exist if not for lessons I learned from the judgment in Samyaza."

Hayak walked to the desk and touched the relic. "I know my trade. I smuggle ancient artifacts. You won't fool me. What is your story?"

"Everyone, slow down, we still have problems." Asitr interrupted when he caught sight of the scrolling email listings on Bill's computer. "We don't want worried listeners to call the police. Lock? See if you can answer those emails. Tell them we are having technical issues. Call the guys at the cave, and tell them not to worry. Hayak, tell your guys to keep the grounds covered, but be inconspicuous if the police come. Put someone inside the gate, and tell him what to say. Come back if you can follow the rule. You can't gizmo anyone before a vote."

"Okay," Hayak said dryly, "First we vote, then I gizmo." His wink to Asitr affirmed he would follow the rules. The way he smiled into Alayat's face, before he left to organize his men, raised doubts about how committed he was to his wink of a promise.

On his way out, Hayak jerked the door from its last hinge. He took it with him, dragging it down the hall and to the gate, all the while singing the old Armenian folk song, *'Come on'a my house, to my house. I'm going to give you candy.'*

"It looks like we have a deck with lots of wild-cards," quipped Alayat.

Asitr was uncomfortable with the sudden surprises and Alayat's confident tone. "We should take a breather until Hayak returns," he said. "Everyone relax. We're in for a long night."

Sinking into the couch, Asitr leaned back and shut his eyes. He was tingling and afraid. Something was wrong, and he didn't want anyone to know. Numbness and pain on the left side. Shortness of breath. A cold, prickly sensation working its way across his scalp. Indigestion. Fatigue. Dizziness. After putting his fingers across his wrist, he added irregular heart rhythm to his list of symptoms. *"It's all right,"* He told himself *"Breathe. In through the nose. Out through the mouth. The rhythm of calm."*

Under lids tightly shut, Asitr's eyes ponged rapidly back and forth. The hand checking his pulse slid from his wrist and onto the couch. Like a manic channel changer, his mind flashed incomplete images, then settled into a dream-state panorama of a forest of pre-flood vegetation.

Old Mother Puth was there with a woman he didn't recognize. Puth wasted no time. She put her finger in Asitr's face and admonished him. "You wouldn't have to worry about dying right now if you had eaten your garlic raw."

"I should have, mother. I'm sorry. Am I too late?"

"Well, what do you think, Mr. protected by Heaven so you can do anything you want. How many lives do you need before you listen?"

"I'm sorry. I should have listened."

"I tried my best. Now, you better listen to this lady. She's your first mother."

"Hi, baby. Don't be afraid."

"Mother?"

"Shush, sweety, hush. Listen ..."

"My mother?"

"Yes. I want to tell you something. I didn't give you to the Shinies, baby. From the moment I saw you, I knew I was in the world to raise you into a man."

"I believe you, mother. Are we going home?"

"All of your mothers are waiting for you. None of us gave up on you, even those who know about the lives you hide from Lockjaw."

"Oh, no, no... I feel so ashamed."

"Shush up and listen, little one. Learn your lesson and listen. I was wrong. You were the only thing on my list, and I was wrong. Raising you to manhood isn't what I came into the world to do. Do you understand?"

"Sure. I know. The only thing left on my list." The two mothers began to fade, and Asitr heard himself say the words aloud. "The only thing left on my list."

"Your list?" Lockjaw wasn't sure he heard correctly.

Asitr didn't repeat it. He was struggling to remember his evaporating dream. Like leaves from the windshield of a speeding car, the faster he traveled toward consciousness, the faster the leaves scattered. Each scattered leaf, a page torn from a book, removing part of the story. Finally, the dream was nothing more than words on the tip of the tongue, forgotten but not gone.

When he opened his eyes, Asitr was confused. He didn't know how long he had dreamed, but he knew he lost time. Lockjaw was still at the computer, but Bill sat on one of the footrests, head in hand, and Po stood over him, adjusting his icy turban.

Lock was busy, but he asked again. "What about your list?"

"Nothing, I was talking to myself. There's something ... I don't know. There's something I'm forgetting. I didn't finish with Bobby."

The man with the ice turban spoke. "Robert, damn it. Robert. What do you want? Can it wait for the pain medicine to start working?"

Before Asitr could answer, Lockjaw called for his attention. "Grampy," he said, "We have an email from VanGrada. CSI wants to send a fax. Can we receive it?"

Po, the natural-born facilitator, stepped carefully through the bloody melon field and to the desk. "Skootch over," she told Lock, "I can set that up." Lock skootched all the way over to the couch and Po sat down in her familiar organizing station behind the computer.

Asitr recognized he needed to rush, and he needed to slow down. He recognized old feelings, memories from his other lives, the physical stupor, the dull wonder of fading away, the hyper-awareness of activity speeding around him. It was the pace at the end of the race. His spirit was separating from his soul and only a string tethered the two together. He knew it was the awkward moment of realizing that life was going on without you.

He would have embraced the chance to move on, if not for one thought. *I can't leave until I know why I was here.* Feeling like a child trying to hold on to his balloon at the height of a raging gale, Asitr willed himself to hang on to his thread between worlds.

After inhaling a good tank-full of air, he addressed Robert. "I have more questions, but they can wait until Alayat has his say."

"You don't look good," responded Robert.

"I'm used to it," said Asitr." I've never been handsome." He leaned back to breathe easy, hoping for a little more rest before Hayak returned and the campfire could continue its sober purpose.

Horrific slapstick chaos, the emergence of innocent Bobby McKinney, and a heart attack weren't part of Asitr's planning. His list had only one item remaining; the judgment of Baal Alayat. Gnawing at the forefront of his thinking was the suspicion he wasn't there to judge.

"If you have questions about the baby, ask me now, before Hayak comes back. Our baby has nothing to do with him." Robert's consideration for the child's privacy was well received by Asitr, so he went directly to the heart of his questions.

"Who initiated the sex, Robert?"

Po was shaken by the implications of the question. "Why do you need to know?" She asked. "Do you think we're raising a devil baby?"

Asitr gulped in another air refill and responded, "I have suspicions. Please, either of you, answer the question."

Po knew she fell in love with both Bills. The confident, mysterious Bill fascinated her, but the gentle, boyish Bill melted her heart. The combination of the two was irresistible. "For the love of God Asitr, I did it," she said. "I raped a twelve-year-old boy in a fifty-six-year-old man's body. I'm a sugar-daddy-craving minx with a flair for pedophilia. Hotchacha. Call the lobotomy squad."

Po's sarcasm confused and agitated Bobby. He tried to do what he felt a man should do. He came to the defense of his woman. The moment was awkward. "I wanted to. It's not her fault, I wanted to. I got a ... a hard ... a hard ..."

"An erection?" Asitr was embarrassed by Bobby's discomfort and didn't want him to think he was being made sport of. "Okay, that was helpful," he added. "So, you came together in an unplanned, natural attraction between two consenting adults. I'm sorry you feel like I'm prying but ..."

Hayak arrived from the hallway with an armload of towels and spoke from the door-less entrance. "What's all this about sugar daddy minxes with the hotchacha? What has happened?"

"I can explain it all, without the silly need for verbal fig leaves." Alayat was once again speaking through Robert's mouth. "Asitr is worried about a new age of Anakim. He thinks I'm on a mission to breed a stable of smarter humans for possession. Let me tell my story, then we can all go home."

With all eyes and ears focused on him, Alayat understood the rhythm of the campfire was now in his hands.

*   *   *

ALAYAT SPINS HIS STORY

"When Asitr began his story last Monday, he didn't start at the beginning. He began at a point in time with no bearing on the real reasons he was on my show. Why? He wasn't being truthful. He needed to hide dirty little details, furtive plans, and deadly intentions.

"I don't have a need to manipulate an outcome. I have a need for mercy, spilling over me from the seat of mercy. I need judgment from the Lord.

"Before falling into darkness, I was a creature born in the light of fire, with a perfect body, a clear purpose, and equipped with a mind capable for my tasks. I was to be a watcher of and guardian for a race not yet created.

"An entire world was made to house the coming human. I had my hand in the construction. My pact mate, Alazam, and I assisted in laying the earliest building blocks of an ecological design made for an environment constructed with organic media.

"On our days of rest, we contested in games of sport with the mighty Leviathan. We conversed among the dancing lights of all the borealis and we speculated on the nature of the being for whom such an incomparable world was being readied.

"We assumed the new beings would add luster to the world we helped prepare. We anticipated, one day, we would flare out in songs so exultatious they couldn't be written prior to the inspiration of meeting the human. When the day of the Adam arrived, we flared out into cries of disgust upon realizing the loathsome nature of the creature we were to serve.

"Soon after, the mighty fallen ones arrived from heaven, looking powerful and acting superior. By clever temptation, they broke the human of his obedience, and they turned the Adam to their own purposes. The big-wings did whatever they willed to do. Many watchers left their stations to join them.

"Alazam made a pact with the sect led by Marduk. I made my pact to remain with Alazam. We were now Baals, and after I compared the excellence of the works of heaven to the self-destructive works of man and rebel, I was mortified by my mistake.

"Even before I saw my first Bombag, I was a homeless ghost, trying to keep myself in life while trying to find my way back home.

"It was illogical to ignore a Godless future and sort the possible from the inevitable. At least, that was the thought that sired my repentance, as I stood with a baby in my arms, ready to conduct my first sacrifice to Baal Zebub.

"The loud, kicking baby named Asitr wasn't impressive. I smelled the excrement sticking to his skin, I saw the snot dripping down his face and into his crying mouth. He peed on me. In his eyes I saw a single-minded message, *'I don't like this ... I don't like this ... I don't like this.* I wondered what he would become if I allowed him the time to become more, so I blinked out, left his fate to chance, and now, I know what's become of him. He has come to write me from the book of life.

"How can I put this? *Hooga mushka er hoobida. Hoobida Samyaza,* Understand?

Asitr does. His wife, Gaut, wrote those words in the book decorated with a circle of hands. Asitr calls it *The Nameless Book.*

"The book is a collection of stories featuring Baal Zebub, Alayat, Alazam, Herakles, Azazel, Enoch, Methuselah, Noah, and the lesser known, Foop. In the details of those stories are descriptions of a war with Heaven, fought in the sky, and the judgment following Heaven's victory.

"Asitr didn't know these stories. He died before the war was declared. He missed the war, the judgment, and the flood, but Gaut sent him the news. Over the thousands of years between flood and now, Asitr has finally heard the news and received her warnings.

"*Hooga mushka er hoobida. Hoobida Samyaza* ... Never see Heaven, but hoobida be yours. Hoobida for all who act against the judgment of Samyaza ... These words are a sword with two edges. One edge is for the condemned, who must accept their fate without further crimes. I am one of those who have been condemned. The other edge is for those who, out of personal needs, like vengeance, act to add additional punishments. I believe that edge is for you. Hoobida for both, the book says.

317

"Hoobida is the double death. Loss of soul in the short life. A wandering spirit with no hope of seeing Heaven in the next. Past and present, bound in the curse of being erased from the archives of Heaven and the minds of those who knew you. Only God will know you ever existed. You will try to reach him for one more chance, but he will choose to forget you. Hoobida. The double death.

"Is anything worth the risk of being written from all worlds, while howling to enter just one? Vengeance for age-old myths? Punishment for phantom wrongdoings? Bad man almost hurt my Grampy?

"Let's talk double jeopardy. I have been judged, punished, and put on probation by the Lord, himself. Where have I broken probation? What additional punishment do you seek? Why are you so high as to amend the judgment at Samyaza?

"Robert said I once had superpowers. There is nothing super about me anymore. I can no longer glow to impress you. I can no longer blink out. There was a time I could move invisibly among angels of a lower rank. Now, I am invisible only to the human. Flight was exhilarating. Now, I only fly in my laughing-weed-fueled mind. I have arthritis, gas, and hair grows from my ears. The ethers have become impossible obstacles, and I'm cursed with the need to reason through an organic thinking device which denies access to ninety percent of its capacity.

"I am punished. Who will risk hoobida to punish me again?

"Where are my ongoing acts of evil?

"Show me the gizmos, gentlemen, or drop the threat. The only decision left for you to make is between parting as friends or making the biggest mistake of your lives. My judgment both punishes and defends me. Poof, Asitr, your reason for being here is gone. We both have the protection of Heaven."

*   *   *

Asitr read his *Nameless Book* while transcribing the script in Babylon. He learned the meaning of the words when he awoke to his last life in Eden. When it was clear that Alayat believed he didn't know what the book said, he let him go on with his misunderstanding. Perhaps he would lie about the contents and reveal his true nature.

In the old language, there was very little gray area needing interpretation, so he was clear about his boundaries. All his discussions with Lockjaw over the last forty years left him feeling practiced in the details of Alayat's prosecution, but the barriers restricted him. To condemn and execute a judgment that amended God's own sentence called for a standard much higher than a reasonable doubt, and for more cause than a rehashing of old crimes, already judged.

The campfire hadn't burned out yet, and he wasn't ready to part as friends, but he knew he had to be right, and he needed stamina for the task of working through several issues.

In spite of feeling prepared to answer Alayat's points of order, he realized he wasn't very sharp when he leaned forward and attempted to speak. He barely moved. Suddenly, Asitr realized his mind was fading. Hayak saved him from trying to formulate a sentence.

"A question," Hayak began. "A simple matter of time-lines. First is judgment in Samyaza, next is flood?"

Alayat knew what was coming, so he met the intent of the question head on. "You are concerned the acts of the Baals, after judgment, crossed the line into further acts of evil. Allow me to tell you about the time between Methusaleh's death and the birth of Armenia. Will you listen with an open mind?"

"Consider me interested," Hayak said. "Opening up my mind will depend on what you are putting in."

*   *   *

ALAYAT'S ARMENIAN DEFENSE

"In the war, Baal Zebub was blown from his fortress on Tiamat. All of his followers were written out of life on that planet. All but the two who watched from earth. Alazam and I were the only little-winged Baals to be judged in Samyaza. On that day, I learned the human condition you call panic.

While my abilities were being removed, I was also losing my senses. Not all of them, I could still see, so I could be punished with unrequited coveting. My hearing remained, so I could hear the world around me reacting to life with feelings I no longer had.

"The day after Methuselah died, the deluge arrived, and I thanked God for my judgment. I thanked him for being unable to feel the emotions of those who screamed in terror.

"While the age of ice persisted, I had no other thing to do but think. Somewhere, Alazam was doing the same thing. What else could anyone do? There was only wind to listen to, nothing breathing air was alive, and there was only the ark worth searching for.

"In my mind, the ark was a conveyance for frozen sparks, destined to remain cryogenic until the water softened, and the ark could bob its way across the liquid toward the exposed peak of Ararat.

"I was desperate to be near the human when he thrived again. This made me realize the proportion of my ludicrous decision to second-guess the creator. Humans, the creature I once loathed were now my greatest comfort. A life of hearing and seeing without emotional involvement was uncomfortably close to hoobida, but still, it was life, and more than I deserved.

"It wasn't until the ark made landfall, and the frozen sparks burst back into flame that I learned how the Lord offered a doorway to becoming more. Alazam found me, and he enlightened me about the doorway to possession of a human soul. If it is the Lord's will that I take back a richer life from someone willing to sell their inheritance for a bowl of soup, then who can argue?

"Hearing me say that, while Robert is my host, may shock you, but it is true. I easily accepted the option of more life, and I swore to use it to please Heaven. With acceptance of new responsibilities, my education in what it's like to be human began.

"I chose to possess a young farmer who was suicidal after losing his wife to the lure of service in the temple of Marduk. The temple was located in the brand-new city of Babylon. Her husband, Haik, forbade her, but she followed the bling and the seductive charms of Nimrod, the mighty hunter, builder, and dictator of his tribe. In payment for claiming his bride, Nimrod gave Haik a special bracelet made of three materials, bronze, gold, and flint. The weave of materials in the bracelet was long ago accomplished in Azazel's crafting class by Enoch, himself.

"Nimrod tossed the bracelet to young Haik with the finality of a deal being finished. 'A lasting treasure for you,' he said. 'In return I devour the youth of your wife.'

"To Hayak, it was an ugly, heart-breaking offer for which he had no option to refuse. He smashed the bracelet between rocks. When he clenched the pieces in his fists, he cut himself, adding sharp physical pain to his flaming emotional misery.

"I heard him cry out to have revenge or die. Refusing submission, but not imagining an opportunity for revenge, he chose to die. He would have ended his life, if not for my offer to save him.

"I spoke to Alazam after possessing Haik. Our reactions to our first possessions were similar in nature but digested very differently.

"They were similar in the sense — we had the same initial reaction. We threw up. Suddenly, our sense of smell was working against us. Next came the realization of a hit to our math skills and our ability to think logically. We were dull and inhibited while trying to access our old reliable data base. Neither of us could carry a tune. The only positive was the ability to feel emotions again.

'So this is what it's like to be human,' Alazam complained. 'Stinking Dirtwings is what we are... without the wings. We're dirt. There must be more to being human than this.'

"I believe he put his finger right on top of the big picture without knowing it. I felt privileged to have a chance to watch humans become more, but Alazam refused to acknowledge your potential. His only interest in serving you was as an item on the menu.

"Alazam used his hosts to to pleasure himself with depraved sensations. He delighted at basking in the emotions of chaos. He favored the inhalation of infant fear as his greatest indulgence. It wasn't long before we clashed over our principles. Soon, we were at war.

"After Nimrod died, Alazam murdered his way into the office of leadership in Babylon. He took the name Baal, and he ruled like he was a god.

"Through my own work, I made the house of Haik into the finest house in the city. We gathered to discuss the notion of the one God. My flocks grew numerous, my farms multiplied, and my people were happy. I gave the men training and the tools to keep what was ours. When my army grew to the size of two hundred reliable men under arms, I announced to Alazam my intentions to leave Babylon. 'This portion of survivors, offspring of those who walked down the southern face of Ararat will disperse as the Lord wishes,' I told him.

"Alazam told me he would never let us leave.

"To add insult to his attack on free will, he spoke down to me. 'Little brother,' he said. "I'm not going to finish that sentence. I've told you what you don't know about the founding of Armenia. We have Hayak here with us, namesake of the patriarch Haik, whom I possessed. I would like to hear our modern young Hayak finish the story. A favor for the arrowhead I crafted from the shattered bracelet. Icons are precious in your churches; artifacts are your profession. You must accept my gift, but Hayak, show me you understand. Will you finish the story?"

*   *   *

Inside the studio, there was a sense that something definitive was going to happen. Lockjaw turned to Asitr, and realized he was pale. Using a hushed tone to avoid breaking the spell of rapt attention obvious in the faces of everyone waiting for Hayak to speak, he whispered, "Grampy."

Asitr turned to his grandson, knowing Lock must be worried about him if he looked as bad as he felt, so he put two thumbs up and smiled. His smile was forced, and his eyes didn't shine, but Asitr hid the deadness in them with a wink. He was convincing enough to allow Lock to return his attention to Hayak. Asitr turned his attention back to controlled breathing.

In the room, a hushed wait for Hayak to speak spawned multiplying questions. When he did speak, his cockiness was noticeably more subdued.

*   *   *

HAYAK ABSTAINS

"As my ancestors tell the story, Baal doesn't give his 'little brother' permission to leave Babylon.

"Haik, he was insistent, 'Go we will,' he said, and go they did.

"Animals and people, they walk up the foothills of Ararat. We settle in a land of spring-fed rivers, deep lakes, and magnificent forests.

"The early ones called themselves Armens, after Methusaleh's sun god, and made homes by the shores of Lake Van. There was good soil in wide swaths. Everywhere, stone and timbers aplenty to build with. The game was plentiful, and dangerous wild beasts were few. The Armens could raise their eyes up and see the peak of Ararat. When I travel back home, I have pains in my heart from seeing what the little satans have done to us, but I thrill with my ancestors to gaze on Ararat.

"Here's something my ancestors don't say. It is the why, so I don't know why, but after a time, Baal came to Lake Van with his army. 'Little brother, go home,' he says.

"Haik, he offers hospitality. 'Come visit me in peace,' say Haik. 'We are making a peaceful land with love for all. Give up old violent ways.'

"Baal, with his big army, he attacks, and he learns how men fight when they love a life put in danger. Haik, he understands that a good fight is second prize to winning, and big armies can beat small armies, so he makes his arrow.

"This arrowhead, with three edges, is heavy in weight. It must be mounted on thick shaft and launched with a special long bow. The arrowhead, just so balanced for straight flying. Still, the archer must have all the luck, or a good blessing from the angels.

"Haik, he used the right materials, he crafted well, and he shot his arrow far enough. The blessing from an angel must surely have been given. At great distance, at the time of the Babylonian surge, Haik, he let go his string and stood still before both armies to wait the landing.

"My great-grandmother, who survived the Turks, she liked the story and she added something to make the telling more exciting. I like as well. She tells all the little ones the arrow go so high it bounce from a cloud and veer down, back to earth, with the added weight of dew from Heaven. The new weight is enough to split the breast plate of Baal and open a door for three cutting edges to kill the devil. I mean different than you when I say the words, 'Give the devil his *dew.*' I mean to hell with him.

"The story of the dew from Heaven. We like it so much. Now, the little ones today, they think it true. This is my problem. Anyone can add to a story. I believe the legend is true enough to stay proud of my name. When I have little ones, they will hear all of it, from what was told as news of the day, all the way to the wrinkle in the skin added by a sweet storyteller.

"Let me tell us this. I think, maybe, I have put my face in something I can't feel is gelling between my ears. My scales are unbalanced from the weight of what has become of my people, and I want to avenge them more than I want to do the right thing.

"The voices of one hundred and sixty thousand Armenian men conscripted into the Turkish army, then murdered, to the last of them, call me to act. Defenseless women and children left unprotected by the slaughter, they ask me questions. Why, they want to know, were we marched into the Syrian Desert, past cities and temples named to honor Baal the bloodthirsty? Where were our neighbors when the last shriveled children, too weak to move, lay in sight of the temple of Baalshamin in Palmyra? Who speak condemnation of Turkish officials when they teased dying children to make the last little distance by holding loaves of bread in front of them and assaulted their ears with laughter? Who saw this and not think to bring food and water? My heart shouts to me, gizmo, gizmo. My spirit say don't believe you know all the story, but my mind on this is a dull third edge.

"I know I must see the murder of two million as same crime as the murder of one. My spirit tells me this, so I'm ashamed to falsely accuse one Baal for the crimes of so many Satans. Maybe I should return to the street with my men. To give this one devil his due process, I think more facts need knowing. Do I wear the name of Haik with pride, as always, or as a reminder that I have been fooled by lies slipping freely from the mouth of Baal?"

✳   ✳   ✳

THE THIRD EDGE

While listening to Hayak share his indecision, Lockjaw surveyed the people at the campfire. From left to right he sized up the reactions to Hayak's loss of certainty.

Hayak, himself, looked sheepishly toward Asitr and shrugged.

Po was still in Bill's chair, but she rolled to the couch-side end of the desk to be closer to Hayak while he spoke. When Hayak concluded his admission of confusion, she smiled at him and nodded her approval.

Alayat, even with an ice-pack turban wrapped around his grotesque forehead, appeared pleased. For Lock, the Mona Lisa smile was irritating. The message sent by his twisted lips had none of the charm of the painting, but it telegraphed the same confidence.

Lock twisted a confident smile of his own, convinced Asitr was in a win-win situation. From the book, this is Gaut's advice for interpreting the judgment at Samyaza: *"If you trap a fallen one suspected of ongoing rebellion, gather the sincere to the campfire and judge him. If he is denounced as guilty, destroy him."* The next line of Gaut's advice gave moral guidance for the undecided and timid: *"If perception is clouded, but suspicion is strong, the verdict must be to set the captive free"*

Her final line of advice supplied the reason for confidence. *"If there still exists a witness alive, who lived in the days of rule by the fallen, give the captive to him for a decision. He must set him free or*

325

call for an attending angel to carry him to the throne for perfect judgment."

Asitr believed his streak of good facts and bad conclusions would end. Gaut's words left him confident. Through them, the burden of judgment felt lighter.

When Robert presented the book to Asitr, questions were answered. When he discussed the book with Robert over brunch, he came away with the opinion Robert hadn't read Gaut's advice for judging the fallen. Bill, however, had to know.

According to plan, there was more dancing to do. Lines of questioning were waiting to be opened. A lie, a single lie, would continue to be mined for in Alayat's answers, but in the long game, Lock and Asitr believed being out-danced at the campfire didn't look like an unacceptable outcome. Sending Alayat to appear before the perfect judge sounded like the greatest fallback plan of all time.

On the moon, Kae'Lairy told his listeners, "Lockjaw's faith in the third option of a hung campfire isn't the win-win he and Asitr secretly celebrated. Their third option could lead to the end of any chance for humans to remain in the short life. If not for my own patience, you would look toward earth, today, and see another debris field."

In Bill's office, decision time was coming too fast for Asitr. The plans for judgment didn't take into account the barrier of time. Now he wondered. *Is there enough time to argue for an agreement on possession being an act of evil? Robert justified his own possession as an act of protection for the innocent.*

Asitr had to weigh the odds for winning the argument against the time he had left. It was, he decided, time to move on from finding a reason to gizmo.

"Just a couple more questions," Asitr said, while rising from the couch. His color was returning. The voice was stronger

Alayat smiled his first genuine smile of the night. "You've made your decision. I'm ready. Bobby won't like it, but I'm ready. What do you want to ask?"

Asitr walked to the desk and picked up the arrowhead, thinking about the craftsmanship Enoch showed as an artificer in

Samyaza. The crafting of the arrowhead wasn't Enoch's work, but clearly, it was the work of a master artificer.

The bronze made a strong foundation for mounting the arrowhead to the shaft, and bound the flint tightly, while leaving the sharp stone edges exposed at the point of contact. The edges of the flint were left bare for deep penetration. The gold was both decorative embroidery and soft glue. Applied sparingly, over both bronze and stone, the soft metal was protection for the hard stone, helping to absorb some of the shock of impact.

Spinning the masterpiece in his fingers, so he could see all sides, Asitr discovered something else. The surprise at what he saw changed the question he meant to ask Alayat. The lattice of gold was more than a decorative shock absorber. The flowing design was a fanciful script. *Ru Beswan Ru ... Die Dirtwing Die.*

Impatience crept into the voice of the waiting Alayat. "Do you know what you want to ask me, Asitr?"

"As Mazgabar, I witnessed your reunion with Alazam. You embraced as brothers. I had the impression he was the little wing in your relationship. Was I wrong?"

"No, Asitr, you are perversely correct. I had the upper hand because I no longer cared to stay in life. Not caring what happens is a very empowering attitude."

"You felt empowered by hitting rock-bottom? Who do you blame for the fall?"

"I blame myself for joining in the pact with my brother Alazam. I blame Alazam for ongoing acts of evil, but breaking a pact leads to yet more judgment. Attempt to control Alazam is all I could do. It's been difficult. Shutting him off from the Telstar web may be the best thing ever to happen to this planet. I had to create the world's first ever parental control programming."

Asitr leaned against the desk for support and eyed the smiling Alayat. "We know what was done from the web. Are you going to blame it all on Alazam?"

"Yes, and I'm sorry I didn't catch on quicker. A nuclear submarine was sunk without warning.

"In Central America, a spoiled asset was dethroned by his people. Orders were given to very quietly eliminate him before he told secrets. Alazam changed the orders. A bazooka to the chest, at point blank range, in front of the press, was added to the orders. The "very quietly" was removed.

"An odd aerial photo in the Amazon led to orders sending a specialized map team to the location. Napalm followed.

"Alazam was the first internet junkie on the planet," Allayat continued, "but I managed to shut him out after the Three-Mile Island caper. You're welcome."

"Did you hate him?" Asitr repeated the words on the arrowhead, "Ru Beswan Ru."

"We were pact brothers. I loved him once, but I hated his resistance to rethinking. I was stuck with him."

"Stuck with him?"

"It's not in Gaut's book. You wouldn't understand."

"I think I do understand. You were bound by your pact, a very serious thing among angels. We're tolerated when we break our word, given chances to hit the *do-over* button. I believe you resent our permissive coddling. Do I have it right?"

"Yes, I resent you, but I resented Alazam more than I could tolerate. Did I do wrong to tell him you mentioned Chaco Canyon, knowing he would fly into your trap? Let's go straight to the finish. I can no longer include my audience as voters at the campfire, but you know the remaining members are undecided, or clearly believe in me. We two, we understand what is coming and we embrace it. You, with your life in the times I rebelled, have the only claim to any option other than setting me free. I accept your third option. Call your angel. If he appears, I'll be bound and sent to the Throne for judgment. If the campfire rules were drowned in the Deluge, he will not appear, and I walk away." Spreading his arms to indicate he was speaking to the room, Alayat asked the question, "Are we a hung campfire?"

Glances back and forth confirmed the opinion. Nothing was said, but nodding heads ruled. "We don't even need to hear from Robert, do we?" The width and crookedness of the fallen angel's smile increased.

Asitr knew Alayat was correct. "I don't know" wasn't a judgment, so he made the call. "I'm calling on the attending angel to appear... but first ..."

There were noticeable moments between words when Asitr inhaled gasps of air. In those moments, Kae'Lairy moved too swiftly for Asitr to finish his sentence. Before Asitr managed to announce he wanted to include Robert in the decision, Kae'Lairy gathered Alayat's spirit, Robert's spirit, and Robert's body into the box.

Kae'Lairy explained his rush to rashness on the moon. "I knew, I knew it, I knew it," he said. "The rebel who responded to Asitr's description of the Savant as 'Easy to mislead,' had done it again. I was caught in a loophole. Asitr made his judgment and I was bound to act. If I would have been patient enough to wait for Asitr to speak to Robert, or if Asitr had eaten his garlic raw, things would have been different. In spite of my impatience, and Asitr's early exit, I knew I would never allow the tricky Baal Alayat, the meddling Otis Beckley, or the innocent Bobby McKinney to have access to the throne. In the next few seconds, I would add Asitr to my box."

Asitr's habit of reaching wrong conclusions, based on good facts, was about to end. He owed the moment to his eyes catching the blinking of a red LED light on the Fax machine. The light, flashing behind Po, under the computer screen, went unseen by everyone but the dying man. When photos scrolled from the Fax machine, only Asitr saw the incoming evidence.

The final photo hung from the device like a billboard. There they were, both Baals, Alazam and Alayat, present in a room where a dangling Icarus floated above Bill's desk. Atop the desk, evidence of ongoing acts of evil. The photo screamed a thousand words of ongoing acts of evil. It loosened Asitr's grip on his string to life. His heart seized.

While he pushed out words of irony with the last little puff of air from his final inhalation in life, Kae'Lairy waited for his spirit to cleave from his soul.

"The Fax. Lock, check the Fax," squeaked Asitr. Then he fell, bouncing face first off Bill's desk, and the squeeze from his dying contractions echoed in the room.

His ears never heard the response by Lockjaw, uttered as he pitched forward, "Yes, Grampy," lock said, "we'll check the facts. Which facts?"

*   *   *

DELAYED FLIGHT

This feels different, thought Asitr. *Where is the whoosh, and what is this movement?* The movement was familiar, but not the same sense of motion he felt when returning to his Savant family. It felt like floating downstream. When his visual perception went from black, to snow, to clarity, he relaxed. He was in a canoe, floating down a rock-bottom river fed by springs on either bank.

He looked for a paddle and couldn't find one, but the old up-the-creek scenario didn't bother him. He sat with one hand over the edge, feeling the water slide by, and marveled. On both sides of the stream were trees like he hadn't seen since leaving the Savant glade. Brightly colored birds walked to the ends of their branches to ogle the little man in the canoe. A monkey on the bank tossed his olive drab hat in the air, crossed his arms and laughed.

Asitr waved back and beamed. A celebratory feeling washed over him. He imagined himself as a child, exchanging a string from a withered balloon for a grapevine at its zenith over a spring filled with the waters of life. He anticipated the moment of letting go the vine and immersing himself in the sapphire-colored water.

From the tree where the grapevine swung, he heard a joyful noise. *I'm going to get my big cat back,* he thought. The sound of a purring jaguar, as soft on his ears as glade moss was to the touch, harmonized with the gurgling waters.

"Mom, I'm coming home," Asitr shouted. He was giddy. *If this is the journey, I can't wait to see the destination,* he mused.

Then, the voice. "Asitr, be at peace, you tried your best."

"God?"

"I am the mighty Kae'Lairy, messenger of the Lord, protector of the throne, and bondsman without peer. What you are experiencing is a chemical reaction from dopamine. God has designed it to be released for human comfort during the dying experience. Bless him for the mercy."

"Mister mighty Kae'Lairy," Asitr asked hopefully, "are you guiding me home?"

"I am not. I've placed you in a box with your friend Otis Beckley and the innocent Bobby McKinney. Their bodies are frozen, but their spirits will speak with you. Your own soul is cut from the spirit. It must be. You know too much. Be at peace."

*   *   *

Under any circumstances, Asitr's death was going to affect his grandson, but Lock was jolted to his core. He held onto Asitr's body and cried with deep, agonizing, convulsive sobs. Po rubbed Lock's shoulders to comfort him. She, too, cried. As one, Po, Hayak, and Lockjaw mourned in shock for the little man with so many lives.

Hayak watched forlornly until he noticed the image of the picture dangling from the Fax machine. When he recognized the room, the two Baals, the medical equipment, the soup spoons on napkins, and the moist eyes of a caged infant, he exploded in rage, spinning around the room, gizmo in hand, power on, screaming, "Where is the damned Baal!"

Po looked at him like he was a crazy man, until she too was shocked to notice, no Bill, neither Alayat nor Bobby was in the room. Her eyeball search stopped at the offensive image and she moved to get a closer look. Words failed her, and she let out a garbled growl, ending in a shout. "Damn you Baal Alayat!"

The three-part disharmony built to the big finish when Lock, on his knees with Grampy in his arms, peeked past the desk and focused in on the image. His life-long control over the impulses to avoid the language of empty invective eluded him.

Lock took Grampy's gizmo from his pocket and fired, both his and Asitr's weapons, into every corner of the room, two guns, blazing away, hoping to hit an invisible target.

Hayak ran from the room to the courtyard, screaming from the gate to his crew, "Come hot, come now, light it up!" Then he ran back to the studio while his boys did their calm best to carry out the plan they trained for. Every inch of Bill Elliot's home was covered in a shrinking circle of sweeping, sonic, death rays. The arcs of vibration moved from the street to the yard, then into the house.

Po dropped to her knees and squealed.

Despite the squealing, growling, spinning, and cursing, Alayat escaped the room. He would never escape the box, however, if Kae'Lairy had his way. None of them would. Three of his prisoners knew too much, the other, a" malicious spirit with a greasy smile," knew everything.

For the comfort of the three innocents in the box, Kae'Lairy bound the mouth of Baal Alayat, but couldn't hide from his own senses Alayat's irritating vibration of satisfaction.

The first of the three innocents to speak was Bobby. "What did I do? I'm sorry. I didn't mean to know too much. Can I take it back? What can I do?"

Thus began twenty years of imprisonment inside a bondsman's box, destined to finally arrive at some answers at another campfire, not too far away from here, Doc. Relatively speaking.

39

AT A CAMPFIRE IN ILLINOIS

"I WISH THEY WOULD CALL," said Jack VanGrada, "so we know everything is going well."

"Let's all take a moment and give some credit to my friends from the crime lab," said the CSI prematurely. "They didn't need to take the time to send Goodhope's complete files."

"Bloody right," Guglielmo responded, "To old friends, with time to help."

"To old friends," chimed in FSU, "and success on the dig."

Guglielmo stretched the premature speculation a little further. "Shall we add a little Irish whiskey to the cup? What could go wrong?"

ABOUT THE AUTHOR

Paul Moore was born in the Missouri Ozarks, raised in St. Louis, and eventually settled in the sand of central Florida. He calls each of these places home.

His inner mix of hillbilly river rat, lowlands daydreamer, sand road hermit, and reader of nineteenth-century history writers form the base of a non-elite education. These roots allow imagination to turn historic events into serendipitous thoughts. Those thoughts organize into stories, and stories become novels.

With the remedial help of a good critique group, and the birth of publishing companies that read a manuscript without asking first, "What are your credentials?", he's found a voice to share those stories.

www.ingramcontent.com/pod-product-compliance
Lightning Source LLC
Chambersburg PA
CBHW021446240626
47153CB00001B/312